GETTING LUCKY

SAPPHIRE FALLS

ERIN NICHOLAS

ABOUT GETTING LUCKY

TJ Bennett knows one thing for certain—being in love isn't for him. Been there, done that, has the scars to prove it.

But that's before the colorful and sweet, free-spirited Hope Daniels lands on his doorstep looking for another man.

Hope is only in town for one reason—to find the man who stole her mother's heart twenty six summers ago. She isn't looking to make up for lost time or a date to a Father-Daughter dance, she simply wants to have a cup of coffee with the father she's never known.

But when her directions lead her to TJ's house instead, everything becomes a lot more complicated... and a lot more interesting. Because there's nothing like a big gruff introvert to push this extrovert's let-me-make-it-all-better buttons.

All of TJ's plans to stay uninvolved and out of her way evaporate quickly and before he knows it, Hope's got him thinking differently about everything—family, home, heartbreak and maybe even the fact that he's never actually been in love...before now.

ISBN: 978-0-9863245-7-4

Editors: Heidi Moore, Kelli Collins

Cover by Qamber Designs & Media

1

Her bare feet had bright-pink nails and multiple toe rings. Her long, tanned legs stretched out beneath the flowing multicolored skirt that had been hiked to mid-thigh to expose the smooth skin to the sun, and various bracelets circled her ankles. Her midriff was bare below a white blousy top that was filled with a pair of luscious, firm breasts. Her silky blond hair was so light it was almost white—which made the vivid pink tips all the more noticeable—and curled tantalizingly against the one shoulder left bare by the top. A variety of bracelets wrapped around delicate wrists, multiple rings adorned slender fingers and a line of six earrings sparkled from the sexy curve of her ear.

Sexy curve of her *ear*?

What the hell was *that*?

She looked like a damn hippie.

TJ completed the inventory of the woman who was reclining on the hood of a little yellow car attached to the tiniest camper he had ever seen. Her eyes were hidden behind a humongous pair of sunglasses, the frames also bright pink—

to match her toenails and hair, evidently. Her lips were parted slightly and he thought she was maybe dozing.

Dozing on the hood of the yellow car that was parked in the half-circle drive in front of his house, under his favorite tree.

He'd been distracted by the legs and breasts and, apparently, her ear, but now TJ felt his frown forming. Who the hell was this and why was she parked under his tree?

There was a lot of...color here. He preferred brown. Maybe green. Like dirt and grass. Women with pink streaks in their hair, who wore multicolored skirts and drove yellow cars, were not his type.

He liked farm girls. Girls who wore boots and blue jeans and knew that all those bracelets and rings could be downright dangerous on a farm. There were too many things for them to get caught on, and serious injuries could occur.

So he was *not* going to be attracted to this woman. Whoever she was. Period.

"Can I help you?" He knew it sounded less like a question and more like a demand.

The woman rolled her head to look at him, a smile in place. Then the smile died, and she slowly pushed her sunglasses to the top of her head as she came up to a sitting position.

She looked stunned. Or something. "Holy crap." She said it softly, almost to herself.

"Are you okay?" He put his good hand on his hip, annoyed by the arm sling yet again. He wasn't exactly concerned about her mental health. He was concerned about getting her and her car and her camper off his property before that mental health, or possible lack thereof, became his problem.

She turned to face him and tucked her legs under her like kids did. The move made her plethora of jewelry tinkle like little bells. It also shifted the skirt over most of her legs, and TJ worked on not being disappointed about that.

Then she smiled at him. And he promptly forgot even the color of the car she'd parked under his favorite tree.

"I'm looking for Thomas John Bennett."

"What for?" He didn't have to be polite. She was on his property uninvited. And when she'd moved, the skirt had pulled down and her top had pulled up, and he'd noticed there was a tattoo running along the side of her torso. If his neurons weren't firing perfectly, surely he could be forgiven?

The tattoo was a swirling pattern that, from where he stood, could be a design of some kind but could also be words in a script font. He wanted to find out which it was. Personally, up close, with his own two eyes.

Fuck.

He didn't have time for this.

"It's personal, actually," she answered.

His gaze snapped back to her face. Which was just as distracting, frankly. She had a cute nose that went with the cute ear he'd already noticed, and she had the biggest, roundest eyes he'd ever seen. He wasn't close enough to see the color. But he really wanted to be.

She looked like a pixie. And if that was the damnedest thing he'd ever thought, he didn't know what was.

He wasn't a romantic, whimsical kind of guy. Which was exactly why her jingling bracelets and flimsy skirt and pink toes and hair did *not* do it for him.

Not at all.

But she was looking for him for a personal reason? That was interesting.

And interesting was the last thing TJ wanted this woman— or any woman—to be.

His grumpy bachelorhood was firmly in place. He didn't do *personal* anymore. Impersonal one-night stands, sure. Personal? No way.

"I can assure you he's not buying or hiring," he said. He

needed to get rid of her. He had work to do. And his shoulder was killing him.

He'd let his mother and Delaney, his brother's fiancée, talk him into undergoing the scope to clean up the bone spur and arthritis in his shoulder. Now he was stiff and sore and stuck in a sling and unable to take the pain medications because they made him groggy.

So he'd settled on being pissy instead.

It wasn't that different from how he usually was, in all honesty. He liked to keep to himself most of the time anyway. Being an asshole to everyone who cared about him over the past week had ensured a lot of alone time.

Only his mother and Delaney were tough enough to put up with his crabby ass. He hadn't even seen his brothers in days.

And now this.

A distracting woman who had clearly never set foot on a farm had her car and camper parked on his land and was looking for him for *personal* reasons.

He *really* didn't have the time, or temper, for this.

"So you do know him?" she asked.

He nodded without thinking.

"So you can tell me where to find him."

"Why would I do that?" he asked. "You're a total stranger, and I don't know why you need to find him."

She chewed on the inside of her cheek for a moment, watching him. Actually, she was checking him out, if he wasn't mistaken. Her gaze roamed from his ball cap to the tips of his boots. Slowly.

"Why don't you tell me who *you* are," she finally said.

He almost laughed at that. "No. For the same reasons."

"I'm not here selling anything."

"Okay."

She sighed. "I know an old friend of his. She just passed away and I thought he would maybe like to know."

TJ frowned. "Who?" He couldn't imagine who this girl might know. Most of his friends—old and new—lived right here in Sapphire Falls. But he did have some buddies who he'd met during his stint in the Army National Guard. He'd lost touch with a couple of them.

The girl swallowed. And she really was a girl. She couldn't have been more than twenty-five, if that. If she was a wife or girlfriend of one of his Guard buddies, the guy had gone about nine years younger.

"Melody Daniels."

Didn't sound familiar at all. "Sorry, I don't know her."

The pixie frowned at him. "I don't care if *you* know her. I'm here to talk to Thomas Bennett."

"You're talkin' to him."

Okay, so there *was* another Thomas John Bennett in town. And TJ had a bad feeling in his gut suddenly. Who was this girl? And who was Melody Daniels? She wasn't from here. TJ knew everyone in Sapphire Falls. There were no Daniels here at all and hadn't been in his lifetime.

Of course, there was another Thomas's lifetime that might be important here.

The girl was giving him an irritated look now. "You can't be Thomas Bennett."

He shrugged. "I am. I promise you."

"Thomas John Bennett," she clarified.

"I go by TJ. But, yes."

She shook her head. "But...you can't be." She reached behind her for a cloth bag. She lifted it into her lap and started digging through it. "Here." She pulled something from the depths and tossed the bag back onto the hood. She slid to the ground, her bracelets all jingling like she was covered in sleigh bells.

The skirt swung down, covering her legs to her ankles, but it hung low enough from her slim hips to widen the strip of bare stomach and show more of that damn tattoo. Any hope he'd had that the top would also shift and cover more of her was dashed. Seemed the white blouse thingy was intentionally short. It fell just below her breasts and still hung off one shoulder.

TJ's mind started to wander. How far did the tattoo extend up and down? Did she have others? Where were those and what were they of?

"This says Thomas John Bennett on the back." She held up an old photograph.

His attention was right back on their conversation with that.

He held out a hand and she came forward on bare feet, ignoring the pair of flip-flops—pink, of course—lying next to the wheel of her car.

Green. Her eyes were green. And she had a light sprinkling of freckles on her nose.

He kept his eyes off of the tattoo. Somehow.

He took the photo from her, dreading it for some reason. Looking down, he saw a younger version of his dad and his dad's best friend, Dan. Between them was a beautiful girl who TJ had never seen. A girl who looked a lot like the one in front of him.

The dread in his gut increased.

"Where did you get this?" he asked.

"From Melody." She leaned in to point at the woman in the photo.

She smelled like flowers. Wild flowers. And fresh air.

TJ cleared his throat. Jesus.

"And who is Melody, exactly?" he asked.

The girl looked up at him. She crossed her arms. "You know, you're a total stranger to me too."

"You know my name is TJ Bennett and where I live. I'd say you're a little ahead here."

She sighed and took the photo back from him. "Okay, fine.

Melody was my mom. I'm here to find Thomas because she…"
She stopped and cleared her throat, staring down at the photo
instead of looking at TJ. "She passed away recently. She used to
talk about Sapphire Falls all the time. Always very fondly. And
then I found this photo in her stuff. There were lots of photos,
but this was the only one with a name on it. So I wanted to
come and meet him." She lifted her eyes to TJ's. "But you're
obviously not the Thomas John I'm looking for."

"Obviously." The Thomas John in the photo was clearly his
father. About twenty-five years ago.

Yep, that ball of dread kept getting bigger and bigger.

And she'd just lost her mom. God. Any thought of tossing
her back onto the gravel road leading *away* from his house was
gone with that. Her mom had died recently, and she was here
wanting to meet his father. There was really only one conclu-
sion to reach, but he stubbornly ignored it.

Not that it mattered.

There was a beautiful woman in need on his doorstep.
Another beautiful woman in need. He'd been there and had the
T-shirt.

This had all the makings of a big, dramatic emotional
entanglement. Exactly the last thing TJ wanted. Ever again.

"You look a lot like him though," the woman said, studying
TJ.

He shifted his weight. Fuck. He did *not* want to do this. He
had work to do that would take him twice as long with one arm.
He had a mother to convince that he was fine. He had grumpiness to practice.

And he wouldn't want to do this even if he felt great and
had nothing else to do.

This was trouble. He sensed it.

"He's your dad, right?" she finally asked.

What was he going to do here? TJ nodded.

"Is he…still alive?" she asked carefully.

He actually snorted at that. "Uh, yeah. Very." His dad was a big, tough, outgoing smart-ass. He couldn't imagine anything taking him down. Ever.

She looked relieved at that. "And he still lives here?"

That meant she hadn't spent much time in town. It would take her about three seconds in the gas station, diner, grocery store or bakery to find out all of that information. Or it was very possible she'd run into Thomas himself at the gas station, diner, grocery store or bakery.

Sapphire Falls was a small town with very few secrets.

Except...maybe there were a few skeletons in closets around here. He could only hope the closet wasn't his father's.

TJ sighed. "He still lives here. Why do you really want to find him though? Not just to reminisce about your mom, I'm guessing."

He didn't want to hear this.

She swallowed and looked hesitant. Those big round emerald eyes were easy to read. She recognized that he wasn't going to like whatever she was about to say.

"What's your name?" he asked when she hadn't answered.

Her lack of answer was kind of answer in and of itself.

"Hope."

He stared at her. Hope.

Well, of course it was. Because he hadn't had hope in a really long time. And now Hope was right in front of him and he still couldn't have it—her—because...

"I think he might be my father."

Hearing it was way worse than thinking it.

TJ took a step back, out of reach of her flowery scent, away from the freckles and the pixie ears and the tattoo that he *still* wanted to see closer.

Fuck.

Things really did keep getting better and better.

He was stirred by the first woman in a long time and she might just be his *sister*.

T he look on TJ Bennett's face was a mix of shock, frustration and pain.

The pain, she didn't really get.

Except that she was feeling a pain of her own.

The man was hot. Really hot. Big and solid, with an attitude that said most people listened to him and no one messed with him. He wore a ball cap instead of a cowboy hat, but otherwise he looked the part of a country boy she'd always imagined— blue jeans, T-shirt and boots. And muscles and tanned skin and scruffy jaw...and muscles.

The word *rugged* suddenly had a very visual definition.

And he might be her *brother*.

Ew.

It was so unfair. She hadn't been attracted to anyone in a long time and her life had really sucked lately. The idea of spending some time in the little town that had changed her mother's life had seemed like the perfect solution.

Hope knew she had been conceived in Sapphire Falls. She also knew this photo was the only one her mother had kept in a special place in her journal and looked at regularly. Only one man's name was written on the back. Thomas John Bennett. He had to be the one. The guy Melody had loved. Hope's father.

So she'd let her company know she was taking some time off, packed her mom's stuff—her clothes, her books, her journals—into her mom's teeny tiny camper and had headed for Sapphire Falls.

Of course, Hope hadn't ever used the camper before, and she hadn't realized just how teeny tiny the camper really was. Melody had been all about a minimalist lifestyle, not becoming dependent on material things, trusting the universe to bring her what she needed when she needed it.

Living like her mom, even for a summer, was going to take some getting used to.

And then there was the idea of meeting her father.

That was also going to take some getting used to.

It had always just been her and her mom. She knew that her father knew nothing about her and she'd always accepted Melody's assertion that the universe had given Hope to Melody, not to them as a couple. The summer had changed Melody's life, not her father's life. It had always seemed normal and happy to have only a mother. Lots of kids she knew had unique family situations. It had never fazed Hope a bit.

Until her mom died.

Now Hope was filling the summer with things that had been important to her mom to try to understand her better. They had gone through many of the typical mother-daughter phases. Like Hope rebelling against her mother's practices and beliefs simply because they were her mother's practices and beliefs. They just hadn't had a chance to get to that phase where the daughter came back around and realized how much they had in common and that her mom was a really amazing person after all.

Some of her hopes for the summer came from grief. Absolutely. But some of it was the self-awareness that Melody had possessed a wisdom and confidence and peace that Hope wanted. She'd expected once she was an adult and had experiences and adventures of her own, she and her mom would find common ground.

Now they would never get to that point.

The woman Hope had adored and who had challenged her and driven her crazy was gone.

Hope had more growing to do. She wasn't sure she knew how to do it without her mom.

So she was living life in Melody's footsteps this summer. Living the way Melody had and visiting the places and people who had been important to Melody in her life.

Including Hope's dad.

"How old are you?"

Hope focused on the big man still frowning down at her.

"Twenty-five."

He stood looking at her, saying nothing else.

"So..." Hope said into the silence that stretched between her and TJ Bennett. The younger Thomas John. The son of Thomas John Bennett.

Her maybe half-brother.

Yeah, still *ew*.

She'd definitely been having lusty thoughts about him. He was just so...there. No woman could ignore this guy. He took up space like he owned it, like the space molded around him, wanting to be close.

Holy crap.

"Can you tell me where he lives?" she asked, concentrating on the thing that had brought her here from Arizona. Not big, bulging biceps, not wide shoulders, not dark-blue eyes that somehow seemed suspicious and inviting at the same time.

TJ's eyes narrowed. "No."

Hope felt her eyebrows arch. "No?"

It was a small town. Surely she could ask the first person she saw on the street. Of course, the lady at the bakery had been super friendly but had sent her *here* instead of to the elder Thomas. Maybe she'd misunderstood Hope when she asked where Thomas John Bennett lived. Maybe she'd assumed Hope was looking for TJ. She supposed that was possible. He was closer to her age, and she figured there were women wanting to find this Thomas all the time.

"No."

Clearly, her possible half-brother wasn't the type to go on and on and on.

"Why not?"

"There is no way in *hell* I'm letting you waltz your pretty butt up onto my dad's front porch and screw everything up unless you know *for sure* what happened between him and your mom."

Her pretty butt? Those three words were so distracting that Hope had to shake her head and replay the last couple of minutes to remember that he was saying *no* to her request to meet the man who she'd traveled over a thousand miles in a *Fiat* to meet.

A Fiat. Did TJ have any idea how small a Fiat really was?

Looking him up and down now, she realized he wouldn't even fit in her car. Her *mother's* car. Hope had a Jeep. A nice, tough, four-wheel-drive Jeep that she could take up into the hills or out into the desert with no problem.

Her mother, on the other hand, loved the tiny, colorful, fuel-efficient Fiat.

Cute. That's what she'd called it.

Hope called it girlie.

But the bright sunshine-yellow always made her smile. It was so Melody.

She focused on TJ. "I don't want to screw anything up for him." She really didn't, but she did acknowledge that learning about a twenty-five-year-old daughter might be a bit of a shock.

"My father has spent his life in this town. He and my mom have been married for thirty-five years. They have four sons, a daughter-in-law, a grandchild on the way, another soon-to-be daughter-in-law and four adopted grandsons. They are pillars of this community." TJ shoved a hand through his hair and took a deep breath. "My grandmother is still alive," he said.

Wow. That was a lot of people. A lot of family.

Hope didn't really know how that stuff worked. It had

always been her and her mom. She had grandparents, but she rarely saw them. Her mom had kind of been an afterthought in their relationship. Their only child, she'd been raised to be incredibly independent and self-sufficient. Melody had never said as much, but Hope got the idea that they'd done so in order to be less burdened themselves. And it had worked. Melody rarely talked to them, almost never saw them and had never ever asked them for anything.

Then it hit her—TJ had a grandmother.

"Is she your dad's mom or your mom's mom?"

He narrowed his eyes, as if knowing what she was thinking. He sighed and answered anyway. "My dad's."

She could have another grandmother. The kind that saw her grandkids. The kind that her grown grandsons loved enough to protect her from crazy women who showed up in yellow Fiats wanting to claim a branch of the family tree.

She took a deep breath. "I see."

"I don't think you do." He was clearly frustrated. "You show up here, out of the blue, claiming you think my dad is your father simply because you have a photograph with his name on the back. I can't let you stir all of this up without knowing for sure."

Of course, she understood that her showing up like this might stir up some things for this family.

She stepped closer, wanting to see his eyes more clearly. She peered up at him, realizing that he was easily eight or nine inches taller than she was. She was an averaged-sized woman, about five-six in her mother's flip-flops. But TJ was an above-average-sized man. He had to be six-three, maybe more. And his hands were *huge*.

And her reaction to that revelation was *completely* inappropriate.

Not only because they'd just met, but because of the whole maybe-related thing.

Since she hadn't yet met the senior Thomas Bennett and had spent all twenty-five years of her life without a father and had turned out just fine, thank you very much, she allowed herself a moment of hoping it wasn't true. Maybe Thomas Bennett was not her father.

That would mean her inappropriate attraction to TJ was not inappropriate at all.

TJ looked a lot like his dad. They had the same dark-brown hair, the same eyes, though TJ's were darker. They were built alike too, from what she could see in the photo. The photo showed Thomas, Melody and the other man from about mid-thigh up. The guys had their arms around Melody's shoulders and she had an arm around each of their waists. They were smiling widely, looking very happy.

Hope wondered if the two Thomas Bennetts shared the same smile. She definitely hadn't seen TJ's yet. But his father was a good-looking guy. This son had definitely taken after him in that department. And TJ had mentioned four sons. He had three brothers? Good Lord, if they were half as hot as TJ, she felt sorry for the females in Sapphire Falls. And the mother who had likely been chasing girls off for years.

But there was nothing about *her* looks that linked her to the man in the photo. Of course, she and her mother could have been twins. Especially considering Melody had looked fifteen years younger than she was, and she'd had Hope when she'd been only nineteen.

"Okay, I get it. I need to know for sure before I introduce myself as his long-lost daughter. How do you suggest I get sure?"

TJ scrubbed his hand over his face. "I don't have time for this," he muttered.

She frowned. That kind of stung. But, yeah, okay, this wasn't really his problem. She'd been directed to the wrong guy by the lady at the bakery, and Thomas was TJ's dad, but that didn't exactly make any of this his issue.

"Yeah, I should just go." She turned and crossed to where her flip-flops lay in the dirt. She slipped them on and started to reach for the car door.

A big hand wrapped around her wrist.

A *big*, hot, heavy hand.

Whoa.

She looked up at TJ, startled.

"You can't leave." He didn't look happy about that. Resigned. That was the best way to describe his expression.

"Excuse me?"

Honestly, the showing-up-on-a-stranger's-doorstep thing hadn't occurred to her as a bad idea. Her mother had talked about Sapphire Falls with a wistful affection that had Hope believing it was some magical place where everything went right, everyone was generous and kind and there was nothing to fear.

Some people might have thought that was a strange reaction for a girl who had ended up in town due to car trouble, had gotten pregnant and then had to raise the child alone. But Melody had been thrilled. She'd never thought about needing anyone else or even wanting Hope's father involved. The universe had given her the chance to be a mother. She'd reveled in it all.

That was Melody.

Hope didn't look at the world with quite the rose-colored glasses her mother had always worn. Melody had found bright sides and silver linings everywhere. Hope liked to think she was more realistic than that.

"You can't... I can't let you leave," TJ said, still holding her wrist.

Hope's eyes widened. She also hadn't thought for a second

that she might run into a big, hunky farmer who would physically restrain her.

Nor had she thought she would be a little turned-on by that.

Should she be afraid of TJ, or at least intimidated? Maybe. They were strangers. He lived on a farm, miles from the nearest neighbor. And no one knew she was here. There were probably acres on which he could bury a body.

But all she felt with him touching her was heat. Intense, blood-pounding heat.

Half-brother. Half-brother, she tried to remind herself. But all she really heard was *maybe*.

"You can't let me leave?" she repeated. "Why not?"

He felt the heat too?

"Because I don't know you. You could head straight to my dad's house and still fuck everything up."

Ah. Not heat. Distrust and suspicion. Got it.

"I won't," she said. But what would she do? She'd come a thousand miles. She really wanted to meet this guy. This might be her *father* they were talking about here.

TJ wasn't buying it either. "You need to stay here."

Her eyes widened again. She glanced toward the house, then back to him. "Here?"

His gaze dropped to her mouth and he let go of her wrist quickly. "Well, nearby."

All he'd done was look at her lips and they were tingling. Hope pressed them together and ran a hand through her hair. What was happening here? He was practically stumbling over his words. Hope had the definite impression that TJ Bennett always knew what he was going to say and always meant it. Stuttering and stammering were not his style. And she'd only known him for a few minutes.

So maybe not *just* distrust and suspicion. Though those were there too, she knew. And she couldn't really blame him.

"Nearby?"

He looked at her camper. "You can kind of stay anywhere with that thing, right?"

She shrugged. It was not the Ritz-Carlton, but it was shelter. "Yeah, I guess."

"So you can—" He cleared his throat. "Keep it here. Until we can get some answers."

She could keep her camper parked here and stay until they could figure out if Thomas Bennett was her father. Huh.

"We?" she asked. "You're going to help me?"

He sighed. "How do you think *you're* going to get a DNA sample from my father?"

"*You're* going to get one?"

"Someone has to."

His expression still clearly said he didn't have time for this. But he was offering. And he had a point.

"We could do it with a kit. You can get them online. It's just a swab—"

"I know."

She blinked. "You do?"

"Let me handle it. But it can take a week to get the results."

She nodded. "I read that."

He looked her up and down. His gaze traveled from the top of her head to the tips of her toes, and he took his time on various parts in between. In fact, his attention seemed to pause on her tattoo longer than even on her breasts.

She was tingling all over by the time he was done, and again there was a flitting thought of, *Please, please don't let me be related to this guy.*

"You're going to have to stay here," he finally said.

She nodded. "I'm not going anywhere until I know one way or another."

She wasn't here to fill a gap in her life left by her father. She couldn't miss something she'd never had. She'd been loved and cared for. She'd wondered about her dad from time to time, but she'd never felt a deficit in her life.

But this man had been important to her mother. Melody had spent a summer here and had remembered it fondly for twenty-five years.

Hope just wanted to meet him and experience this place.

But she understood that the news of her existence might be a bigger deal for the others involved.

So there hadn't been a lot of thought and planning put into this trip. So what? Melody had always done things by the seat of her pants, gone with the flow, wherever the wind blew her— and any number of other clichés. Hope wanted to live her mother's life for the summer and planning and forethought would definitely not be faithful to that experiment.

"Okay, but I mean you have to stay *here*," TJ said, his eyes finally back on her face.

"Here? As in *here*, on your farm in my camper?"

He nodded. "You will...attract a lot of attention if you go anywhere else."

A corner of her mouth curled at that. "You think so?"

He lifted an eyebrow. "Uh, yeah."

For some reason, that made her feel warm. TJ maybe hadn't meant it as a compliment, but she took it as one. If she'd been in her own clothes, doing her own thing, being the real Hope Daniels, she would have been able to blend in. She had been raised in an unconventional lifestyle by an unconventional woman, but ever since she'd *insisted* on going to public school starting in ninth grade, Hope had been very aware of how *regular* people dressed and ate and acted. Hope was still a vegetarian and loved yoga and her mother's homemade, organic shampoos, soaps and lotions. But she also knew when to downplay her hippie-Earth-girl upbringing and habits and be *normal*.

But if she was going to live and act like Melody, Hope would stand out. Melody always had. It wasn't just how she dressed, it was how she *was*. How she'd looked at things, how she'd approached things, how she'd lived. She'd always had a glow about her that had drawn people to her.

It had driven Hope crazy.

Her mother had never gone anywhere without meeting someone interesting. She would strike up conversations everywhere and errands that should have taken ten minutes often turned into hour-long adventures into someone else's life.

Looking at TJ now, Hope felt an inkling of understanding. She could see the appeal in being adventurous.

It was...strange. There was no better word for it. She didn't know him. He didn't really want her here. She was—potentially anyway—about to stir up some big things for his family, and he might even *be* her family, but she still had an impulse to be in his world for a bit.

Her mom would have gone for it. Impulses were signals, signs of something your soul knew it needed. God, how many times had Hope heard that? How many times had Melody used that to excuse something—quitting a job with benefits, breaking up with a great guy for another not-as-great guy, taking off at midnight for a road trip to the mountains, selling their house for a trailer because she had the *impulse* to minimize her material possessions and simplify her life.

So many times.

And yet Hope had never been able to look at her mother with anything less than resigned affection. Melody had been the happiest person Hope had ever known. She'd embraced everything that had come at her as a chance to learn something and be new and better than she had been before. Her optimism had been boundless.

Not for the first time in her life, Hope wondered if her mom hadn't actually held the secret to life, the universe and everything.

Be happy. No matter what. No matter where.

So maybe right here, right now, was Hope's chance to just be happy. To let go of all the niggling doubts and the little voice that said this wasn't *normal* and just be for a while.

With TJ Bennett.

She shook her head.

Yikes.

Maybe she needed to lay off her mother's home-blended tea she'd been drinking instead of her coffee. Coffee was good. Caffeine was good. She was still going through withdrawals obviously.

"And that's bad?" she finally asked. "To attract attention?"

"Yes." He said it firmly and without hesitation.

She smiled. "Why is that?"

"Because here, people don't just look or talk behind your back. They'll corner you, demand to know who you are, where you're from, what you want and how long you're staying."

She thought about that. Sapphire Falls was a small town in Nebraska. She admittedly knew nothing about those. Sedona wasn't a huge town, but they had millions of tourists every year. Even without the visitors, though, Sedona was almost ten times the size of Sapphire Falls.

"I'm a friendly person," she said. On the friendly-and-interested-in-others spectrum, where her mother was a ten, Hope was about a six, but she did actually like other people. Part of her following in her mother's footsteps this summer was embracing new situations. Learning about small-town life in the Midwest could absolutely be part of that.

"Do you have answers to those questions?" TJ asked.

She thought about the questions again—who she was, where she was from, what she wanted and how long she was staying. "Three of the four," she said.

"Really?"

"I'm Hope Daniels from Sedona, Arizona, and I'm staying for the rest of the summer."

TJ's brows pulled together in a frown. "The rest of the summer?"

"Yes."

He stared at her. "Why?"

She had an answer to that too, but it was complicated. "My mother loved it here. I'd..." She took a deep breath. "I want to experience some of the things that she did, that meant a lot to her. She spent a summer here and said it was the best summer of her life."

TJ didn't say anything for almost a full half minute. "And you're looking for the best summer of your life?"

Something about that question from him made her tingle. She nodded. "Definitely."

He seemed to think about that. His gaze softened slightly. "This is a good place for having amazing summers."

She was taken aback. That was pretty...warm of him. "Good. Amazing sounds like exactly what I need."

And she thought maybe, just maybe, the corner of his mouth curled slightly.

"But I do understand I could be complicating some things by being here," she added.

The softness left his eyes and mouth. "Yeah, you could."

Damn.

"I'm sorry about that," she said sincerely. "I don't want to upset anyone. I guess, I just want to know. Just know who he is for sure. Maybe just meet him. I'm not really looking for someone to spend holidays with or to send Father's Day cards to."

And she wasn't. She knew Father's Day was sometime in June, but she wasn't looking for a *father* exactly. She was twenty-five. She didn't need a father for anything. She had a job with benefits and her own condo. She had no debt. She knew how to take care of herself. She'd never had fatherly advice. Hell, she'd never had a lot of motherly advice either. Her mom had taught her things, exposed her to ideas, given her expectations and then let Hope make her own decisions.

TJ didn't look convinced that she wasn't looking for more than she claimed, but he gave her a nod. "How about we figure out if my dad is..." he coughed, "...yours and we'll go from there."

She understood that this was uncomfortable. Bizarre even. And that TJ wished he hadn't been dragged into it. But she did appreciate the offer of help.

"Okay."

"I'm going over there for dinner tonight. I'll talk to him."

"You're going to tell him?"

"How else will I have a chance to swab his cheek?"

So TJ really did know about DNA tests. That was interesting. "What will he say?" she asked.

TJ shook his head. "I have absolutely no idea."

"But you're not going to tell him in front of your mom or anyone." A sudden thought occurred to her, and she looked toward his house again. "Are you married?"

"No."

"Girlfriend?" she ventured to ask.

"No."

"Good."

He arched a brow, but only said, "I'm not going to tell him in front of anyone. I'll do it in private." He shoved a hand through hair. "Though God knows how I'm going to bring it up."

She pondered her next suggestion for several long seconds. Then she thought about her mom. Melody had been a kind, warm person, but she hadn't had much of a filter. She'd worn her emotions on her sleeve, and if she had a thought, it usually made it out of her mouth without much contemplation. "Maybe I could come."

"To dinner?" TJ asked, clearly thinking that was the worst idea he'd ever heard.

She shrugged. "Yeah. Maybe that would be enough. I could meet him. Talk with him. But he wouldn't have to know who I was."

"First of all, that's crazy. I can't just show up there with a strange woman and no good explanation," TJ said. "And secondly, what if it's not him?"

What if it wasn't him?

Hope looked down at the photo in her hand. She wanted it to be him. That was absolutely the dumbest thing ever. From a photo? Really? But he looked like such a nice guy and he had raised this protective-of-his-family, help-a-stranger-out guy. That had to mean something.

She shrugged. "Maybe I'll just pretend it's him."

"No." TJ's answer was swift and firm.

"Why not?"

"Because then—" He bit off what he was going to say. His jaw tightened. "No. We need to know for sure."

We? But she didn't question that. Now that he knew there was a possibility he had a sister—*oh God*—maybe he *did* need to know for sure.

"Maybe I don't," she finally said. "I've lived this long without him." And if her mom hadn't died, she wouldn't be here right now.

Again, TJ's gaze softened, and Hope felt her breath catch for a millisecond. Hot *and* sweet? Even if it was deep, deep down underneath things? That would be a hard-to-resist combination.

Unless he was her *brother*.

Okay, yeah, maybe she did need to know.

"Hope," TJ said, his voice low. "If you're my father's daughter, he would want to know."

She knew she was staring again, but damn, that was the first time TJ had used her name, and it made something hot and tight settle deep inside her. Something dangerous.

"You sure?" she managed.

He nodded. "Very."

She believed him. She could get in her car and head back to Arizona. Or head to Texas or Florida or New York. Point being, she could *leave* and live like her mom, free on the road, taking the adventures as they came. It would be less complicated. Obviously something she could have thought through before she'd gotten here, but still—she could avoid disrupting this family.

But instead, she heard herself say, "Okay."

"So stay here tonight. I'll go to dinner and...figure something out."

She nodded. "Okay."

He looked as if he was about to say something else but thought better of it. Instead, he moved past her and her car and her camper and headed into the house.

God, please don't let him be my brother.

Because her thoughts about how great he looked walking away in those blue jeans were *not* sisterly. At all.

2

How had this happened?

One minute, he'd been in town picking up the pain pills he was going to try at night because he couldn't sleep worth a shit with his shoulder throbbing, and the next, he had a gigantic pain in another part of his anatomy.

Well, two other parts.

Both below his belt. One in his ass and one...on the opposite side.

TJ stood in front of his kitchen sink, looking out the window. He could just barely see the back of the camper Hope had pulled into his yard. From this vantage point, he couldn't see her car. Thank God. She was again reclining on the hood, reading a book, her skirt hiked up to bare her legs to the sun.

It had taken a lot of will power to drink his iced tea in the kitchen instead of in the living room, in front of the huge picture window that would have given him a perfect view.

He could *not* be attracted to this woman. At least until he knew if his father was her father.

He couldn't use the word *sister*. It gave him the heebie-jeebies.

It was about three in the afternoon, which meant his dad was probably out in his workshop in the barn tinkering with something. TJ could head over there and start the conversation that he was both dreading and wanting to get through as soon as possible. But there was always the chance that someone would come in and overhear something.

There was also the issue of leaving Hope here alone.

She might take off and try to find some answers herself. He couldn't have her wandering Sapphire Falls, asking every guy over the age of forty-five if he'd had a fling with a beautiful blond passing through town twenty-five years ago.

There was also the chance—a very good one, in fact—that someone might show up here unexpectedly. No one called ahead in Sapphire Falls, especially in his family. His mother and Delaney, in particular, had been stopping by on a regular basis, and sooner or later everyone else would get brave and want to see for themselves that he was okay. The minute someone drove up his lane, they would see Hope's bright-yellow car. Not to mention *her*.

And leaving a total stranger alone at his house didn't seem like a good idea. She certainly didn't seem like a thief or a squatter. But what did he know? She was making do with a Fiat and the tiniest camper he'd ever seen. Maybe she'd been counting on getting an invitation to stay in a big, comfortable farmhouse with a clean bed and home-cooked meals. Maybe she did this all the time. Maybe the story about trying to find her father was nothing but a story.

That didn't explain the photo, of course.

He needed some answers. He hit speed dial number three on his phone for his dad's cell.

"Hey, TJ."

"Hey, Dad, I need some help with something. You free right now?" He didn't even feel guilty that his father would assume he needed help because of his shoulder.

"Of course. I'll be right over."

TJ turned away from the window and settled his butt against the counter behind him. He downed the rest of his tea and waited. His dad was about six minutes away.

Sure enough, TJ heard his truck coming a few minutes later.

TJ pushed away from the counter and headed for the front door.

Predictably, his father and Hope met before he even hit the first porch step.

They were smiling at each other. His dad looked simply friendly, like he would meeting anyone new. But Hope looked —excited and nervous.

"Hey, Dad."

"Son."

"This is Hope."

"Yes, we've been introduced." Thomas glanced at the license plate on the front of her car. "Arizona?"

Hope nodded. "Road trip."

"Let's go inside," TJ said to his dad. His gaze went to Hope.

She nodded and TJ motioned for his dad to head into the house. He started after him but turned back and said, "I just need to—"

"It's okay," she said. "I understand."

He gave her a single nod and then followed his father into the house. How could he feel bad about leaving her out of this conversation? He didn't *know* her. This was his dad. He needed to protect his father first, and Thomas should have the chance to explain before it was in front of anyone else. Even his daughter.

Thomas settled at TJ's kitchen table.

"Is everything okay?" Thomas asked as TJ took a seat.

TJ wasn't going to lie now. "I don't know."

"What do you need?"

TJ's chest tightened. Thomas would do or give anything he could to make his sons and their families happy, safe and healthy.

If he had a daughter, he would want to know. TJ knew that.

He decided to jump right in. "Does the name Melody Daniels ring a bell?"

Thomas frowned slightly. "No. Why?"

"You *don't* know a girl named Melody who spent a summer here twenty-six years ago?" TJ asked.

Thomas's surprise was clear. "I do. I don't recall her last name being Daniels. But, yes, I remember Melody."

TJ took a deep breath. "Hope is her daughter."

Thomas smiled. "She looks just like her. I had a flash of déjà vu when I saw her."

"She's twenty-five," TJ said. "Never knew her dad. Says her mom told her he's here in Sapphire Falls."

Thomas sat up straighter. "Oh."

Oh? TJ frowned. "That's it?"

Thomas's gaze was focused on the fridge across the room. He was clearly lost in thought.

"Dad?"

Thomas focused on TJ again. "Yeah?"

"Dad..." TJ took a deep breath. "Is it possible that you're her father?"

Thomas jerked at that. "What? Melody said that?"

TJ shook his head. "Melody passed away. She never told Hope her dad's name. But she has a photograph of her mom with you and Uncle Dan. Your name is the only thing on the back."

"And you think that means *I'm* her *father*?" Thomas asked.

"Hope thinks that's what it means. Actually," TJ said, "I think she *hopes* that's what it means."

"TJ, I knew Melody. So did your mother. We were married with all four of you boys by then."

"I know. But...things happen."

"And you thought things might have happened between me and Melody?" Thomas asked with mild disbelief.

"I don't know what to think. Hope was sitting in my front yard when I got home today, and she dumped all of this on me. She was actually looking for you and got to me by mistake."

"And as soon as you heard she needed help, you volunteered," Thomas said.

"No." He was helping Hope only because it directly impacted his family. He wasn't being suckered in by a pretty face. This time. "I wanted to keep her from showing up at *your* house. I wanted to talk to you first. Let you decide how you wanted to handle it."

Thomas nodded. "Well, thank you. But there's nothing to handle."

"What do you think of doing a paternity test?" TJ asked. "A simple cheek swab. We can do it here. No one has to know anything until we know for sure. Results take about a week."

TJ knew more than he'd like to about how the DNA tests for paternity worked, and knew personally how long that week could feel.

"There's no reason for that," Thomas said. "I am not Hope's father."

"Dad, I know this is awkward. But we all screw up sometimes." His father knew exactly how familiar TJ was with this kind of stuff. "I know it will take getting used to—"

"TJ," his dad cut him off firmly. "I am *not* Hope's father. I can promise you that."

TJ pulled a breath in through his nose. His father's word was worth the world. Integrity was one of the top three words TJ would use to describe his father if asked. Finally, he nodded. "Okay."

Damn.

He was so conflicted. He didn't want his father to be Hope's.

It meant Thomas had not cheated and TJ didn't have a sister he hadn't known about for twenty-five years.

And that his crazy attraction for her was okay.

God, *that* was a relief.

In fact, his body surged with the sudden realization that everything he'd felt was perfectly fine.

He looked at his dad. "Totally one hundred percent positive?"

"One hundred percent," Thomas said firmly. He got up from the table and headed for the front door. TJ sighed and followed. Thomas was upset that TJ had doubted him. He understood that, but he still needed his dad's help.

"Dad—"

"Hope," Thomas called from the porch. "I think you should join us."

Hope looked surprised, but she slid off of the hood of the car. "Are you sure?" Her gaze went to TJ.

TJ nodded. If his father was good with her hearing this, then TJ was. This was Thomas's story now.

TJ and Thomas stepped back for Hope to enter the house ahead of them. Back in the kitchen, TJ offered them both iced tea. Once everyone had a glass and was seated, Thomas took over the conversation.

"Hope," he said gently. "I knew your mom. But I'm not your father."

Hope looked at Thomas as she processed that. Finally, she nodded. "Okay."

"You were with mom," TJ said. He trusted that. His parents were very much in love. They were the solid foundation of the Bennett family.

Thomas nodded, but his gaze was still on Hope. "And Dan was in love with Melody."

TJ started at that and looked at his dad. "Really?"

Hope's eyes widened.

Thomas nodded. "Very. So even if your mom hadn't been a factor, I wouldn't have so much as flirted with Melody. We were all friends. She hung out with us all summer. There are lots of other pictures, but maybe she didn't keep them, or maybe you just haven't found them yet," he said to Hope. "I don't know. But she and Dan had a fling that summer. I would wager this farm that Dan is your father."

TJ felt a strange surge of happiness at that. He'd found Hope's father for her and it wasn't *his* father. Dan was one of Thomas's best friends.

Hope looked thoughtful when TJ glanced at her.

"So we'll introduce her to Uncle Dan," TJ said. "Do you want to give him a call or should I?"

And then she could park her camper and her pretty little butt—and long, silky hair and big green eyes and long legs, tattoo and cute ears—over there. And TJ could get on with his being pissy about his shoulder by himself. Though that was depressing suddenly.

"Neither," Thomas said.

"*Neither*?" He looked at Hope again. "You think she should just go over there?"

"No," Thomas said firmly. "Definitely not."

"We have to introduce them," TJ said.

"Maybe." Thomas looked conflicted now.

"Maybe? This is her *father*. She came all this way to meet him. Her mom is gone. We can't *not* let her meet him."

"Let me think about it," Thomas said again.

"What's going on?" TJ asked.

"Dan and JoEllen were also dating that summer," Thomas said. "Dan broke up with Jo because of Melody."

"He cheated on JoEllen?" TJ asked.

Thomas looked at Hope. "No. At least I don't think so. I think he broke up with Jo before anything really happened with Melody," Thomas said. "He'd asked Melody to stay. But she had no intention of that. She was almost ten years younger than we were. She had a lot of things she wanted to do. She hung out with us because Dan was the one who picked her up when her car broke down. Come to think of it," he said, looking at Hope. "She was pulling a camper like that one."

Hope nodded. "That's Mom's camper." They were the first words she'd spoken.

Thomas smiled. "She said she loved sleeping out under the stars but that the camper would do in the rain."

TJ got the definite impression that his father had liked Melody.

"That sounds like her," Hope said with a smile. "It's called a teardrop camper. There's hardly any room inside for anything more than the bed and a bit of storage, but she only used it when the weather didn't cooperate with sleeping outside." She traced a finger up and down through the condensation on the side of her glass. "I'm guessing she also said something about her summer here being just one adventure of many she needed to go on."

Thomas laughed. "Something like that." He shook his head. "She was...different from the girls here. Sweet, kind, warm, but very...earthy," he said. "Very into self-expression and being free and open. She dressed differently, ate differently, thought differently." Thomas was definitely having a hard time describing Melody, and yet TJ knew what he was saying. "She introduced us to hummus and edamame and *kombucha*."

TJ frowned. He knew edamame and hummus, though he'd never tried hummus. But he had no idea what *kombucha* was.

Hope laughed. "Really? Do you still drink it?"

Thomas shuddered. "No way. Couldn't get into that." He smiled at Hope. "You look just like her."

Hope looked pleased at that comment. "She was a force of nature, that's for sure."

"I'm sorry to hear she's gone," Thomas said. "Are you an only child?"

TJ sat back. Well, this wasn't all bad. He could get to know Hope better this way.

He didn't let himself think too hard about why that was appealing.

Hope nodded. "She never married and never had any more children. It was just her and me all my life."

"Can I ask what happened to her?" Thomas asked. His tone was warm and kind. "If you don't want to talk about it, I understand."

Hope took a deep breath and TJ fought the urge to cover her hand with his.

"She was hiking with a friend," Hope said. "It was a path she'd done a million times. It was totally routine. She felt fine. Everything was great until they got to the point where they were going to turn around. Without any warning, she suddenly passed out. At least that's what her friend thought. Turned out it was a brain aneurysm. She died instantly. It was...strange. Random, really. She had no signs or symptoms, nothing that would have alerted her to a problem. And there was nothing anyone could have done. It was just...her time."

Hope was looking at Thomas as she told the story, but as she finished, she looked to TJ.

"So I totally wasn't ready for her to go. And I'm here now because I want to walk in a few of her footsteps. I want to see and experience and meet people and places that were important to her."

TJ had no idea what to say, and this time he didn't fight the urge to cover her hand. Or maybe he did it before he even felt an urge or thought about it. It was simply an instinct.

"I understand that," Thomas said. "And I'm glad Sapphire Falls meant something to her."

"And Dan," TJ said. "Obviously."

Thomas nodded. "Yeah."

"So we have to introduce them. Dan would want to know Hope, wouldn't he?"

Thomas sighed. "That's complicated." He met Hope's eyes. "It's not about you personally, honey. But your mom broke Dan's heart when she left. He'd ended a three-year relationship with the only other woman he'd ever been with for her, and when she left...it took a long time for him to get over her. In fact, I'm not sure he ever did completely. He eventually got back together with JoEllen, but it was tough, and I think deep down she also believes he's still in love with your mom. He might want to know about you, but it will cause issues with his wife and..." Thomas looked at TJ. "They haven't always had a perfect relationship."

TJ felt Hope squeeze his hand, and he looked at her.

"I don't need to tell him who I am," she said. "I don't want to cause trouble."

TJ felt his heart clench. Damn. He did *not* want to get sucked into a big family drama. But he couldn't lie to Hope either and tell her it would all be okay. Nor could he say that it was a good idea for her to *not* meet Dan. Fuck.

"Jo's bipolar," TJ told her. "And Dan's an alcoholic. Not a great mix. She doesn't take the medication she needs to regulate her disorder. Dan takes care of her. And drinks because of it. And they have a daughter. Who also gives Dan a lot of excuses to drink."

Hope's eyes widened. "Daughter?"

TJ nodded. Her half-sister. "Peyton. Peyton's twenty-one. She's...a wild child. Never thinks things through. She likes to party and maxes out her credit cards and attracts loser guys, and when she gets into trouble she calls her daddy."

TJ glanced at his father. Dan was one of Thomas's best friends, but all of this was common knowledge in Sapphire Falls. He wasn't sure how Thomas would feel about TJ sharing all of Dan's baggage, but somehow he felt Hope deserved to know. Besides, Thomas and Dan's friendship had started a long time ago, before any of that baggage had been an issue. At one time, they'd been two peas in a pod. Now, with Dan's drinking and marital issues, he and Thomas had very little in common.

Except their devotion to family and friends.

The men shared that and it was what kept Thomas around, helping his friend attempt to help his family.

Thomas apparently agreed that Hope needed all of the information. "Dan started drinking after Melody left," he said. "And I really believe that he lets Jo and Peyton walk on him, even to this day, because he feels guilty about his relationship with Melody. It's like he's been trying to make that up to Jo all this time, so he gives in on everything. Neither of them really knows how to parent, so Peyton gets to do whatever she wants."

Hope seemed to be taking it all in. She hardly reacted outwardly though.

TJ of course knew Dan's wife and daughter, but he'd never known the reason behind it all. He loved Dan.

Fortunately for TJ, his own wife had left him, and his brothers had intervened to stop his drinking before it had gotten out of hand. Dan was still with his wife, and his friends' interventions over the years hadn't stuck.

Not that TJ blamed Dan. If he'd still been with Michelle, he and the bottle would be close.

"Finding out that Dan fathered another child, even accidentally, who has grown into a beautiful, independent, responsible woman might be a tough blow," Thomas said. "I'm not saying they shouldn't have to face it and deal with it, but I do worry about the fallout."

Something about that frustrated the hell out of TJ, even as he understood it. He felt like he knew Dan. Dan's friends, including TJ's own father, had never been through some of the stuff that drove Dan to drink and didn't understand him completely. Their marriages were good and their children had turned out well. TJ understood why Dan stayed in the marriage, and he understood why the other man drank. He didn't agree with it or condone it, but he understood it. At the same time, he caught himself feeling sorry for Dan and labeling him as weak. It was a tough position to be in. Especially when TJ also remembered Dan from before he'd gotten married and had Peyton. He'd just been a kid, but he remembered Dan being fun and laughing and playing practical jokes. It had been a long time since he'd seen that side of Dan.

"So what do we do?" TJ asked.

Thomas shook his head and blew out a breath. "Let me think about it."

"I think Dan would want to know her," TJ insisted.

"I think so too. But I don't think Dan would want Jo and Peyton to know."

Could Jo make Dan even more miserable than he was now? Maybe. TJ shuddered with the thought.

"So you want us to wait?" TJ asked. "For how long?"

Thomas sighed. "I don't know. I'll feel things out."

"Do I get a vote?" Hope asked.

They both turned to look at her.

She pulled her hand from TJ's and put both hands around her glass. "I need to think as well."

"You do?" TJ asked.

"I'll admit that coming here was a spontaneous decision. I knew that my father, whoever he was, might be surprised to meet me and maybe wouldn't be thrilled. But it didn't occur to me that I might not want to know him."

TJ frowned. "What does that mean?"

"I don't want to stir up trouble for anyone or mess with anyone's relationships, especially one that's already tenuous. And maybe Dan isn't someone I need to know. I told you before that I'm not really looking for a *father*. I just wanted to meet the guy who was so important to my mom." She looked at Thomas. "It's more about knowing *her* better than it is about knowing him."

Dan was an okay guy. He'd made some poor decisions, he handled confrontation badly, and he had let guilt and grief over Melody turn him into a doormat for his wife and daughter. But he was basically a decent guy. When he wasn't drinking.

But, yeah, okay, maybe he wasn't someone Hope would love getting to know. That sounded horrible, but there it was.

"You came all this way," Thomas said. "You wanted to meet him. Let me figure out a way to make it work."

She looked back at TJ. "Maybe he's not the reason I was supposed to come here."

TJ felt like he'd touched an electric fence—a hot shock burst through his body as he met her eyes.

What the *hell*?

Hope was becoming more and more the *last* type of woman he would ever get involved with. If she thought there was some kind of cosmic force at work here, that fate or some damn thing had brought her here, he was going to stay far, far away.

"Well, it's certainly your choice if you want to meet him and get to know him or not," Thomas said.

"I need to think about it," she said again.

"And I'll think of the best way to handle this with Dan," Thomas said. "Then we can decide what to do."

"Okay," Hope agreed.

"And in the meantime?" TJ asked. This sounded like a lot of thinking and waiting around. Not two of his favorite past times.

"Hope should stay here. Lay low," Thomas said.

So then he could stay as far, far away from her as his own front yard. Dammit.

"Stay here?" Hope repeated.

"If you go into town, everyone is going to notice and want to know who you are and why you're here."

TJ shrugged casually in spite of the chaotic mess of emotions churning in him about all of this. "Told you," he said.

She laughed lightly and TJ felt it all the way to the soles of his feet. *More.* That's all he could think. *I want more of that.*

"Okay, so I'll camp out for another day or so."

She gave him a look that was hard to decipher, and he had to wonder if she was thinking that *this* was why she'd ended up here after all.

Fuck that fate shit. He'd been with a girl who'd given him all of that romantic crap and look how that had turned out.

He stretched to his feet, accepting the fact that he was involved, at least for a few more days. He was anxious to get those days started and over with.

"Let me know," he said to his dad. "And," he hesitated, "I'm sorry I thought…"

"Don't be." Thomas got to his feet as well. "I understand. And we'll figure this out for Hope and Dan. Somehow."

TJ pulled his dad into a quick hug. "You're the best man I know," he said gruffly.

And that was why he still felt a twinge of regret that Thomas was *not* Hope's father. Thomas was definitely a better man than Dan.

Thomas cleared his throat. "Well, I raised some pretty great men too."

TJ blinked and nodded, turning away before he did something really uncomfortable, like cry.

He walked his dad to the front door. Thankfully, Hope stayed in the kitchen, maybe sensing that the men needed a moment alone.

"This all became your project pretty quickly," Thomas commented as they stepped out onto the porch.

"What was I supposed to do?" TJ asked more sharply than he'd intended. "She was in my front yard telling me she thought she was my sister."

Evidently, he could say the word now that he knew it wasn't true.

That comment made Thomas grimace. "I didn't even think of that."

"I couldn't just tell her to hit the road."

Thomas nodded. "Of course not."

"I *am* concerned about her getting close to Dan, now that you pointed out all of the possible complications."

Thomas looked at him. "For Dan or for her?"

Good question. "Both."

"It's not your decision to make, son."

"But we know Dan. It's up to us to be sure that this doesn't hurt Hope."

"Ah, so more *her*."

Dammit.

"You're getting very involved here," Thomas said.

Yeah. He was. Unintentionally. He was going to need to be careful around this woman. With Michelle, he'd gotten involved knowing full well what he was getting into and he'd done it anyway. With Hope, it was happening accidentally. He didn't know her, didn't really know how this was all going to play out. Yet here he was in the middle of it.

"So the sooner we figure this out, the better," TJ said.

"I promise I'll figure something out as soon as I can."

His father left and TJ headed back into the house. Now what? He and Hope were going to have to kill time together for a day or two? Sure, what could possibly go wrong in that plan?

But she was gone when he went back into the kitchen. She must have exited out the back door. TJ breathed deeply. He wasn't disappointed she was gone. Sure, he might be even more intrigued by her now that he knew a little bit about her life, but he didn't want any intrigue in *his* life. He liked things straight-forward and routine. He liked knowing what to expect. Boring was good. Welcome, even, after having Michelle around.

And clearly, Hope needed some space. That made sense. She needed to think about the new information she had as well and make some decisions. If she decided she wanted to leave everything alone and *not* meet Dan, things would be a hell of a lot easier.

At that thought, he glanced back through the living room. Her car was still parked out front, so she hadn't snuck around the side of the house and jumped in her car at the first opportunity. Okay, that was good. Or was it? She was sticking around, at least for now. Was that a good thing?

Hell, he didn't even know how he felt about all of this now. If she left, what difference did it make? She now knew which man in the photo was her father and that he'd been madly in love with her mom. Maybe that was enough for her.

But how could that be enough? TJ couldn't imagine life without his family. Yes, it would be quieter and he'd have a lot less worry and frustration in his life. But he couldn't imagine having a quiet dinner alone *every* night. Or spending holidays without chaos and laughter. Or not having four other houses he could go to at any time and be welcomed and feel completely at home.

Hope had a trailer and a car. Presumably, she had a house or apartment back in Arizona too, but she had no family. Presumably, she also had a job, friends, maybe even a bigger car somewhere. But she still didn't have family. Except for Dan. And Peyton.

TJ blew out a breath. It didn't seem that straightforward and boring were in his near future.

He wanted this woman to know her family. However small and imperfect they might be, they were still hers.

TJ felt strongly about family. Always had. He'd been raised in a solid, loving home where people stood by one another no matter what. He had a lot of friends, but he knew for a fact that wasn't the same as those bound to him by blood. Family was forever. Family was the people there long before and long after most friendships started and ended. He'd also learned a lot about friendship from being with Michelle.

Many of his friends had stood by him when things had gotten crazy and Michelle had turned his life into an episode of the Maury Povich show. Many of them had stood by him when it had all fallen apart and the most private parts of his private life had become public gossip. But with Michelle being a hometown girl—and the *other guy*, Colby, being from Sapphire Falls as well—their group of friends had been divided when their relationship broke apart. The only people he could count on to be there for him, no matter what happened or what was said, was his family and Dan. Dan had been there for him through all of it. They'd shared more than one bottle of whiskey during that time. Dan was a drunk, but he was a good guy.

It made TJ even more determined to figure out a way to make this work for Hope and Dan. Even with his own demons, Dan had been there for TJ, and he would be there for Hope too. And maybe Dan needed someone who would really truly be there for him, as well. God knew Thomas and others had tried. But again, family was stronger. Maybe Hope, his *daughter,* the child created from his one true love match, would give Dan a reason to put the bottle down and would give him some light in his life.

Light seemed like the right word when TJ thought of Hope. She seemed full of light.

And that ridiculous thought went right along with him thinking of pixies.

Jesus. She was making him crazy.

TJ puttered around the house for a while but found himself checking out front every few minutes to see if Hope had come back. Not that he cared. He was just curious.

But by the time an hour had passed since she'd left the

house, and he was watching for her more than he was watching what he was doing inside, he knew he had to go find her.

He had stuff to do. He couldn't go chasing her all over the countryside.

And where was she? There wasn't anything out here but pastures and cornfields and trees and the pond. *He* knew how relaxing and comforting it could be alone out here, but what was the Arizona hippie girl going to do in the middle of a cornfield? And if she'd headed the other way, she would have found the road.

She needed to stay away from the road.

If anyone drove by, they would definitely stop. He wasn't afraid for her safety. It was more the churning of the rumor mill that would result. Even if she were wearing blue jeans and a T-shirt like most of the girls around here, anyone driving by would know she didn't belong. Add in her swirly skirt and her long, white-blond, pink-tipped hair and jingly jewelry and bare stomach and... TJ frowned as he lost his train of thought.

Oh, yeah—she would no way go unnoticed by anyone driving the road past his house.

And if she was walking through the pasture, it would only take her about two miles to end up in Travis's pasture that butted up against TJ's. And if Travis met her... Well, TJ didn't really want to think about how that might go.

That meant TJ had to find her before anyone else did.

She could be walking in the woods that bordered his property, or at the manmade pond he and Travis shared. Either was a great choice for meditative thinking, but they were *his* spots. He didn't share them.

TJ pulled a cap from the hooks by the back door and put it on as he headed out. He should just go check on her. Just to be sure she was okay and hadn't gotten lost on her way back to the house.

The pond was only a five-minute walk from his back door

and he decided to try there first. He'd built a wooden dock on his side to fish and swim from. He could also launch a small boat from the dock to fish in the middle of the pond they had stocked with bluegill, largemouth bass and catfish, but TJ preferred to fish from the dock and the big wooden chairs he'd built for that exact purpose.

As he approached the pond, he heard nothing but the birds and insects and his chairs were empty, but as he stepped up onto the wooden boards and could see over the backs of the chairs, he realized he'd guessed correctly.

Hope was at the end of his dock.

Dammit.

This was his spot. This was where he came to think and be alone. And now *she* was here.

Blowing in, taking over, stirring things up and soaking in to everything. Why did women always do that to him?

As he moved farther down the dock, he saw past the top of her blond head to her bare back.

Bare. She was sunbathing again. Topless this time.

He tripped over one of the wooden slats and the thunk of his boot against the dock as he caught himself got her attention. She was on her stomach, thank God, and she turned her head toward him.

"Hi," she said with a smile.

Hi? Seriously? She was half-naked on his dock—his special, solitary spot—stretched out to soak up the sun like a damn cat.

And then all he could think about was petting her.

Fuck.

"I was starting to worry that you'd gotten lost," he managed.

She started to sit up and he put his hand up.

"No!" he said loudly.

She hesitated and then gave him a grin. She'd been lying on top of her shirt, so she gathered it against her breasts as she sat and tucked her legs under her like she had on the car hood.

Holding the flimsy white top against her breasts was covering herself in only the very strictest terms. Her palms cupped the mounds under the shirt, giving him a perfect image of their size and shape.

He shoved his good hand into his back pocket and resolved to stay where he was. There were at least twenty feet between them, and that didn't seem like quite enough.

"It's gorgeous out here," she said.

More so now ran through his mind, but he just nodded.

"I took a walk and found this place and couldn't make myself leave," she said.

He felt similarly about the spot. Even before there'd been a gorgeous, half-naked woman here. Hell, partly *because* there were no gorgeous half-naked women here. Until now.

"You've been gone for quite a while."

She lifted an eyebrow. "I didn't realize you were keeping track."

"Just got a little worried."

"About me?"

"Well, if you go missing, I'm the first person they're going to suspect, right?"

She laughed and he felt it like a punch to the gut.

"But no one knows I'm even here," she pointed out.

"My dad does."

"He'd cover for you," she said confidently.

TJ chuckled, surprised as he did that she could make him laugh. "Yeah, he would. But now that I know you're okay, I'll leave you alone." He took a step backward, knowing that he should actually *turn* as he walked away but not quite ready to lose the view.

"I've been thinking about everything," she said, getting to her feet.

Damn. She wanted to talk.

Why he felt it was his responsibility to be her sounding board, he couldn't explain, but he stopped walking.

"And?" he asked.

"I'm wondering if there's a way for me to meet him—Dan, I mean—without telling him who I am. Maybe get to know him just a little. I'd love to simply *talk* to the man who my mom fell in love with."

TJ frowned and took a few steps forward without thinking. There were a number of things in her answer that he wanted to know more about. But for some reason, the first thing he said was, "He was madly in love with her. How do you know she was in love with him?"

"The photo."

"The one that has my dad's name on the back?" TJ asked. "Why?"

"I figure she wrote your dad's name because she was afraid she might forget it. She didn't write Dan's—that must mean she knew she'd always remember it. And I found it in her journal. There are other pictures in boxes and stuff, but that was the only one in her journal."

"And all of that means she loved him?" TJ asked.

"And my last name."

TJ took another couple steps forward. "What do you mean?"

"I didn't figure it all out until I was about ten, I guess. I finally put it together that most kids had their dad's last name and that my mom's parents' last name was Warren. I figured Daniels was my dad's last name. When I asked mom about it, she just said that she changed her last name before I was born. She never told me it had to do with my dad, but..."

TJ shoved a hand through his hair. "Wow."

She smiled. "My mom had boyfriends, but no one was ever serious. I think it's because she still loved Dan. Even after all these years."

Or that's what Hope wanted to believe. "Then why did she leave?" he asked.

"She was a wanderer," Hope said. "She always said that if we weren't meant to see the world, it wouldn't have been created so big and diverse. If everything else was just like our own backyard, she'd be content to stay put. But there was always more to see and do and try. Even if she had fallen deeply in love, she would have been grateful for the experience and for the fact that it allowed her to be a mother, but she wouldn't have thought it meant she should stay in one place."

TJ frowned. "It sounds to me like she used all of that to justify her doing whatever she wanted."

He thought Hope could be offended by that observation, but instead, she laughed lightly.

"I know. Trust me, I know."

He found himself taking a couple more steps forward. Now they were more like five feet apart. Way too close. But he couldn't make himself back up.

Red flag, for sure.

But he'd never been real good at obeying red flags.

"You do?" he asked. "You didn't believe all of that?"

She sighed. "I didn't. For a long time, through my teenage years, I thought she was just coming up with excuses to keep from getting serious about anything—and not just guys. I mean, she was always changing something—where we lived, where she worked, what she ate, her hobbies. It was always something new. Do you know that she was within a few hours of finishing four different degrees? But by the time it came down to the final classes, she was bored and on to the next thing. She always said she'd learned what she needed to at that point and was ready for a new challenge."

Hope huffed out a breath, and TJ was reminded she was simply holding her shirt up with her hands, and with one wrong move, that shirt could be floating in the middle of his pond. Not that he needed much reminding.

"She frustrated you." It wasn't a question. It was clear on her face. But that surprised him.

"She did." Hope sighed. "Which is why I'm here."

"What do you mean?"

"I spent my childhood thinking she was the coolest, most fun mom in the world. There was always something new going on. If I wanted to try something or do something or go somewhere, we did it. Life was like this big adventure." A slight frown pulled her eyebrows together. "But when I got to be about twelve, I started to really understand that most moms weren't like her, and instead of thinking she was cool, I thought she was weird. I started wanting to fit in, and she ended up embarrassing me. Then I got older and more responsible and her irresponsibility drove me crazy. When I was old enough, about sixteen or so, people starting coming to *me* when the bills were late or when she hadn't shown up for work. And I started to see her as a little wacky and a lot flaky. I left for college and just kind of reveled in being away from all of that."

TJ was even more surprised. Hope wasn't what she seemed. That was...intriguing.

Dammit.

"But then I grew up even more and I saw some of the depression and cruelty and sadness in the world. I hated that. I longed to be back with my mom, who always saw the positives and truly made everyone around her happy. I decided to go home and get back in touch with some of that and open my mind up to her."

Her voice had gotten husky, and not in a good way. In an I'm-trying-not-to-cry way. TJ instinctually stepped closer. "And did you?"

"For about a month. And then she died."

Well...crap.

TJ took the final two steps between them. He'd stopped trusting his instincts about two and a half years ago, but this one was too strong to resist. He wrapped his good arm around Hope and pulled her into him.

H oly crap, that felt good.

Hope was all for being touchy-feely. She'd been raised by Melody Daniels after all. But dang, touching and feeling TJ Bennett was beyond her experience.

Hot. Hard. Huge.

Those were the first three words that came to mind.

She wrapped her arms around him as well. She had, for sure, never hugged someone as big as TJ.

He was so much taller than her that her chest hit him at about belly-button level.

She breathed in the scent of his laundry detergent and the scent that was all him—a combination of fresh air and cut grass and coffee and something she'd never smelled but that made her want to get even closer.

Though that would require fewer clothes and maybe a firm surface...

"I'm going to talk to my Uncle Dan if Dad doesn't get it done soon," TJ said against the top of her head. "I promise."

That was so nice. He had heard what she'd said about meeting Dan and just getting to know him. He was going to—

Suddenly, she jerked back. "Oh my God!" She covered her mouth with her hands.

Belatedly, she realized that her chest against TJ's midsection had been what was holding her top up since her arms had been around him.

TJ's reflexes had kept the shirt from falling, and he now clutched it against his stomach, frozen.

His gaze on her bare breasts set off fireworks in her. Her

whole body got hot and felt as if it was being touched with the end of a sparkler. Especially her nipples.

She watched him swallow hard and his fist crumpled her blouse. Then he tipped his head back, focused on the sky above and sighed.

"Are you okay?" he asked. His voice sounded strangled.

She didn't answer at first. He was studying the clouds over-head as if they were the most fascinating things he'd ever seen.

And her bare breasts were right in front of him.

Nice.

She crossed her arms. She was very comfortable being naked. Not necessarily in front of everyone or even in front of one guy she'd just met. But she'd been raised in what some of her friends called a *naked house*. Melody had been very free with…everything. Hope didn't have hang-ups about nudity and sex and some of the other things that most people did. It was all completely natural. Plus, she did a lot of yoga and loved kick-boxing and had genetically great skin and breasts. She had no problem being naked.

She and TJ were roughly the same age, healthy, single. There was definitely chemistry between them. Him seeing her naked shouldn't be weird. In fact, it should be a lot of fun.

"Are you okay?" he asked again, since she hadn't answered.

He was still looking up.

"No, actually."

At that answer, his chin came down and he looked at her. To his credit, he focused on her face. First. His gaze did drop lower again, but only for a millisecond. Then he was staring into her eyes as if they held the secrets of the universe.

She shook her head. Either he was *very* much a gentleman or he was a monk.

"What's wrong?" he asked.

He was gripping her shirt so hard she didn't think she'd ever get the wrinkles out.

She was pretty sure he was not a monk. There was a distinct lack of crucifixes in his house, for one thing.

She was attracted to him. *Very* attracted to him. Like rub-herself-all-over-him-like-a-cat attracted to him. And she was now half-naked right in front of him. And he was *not* looking at her half-naked right in front of him. Okay.

Hope took a step closer and TJ quickly stepped back.

She narrowed her eyes and did it again. He took a bigger step this time. He was going to step off the dock into the pond at this rate.

She was about to ask him what his problem was but then she remembered her reason for pulling back in the first place. "Wait, I just realized you're my *cousin*."

And that would make sense why he was stoically looking anywhere *but* at her bare breasts. She covered herself with her hands.

He looked completely confused. "I'm your..." Then understanding dawned on his face. "My Uncle Dan isn't actually my uncle. He's my dad's best friend from high school. We just call him uncle sometimes."

She let those words sink in. Not really his uncle. So she was not really his cousin. So her attraction to him was...fine.

"Thank God," she breathed. Relief flooded through her, even stronger than she would have expected. She let her hands drop. Yes, being attracted to her brother or cousin would have been very, very icky. But her relief wasn't just about it being okay to feel attracted. Her mind—or her body perhaps—instantly recognized the fact that this meant she could *act* on that attraction.

So could he.

He cocked an eyebrow. "That happy to not be related to me?"

Hope had the impression that TJ Bennett really liked and respected honesty. He'd met his dad head-on with the question about being her father, and he'd been upfront about Dan's issues.

"Yes," she said with a nod.

TJ hesitated for a moment. He also kept staring at her face like he'd die if his gaze wandered even a centimeter lower. She found that equally amusing and offensive.

Finally, he asked, "Why is that?"

There was something in his eyes or his tone or maybe the air between them that made her think that he knew the reason for her relief.

But if he didn't...

"Because I've been fighting an attraction that would be inappropriate if we were related."

TJ pulled a long breath in through his nose, held it, then blew it out. "I see."

I see? That was the only reaction?

She waited. She had essentially just given him permission to look at her breasts as much as he wanted.

All at once, he thrust her shirt at her. "Here."

A gentleman. That had to be the reason. He wasn't a monk and they weren't related.

Or he wasn't attracted.

But he didn't seem bored or unimpressed or unaware of her. He was actually acting very aware, and like he was fighting it.

So he was uptight. And that made more sense than the gentleman thing for some reason.

Naked bodies made him uncomfortable.

Yep, that was it. As soon as the thought occurred to her, Hope knew it was right.

Perception, gut instinct, empathy—whatever she called it, she was often right when she had insights about other people.

It had always been that way. But she hadn't understood it was unusual until high school when she'd realized that no one else in her circle of friends had the kind of awareness of other people that Hope did. They also knew nothing about astrological signs or the phases of the moon or people's energies or any of the other things her mother had made a part of her life. So Hope had kept her knowledge to herself.

Keeping it bottled up had nagged at her though. It had also been one of the things she and her mother had fought about most often. Melody had known that Hope was ignoring her insights and she hadn't understood why Hope wouldn't want to embrace them. Finally, when Hope was about twenty, she'd found a way to channel her empathy and need to help others by starting at the local nursing program.

And thankfully, her hypersensitivity didn't happen with everyone. Some people, she felt nothing for.

That was not the case with TJ Bennett.

She felt him. She was drawn to him. Felt the desire to heal him somehow. She also felt that he was drawn to her. And that he was fighting it.

"I'm okay, actually," she said, not taking the shirt from him and stepping back slightly so he could have a better view. She stood with her arms by her sides. "I don't mind if you look at me, TJ."

She knew the use of his name would rattle him, and she saw the way his eyes flashed and his jaw tightened.

He said nothing. And his gaze remained on her face.

"In fact, I wouldn't mind being completely naked and having you look at me." She reached for the tie on the side of her skirt. She meant it. Not only was she comfortable with nudity, she *really* liked the idea of TJ looking at her. Her heart began to race.

"You're actually going to get naked out here in the middle of nowhere with a complete stranger?" he demanded. With a huge frown.

"I'm not afraid of you."

"Don't you think you should be?" he asked. "You don't know me."

That was the weird thing, the thing she couldn't explain and that she knew would sound crazy if she said it out loud— because it had sounded crazy to *her* when her mom had said stuff like this.

"I think I do know you," she said anyway.

He didn't roll his eyes exactly, but everything about his expression said that he wanted to. "Really."

She nodded. "I do. You're a protector. It's obvious in everything about you. You wouldn't hurt me."

"Everything about me?" he repeated.

"You have a positive energy about you. People are drawn to you because of your strength—not just your physical strength, but your loyalty and integrity and even your stubbornness."

"Oh, Jesus," he muttered.

Then he shoved his hand through his hair, muttering something she couldn't hear other than a very clear word at the end. Crazy.

His frown eased, but his expression was not exactly happy. He looked resigned. "I suppose you think you're psychic or something."

"No. Just very, very intuitive," she said, fighting a smile.

"You read auras and stuff?" What he thought of *auras and stuff* was very clear in his tone.

She smiled fully at that. She wondered what he knew about auras. "Not exactly."

"But kind of?"

No, not really. But for some reason, the whole aura-and-stuff thing made TJ uncomfortable too, and she had a sudden flash of awareness that TJ worked really hard to keep his boat from being rocked.

Being rocked might be really good for him.

She nodded. "Kind of." She was perceptive. That was a little like seeing auras.

He sighed again. "Look, you should know that I have a very low tolerance for crazy."

She tipped her head to the side, completely and totally intrigued. "Wow, sounds like there are all kinds of very interesting issues I'd love to know more about."

"I'm a grumpy asshole," he said. "That's all you need to know. You don't want to be naked with me."

"Oh, I'm pretty sure that's not true."

Heat flashed in his eyes. Definite, singe-her-where-she-stood heat. And then it was gone.

"No." That was his only response.

She couldn't help her smile. "Being a grumpy asshole is a choice, not who you really are, you know."

He frowned and tossed her shirt at her. Not *to* her. Definitely *at* her. "Put that on. Now."

And it became suddenly crystal clear. A woman had wrapped him tightly around her finger and then broken his heart.

Dammit. Why did someone have to have hurt him? The wounded thing got to her, no question.

Hope dropped the shirt to the dock at her feet. "You can swear, you can frown, you can be demanding and grumpy, you can even yell, TJ Bennett. But I still trust you."

This time he didn't look away. TJ's gaze raked over her from the top of her head to the bright-pink nail polish on her toes. He touched on every part that was already tingling and wanting to get closer to him, but he lingered on her tattoo and then returned to it again after he'd taken stock of everything else. Hope was breathing harder and her heart was pounding by the time he was done.

"Okay, I've looked," he finally said, his gaze meeting hers. "Now get dressed."

He was very self-disciplined. Hope respected that even as she was *this* close to begging him to now touch her with his hands the way he had with his eyes. She pulled in a deep breath.

"TJ, I—"

A gust of wind blew across the dock and picked her shirt up, sliding it over the wooden planks. She started to grab for it —just as it went over the edge.

Well, crap.

3

Hope moved to look over the end of the dock. Her blouse floated in the water about four feet below where she stood.

"Hold that thought," she said to TJ as she prepared to go for a swim.

But as she was about to jump, she felt TJ grab the back of her skirt.

She looked over her shoulder. "Hey."

"You're just going to jump in?"

She looked back to the water. "Are there things I should be worried about in the water?"

"No. But you didn't know that until right now." He pulled her back from the edge and let go of her. He grabbed a big stick and got down onto his stomach, leaned over the edge, stretched with the stick and snagged her shirt. He pulled the soggy top onto the wooden slats beside him and then pushed back to his feet. And he did it all one-armed.

Wow.

"See?" she said, looking up at him. "A protector. There you go, saving me and fixing things."

"And see?" he returned. "There you go, just jumping in without any thought to consequences and *needing* someone to fix things."

She smiled up at him. "The benefit of growing up with a mother who thought of everything as a life lesson is that I haven't needed someone to fix anything for me for a long time. I've been helping myself since I was a kid."

He looked at her for a moment without reply. "You need to cover up."

He grabbed the back of his shirt with one hand and pulled it over his head. Wincing as he did it, he pulled his good arm out of the sleeve and then wiggled the shirt under his shoulder sling and down his injured arm. When it was free, he handed it to her. "Put that on."

She couldn't.

She suddenly couldn't remember how to do anything but stare.

Clothed, he was big and wide and hard. Without a shirt on, he was...the thing she most wanted to touch—and rub against and lick—in the world. His skin was tanned from the sun and clearly working shirtless more often than not. There was no farmer's tan on this guy. His left shoulder, the one in the sling, had an elaborate tattoo—an ornate letter B. He also had four tiny incisions dotted around and in that B. He had dark hair sprinkled over his massive chest and deliciously defined shoulders, pecs and abs. And once her gaze focused on his lower abs and the V that formed there and dove into the waistband of his jeans, she could not pull her eyes away.

Holy crap.

If her nipples and heart rate hadn't responded to him before now, there wasn't an inch of her body that she wasn't incredibly aware of with TJ Bennett standing in front of her half-naked.

She also had the strangest urge to see his back. She knew

the muscles would be equally impressive there, and she needed a new study of his fine ass. With her hands.

Was she objectifying him because he was showing more skin? Damn right she was.

And enjoying every second of it.

"Hope."

His firm, deep voice pulled her gaze to his face briefly. He was watching her with heat in his eyes and a tightness to his features that seemed like restraint. Restraint that was about two seconds away from snapping.

"Put the shirt on."

She was all for *him* staying shirtless, so she complied. Plus, she suddenly wanted the shirt that was still warm from his body and smelled like him on her.

As the T-shirt settled over her, the neck gaping, the sleeves hitting her at the elbows and the hem at mid-thigh, she took a deep breath and rubbed her hands over the sleeves, sliding the soft cotton against her skin.

"I know what you're doing," he said.

He knew that she was getting turned-on just wearing his T-shirt? "You do?"

"You're trying to distract me."

"Distract you from what?"

"From realizing that you're insinuating yourself into everything."

He was so suspicious, and she *so* wanted to know why. And know everything else about him. "What am I insinuating myself into?" Because if he knew she was thinking about his bed, he was maybe a bit intuitive himself.

"My front yard," he said. "Tiny as it is, your car and camper are taking up space. You've already met my dad and gotten him worked up, and now you're on my dock. Half-naked. And willing to be more naked." He paused and gave her a firm look. "And willing to jump into God knows what."

She didn't think he was talking about the pond.

He was afraid of her getting too involved in his life. He was pushing her away as quickly as possible. He was attracted and fighting it.

So intriguing.

"And you think all of that is intentional? That I'm trying to somehow become important to you?"

He just lifted an eyebrow.

"Why do you think that?" she asked, seriously curious. She wasn't offended by his assumptions. Clearly, someone had done a number on him.

"You're saying it's all a happy coincidence that you're here right now, in this spot, suddenly attracted to me and so content on the dock on my pond?"

"You don't think I'm actually attracted to you?" she asked. Because *that* was ridiculous. She couldn't fake this. And she *wouldn't* fake it anyway.

"It's convenient, don't you think, that you're *so* attracted to the man who you're dependent on to get what you want, that you're willing to undress and get dirty on the dock within hours of meeting him?"

Getting dirty with him did sound nice.

But there were some things to clear up first. She wanted to keep him talking. She couldn't resist. "What I want? You mean meeting Dan?"

He gave one terse nod.

"I could quite easily find and meet Dan without you, TJ," she said. "If I hadn't ended up on your doorstep, it would have been your dad's, and he would have told me everything he told us in your kitchen."

"But you're still here."

"Because *you* asked me to wait to meet Dan until your dad figures out the best way."

"And you're fine with that because you found out that Dan

might not be the guy you were hoping he would be."

"Also because I'm a nice person, and I believe that you want to protect him and his family, and I trust you."

"Also convenient that you're so trusting."

She crossed her arms. "What do you think I was hoping for with Dan?"

"Either a big happy welcome from the father you've never known, or..."

She raised her eyebrows. "Or?"

"Someone who can pay off your maxed-out credit cards or fix some legal problem for you or save you from whatever other trouble you've gotten into."

Whoa. There was a whole lot of something going on inside that good-looking head. "Have you ever heard of the term projection?" she asked. "As in, you're projecting *your* issues onto someone you just met and don't know?"

He didn't reply.

So she went on. "Obviously, there was a woman. Who somehow messed with you and manipulated you with sex," she said.

His eyes narrowed. "Sex was one of the things she used."

Hope was shocked that he'd admitted it that easily. "Wow, you don't seem like the type to open up about something like that."

"You could go have a muffin at the diner and they'd tell you all about it," he said flatly. "It's not a secret."

Her eyes widened. "Wow, I really want to hear this story."

"I don't talk about it."

"Then I'm suddenly in the mood for a muffin."

The corner of his mouth curled up for just an instant. "The diner's on Main. Avoid the coffee."

So there *was* a sense of humor there. That was encouraging.

"Listen," he said. "You're right."

That was also shocking. "I am?"

"About me being a protector. In the past. But I'm over it."

"No, you're not."

He sighed. "I'm trying to be over it."

"And you're going to practice being over it with me?"

"Definitely." He said it quickly and firmly.

She felt her eyes widen. "That was pretty adamant."

"Yes."

That was also very adamant.

"Which must mean I intrigue you a little bit too," she said, realizing it as she said it. She smiled.

He gave a short bark of laughter at that. "Of course you do. I'm very drawn to crazy."

She frowned. "Crazy?" She wasn't crazy, but that might not actually be the most important—or interesting—part of this conversation.

He nodded. "Definitely."

"Why is that?"

"I wish I knew."

She laughed softly, not so much at his words but at the legitimately perplexed look on his face.

"I don't know all the issues that you're dealing with," he said. "And frankly, I don't want to. I'm sorry about your mom. But this isn't my circus...and you are not my monkey."

She tipped her head. "I'm not your *monkey*?"

"Nope. Your care and feeding is someone else's problem."

"Whoa."

"Yeah. Asshole, remember?"

"And where's that come from?"

"My ex-wife."

Okay, she hadn't been expecting *that*. "Wife?"

"*Ex*-wife."

She just stared at him.

"Stop it." He gave her a frown.

"I'm fascinated. I can't help it."

His frown deepened. "By what?"

"You."

"No, you're not."

But she was. "I'm not crazy, by the way."

"You've fixated on me within only a few hours of knowing me."

"I am not fixated." She was intrigued. She was attracted. She wanted to know every single one of his stories and quirks. But she wasn't fixated. Exactly.

"You said fascinated," he pointed out.

"That's not the same thing."

He shrugged. "Potato, potahto."

"I'm *not* fixated." That sounded so much...crazier than fascinated.

"You traveled over a thousand miles, alone, while grieving, to find a man to fill some gaps in your life. You've been thinking about him. Planning the moment you meet him. Listed your questions for him. Now you've found out that he might not be able to be who you need him to be. So you focus on the next guy who can help you and make you feel better and give you a place to belong."

She could have argued. She could have told him that she hadn't planned the trip at all. She'd found the photo of Dan and Thomas and her mom the day before she'd hit the road. She also didn't have any gaps that needed filled. She had a great life that she loved. She did not have a list of questions and she didn't really need Dan to be anything at all.

But there was a little bit of her that thought having concerned and attentive TJ Bennett around might be kind of nice.

And *that* was crazy. She hadn't truly needed anyone in longer than she could remember. And as he'd pointed out, they'd just met.

Yikes.

She took a deep breath. "You sound like a shrink."

"Almost a year of therapy now."

"And yet you're still kind of an asshole."

"I'm not trying to get over *that*."

"Well, I'm very well adjusted, thank you."

"And yet you're standing on the end of my dock willing to take your clothes off and, I'm guessing, do whatever else I ask you to do. You're trying to get closer to me and please me, and the easiest way is through sex."

"You have a lot of sexual energy. I was in the moment. Geez. So sorry to make you look at my boobs." Hope couldn't believe that her pride was feeling piqued. She was typically a live-and-let-live girl. If TJ didn't want to have sex with her, that was his prerogative.

But it irked her.

"If you didn't have an estranged father and plans to stay around for a while, I'd be happy to look at your boobs," he said mildly. "But I like the boobs I get involved with to leave the next morning. You're not going to be doing that. Are you?" He looked almost hopeful.

She frowned. "No."

Probably not. She didn't know. Nothing about the trip had gone according to plan so far. Which just went to show that she was already screwing up the live-like-Melody thing. Melody didn't make plans and was a master at going with the flow.

"Then keep 'em covered up."

"I think I know why you're an asshole," Hope said, crossing her arms.

"Oh?" He didn't look particularly interested in her answer.

"It's because you're conflicted. You *are* a protector, you do want to help me, but for some reason you're trying to fight that."

"Because you can't fix crazy," he said flatly. "I learned that the hard way. Avoiding it is the easiest thing."

"You don't strike me as the type to take the easy way out."

"Let's put it this way—I put my time in."

"In the circus?" she asked.

He nodded. "I've cleaned up more than my share of monkey shit. I'm out. Someone else can worry about your cage."

"Where's your monkey now?" she asked, maybe a little beyond fascinated at the moment.

"Around."

"Does she still make a mess once in a while?"

"She does."

"That you clean up?"

He didn't answer.

So he *did* still clean up after this monkey sometimes. That was interesting.

"She must be something."

"She is." His tone didn't make it sound like it was a compliment.

"I think of monkeys as screechy things that climb all over everything and throw stuff around."

"That's about right."

She smiled up at him. "If you don't want me to be fascinated, you need to stop being interesting."

"You've been on the road a long time by yourself. I'm not that interesting."

"I drove almost straight through. It was only a couple of days. And I had a very nice conversation with an older couple at the truck-stop diner. They were interesting too. You're not the first." But he was the one whose lap she wanted to curl up in while he told her all of his stories.

Hmm. He might not be so far off on the crazy thing.

He frowned. "You just strike up conversations with strangers at truck stops?"

She didn't comment on the fact that he was acting protective again, but she did absorb it. She wasn't the type to need someone to be protective. She wasn't used to it at all and logically thought it was very likely to make her feel claustrophobic pretty quickly.

Still, his comment made her feel warm.

"I strike up conversations with people almost everywhere I go." She'd inherited that from her mother. "Truck stops have the most interesting mix of people to talk to."

"That's not safe." He said it with exasperation.

"I don't take candy from them," she said with a smile. "I talk to them. I don't tell them personal details, I don't leave with them and I don't give them my phone number. I just talk to them."

"Still, they could— Whatever." He shook his head. "Don't care."

He was trying not to care, she'd give him that. But she thought he was kind of failing. And that, stupidly, made her feel even warmer.

"I've heard some amazing stories," she said. "I'll tell you a few if you're nice. I'll tell you about the guy who taught piano lessons for almost forty years before he finally made it to Carnegie Hall. I'll tell you about the woman I met who has lived for a year in every state in the United States. Or the couple who has run a marathon on every continent."

"I won't be that nice."

She didn't know if he meant to be funny, but he was. "You'll find that I'm interesting too."

"Sure. That's one word. And I don't want to be interested."

"Okay." She shrugged. "So tell me more about your monkey. Tell me she's a big old ugly gorilla."

"I don't want to talk about my *ex*-monkey."

"I'll keep my shirt on if you agree to tell me."

"It's my shirt."

"I can put mine back on," she offered, looking at the wet wad at their feet.

It was white. Putting it on would be like standing in front of him naked.

Clearly, he knew that.

"Why do you want to talk about her?"

Because she might be becoming a little fixated on him. "What kind of monkey is she? An orangutan? A baboon?"

The corner of his lips twitched again. "She's whatever type of monkey Curious George is."

Hope frowned even though his sort-of smile made her stomach flip. "He was pretty cute."

"Yep," TJ agreed.

Oh, great, so the ex was cute.

"And a huge troublemaker," TJ said. "Cute only goes so far."

She studied his face. He didn't look heartbroken right now. He looked mildly annoyed. That meant he didn't hate this woman. She reminded him of a cute, if somewhat troublesome little monkey. Great.

"But you're divorced. So the cute didn't go far enough," Hope pointed out.

"We're divorced because she fell in love with someone else."

Oh. Well, shit. Still, she couldn't help it—she wanted to keep him talking. "So why are you still cleaning up after her?"

His jaw tightened for just a moment, but then he said easily, "She calls me to piss him off."

"Does it work?"

"Every time."

"Why do you keep answering?"

"Because I don't care if he's pissed off."

Seriously, this was interesting. How could he not see that? "What kind of cleanup jobs are we talking here?"

He sighed.

"I can take this shirt right back off." She raised the hem a couple of inches.

He rolled his eyes. "She gets into squabbles in public."

"Squabbles? Like arguments?"

"Like someone ends up with beer dumped on their heads."

Hope felt her eyes widen. "What else?"

"She gets stranded by her *friends* at bars, she runs out of gas, she gets lost, she runs out of money in L.A. and has no way to get home, she gets arrested for breaking into someone's apartment because the key wouldn't work—because she was at the wrong building. That kind of stuff."

Hope blinked at him. Wow. That was...beyond Curious George. And there TJ was, the big protector, the big hero, no matter what he said.

"That's quite a circus."

"That's what I'm saying."

She grinned in spite of herself. "You couldn't just walk away from the monkey crap?"

"The lights, music and cotton candy kept me sucked in for a long time."

Yeah, she wasn't going to delve into what kind of cotton candy he was talking about. At least, not yet.

There were things swirling under the surface with TJ Bennett. Lots of things. Things Hope thought she wouldn't mind having swirling around her.

She frowned at that thought. She was not the type of woman to get into trouble like the ex-monkey did. No way. None of that would ever happen. Which meant there would be nothing for TJ to clean up. That sounded like it would be perfect—what with his aversion to cleaning up monkey crap now. But she knew that wasn't the case. TJ wasn't simply the monkey keeper. He was the ringmaster. No matter what he told himself.

"So what kind of monkey am I?"

That corner of his mouth ticked again. "A capuchin. For sure."

"Those are the ones that organ grinders use, right?"

His smile increased slightly. "Yes."

"They're cute."

"They are."

Well, that was nice. "I've only ever seen them being cute and sweet," she said with a shrug.

"Oh, they're a pretty aggressive breed."

"Is that right?" What did that mean?

"Yep, they're very territorial. They pee all over to mark their space."

She gave him a look. "And what about that reminds you of me?" Territorial, she was not. She'd never been jealous or possessive about anything she could think of.

"The noise," he said.

"The noise?"

"They make a lot of noise."

She narrowed her eyes. "You're quite the expert on monkeys."

"Lots of experience."

He said it blandly, but she got the impression he was amused. As was she. Except for the comparison with the crazy ex and the noisy monkey.

"How'd you get hooked up with your ex-monkey anyway?" She had to ask.

He didn't answer at first, and she reached for the hem of the shirt again.

He sighed. "We were young. Met her in high school," he said. "And she was cute. I had a crush. She needed some help, so I stepped in and we started a crazy, bad pattern."

"What kind of help?"

He clearly didn't want to answer, but he did anyway. "Her stepdad was abusive. He hit her, I went over and beat the crap out of him and told him if he ever touched her again, I'd make it worse. He believed me and it never happened again. She was," he cleared his throat, "grateful."

"She married you because she was grateful?"

"You're nosy, you know that?"

"You're interesting."

"I don't want to talk about this."

She again started to lift her shirt.

"She broke my heart in high school. Twice. Then came back to me when her life went to hell and she needed someone. That time she stayed. She was unpredictable, fun, wild. I was her hero. Then I realized that's all I was. And that she fabricated about seventy-five percent of the crap she got into to keep things working between us. All we had was the victim-hero thing. She was only turned-on by me when I was swooping in to fix things. Eventually, it fizzled out."

"Wow, you seriously are—"

"Over it," he said firmly. "No more drama, no more craziness."

"I am not dramatic and crazy," Hope protested.

"Oh sure, the pretty hippie girl who showed up on my front lawn out of the blue looking for her estranged father, who's willing to take her shirt off for me within a few hours of meeting me, who talks about auras and is already nosing into my personal life, isn't a bit crazy. That's all totally normal. Plus, the long-lost family you came to meet is a mess. Honey, you have drama written all over you."

Well, at least he thought she was pretty.

She frowned. "No." She shook her head. "I'm very self-sufficient. I don't get caught up in drama. I'm the one who helps other people." And she wasn't a hippie. Exactly. That was kind of a gray area, so she let it go.

He leaned in as if he was going to tell her a secret. "The crazy ones always say that."

She blew out a breath. "I'm not crazy and I'm not undressing just to manipulate you."

"You did it because you want to have sex with me? After

knowing me for three hours and me being an ass for two of those three?"

"Two and a half," she said. "And, yeah." She shrugged. "We have chemistry. I'm drawn to your positive energies and power." There, that would make him roll his eyes.

It did. "You're in Nebraska. You can't go around stripping and talking about positive energies."

She laughed. "People in Nebraska don't know about nudity and energy?"

"Not your kind of nudity and energy."

"What kind is that?"

"Crazy."

"Argh."

He finally gave her a full smile at that. "Okay, let's go, Looney Tunes."

The crazy theme was gonna have to go. But TJ seemed more the show-versus-tell type of guy. "Where?"

"To the house. Enough getting your energies all over my dock."

"Just one more thing," she said, stepping close.

When he didn't step away from her, she let out the breath she hadn't realized she was holding. She moved to his side. He simply watched her out of the corner of his eye. As if he was sure she was about to do something he wouldn't like.

That might be true.

His injured shoulder was in front of her, with the four tiny scars that were freshly healed marring the otherwise beautiful tattoo. She reached up and touched one. He flinched, but she didn't think it was from pain.

She flattened her hand and laid it on his skin. "Scope?" she asked. Clearly whatever he'd had done had been done arthroscopically versus cutting him open.

"Yeah."

"Rotator cuff?" she asked. He was immobilized with a sling

but the muscle tone of the shoulder was really good for a repair like that.

"Bone spur, some arthritis," he said. His voice was a little rougher now.

So they'd just debrided the area, smoothing the bone and tendon where wear and tear had roughened it, causing increased friction and pain when he moved. She rubbed her hand over the tiny scars. "How long ago?" It had to be at least two weeks based on how healed the incisions were.

"Three weeks."

She frowned. "You're still in the sling?"

"Still hurting like a bitch and doc doesn't know what to do."

Hope put her other hand on his shoulder too. His skin was so hot. Or maybe she just felt really hot touching him. It was a shoulder. An injured one at that. She was a nurse. She'd seen thousands of shoulders. Touched thousands. Even some attached to really good-looking guys.

Her hands had never shaken and her heart had never pounded while touching those shoulders.

They were now.

"What have you tried for pain?" she asked. She kept her eyes on his shoulder. She could feel him watching her, and for some reason, she didn't want to meet his gaze.

Hope moved her hands over his shoulder, massaging the muscles, moving the scars.

He cleared his throat. "All the over-the-counter stuff. Ice, heat. Anything and everything."

"Nothing stronger than ibuprofen?" she asked.

"Can't do it," he said. "Makes me goofy."

She smiled at that. She'd kind of love to see him goofy.

"You think I'm a pain in the ass now?" he asked. "You should see me on morphine."

She finally looked up. "Pain in the ass and goofy aren't the same thing."

He met her gaze. "I lose my inhibitions. It could go either way, depending on the situation and who you are."

Hope licked her lips subconsciously when his gaze settled on her mouth.

She couldn't remember the last time she'd felt subconscious. Dang, she didn't like that. "So you say whatever you really think?" she asked.

"Among other things."

"Like if you thought someone reminded you of a capuchin monkey, you'd just tell that person?"

Then the most devastating thing happened. TJ Bennett grinned at her. Up close. With her hands on his body.

She almost had an orgasm right then and there.

"Holy crap."

"What?"

She realized she'd spoken out loud. She shook her head. "I guess I lose a few inhibitions when you smile at me like that."

His grin faded, but the heat in his eyes flared.

Now when his gaze went to her mouth, all she could think was, *Holy hell, yes, right now.*

He blinked, took a deep breath and asked, "You have inhibitions?"

Okay, so maybe not right now. She chuckled. "Not many." She'd continued to massage his shoulder as they'd talked. "You need to get out of this sling," she said.

"Doc says if my pain is still bothering me, I should rest it."

She nodded. "I'm not saying you should throw hay bales around." She tipped her head. "Do you actually throw hay bales around?"

He almost smiled again. Almost. "Yes."

"So you shouldn't do that right now, but you need to start moving it. That would help."

"Actually, your hands on me seem to help."

Her hands stopped rubbing. She didn't take her hands off

him though. "See?" she asked softly. "Maybe having me distracting you isn't all bad."

There was that hot flare in his eyes again. "Is that all that is? Distraction from the pain?"

She shook her head. "No. Scar tissues can penetrate deep, even from small incisions. It's important to move them to heal everything around them."

She didn't miss the fact that all of that was a pretty good metaphor for emotional scars and healing too. And she was pretty sure TJ caught it as well.

She put the pad of her finger against one of the marks and moved it side-to-side, sliding the skin and the tissue underneath. "See? Moving it gently a little at a time doesn't hurt and helps with healing."

He was watching her when she looked up again.

"Having you move it feels good."

Maybe he'd let her move him gently toward other healing. Keeping her gaze on his, she leaned in and put her lips against the scar. She resisted licking the letter B. Barely.

He sucked in a quick breath.

"There, that should feel better for a while," she said.

She stepped back. TJ was a tough guy. Stubborn, sure of what he wanted and what he didn't, protective, suspicious and wounded. If she was going to help him, she'd have to go slow and gentle. She could do that. Because not doing anything at all, just like with his shoulder, was only going to hurt him in the long-term.

She took another step back before she put her lips on skin in other places. Like those abs. Damn.

Because if she did that, TJ would think she was using sex to get something more from him. She was going to have to tamp down her urges to jump him. Because she wanted to jump him. For no other reason than the jumping.

"I have some other stuff that can help," Hope heard herself say.

She sighed internally even as she made the offer. But she'd promised herself that she would embrace her mother's approach to things, and that meant more than her approach to a good time in Sapphire Falls with a hot farmer.

She really was committed to giving her mom's approach to life a try. And she couldn't argue with a lot of it. Melody had not only been happier than anyone Hope had ever met, she'd also been healthier, physically and mentally, than the majority of the people Hope had run into. Granted, Hope was a nurse, so that meant she spent a lot of time around people with health issues of all kinds, but if she was honest about her mom—and she was really trying to be more honest about her mom— Melody had clearly had some things figured out.

Besides, TJ had been trying Hope's form of medicine— surgery, heat, cold, rest, medications—and it wasn't working. He was hurting and she had an intense desire to help him. Almost as intense as the desire to run her tongue over his abs. And that was very intense.

"What kind of stuff?" he asked. Again suspicious.

She rolled her eyes. She was going to get past that what-are-you-up-to wall he'd constructed so high and wide against her gender. "Some teas that can help with inflammation and healing. Some creams that can increase circulation in the tissues and help with the pain."

If Hope could figure out what to put in the cream.

Melody had always made everything at home from scratch. Hope had her mother's recipes, but the instructions for her concoctions were mixed into her journal along with poems, song lyrics, notes and thoughts, drawings, people's names and seemingly random dates. Oh, and the recipes weren't always labeled.

Still, it was cream. It's not like she was going to have him eat it. It wouldn't *hurt* him and could maybe help. She knew very well that the placebo effect was a real thing. If she sold it and he believed it, he might feel better even if she messed up the mixture. And she'd gladly rub it in. At least that would feel good. To TJ too.

Melody would be so happy. She was probably dancing wherever she was, Hope thought. She and her mother had gone round and round about the body and what it took to heal. Melody's natural methods versus Hope's Western-medicine approach.

But no matter what, Hope couldn't deny that she hadn't been sick much as a kid. And when she was feeling under the weather, her mom's soup, tea and essential oils did help.

"Do I strike you as the tea type?" TJ asked.

She smiled at him. "Do you really want to know what type you strike me as?"

She was fine with telling him that she found his uptight, distrustful and grumpy outer layer nothing but a challenge, and that she was quite a fan of him without his shirt on.

He started to reply but then apparently thought better of it. He shook his head. "Probably not."

She chuckled. He was also kind of a chicken. She knew that he knew where her thoughts had gone.

"I'll get some stuff together when we get back to the house," she said. "I should have most of the ingredients in the camper."

Her mother had any number of vials and bottles and jars in a big wooden apothecary chest that had always sat in the corner of their kitchen. It was a handmade, hand-painted box with flowers and trees and butterflies on it. It was done in a myriad of colors and it had been as much a fixture in Hope's life as the wooden table and chairs she and her mother had used for every meal and every important project or talk in Hope's life.

Hope hadn't even considered not taking the box with her.

The thing held eighteen small glass bottles, four big glass jars and had eight drawers. Hope was actually excited to open it up and play. She loved the hand cream and mud facial masks she made for herself and the cleaning solution her mother had made for household cleaning. How different could medicinal cream be?

"You have the ingredients in the camper?" TJ repeated, disbelief in his tone.

"Yes. Hopefully. Or I'm hoping I can find what I need here." Her mother hadn't traveled with the more common things like lemons or vinegar or honey since those could be fairly easily found wherever she was.

"You're going to *make* this cream?"

She laughed. For some reason, TJ Bennett and his skepticism amused her. It wasn't as if he was the first skeptic she'd ever come across. Hell, she'd been one of the skeptics for much of her teenage years. But she enjoyed ruffling him. Something about that felt right. She wanted to ruffle him, make him think of things in a new way, open up his mind.

Like she was opening hers to new things.

Looking at him now, with all of that hot, tanned skin and those glorious muscles, she thought that her mom really had been on to something—new adventures were all around, it was simply a question of if she was going to embark on one or not.

"I'm going to make this cream," she said. "Nothing like homemade from scratch with plenty of TLC added in."

His eyes narrowed. "Maybe I'm the crazy one."

"Why is that?"

"Because I'm going to let a hippie girl I just met rub some mystery homemade cream all over me."

Rub. All over. Those were nice words.

"I can definitely make a cream for that too," she said, dropping her voice just enough that he would know exactly what she was talking about.

He didn't look confused, that was for sure. "Massage cream for all over the body, huh?"

"There are several essential oils that act as aphrodisiacs and that can increase sexual pleasure."

He lifted one eyebrow. "Funny, I've never felt the need for essential oils to have a good time."

"You don't know what you're missing."

There was a long, heated moment between them, and for a second, Hope thought he was going to kiss her.

But again, his restraint was remarkable.

That or he was really bad at reading *her* energies. Because they were saying *I'm all yours.*

"Maybe we should stick to my shoulder."

He didn't add *for now* but Hope decided to believe it was implied. "Hey, I'm all for rubbing whatever of yours I can get."

He blinked and she almost regretted her words. She didn't want to scare him off. She really did want to help him with his shoulder.

The idea that the big, tough farmer with the emotional barricade firmly in place could be scared off was amusing, but Hope definitely sensed it. He was drawn to her, but he was still sure it was a bad idea to do anything about it.

"I'll keep that in mind," he finally said.

Now it was her turn to blink. Not only was he not scared off, he'd given a sort-of flirtatious comeback. She was making progress.

Progress toward what exactly? she asked herself. But she wasn't sure she could, or should, specifically answer that. She wanted to help him. His shoulder hurt—she could do something about that. His heart hurt too, but what was she going to do about that? What did she *want* to do about that? Maybe she wanted to fix that too.

She wasn't hoping to become wife number two or anything, but another Melody lesson was that relationships were about people relating. Period. They didn't have time frames, they didn't have specific objectives. They were just about people connecting.

Could she connect with TJ Bennett beyond helping him with his shoulder pain?

Oh, yeah she could.

Happily.

"You just let me know," she said. "I'm actually a professional rubber."

"Are you now?"

She nodded. "I have my massage therapy license." True story. She'd done that before starting the nursing program. She'd loved massage and had kept her license active. There was nothing like human touch to restore all kinds of good things in a body.

That and aromatherapy were two things she and her mother *had* seen eye to eye on. Hope loved essential oils and used them herself in any number of ways. She didn't know as much as Melody had. Hope stuck with the basics.

"Makes sense why my shoulder feels so good now," he said.

"Well, that and the fact that you like me touching you," she said. If they were going to connect, then TJ was going to be as aware of it as she was. Even if she had to spell it all out every step of the way. "Being aroused helps decrease your pain levels."

TJ turned to face her fully. "Is that right?"

She nodded. "Oxytocin. Leads to a release of endorphins."

"You know all kinds of things."

"You have no idea." Did she sound breathless? She felt breathless.

"I think this would be a good time to go back to the house."

Or get naked. She could really go either direction.

"Hope." His voice was soft but firm.

She realized she was staring at his abs again. She lifted her gaze to his, reluctantly.

"Time to go."

"You sure?" she asked.

"I'm having a hard time even remembering I have a shoulder right now."

Good. The oxytocin was working. "So we could—"

"Go."

4

_____

TJ started off the dock and Hope had little choice but to follow.

She grabbed her soggy shirt and slipped into her flip-flops, then padded down the wooden slats behind him. Without him there, the dock had lost a lot of its appeal anyway.

Hope followed TJ over the grass and dirt leading away from the pond. She was treated to a very nice view of his naked back and denim-clad ass, and she realized there were advantages to having him walk away from her. But after a few yards, he slowed his long strides so that she could catch up and walk next to him.

"So how many ex monkeys do you have?" she asked in the silence.

He sighed.

"Is there a chance I might run into the orangutan? Or one of the other monkeys?"

"I didn't say she was an orangutan."

"That's how I'm imagining her," Hope said with a shrug. She realized she was way too interested in all of this.

"I changed my mind."

"Orangutan is more accurate, right?"

"About *you*," he said. "You're more like one of the fluffy yippy dogs. The ones that run around your heels and bounce up and down and yap for attention."

She frowned at him, but he didn't even glance at her. "You should be flattered I want your attention," she said.

"Uh huh," was all she got in reply.

She was wondering what was next—and how she could make what was next what she wanted it to be—when they hit the side yard.

He suddenly stopped and took her upper arm. "I have to know," he said, turning her to face him.

"Know what?" What it was like to kiss her? Because she was definitely wondering about that herself.

"What this says." He took the side of his T-shirt in his hand and tugged her closer.

She took the step without a single hesitation.

He slowly began to pull it up her body, watching her face carefully. She knew that he would stop if she told him to. But why in the hell would she stop him?

The cotton slid along her skin, but the shirt was baggy enough on her that his fingers didn't even brush against her. Dammit.

Once the shirt slid past the end of the tattoo, he stopped. The last curl on the last letter ended just below where her bra would hit. If she were wearing one. Which she was not. And she had never been more aware of that in her life.

Going without bras and panties was another Melody thing. She hadn't liked to be confined in any way. Hence the flowy skirts and blousy tops and flip-flops. In fact, Melody preferred to be barefoot whenever possible.

Hope had to admit it was all very freeing. She could get used to the no-panty-and-bra thing. Though when TJ was around, she was *really* aware of her bare parts rubbing against her clothing.

His gaze went from her face to the ink that swirled up her side.

Without a word, she pulled the top of her skirt down so he could see the beginning of the letters just below her hip bone.

He swallowed hard and then read out loud, "Your life is an occasion. Rise to it."

He looked at her again.

"Is there any chance that you know what movie that quote is from?" she asked. If he did, she just might marry him. A hot, grumpy farmer who made her melt with only a look and who was whimsical enough to know that movie would get whatever he wanted from her.

"Sorry, no." He let go of her shirt.

Damn.

She caught the shirt and held it up. "*Mr. Magorium's Wonder Emporium.*"

He lifted an eyebrow.

Yeah, it didn't sound like his type of movie to her either, and she'd just met him. "My mom and I loved it. I've seen it probably thirty times."

He studied the tattoo again and she felt goose bumps erupt all over her body.

"Dustin Hoffman," she said. She definitely sounded breathless this time. "Natalie Portman. And—"

She sucked in a quick breath as TJ lifted a hand and traced his finger over the letters on her skin.

She coughed, worked on breathing and then said, "Jason Bateman."

It was a very ornate script font and there were lots of curls and loops. The pad of his finger was rough against her skin, and every drag on every dip made her breathing speed up and her temperature rise.

One finger. That was all that was touching her, and she felt as if he was stroking her clit and nipples at the same time.

"TJ—"

That was all the plea for more she got out before he put his big hand at the back of her neck and pulled her in as he lowered his head.

His lips were hot and greedy. He didn't lead up to anything, didn't tease and coax, didn't ease in. He took over, plundered, dove right in. And nothing could have turned Hope on more.

She gripped his shoulders and lifted onto her tiptoes, needing to be closer, needing to be *taller*. She was too fricking short to get close enough and there was a definite lack of higher surfaces to boost herself onto out here in the middle of his yard.

TJ swept his tongue over her bottom lip and nipped the flesh lightly, making her groan and give him full access to her mouth. He stroked his tongue over hers as he slid his fingers up into her hair and tugged slightly, making her moan again as her head fell back. He dipped his knees and dragged his mouth down the length of her throat. If her eyes hadn't been closed, they would have crossed.

"Hi!"

A voice broke into the moment.

TJ froze.

Hope did too, but it took a few seconds for it to sink in that someone else was here. Her whole body was humming, and all her brain synapses were firing messages like, *Get closer*, *Take him deeper*, *Too many clothes* and *He really is big and hard all over*.

All other stimuli were coming into her consciousness very slowly.

TJ groaned and rested his forehead against hers for a moment. He slid his hand out of her hair, let her settle back onto her feet and then stepped away from her, breaking all contact.

She blinked, breathed and studied his face.

Oh, yeah, he was having some trouble getting beyond the closer, deep, hard stuff too.

"Hey, TJ."

Hope looked from his face toward the new arrival.

A beautiful blond was coming toward them, a covered dish in her hands and a good-looking guy with a huge grin a step behind her.

"Fuck," TJ muttered.

There was no way these people hadn't seen the kiss. Or couldn't see she was wearing his T-shirt and that he was naked from the waist up.

Yeah, that would be hard to miss.

"Hope, this is my sister-in-law Delaney and my brother Tucker," TJ said, turning toward the two people coming toward them.

"Almost-sister-in-law," Delaney corrected with a big smile. "And you are?"

Hope licked her lips and glanced from Delaney to TJ and back again. "I'm Hope."

Delaney seemed friendly and very, very curious. Tucker looked friendly and not curious so much as...knowing.

Delaney looked at TJ expectantly. Hope did too. Now what?

Then TJ surprised them all, including Hope—*especially* Hope—by putting his arm around her and pulling her against his side.

"Hope is my girlfriend."

Fucking karma.

TJ couldn't believe that Delaney and Tucker were here.

They were interrupting him in the midst of doing something really stupid with a woman he'd just met.

Exactly like he had interrupted *them* the first night Delaney was in town and in the midst of an emotional crisis.

Of course, that hadn't stopped Tucker from doing something stupid...like falling in love with her.

And it had turned out not to be all that stupid.

Which did *not* help TJ's mental state in regards to Hope.

But they were here, and the fact that it had surprised him to see them just went to show how far gone he was with Hope around.

"Your girlfriend?" Delaney repeated.

TJ stepped forward to take the casserole dish from her hands before she dropped it. No sense wasting his mother's cooking because he'd shocked his almost-sister-in-law.

And the dish had to be from his mother. Delaney didn't cook. She did, however, butt into his business.

Delaney frowned up at him. "I can't believe you have a girlfriend you haven't told us about."

Okay, she didn't look *shocked* exactly. But she did look annoyed.

Tucker stepped forward with a huge grin. He stuck his hand out to Hope. "Hi. Welcome. Nice to meet you." He nudged Delaney in the back and she shook her head and smiled at Hope.

"Yes, definitely nice to meet you."

Now TJ almost felt like he should apologize to his brother. Emotional crisis or not, stranger or not, kissing Hope had just rocked his world.

Or maybe he should be *thanking* Tucker and Delaney. He wasn't really a fan of having his world rocked.

"We brought dinner. Mom was worried," Tucker said.

TJ had no idea what time it was. He and Hope had been out on the dock for a while. Half-naked. He could close his eyes and picture every inch of her, from the top of her head to the colorful skirt she wore. He knew the exact shade of her nipples.

He knew the exact texture of her lips. He knew the feel of her hair.

He resolutely kept his eyes open.

"Didn't mean to worry anyone." Hell, he'd been worrying himself since Hope had shown up. Now he'd gotten to know her—and *see* her—and he was deeply concerned.

"Well, you didn't show for dinner, and Dad told Mom not to worry and to leave you alone. So, she got more worried," Tucker said.

"And then Adrianne called and asked me who the girl was who had been looking for you earlier," Delaney said. "We immediately volunteered to bring dinner over." She gave TJ a grin.

"That's very thoughtful of you." He tried not to grit his teeth as he said it. Shit, Adrianne knew about Hope. Had met her. Who else had been in the bakery? Maybe half the town already knew that Hope was here.

"Well, we didn't want Mom walking in on something she shouldn't see," Tucker said with a chuckle.

Yeah, this was all too familiar. TJ had volunteered to bring dessert to the two of them when Delaney and Tucker had been alone long enough to get into trouble.

"Let's go in and have some," Delaney said, watching Hope as if she'd just discovered a shiny new toy.

"Would you go in and get the table set?" TJ asked. "I just need to check one more thing on Hope's camper for her."

Delaney looked from TJ to Hope and back.

Tucker was finally the one who said, "Sure. See you in five minutes."

"Give us ten."

Tucker nodded with a grin. He grabbed the casserole dish from TJ with one hand and Delaney's hand with the other, pulling her with him toward the house.

Damn, now he was definitely going to have to apologize to Tucker for interrupting him and Delaney that first night.

TJ sighed. He loved Delaney and Tucker and he fucking hated lying. But the truth about who Hope was and why she was here wasn't his secret to tell.

And of course, all of this was already complicated and, yes, crazy. Of course, getting involved with Hope from the beginning was a bad idea. And of course, he'd realized that *after* he'd opened his big mouth to help.

He'd thought he'd given up keeping secrets the night Michelle had walked out of his house for the last time. Secrets hurt, and they never stayed secrets.

Fuck. This was all a mess.

The minute he'd felt his dick stir, he should have known it would be.

When the front screen door bumped shut behind Tucker and Delaney, TJ turned to Hope. "I should have run the girlfriend idea by you before I said it," he started.

Where the hell else was he going to start? *I need you to leave now before things get more difficult* or *take your clothes off?* Those were the only other things going through his mind at the moment.

"I'm surprised, but not upset," Hope told him.

He could not look away from her lips.

He was a breast man and Hope had *very* nice ones, but damn, there was something about her mouth. He was a little obsessed with it. And considering she had been using it to talk almost nonstop about things he didn't talk about with anyone, that was nothing short of amazing.

"You're not upset?"

"I figure you had a good reason for saying it."

It was *that*—the confidence she seemed to have in him and the sense that she knew him—that was driving him the most nuts. How could she know him? How could she trust him already? How could she have him pegged? He knew for a fact he was hard to figure out. He'd been told so on multiple occasions by a variety of people. It was a badge of honor of sorts after having his entire private life spilled all over town.

But Hope definitely wasn't put off by his surly, complex façade.

"And you just trust my reason?" he asked, kind of wanting to hear her say it.

"They're your family and this is your house. I'll follow your lead."

"It was the easiest way to explain why you're here and that we were..."

"Kissing," she supplied when he trailed off.

That had been more than kissing. He'd been trying to drink her in. He'd been trying to absorb her and possess her. Given one less layer of clothing, one firm surface or three more minutes, and he would have been buried deep in her body and fucking her brains out.

He wondered what she'd think if he told her that.

But looking into her huge green eyes, he knew she would love it.

So maybe the crazy notion of her already knowing him wasn't so crazy. He definitely felt as if he was figuring her out quickly. Maybe she didn't have many inhibitions, but there was more to her than the hippie he saw on the outside.

That did not, however, mean she wasn't crazy.

Hell, his intense attraction to her was the first clue that she had to be crazy. That was his type. At least that was the type he was naturally drawn to. A guy could change though.

And a guy could only be grateful he wasn't dead, in prison or addicted to something so many times before he wised up.

Crazy girls would be the death of him if he let them.

"Yeah, the kissing," he finally said. "Hard to explain that any other way."

"Except that there *is* another explanation." She moved in closer. "We are very attracted to one another, the opportunity presented itself, and it felt really good."

That was the biggest understatement he'd heard in a very, very long time.

"That will still lead back to the question of what you're doing here in the first place."

"You don't want them to know about me and Dan?"

"You and Dan are between you and Dan," TJ said, really wishing that was true. Unfortunately, in Sapphire Falls, and particularly in the Bennett family, everything was between everyone. Dan wasn't technically a Bennett, but he was a close family friend. Once you were important to one Bennett, you were important to all of them. And that meant your business was their business. "It's a touchy situation. I think you and Dan need to meet and talk before anyone else gets involved. If he wants to keep Jo and Peyton out of it, then I'll respect that. I hope you will too."

She pulled her bottom lip between her teeth and thought about that. Finally, she said, "Yes, I will. Of course I will." She shrugged. "I don't really have a lot of experience with family dynamics. You, on the other hand, seem to have *a lot*. I'll take your advice here."

A lot of experience with family dynamics? Yeah, that was one way of putting it.

"Thank you," he said sincerely.

"And I don't mind playing your girlfriend for a bit," she said. "Especially after that kiss."

That kiss. The kiss that was going to haunt him for days—and nights—to come. "Thanks." But he was hesitant to be too enthusiastic. After all, the girl was crazy.

"I should warn you, though," she said.

And here it came.

"I'm a very touchy-feely girlfriend." Hope ran her hand over his abs and up to his chest.

He grabbed her wrist before she could do it again. As it was, his entire body was hard and pulsing with the need to be up next to—and inside of—hers.

"I'm not a very touchy-feely boyfriend though," he said. Which wasn't true either. Not that he'd been a boyfriend in a long time. He had a possessive streak though, and public displays of affection were a by-product of that. He also had a very healthy sex drive. Private displays of affection were a by-product of *that*.

But he was a *fake* boyfriend in this case, so the displays of affection would—and *should be*—limited.

"That's okay," she said cheerfully. "I'll follow your lead on the family stuff and the story and you can follow my lead on the touchy-feely stuff."

And saying she was his girlfriend suddenly made the list of dumbest things he'd ever done. That was an impressive list, too.

"How about you pretend you're shy and quiet?" he asked. "Let me do all the talking."

He knew even as he said it that his suggestion was like asking a tornado to come and go quietly without damaging anything. It just wasn't how nature worked.

Hope laughed. "Come on, TJ, they wouldn't believe it if I played shy and quiet."

"You're not that good of an actress?" If that was true, he was actually glad. He'd had his share of women's theatrical performances.

"They know *you* too well. You don't go for shy and quiet. You go for extroverts who have a little wild streak. Or a big wild streak."

He blinked at her. "It would be great if we could convince them that was no longer true."

She shook her head. "It's going to be hard enough to

convince them that you've got a girlfriend you haven't mentioned."

"They don't know everything about me," he grumbled. But they did. They didn't necessarily know the names of all the girls he dated—or more specifically, slept with—because he never dated anyone from Sapphire Falls. Not anymore. But they knew those women were casual affairs, on both parts. They also knew he didn't intend to get serious about anyone again. He hadn't been kidding about the circus and monkeys. Delaney hadn't been there for all of that, but Tucker and the rest of his family had been. He wasn't dragging them into anymore Big-Top shows.

"You and I both know that's not true," Hope said.

She turned and headed toward the camper. He followed. Like a damn puppy.

"How do *you* know it's not true?" he asked. "You just met them."

"There's a vibe," she said with a shrug.

She opened the camper door and TJ was struck again by how tiny the thing was. It held a queen-size mattress with maybe two feet of space at the front and a few cupboards and cubbies. Otherwise, the mattress was all there was room for. No one but a child could stand up inside of it. And there was no way TJ would fit in the thing. No way.

"It was there with your dad, too," she said as she rummaged in a duffle bag on the floor of the camper. "Obviously, you're close to your family. You wouldn't keep a serious girlfriend from them." She pulled a black tank top out.

He narrowed his eyes. "I thought you were *not* psychic."

"I'm not. But I am very, very—"

"Intuitive," he finished for her. "Yeah, okay."

Maybe he didn't know the full definition of that word.

Or maybe he wasn't used to a woman being quite so focused and interested in him. That sounded stupid. He'd always had plenty of female attention, and he'd known his two most serious girlfriends—including the one who had turned into a wife—for most of his life. They knew him.

But he couldn't shake the idea that Hope *knew* him. And wanted to know everything. And would keep studying him until she did.

That should feel creepy, especially considering they'd met today and she could have an APB out for her arrest for all he knew.

But it didn't feel creepy. It felt nice. A lot like it had when she'd been massaging his shoulder by the pond. As if things were releasing, as if things were flowing better in him, as if he was letting go of stuff.

Which was *not* how he'd felt kissing her. That had been about things getting tight and hard and hot.

TJ shook his head. Maybe she wasn't a psychic. Maybe she was a witch or something. Or maybe all hippies were like this.

He sighed. He'd grown up in small-town America, which meant that he had seen a lot of the same things, the same type of people, over and over. And over. But he knew that just because someone wore a lot of bracelets, it didn't make them a hippie.

There was, however, an air about her that felt a little magical.

And that could completely be the kiss they'd shared, and that he wanted about a thousand more of.

Then she pulled his shirt off to replace it with the tank top. Just stripped the shirt off. Leaving herself naked from the waist up. Again.

Her breasts were no less spectacular this time around. Maybe more so. Because he'd kissed her. He'd broken through that no-physical-contact wall, and now his body didn't understand why it couldn't be up against her, wrapped around her and embedded deep inside of her right now.

Thankfully, she pulled the tank over her head and then down over her breasts and stomach. But she wasn't wearing a bra and her sweet nipples poked against the cotton, begging him for attention.

"You don't believe in bras?" he asked, his tone harsher than he'd meant it to be.

She shook her head. "They're very constricting."

"Well, you need to cover those up. My brother won't be able to walk without tripping over his tongue."

"Your brother who is madly in love with Delaney, you mean?" Hope asked, reaching back into the camper.

TJ didn't question how she knew Tucker was madly in love. A person didn't need to be psychic or even very, very intuitive to know that Tucker was head over heels for Delaney. "He's in love, not dead."

She shrugged into a bright-pink linen vest that hung past her butt and had sparkly beading down the front. "Better?" she asked.

He nodded. "A little." The thing was, Hope was beautiful and very much not his typical physical type, and his brother would be as interested in *that* as he would be in her breasts. Or almost as interested, anyway.

He yanked his shirt back over his head, inundated with the scent of her that had already seeped into the fabric and the warmth from her body. "You're right," TJ said. "Shy and quiet and sweet are not my type." It was a good reminder for *him* as well.

She frowned. "I didn't put sweet on my list."

"Trust me, sweet isn't my type."

"I'm sweet."

And oh God, she felt like his type. He shook his head. "Doesn't matter, because you're not really my girlfriend."

She didn't say anything to that.

"But you're also right that I wouldn't keep a serious girlfriend from them, so we're going to have to have a reason that they didn't know about you."

"I'll do whatever you want me to do, TJ."

And whether the huskiness in her voice was real or imagined, it still worked to rev TJ right back to the place he'd been when they'd been interrupted.

"Does Adrianne know you're from Arizona?" he asked.

"Who's Adrianne?"

"At the bakery. Delaney said you met her this morning."

"Oh, yeah, she was the one who gave me directions to your house."

"Does she know where you're from?"

"Yes."

He sighed. Of course she did. Hope probably knew all about Adrianne too. She'd probably asked Adrianne question after question, delving into the deep, dark secrets of her... Okay, Adrianne might not have personal deep, dark secrets. Or maybe she wasn't a sucker for blonds with gorgeous breasts and big green eyes. Either way, it was possible he was the only one spilling his guts to Hope.

"How are we going to explain me knowing you if you're from Arizona?"

"Online dating."

He looked at her. "What?"

"We could have met on an online dating site. We got to chatting, we hit it off, I found out you had shoulder surgery and I wanted to come and take care of you."

TJ blinked at her. Wow, that fully formed, even slightly plausible story had just rolled right out. Maybe she had more in common with the girls he was used to after all. Michelle had been able to keep track of an astonishing number of details in her lies.

He shook his head. That wasn't fair. *He'd* started this lie, and Hope was just following his lead as he'd asked. He nodded.

"Okay, fine. That will work. We can tell them we haven't been talking to each other long—which is true—and don't know much about each other—also true. And that's why I haven't mentioned you."

"So if we haven't been talking long, why would I just pack up and come to stay for the summer without an invitation?"

He couldn't help the grin he felt curling his lips. "Crazy, remember?"

Her eyes narrowed again and she studied him in that way that made him certain she was reading him perfectly. Then her expression relaxed and she nodded. "You know, you might be on to something there."

Uh oh. There was a definite twinge of trepidation in his gut at that. "What do you mean?"

"I'm thinking being a little crazy could be very freeing. And fun."

He was thinking she was right. And that this suddenly wasn't such a great idea.

"Maybe—"

She'd already twirled and was heading for the house.

"Hope!" he called after her.

She stopped on the top step to his porch and looked back.

"So you're going to..."

He hoped she'd fill in the blanks.

She didn't. She winked.

And his body reacted as if she'd stroked his cock.

Damn.

"And the kiss..."

"Was amazing."

Since when was he unable to complete a full sentence?

She was messing with him. This wasn't good.

But it had been just a kiss. And it *had* been amazing. "Yeah?"

Her smile changed. Just slightly. Hardly at all. But something in *this* smile didn't make him smile back—it made him want her even more.

"Yeah," she said softly.

Okay. Good. Maybe even very good. He started after her, realizing that he was already planning how to get rid of Delaney and Tucker. Quickly.

"So how did you two meet?" was the very first question out of Delaney's mouth when they were all seated around TJ's table.

Delaney and Tucker had already eaten so were enjoying coffee and dessert—the package of Double Stuf Oreo cookies that was a staple in TJ's kitchen—while he and Delaney ate baked pork chops on top of mashed potatoes and roasted carrots fresh from his mother's garden.

Or while *he* did, and while Hope pushed the food around her plate with her fork and gazed at him with a dopey smile.

"I believe the universe brought us together," Hope said. Her tone was not dopey.

And TJ kind of wished it was. She sounded sincere, and he really hated that he couldn't tell if this was part of her act or not. She might have agreed to go with the coo-coo story, but he knew there really was a little true coo-coo in there somewhere. What if she actually believed that fate had somehow brought her here?

He was also secretly grateful. It was a technicality, but if he wasn't the one voicing the lies to his brother and a woman who he considered a very close friend, he felt better.

"The universe?" Tucker asked, meeting TJ's eyes. There was humor there. Lots and lots of humor.

"Fate. Destiny," Hope filled in. "I was meant to meet TJ."

See, like that. That sounded so...true.

"You just threw a dart at a map and drove until you got here?" Tucker asked.

TJ lifted his glass of tea to hide his smile. His brother was definitely buying the crazy thing, judging by the look on his face. Of course, he was finding it all very amusing. And intriguing. Tucker had hardly taken his eyes off of Hope.

She seemed to have that effect on people.

"Oh, no, we started talking online."

Delaney stopped with her cookie halfway to her mouth. "Online?" she repeated.

Hope had a huge grin on her face as she nodded. Thankfully, Delaney and Tucker didn't know her well enough to know that her grin was more amused than kooky. TJ frowned. How did *he* know that? He hadn't known her long enough, or well enough, to know the differences in her smiles.

But, still, he could tell she thought this was funny.

"In a chat room on *Perfect Pick*," Hope added.

"*Perfect Pick*?" Tucker asked. "The online dating site?"

TJ was surprised. "How do you know what *Perfect Pick* is?" She was using the name of a *real* site? A site where they could go look for his profile? And TJ knew Tucker. He'd definitely look for TJ's profile. He'd invite Travis and a bunch of their friends over and make it a party.

"I've seen the commercials. I had no idea you were signed up with a site like that," he said to TJ.

Yeah, that didn't sound like him. At all.

"Well, he's not anymore, of course," Hope said, putting her hand on his thigh.

They were sitting next to one another across the table from Delaney and Tucker. TJ was regretting that choice already. Not only could he smell her fresh, flowery scent, but he was acutely aware of everything from the way she sat with one foot tucked underneath her on the chair to the fact that the six earrings that adorned her ear were made up of two stars, a moon, a butterfly, a pink gem and a tiny cross. In that order, from top to bottom.

And she'd meant the touchy-feely thing. She'd put her hand on his shoulder, brushed over the top of his hand, run her hand up and down his back and now had it resting on his thigh. And they'd been inside for no more than ten minutes.

He was wound up and ready to go, completely aware that *going* anywhere with Hope was a bad idea, and on the verge of saying to hell with it anyway.

Old, bad patterns died hard.

"He's not on the site anymore?" Delaney asked.

"Well, we've found our perfect picks," Hope said, inching her hand higher on his thigh. "No need for us to still be looking."

She'd instantly solved the issue of Tucker and Delaney trying to find their profiles online, but he could barely spare the brain cells to really appreciate that, considering her hand was getting ever closer to his cock. His cock was straining to be closer to her hand, too.

And none of her stroking his thigh was for show. Tucker and Delaney couldn't even see her hand from their side of the table.

But he also couldn't remove her hand or move away from her because Tucker and Delaney would see *that*.

Great.

"And now you're here," Delaney said, her smile clearly forced. "How nice. It must be...serious."

Hope turned to gaze up at TJ. "Well, once I knew TJ was hurting and needed help, there was nowhere else I could imagine being."

There was another one of those statements he could take seriously if he wanted to. Which he didn't, of course. But even though she'd just found out about his shoulder, she *had* seemed concerned.

"Then you'll be staying for a while," Tucker said.

"As long as needed," Hope answered.

"Well, you should know that TJ has a lot of people around here to help him," Delaney said, a note of protectiveness in her tone.

TJ had to fight another smile. Delaney was the best. Even if her protectiveness was misplaced.

"I'm sure," Hope said. "But no one can help him like I can."

TJ's imagination definitely took *that* for a ride until he reined it in. Tucker's too, it seemed, as his brother choked on his iced tea and covered with a cough.

"And TJ is saving me too." Hope moved her hand from his thigh and looped her arm through his, leaning into his side affectionately. "We need each other. Where else would I be but right by his side?"

TJ missed her touch on his leg but was placated by the feel of her breast against his biceps.

"He's saving you too?" Delaney asked, glancing at TJ.

He tried not to show how interested *he* was in Hope explaining that statement further as well.

"Ever since my mom passed away, I've been looking for... something. And I think I might just have found it here in Sapphire Falls."

For just a flash, he thought he should be appalled that she was using her dead mother to get Tucker and Delaney's sympathy and further the lie. But before that thought was even fully formed, he knew that wasn't the case. How he knew that so easily and so certainly, he didn't really want to examine, but he knew that Hope meant what she said in this case.

That also stupidly made a whole lot of protective instincts rear their heads.

The next thought that flashed through his mind was that Hope would know that. She had already pegged him as a protector. She had to know that a comment like that would make him all too ready to jump in to help her find whatever it was she was looking for. He didn't like being so easy to read.

But he was already working on reconnecting her with her dad. That was what she meant, he was sure.

He was pretty sure anyway.

But what if there was more?

TJ gripped his tea glass and worked on taking a deep breath.

She meant her dad. That was all she meant. That was all he was going to help her with. That was complicated enough.

"Your mom passed away?"

Immediately, any skepticism Delaney might have felt in regards to Hope, and any thoughts she'd had of protecting him *from* Hope, clearly evaporated.

Delaney reached out and took Hope's hand. "I'm so sorry."

A look of sadness passed over Hope's face, and it felt like she'd punched him in the gut. TJ had to clear his throat and consciously stay put to keep from pulling her into his lap.

"I just lost my sister and brother-in-law a few months ago," Delaney told Hope softly. "If you need anyone to talk to, I'm here."

Hope gave her a sincere, sweet smile, and TJ felt *that* like a punch to his gut as well.

"I'm so sorry about your loss, too," Hope said, curling her fingers around Delaney's.

TJ looked from one woman to the other, then at his brother. Tucker was clearly battling the same urges to comfort and shelter. Tucker's jaw was tight, his eyes trained on Delaney, his hand rubbing her back. It was amazing seeing his brother in love, and he knew that Tucker hurt when Delaney hurt.

TJ followed Tucker's example, moving his arm around Hope and hugging her against him.

If she thought it was strange, she didn't show it. She didn't hesitate to press against him as if that was where she belonged.

Of course, that could all be a part of the act too.

He was hating this whole situation more and more. It was one thing to tell a white lie to protect a couple of people's privacy. It was another for this thing to get *his* thoughts and feelings all twisted up, and for him to not know what was real and what wasn't. That was just too familiar. Because there was no way out here either. Hope needed an ally in town while she sorted through her stuff.

TJ knew on some level that he could turn her over to Delaney or Adrianne or any of the other women. His friend Phoebe knew Dan and she was something of a schemer. She could no doubt come up with a way of getting Hope and Dan together while preserving the confidentiality of the situation.

But he wasn't turning this over.

He knew that with a certainty that also concerned him. But there it was.

He was officially involved with another crazy girl.

"Do you have other family?" Hope asked Delaney.

"My mom and dad, but we're not close at all. How about you?"

Hope shook her head. "Grandparents I barely know. My mom was raised to be very independent, to figure things out on her own. When she was eighteen, she left home and started traveling." A faint smile touched Hope's lips and TJ found himself mesmerized and wanting to know more. Wanting to know everything.

It was strange, actually. He'd only ever been seriously involved with women he'd known his whole life. He'd already known all about them and their pasts. It was simply impossible to have a history of any kind that wasn't common knowledge in Sapphire Falls.

The notion of getting to know this woman, of hearing her stories, asking her questions, telling her his...it was all strangely...tempting. Michelle had also known him, or had thought she did, and had never asked him a question other than asking him to come get her or asking him to help with something.

Hope shook her head and it pulled TJ away from the swirling thoughts of the past.

"Anyway," she said. "She raised me similarly. She felt like teaching me to solve my own problems did me more good than solving them for me. So I'm pretty self-reliant. I would have thought that would mean I wouldn't miss her as much or wouldn't...notice her being gone as much..." She shook her head. "That sounds cold. I don't mean it like that. I've been living on my own, in another city. And I missed her while I was gone, but she was always just a phone call away. Now..." Hope trailed off and her smile was definitely sad this time. "Now she's not, and it *feels* different."

TJ felt as if his insides were being pulled in a million directions. Michelle had certainly had her emotional turmoil, but he didn't remember feeling connected to those emotions himself, as if he was being stretched tight and twisted along with her.

"I know exactly what you mean," Delaney said. "I positively ache sometimes with how much I miss my sister and Rafe. Without them here...everything is different."

Hope nodded. "The world changed in a heartbeat."

TJ curled his fingers into her side where his hand rested and he cleared his throat. He wanted to make this better but was at a loss. He might need to pull Tucker aside later for some tips about comforting a woman who had lost someone close. He had experience with distraught women. One at least.

Michelle had certainly shed her share of tears. But he didn't know what to do with a woman who had an actual problem, who'd had a true loss. Michelle had cried to get his attention, to keep him close, to be sure she was his priority and that he knew she needed him. Hope was here, in his kitchen, in his *life*, because she wanted to meet her father and his happened to be the house where she'd landed. She hadn't come to TJ specifically. She hadn't come to Sapphire Falls for help or support or sympathy. And she wasn't trying to wrap TJ around her finger so that she would never be alone and would never have to face her mistakes or responsibilities on her own.

Hope was not Michelle. That was a good thing.

He didn't know what to do with a woman like Hope, because she was not like Michelle. That was probably *not* a good thing.

"It's funny the things I miss," Hope said. "Not the big things as much as hearing her singing while she gardened, her homemade lavender ice cream and the way she always got the words wrong to 'Burning Love'. Things that didn't seem important at the time but now…"

"'Burning Love'?" TJ asked, desperate to take the sadness out of her voice and eyes. "The Elvis song?"

Hope smiled at him and nodded. "Yep. It was always Elvis in the garden."

"*Lavender* ice cream?" Delaney asked.

"It's so good," Hope said, enthusiasm sneaking into her tone. "And lavender is so good for so many things. Definitely for relaxation and soothing your senses. Have you ever used it?" she asked Delaney.

"Used lavender?" Delaney asked. "I don't think so. What do you mean?"

"How do you cope?" Hope asked Delaney. "When the sadness gets so strong or when you can't sleep at night because of the memories? Or when you're not sleeping because you're worried about your responsibilities now that they're gone?"

A flicker of surprise crossed Delaney's face. "How did you know that?"

"Know what?" Hope asked.

"That I have responsibilities that I'm worried about since they died?"

Hope straightened and TJ saw a flash of surprise in her eyes as well. She glanced at TJ and then cleared her throat. "Um, I...sensed it."

"Sensed what?" Tucker asked.

Hope sighed, almost as if she didn't want to answer. TJ stroked his hand up and down her side and felt her relax.

"I sensed that she has heightened anxiety when talking about her sister and her husband not being here."

Tucker shifted on his seat and it was clear he was agitated. "Of course she has anxiety about that. She's sad. She lost her sister and best friend."

Hope hesitated. She pressed her lips together and said nothing. But TJ saw concern in her eyes as she looked at Delaney. Her concern was for Delaney, not about Tucker's reaction. But she was trying to respect Tucker as well.

That made TJ's heart twinge. He loved Delaney. She was one of his closest friends, was making his brother incredibly happy and was the caretaker for four young boys TJ loved dearly. He wanted her to be happy, and if Hope was concerned about her, so was he.

Crazy as that seemed.

Again, he ran his hand up and down her side. "It's okay," he told her. He focused on Tucker. "Hope is very intuitive. Just listen."

Tucker didn't say anything, but his concerned frown didn't ease much.

Delaney met Hope's gaze. "What were you going to say?"

Hope glanced at TJ and he gave her a nod.

She took a deep breath. "I know you're sad. And you miss them. But your emotion changes when you talk about them being gone. Not about losing them or missing them, but the idea of being without them. That's different, right?" she asked gently.

Delaney nodded.

"What do you think about when you think about them being gone?" Hope asked.

"I became the guardian to my four nephews," she said. "I worry about them."

TJ saw the tension in Tucker's body and he sympathized with his brother. He knew that Tucker wanted to take care of Delaney and the boys and he wanted to believe he was making everything better for them. And he was. There was no question there. Delaney would be the first to say so. But that didn't mean she didn't worry. TJ got that. He knew Tucker got that. Even their own mother, who had four grown sons, all of whom were doing very well for themselves, still worried.

"Of course you do," Hope said. "And that's natural. You need to stop fighting it."

Delaney's eyes widened. "What?"

Hope nodded. "You worry. Then you fight to *not* worry because you want to trust that everything is okay. You think if you're worried, you're not trusting. But it's normal to worry, so ignoring it and fighting it and telling yourself that by worrying, you're somehow failing, is tying you up."

There were several long seconds of silence, and TJ felt a little tied up himself. He didn't want Hope pissing Tucker off or hurting Delaney, but for some reason he didn't want her to keep quiet either. No one had talked to him more than this woman in months. Maybe ever. Most people respected his silence and clear desire to deal with things on his own. No one kept at him after he flat-out said he didn't want to talk about something, not even his brothers.

And yet talking wasn't so painful with Hope. Maybe because he sensed that she truly cared and was talking to him because she was interested and wanted to help.

Maybe because he sensed she was right.

About him. And about Delaney.

Delaney was happy here, and was healthier and more at

peace than when she'd arrived by far, but there were still dark circles under her eyes at times and worry lines around her eyes. He supposed that was normal in a mom of four. No matter how many other people she had helping her and supporting her.

"That's exactly what I do," Delaney finally said quietly.

Tucker made a soft growling sound. "Laney—"

She turned to him. "I fight it because I know that I don't really need to worry. The boys are great. You're amazing, Tuck. Everyone is happy and healthy and safe. But it's like I can't turn it off. So then I try to turn it off. I tell myself it's stupid and I have to stop, but that almost makes it worse."

Tucker stared at her for a long moment. Finally, he breathed out. "I worry too. And fight it."

Delaney's smile spread slowly but surely. "You do?"

"Of course. I worry about them and you and about you worrying about them."

Delaney put her hand on his cheek. "I love you."

"I know."

The look that passed between them was intimate and intense and full of love and happiness, and for a moment, TJ's heart clenched hard. He heard Hope sigh beside him and he looked at her. She was smiling at Tucker and Delaney.

Delaney finally turned back to Hope. "Why do I feel like you have a solution to my sleeplessness and worry?"

Hope shook her head. "I can't take the worry away. Like I said, that's normal. But I can teach you to put it into perspective and not let it rule your sleep and not let it take over. You have to stop *fighting* and accept it. Acknowledge it."

"How?"

"Meditation. Yoga. Some essential oils."

Delaney looked intrigued. "Really?"

"Absolutely."

"I know nothing about essential oils."

"I know *a lot* about essential oils," Hope said with a light laugh. "I'm a healer. Been practicing all my life."

There was a heartbeat where no one seemed to know what to say. TJ wanted *someone* to ask her what she meant, but it couldn't be him. He was supposed to know some of this about her. Wasn't he?

"Healer?" Tucker finally asked. "You're a doctor?"

Hope shook her head. She reached for Delaney's hand again and turned it over, palm up. She pressed her thumb into Delaney's hand just below *her* thumb and rubbed slowly. "A nurse, actually."

Tucker's eyes widened and TJ worked not to react. She was a nurse? A *real* nurse?

"No kidding," Tucker replied.

Hope nodded. "Finished my nursing degree almost two years ago. I've been working with a company since then, taking various short-term assignments in different places."

"In hospitals?" Delaney clarified.

"A couple of hospitals. A couple of clinics. Usually they send us to fill in temporarily in understaffed areas. I've been on an Indian Reservation, in rural Iowa, in the inner city in Atlanta. All over. It's been amazing," Hope said.

"And most recently you were back home with your mom?" Tucker asked.

TJ liked this. Like when his father had been here, this was a chance for him to learn about Hope.

She nodded, still rubbing Delaney's hand. "I'd seen a variety conditions and situations, and I saw what our medical model can do—and what it can't." She took a deep breath. "My mom has always been a healer. She's the one people come to when all else fails. She *was* the one," Hope corrected herself.

Delaney reached out with her other hand and squeezed Hope's hand.

Hope looked at her. "Damn, it's hard to get used to talking about her in the past tense."

Delaney gave her a smile. "I still talk about Chelsea and Rafe like they're here."

Hope breathed deeply again and TJ worked on not digging his fingers into her as he held her. His arm wasn't around her because she needed his comfort. It was a show. But there was no denying the urge to pull her into his lap and hold her tight.

"Anyway, my mom was a holistic healer. I grew up with the role model of helping others heal," Hope went on. She moved Delaney's hands so that she could press and rub on the other one. "She taught meditation and knew everything about herbs and oils and natural remedies. She was also an amazing listener. She could get anyone to open up to her about anything."

Like mother like daughter, TJ thought.

"Holy crap, that feels so good," Delaney said, staring at her hands. "I actually—" She looked up at Hope with a puzzled frown. "I feel less tension in my shoulders."

Hope smiled as if that was exactly what she'd expected. "Acupressure points for stress and anxiety. I can teach you. Give me your foot."

Delaney immediately kicked her sandals off. Hope scooted her chair back, moving closer to TJ, and patted her lap. Delany put her foot up on Hope's leg.

Hope put the pad of her thumb on the bottom of Delaney's foot between her second and third toes. She dragged her thumb about a third of the way down Delaney's foot and then pressed.

Delaney moaned. "Oh my God."

Tucker looked at her, seeming concerned and very interested at the same time. "Feel good, babe?"

Delaney's head fell back and she closed her eyes. "So good."

Tucker turned wide eyes to Hope. "Wow."

Hope chuckled and continued kneading the bottom of Delaney's foot. "Acupressure can be amazing. For a lot of things. There are points for sinus congestion, nausea, fear, quitting smoking, libido."

"Libido?" Tucker asked. "As in sex drive?"

Hope nodded. "Definitely. Acupressure on the right points can increase the drive and can make orgasms stronger."

"You don't need to push on any special spots," Delaney told him teasingly.

"Oh, I just happen to know all of *your* special spots," Tucker replied easily.

"Well," Hope said. "It won't *hurt* to press on a few specific places." She gave Tucker a wink.

"You can teach me those spots?" he asked.

"Or I can teach Delaney and she can push on her own spots," Hope said lightly.

Tucker gave her a full-blown, sincere smile. "You have that knowledge and you went into the medical field instead of acupressure and herbs and stuff?" Tucker asked.

"I, like so many people, was skeptical." Hope motioned Tucker forward. She stood and let Tucker slide into her chair. TJ straightened, missing having her close within seconds.

Crazy.

Hope put Delaney's other foot in Tucker's lap and then guided his thumb to the same spot she'd been pressing on. "Press firmly but gently for about thirty seconds, then knead deeply. At least two minutes."

Tucker followed her instructions exactly and they all watched Delaney turn into a wet noodle in front of their eyes.

Hope moved behind Tucker's chair and put her hands on his ears.

TJ's lips twitched at the look of sudden uncertainty on his brother's face. Tucker's eyes widened even farther as Hope began rubbing his ears, stroking down and pulling on his lobes, then repeating the pattern.

"It's silly now as I look back," Hope continued, as if rubbing a stranger's ears was completely normal. "I mean, I saw the things she did work for people. But there wasn't a lot of science and proof, and I went through a phase where I questioned everything she taught me, doubting and rebelling. But I couldn't ignore that I felt compelled to help people, to somehow make things better around me. Nursing seemed like the perfect fit."

"But now you don't think so?" Delaney asked. Even her voice sounded more relaxed, and she didn't seem to have a problem with another woman rubbing Tucker's ears.

TJ took another look at Tucker's face and found that his brother seemed to have no problem with it either. Tucker looked positively blissful.

Hope shook her head. "Actually, I think I have a unique opportunity to combine the two worlds I know. I understand and respect the science behind our Western medicine, but I also know that it doesn't always work. I think there's a place for the things my mother used too. That's part of my journey now. I'd hoped to do it with her, but now I'm on a quest to really figure out where she was coming from, learn what she knew, live it myself."

"So the oils and herbs and yoga are all new?" Tucker asked. His head had fallen forward and his voice was muffled slightly. "You don't really understand it?"

Delaney nudged him with her foot. "Tucker."

Hope laughed. "It's okay. I'm used to people doubting. I doubted for a long time. No," she said, addressing Tucker directly. "I do understand it. I've been around it all my life. But it was so commonplace that I didn't really think about it. I used ginger when I had an upset stomach and peppermint for headaches. I meditated. I did yoga. We never had white sugar in the house. That was all just my life, our usual routine and habit, so I never really *learned* it. Now I'm working on that. And working on seeing things the way my mom did."

TJ pulled his eyes from Hope somehow. She was glowing, talking about all of it. There was a touch of sadness around her eyes when she talked about her mom, but there was excitement in her tone as she told them how she was going to combine her knowledge and help people going forward.

Tucker had turned into a lump of Jell-O in the chair, but Delaney was watching her with the same wonder TJ felt. As if she didn't quite believe Hope was real and saying these things, but like she kind of wanted her words to be true.

Magical.

That damn word popped into his head again.

Then Hope shocked him by taking her hands off Tucker and moving to sit on TJ's lap. True, Tucker was occupying her chair and his empty chair was clear on the other side of the table. But it seemed she'd given it no thought. As if she'd sat in his lap a million times before.

She was a good actress.

Even so, TJ didn't hesitate to wrap his arm around her waist and pull her back against his chest. He could play the part too. And if he looked pleased and turned-on when she rested her hands on his arm that crossed protectively in front of her, that was even better for their story.

"Want to have coffee tomorrow?" Delaney asked.

TJ shifted Hope so he could see her face. And so she wasn't pressing quite so firmly against his cock.

She looked surprised but pleased by Delaney's invitation. "I don't drink coffee."

Having apparently gathered his composure from her ear massage, Tucker asked, "And you don't eat food?" He looked down at Hope's still mostly full plate.

She gave him a sheepish smile. "I'm...a vegetarian."

Of course she was. TJ resisted an eye roll.

"Ah, my mom will be...thrilled," Tucker said.

"Yeah." She looked a little apologetic with that. "How's your head?" she asked Tucker.

"Great. Headache is totally gone." He peered at her. "How did you know I had a headache?"

"You're the new dad of four boys," she said, lifting a shoulder. "And your body language and expressions while watching Delaney told me that you're very concerned with *her* being happy. I'm guessing tension headaches are common. Plus, you had a tightness around your eyes and your shoulders were practically up at your ears."

Tucker seemed unable to argue with any of that.

Delaney moved her foot from his leg and leaned in. She took his hand and lifted it to her mouth. She pressed a kiss on Tucker's hand and said, "I'll learn how to rub your ears."

He gave her a smile. "Deal."

Again, there was that sense that Delaney and Tucker had momentarily forgotten anyone else was in the room with them.

"You didn't eat the carrots or potatoes either?" TJ asked Hope.

She glanced at him and it was clear she didn't want to answer. "I'm actually vegan. And only eat organic produce."

TJ sighed. Of course she was. Just when he'd started thinking this might all be okay. No one was going to actually believe he was in love with a vegan.

"The mashed potatoes were made with milk," he acknowledged. Which meant she wouldn't eat them either. "But it doesn't get more organic than my mother's garden," he said.

"She grew the carrots?" Hope asked, her eyes lighting up.

Well, yeah, she was probably hungry. He hadn't seen her eat anything all day.

"Yes. The garden is her pride and joy. Even above the four of us boys," Tucker said.

Hope reached out and stabbed a carrot on her plate with her fork and bit into it. She groaned.

Her moan of pleasure shot straight through TJ to his groin and he had to shift on the chair as his cock pressed against his fly.

Hope pulled her plate closer to where she now sat.

"So how about tea tomorrow then?" Delaney asked. "At the bakery in town. I have a couple of friends who I think would love to learn about essential oils and stuff. They have kids too and are working moms. We all have the typical fatigue and stress and stuff."

"I'd love to," Hope said around bites of the vegetables that she was suddenly eating with enthusiasm.

TJ had the stupid urge to go get her some lettuce and tomatoes. Hell, he could get them out of his own garden except he wasn't sure what was growing out there. He hadn't been able to tend to it with his shoulder, and with all the things that needed done on the farm, his vegetable patch was pretty far down the priority list.

Then he frowned as he replayed Delaney's invitation. Hope was going to meet Adrianne and Phoebe and Lauren and Kate? Because he knew those were the women that would be included in their little tea party.

"I don't know if Hope will have time," he said. He surreptitiously shifted his remaining carrots onto her plate.

Hope looked from the carrots to his face with a small smile. Yeah, yeah, so he was taking care of her again. Whatever. They were carrots.

She popped one of his carrots into her mouth. "Really? What am I going to be doing?"

He actually did suddenly have a few ideas. But they were all really bad, considering they would both be naked and his dick would be in charge. That was never a good thing.

Delaney and Tucker both looked at him with interest as well.

Fuck.

"I... He sighed in defeat. "I guess you could go have tea."

What could that hurt? She was going to talk about yoga and oil. That was harmless.

Besides, she was clearly a very good liar. No one would catch on to anything over a teatime chat about meditation. But that thought immediately made him cringe internally. Again, the lie was his invention. And the only thing she'd said to Delaney that didn't seem completely true was that they'd met online. The rest had seemed completely sincere.

Yoga. Meditation. Oils. Vegan. Acupressure for orgasms. Everything.

"You know what though?" Hope said, suddenly bouncing up from his lap. "I have something I can give you tonight to try," she told Delaney as she started for the door.

"Where are you going?" TJ asked.

"To the camper. I'll be right back."

5

The back door thumped shut behind her and absolute silence filled the kitchen. The lack of noise was especially noticeable now that even Hope's jingling bracelets were gone.

"What in the *hell* is going on?" Delaney finally asked.

TJ grimaced and faced his friend. "What?"

"An online girlfriend who shows up here out of the blue acting like she's psychic and talking about essential oils and stuff?" Delaney asked.

TJ sighed. "She didn't say she's psychic. And essential oils are a real thing." Of course, that was the extent of his knowledge about the topic—that they were real.

Tucker shook his head. "Hey, she's very...interesting. And damn, my headache really is totally gone. She can rub my ears anytime," he said in typical Tucker fashion. He simply chuckled when Delaney nudged him with her foot. He looked at TJ. "But what are *you* doing with her? She's gotta be driving you nuts."

Yeah, she should be. She was. Kind of. But it wasn't how nosy she'd been about his personal life or how she'd snubbed his mother's pork chops or her crazy talk about *knowing* him that he thought about. Instead, it was her bright smile and the way she'd immediately been concerned about his shoulder and that she was a nurse who had been traveling and working in underserved areas that came to mind. And how she was willing to put up with all of this craziness to protect Dan and his family from the repercussions of her sudden appearance in their lives. And the way she'd taken Delaney's hand and talked about how Delaney felt and what she needed when she had also just lost someone she loved very much.

Damn. She wasn't driving him nuts so much as she was... driving him nuts. Getting under his skin. Wrapping him up, distracting him and making him want to spend twenty-four-seven with her just talking and kissing and...talking some more.

TJ didn't talk. And that was about all he'd done since Hope had shown up.

But even if he hadn't been a bit *fascinated* himself, one look at Delaney's face would have convinced him that Hope Daniels was more than something. She was special.

Delaney and Tucker were definitely fascinated. So maybe TJ's fascination was okay. Unavoidable even.

"I think she's amazing and interesting," Delaney said. "She's got this...*something*." Delaney looked at TJ. "You know what I mean?"

The something that was impossible to ignore and even more impossible to explain? Yeah, he knew what she meant. "She's definitely something."

"Like completely opposite from your usual type," Tucker said. "But that's probably not a bad thing," he added with a shrug.

TJ wanted to laugh at that understatement. "I don't know her that well. She just showed up today. And this is a temporary stop. Just a visit."

Delaney was watching him closely, so TJ carefully kept his expression bland.

"And you're sure she's not a nut job?" Tucker asked. "All this hocus-pocus herb talk doesn't make you worry she might pull out a dead chicken for some ritual or something?"

TJ lifted an eyebrow. "Mom pulls out dead chickens for dinner twice a week."

"You know what I mean," Tucker said. "And maybe it's a *live* chicken for rituals."

Delaney frowned at him. "Stop it." Then to TJ she said, "You trust her?"

Somehow, when faced with that very direct question, he knew his answer was yes.

"I do. I'm not worried about being here with her anyway."

"She could be a serial killer. She could have escaped from a mental institution. She could be casting a spell over your house right now," Tucker said. His tone didn't indicate he was truly concerned about any of that though.

She was blond and had rubbed his earlobes. Tucker was a fan of Hope's no matter what she did with chickens.

Hope was casting a spell all right.

"Don't be stupid," TJ told Tucker. "She's different. That doesn't mean she's dangerous."

"You don't think she's a little crazy?" Tucker asked, twirling his finger near his temple.

TJ started to reply but realized he had no answer. He had thought that convincing everyone that Hope was obsessed with him and had shown up out of the blue was a good plan. That it would throw them off the scent of the real reason for her presence in Sapphire Falls, and she could covertly meet Dan and go from there. And it would give TJ a reason to keep touching and kissing her—at least when other people were around.

Touching her and kissing her when they were alone was a bad idea. Once his cock got involved, all bets were off as to how well he would handle anything about Hope being here. Once he was inside of that soft, sweet-smelling, tight body—

"TJ," Tucker said, snapping his fingers in front of TJ's face. "You okay?"

TJ frowned at him. "Yeah, fine." Because he *hadn't* involved his cock. Yet.

He was feeling crazy—turned around and inside out. But did he actually think *Hope* was crazy? No. In fact, hearing her talk about her work as a nurse, her connection to helping people and her desire to understand her mother better, he was starting to think she was one of the sanest people he knew.

That was not good.

"She's...unconventional," he said. "But maybe that's what I need for a few days—something different, out of the ordinary."

A very *few* days.

"Well, I'd say you're gonna get that," Tucker said with a chuckle.

"I'm going to go check on her," TJ said, shoving back from the table. "I'll give you two a couple of minutes to talk about us without us here."

"Finally," Delaney said.

TJ rolled his eyes and headed outside through the back door. He wanted a few minutes with Hope alone too. Sure, he'd get that later when Delaney and Tucker left, but he couldn't wait. She'd been gone from him for less than ten minutes and he had to go after her.

Fuck.

He rounded the side of the house and found Hope standing behind the camper. The back end was propped open to reveal a countertop and sink and various drawers and cubbies. He'd wondered if she could store or prepare food with this thing. Apparently, there was a built-in tiny kitchen. Tiny being the operative word.

She had a wooden box sitting on the counter. The front of

the box opened like a set of French doors, revealing a collection of glass bottles and jars inside.

"Hey."

"Hey." She gave him a grin as she replaced the top on one of the jars and opened a bottle. She poured a bit of oil into the bowl she was holding.

Whatever it was smelled good. Like peppermint. "Is Tucker pretty convinced I'm crazy?"

"Tucker is..." TJ thought about how to answer that. Finally, he said, "Tucker is like everyone else in this town. We've seen a lot of the same things and same types over and over."

"And I'm different."

"Very."

"And he's suspicious of me because of that?" She stirred whatever the concoction was in the bowl as she watched TJ.

TJ shook his head. "I think he's *fascinated*. Just like everyone else will be."

She smiled at his use of her favorite word. "Everyone else?"

Meaning including him. Absolutely. "Yes. You're going to get a lot of attention."

She poured the mixture from the bowl into an empty bottle and pressed a stopper into the top. "But as long as I keep the attention on things like herbs and yoga and almost-psychic readings, it will keep the attention *off* my connection with Dan and will keep JoEllen happy."

And that irked TJ suddenly. Why was JoEllen's happiness so much more important than Hope's? Hope was Dan's daughter, and she deserved to know her dad and have a family.

"For now," he said grudgingly. "But we'll figure that out, okay?"

She nodded and tucked the glass bottle into the pocket of her skirt and started closing the box. "I'm not worried. This girlfriend thing could work for the next couple of days and then I'll hit the road and everything will be fine."

Yeah, and *that* irked him too. She was so prepared to just leave? She'd only gotten here today. She hadn't even really gotten to know anyone or the town. "Thought you were talking about staying for the rest of the summer?"

"I guess in my mind I was going to have a summer like my mom did here. But," she shrugged, "that's not very realistic. I realize that now."

"What do you think her summer was like?" TJ asked.

She closed the back of the camper and turned to him. "New friends, parties, new love. A carefree summer. A new adventure. A bunch of memories she carried with her for the rest of her life." Her voice caught at the end.

"Dammit," TJ muttered and reached for her.

He just wasn't sure he was cursing the incessant need he felt to comfort her or the fact that she had just laid out everything she wanted and needed that summer—and he wanted to be the one to give it to her.

Hope seemed happy to be in his arms, and TJ felt her big sigh.

He stroked his hand over her hair. "Why do you think all of that is unrealistic?"

She didn't say anything for a moment. Then softly, she said, "Sometimes magic just happens. You can't force it. You can't create it. That's what makes it magical."

Magic. That word again.

"You think your mom's time in Sapphire Falls was magic?" He marveled that he could say that word with a straight face. That word was not a part of his normal vocabulary. But it felt completely serious right now.

"She said so herself," Hope said against his chest. "She talked about long walks and the sky and the air. She loved nature, loved being in it. Camping out by herself just to be a part of it all was something she did a lot. Something that always amazed her was that we could all be looking at the same sky, the same stars and moon, but that everywhere she went it seemed different. Beautiful in a new way. Like looking at the same painting done by different artists."

TJ kept stroking her hair.

"That's what made me want to travel like she did for a while. I want to see things her way."

"It sounds like you understood her really well and that you had a lot in common," he said. "The oils and herbs and stuff."

Hope laughed lightly. "I know all about it. I don't know if I'd say I *understand* it. That's what I'm looking for."

"You were both interested in healing and helping people," he pointed out. "That must give you an understanding."

"I understand her desire to help people. But while we were interested in the same destination, our paths were pretty different. I want to see the scenery she saw along her path," Hope said. "My mom's experiences were a part of who she was and the things she did. It was as if she had this scrapbook in her mind with pictures and pieces of all the places she'd been and the people she'd met. I know she had more she wanted to do, but I also know she didn't have any regrets."

TJ didn't say anything. In fact, he was fighting to swallow against the tightness in his throat. Not having regrets at the end was an incredible accomplishment.

"You should stay for a little while," TJ heard himself say after a few moments.

Hope lifted her head and looked up at him. "Stay?"

"In Sapphire Falls. Meet some new people, do some new things. Make some memories."

What was he doing?

"You can't force magic," she said, her voice wistful.

"Is magic always immediately obvious?" he asked.

If anyone who knew him heard him say something like that, they would insist he check with his doctor. Right away.

Hope stood looking at him, blinking, clearly replaying his words. Then she shook her head. "Maybe not."

She gave him a soft smile and TJ instantly felt everything in him harden and heat.

Without warning, Hope lifted onto her tiptoes and pressed her lips to his.

TJ's body reacted as if she'd touched a flame to a fuse. His hand cupped her head and he deepened the kiss immediately, opening his mouth on hers, his tongue urging her lips to part and then stroking deep when they did.

He felt her arms go around his neck and her body melt against his.

Speaking of good times...

The sound of his back screen door slamming made TJ lift his head.

"Come here." He took her hand and pulled her around the opposite side of the house and into the shadows. He wasn't quite ready to share her. He pressed her back against the house and crowded close so they could whisper. He felt like he was playing hide and seek from his brother. He'd always won when they'd played as kids. Even then, he'd been good at being quiet and keeping to himself for long periods of time.

"What's going on?" Hope asked.

TJ put a finger against her lips. "Tucker's being nosy. He's going to try to stall me out here while you go back inside," TJ told her softly, certain he was right. Because that's what he would have done if he'd been the one inside and one of his brothers was taking a long time alone with a new pretty girl.

Hope surprised him by grasping his wrist, and his fingertip. "I thought I gave him time to grill you about me when I came out here to mix the oil for Delaney," she whispered.

He actually smiled at that. She'd understood that Tucker and Delaney would want to talk to him in private.

"You did," he said. "But he's planning on you going into the house ahead of me. Where Delaney is. Time for girl talk."

Hope raised an eyebrow. "Delaney wants to talk to me?"

"I guarantee it."

"Like about menstrual cramps and shoes sales?"

He leaned back and looked down at her feet. "I don't see you being big on shoe sales. Or shoes. And I'm guessing you have a tea or a cream or an oil for the cramps."

"I'm not. And I do."

She grinned at him and TJ wanted to kiss the hell out of her. Again.

"I don't like lying to them," Hope said. "They're sweet and they're concerned about you now for no reason."

He appreciated that she didn't like lying. He wasn't feeling so great about it either. "No reason?"

"Well, I'm not really some girl who just packed up and came all the way to Nebraska expecting to move in for the summer after having just met you online. They don't actually need to worry."

"No, you're some girl who packed up and came all the way to Nebraska expecting to stay for the summer having never met anyone here in any way at all."

Hope frowned at him. "Well, when you say it like *that*."

He laughed softly. "Which part of that is untrue?"

"Still, I'm not here because I have some strange infatuation with you."

TJ braced his hand on the side of the house next to her ear. "Thought you said you were fascinated?"

Her breathing changed minutely, and if they hadn't been standing so close, he probably wouldn't have noticed. But he did. And he liked it. He liked affecting her.

"Sure, *now* I am," she said quietly.

"The feeling is mutual." It must have been the hiding. Or

the whispering. Or that it was very true. Whatever it was, he was surprised to hear himself say it out loud.

He was rewarded with a smile that was stunning. "I like that," she said.

He wanted to kiss her again. "As for lying to them," he said, forcing himself back on a safer track. "We can tell them the truth. They'll keep your confidence. But we'll also be asking them to lie to other people they care about."

Hope nodded and sighed. "We can't ask that." She shrugged. "Besides, the kooky thing could really help Delaney out."

TJ cocked an eyebrow. "You being kooky could help *Delaney* out?"

"Definitely. I really think I have some things that could help with her stress and confidence. A lot of people think about this stuff too hard."

"Stuff like herbs and oils?" he clarified.

"Right. They overthink. And second guess. But if I'm just your goofy girlfriend, she'll try this stuff to be nice to me, and then she'll find out it actually works."

TJ thought about that. "You really think you can help her?"
"I do."

Hope said it with quiet confidence that he had to believe.

"Okay, then our secret is just our secret." He acknowledged that even that much was a kind of bond and wondered if he was making a big mistake.

"So my conversation with Delaney will be short," Hope said.

"Oh, I'm guessing the girl talk with Delaney will be about me," TJ said.

Hope peered up at him. "And that's not such a short conversation?"

"Depends on how much one of my closest friends is willing to share about me with a virtual stranger."

Hope gave him a sly smile. "I can be very charming and persuasive."

He finally leaned back and shook his head. "That's what I'm worried about."

"Are there things you don't want me to know?"

He thought about that. "Maybe."

"Why?"

"I wasn't someone I'm proud of when I was with my...monkey."

"Or after, I'm guessing."

She'd surprised him again. He wondered if she was going to keep doing that.

Then he worried that she was going to keep doing that.

"Wow. Thanks," he said dryly.

"Well, you're not with her now but you're still a grumpy asshole. I'm thinking those things are connected."

She made him want to laugh. He didn't, but he wanted to.

"People can be grumpy assholes for reasons other than a breakup."

"TJ, I'm not going to claim to know everything about you, but I've gotten a look into your life. You have a gorgeous farm you're obviously proud of and you have a great family who loves and respects you. Those are the kinds of things that make a guy *happy*." She paused and then added, "And you're single."

"So?"

"So you're a protector, you're smart, you have a sense of humor, you're good-looking and you kiss like..." She cleared her throat. "You're a good kisser. You're only single because you want to be."

He wasn't sure what to say to all of that. He did want to be single. There were women who wanted more from him. But he didn't want anyone to want things from him anymore.

No, that wasn't true. He wanted his family to depend on

him. He wanted his friends to know he was there for them. He just didn't want to fall in love again.

He was a very focused guy. Intense was a word often applied to him that he could agree with. When he was in love, it was one-hundred percent. If the woman was happy, he wanted to be a part of it. If she was unhappy, he wanted to fix it. He became an enabler of anything that made her feel good and he'd do anything to keep her from feeling sad, upset or worried, and he'd do anything to right any wrongs—even the ones she caused.

TJ was also intelligent, enough to know that not every woman would use and manipulate those aspects of his personality as much as Michelle had. But he was spooked now. His desire to make and keep her happy had facilitated Michelle making some very bad choices, and his need to make it all right for her after she'd messed up had screwed up some of the relationships he had with other people.

Yes, she'd also screwed up his heart. But also his ability to trust himself. And *that* was what he couldn't get over.

He didn't want to be that guy again. He didn't want to be the reason the love of his life engaged in stupid, risky behavior, and he didn't want to be the guy making excuses and cleaning up her messes afterward.

"You're right. I want to be single," he finally said.

Hope nodded. "I figured." She glanced toward the front of the house. "Delaney loves you and is protective of you. I think the direction of our conversation might be more along the lines of, 'If you hurt him, I'll kill you'."

Even as the words formed on his tongue, TJ knew he shouldn't say them. But he did anyway. "You're not going to be able to hurt me."

Hope's eyes widened slightly. "Okay. Good. I don't want you to be hurt."

He believed her. Or at least believed that *she* believed she felt that way at the moment.

"Because you're not calling any shots around here," he continued. Saying it out loud was a good reminder for him too. He needed to stay as uninvolved as possible. And in the things he *was* involved in, he needed to maintain control over how he was going to give Hope what she needed.

Michelle had needed attention, his adoration, to know that she would always be safe and that someone would be there no matter how stupid or bitchy or irresponsible she was. It went deep and far back into her childhood, and he got that. It made it hard—impossible—to turn his back on her entirely. Even when that inability made him feel pathetic and stupid. He'd been in too deep, he'd become her hero when he was too young and too naïve to realize that she was using him and that what *he* needed out of the relationship would never matter.

He was smarter now. Cynical even. And there was no way he was going to let Hope run the show. If she needed his help, she'd have it. On his terms. His way.

"I'm going to help you, but that means I need your *total* trust. I need you to let me do this the way I think it needs to be done," he said.

Hope was studying him in that way she had that made him sure she could read his thoughts. "This?"

"Helping you with what you need this summer."

"As in, you're going to *make* this summer great. You're going to help me recreate the summer my mom had?"

TJ nodded. "I can do that. I've spent thirty-four summers here."

She smiled up at him. "I think that's missing the point. Part of the...magic...is letting things happen. Going with the flow. Taking each experience as it comes."

Yeah. He couldn't do that.

The phrase "throwing caution to the wind" made him

twitchy, and he was allergic to the word impulsive. "I don't...flow."

Hope didn't seem surprised. "Anymore," she added.

He frowned.

"I'm guessing you flowed in the past and it didn't go well," she explained.

"Something like that."

"Hmmm."

"You can...flow without me." He hated that idea. A lot. Intensely.

Hope tipped her head to one side. "If I stick around for a while and...flow...you'll just sit on the banks of this metaphoric river and watch me go by?"

He already had the feeling she knew what his answer would be.

Could he just let her go? Leave her alone to hang out with other guys in Sapphire Falls? Make memories in his hometown without him?

Fuck.

Somehow, Hope had already figured him out.

"I'd like to say yes," he finally admitted. "I'd love to be able to put your butt in your silly little car and wave while you drive off to whatever or whoever is down the road."

"But?" she prompted with a small, knowing smile.

"Not going to happen."

"But you'll be miserable if I'm doing things my way?" she asked.

He shouldn't be. He knew that. He knew that just because Michelle had taken every advantage of him didn't mean that Hope would. And he also knew that he should just leave her the hell alone.

Problem was, beyond connecting with Dan, she had other hopes for a summer in Sapphire Falls. And well...that was all he really needed to know to want to be a part of it.

"I prefer to be in charge," he said. Not that he'd ever been in charge with Michelle.

"That seems like a win-win," Hope said. "If I turn everything over to you, I can relax and let things happen, and you can do everything your way."

TJ stood looking down at her. She seemed oblivious to the heat and desire her words stirred up—sexually and otherwise. But he still had a feeling she knew. Somehow.

He wanted that total trust. He wanted to be the one she thought back on when she remembered Sapphire Falls. But he could *not* get lost in her. He couldn't be led around by the balls again.

He felt himself nod slowly. "Yeah. Win-win."

He ignored the niggle in the back of his mind that said being in total control around Hope Daniels might be a pipe dream.

"Okay."

One simple word that TJ felt reverberate through his whole body.

However, he was cynical enough to be skeptical of her easy agreement, too. Arguing, he knew. Arguing and tears. Those he could deal with. A woman who was laid-back and trusted him to do things his way? Not so much.

"Totally my way," he reiterated.

She nodded with a big smile. "Totally your way."

He narrowed his eyes and gave her what he hoped was a don't-you-dare-lie-to-me look. "You're fine with this?"

"Completely fine."

Yeah, sure. A woman who had been raised to be fully self-sufficient, who traveled all over by herself, who was obviously very good at wrapping people around her finger within minutes of meeting them—if he and Delaney and Tucker were any indication anyway—was completely fine with him calling all the shots while she was in Sapphire Falls.

They'd see about that.

In fact, the sooner they saw about it, the better. He didn't want to entertain too many thoughts of running the Hope Show only to find out she wasn't going to take it. The idea of her doing *anything* he wanted was too damned tempting as it was.

"Okay, so starting now," he said. "Talk to Delaney. Reassure her that you're going to take really good care of me. Then get her to go home so you can work on my shoulder." It really did feel a hell of a lot better since she'd massaged it. And to get her hands on him again, he'd put up with whatever smelly lotion stuff she was going to concoct.

"What if she asks what taking 'really good care' of you means?" Hope asked.

The question sounded completely innocent, and if it had been just a bit darker, he wouldn't have been able to see the tiny sly smile that curled her lips.

And suddenly he wanted nothing more than to see her bent over his kitchen table with that flowery skirt flipped up over her gorgeous ass. "Anything I ask you to."

There was no way Hope didn't notice the air between them heating several degrees. She stared at him, her lips parted slightly.

"Give me ten minutes." She spun away from him and headed for the front of the house.

He appreciated her enthusiasm. But he needed a couple of minutes on his own to gather his thoughts and calm his racing heart. He felt as if a tornado had just touched down and he was being swirled around in the storm.

Finally, he followed her, wishing he knew for sure how to keep from doing anything *she* wanted *him* to do.

6

Hope passed Tucker sitting on the front porch steps.

"How's your head feel?" She knew she'd won him over with the massage. Her mom had done the ear thing to her easily a hundred times in her life, and she knew more than pain relief, it worked to calm and soothe. It was no wonder dogs liked having their ear rubbed.

"I feel great," Tucker admitted, looking up at her.

"Well, let me know if you have any other aches or pains."

"How about ass pains?" Tucker asked.

She smiled. "I'm guessing yours is pretty big and has been there a while?"

"About six-five and all my life."

She laughed. "That might be out of my scope of practice."

Tucker regarded her with a thoughtful look. "I don't know, Hope. If anyone can help ease that pain, I think it might be you."

Hope felt her eyes widen. Wow. That was nice. And...intense.

Especially from TJ's *brother*.

There were a lot of people in TJ Bennett's life. People who

were really involved and really cared. She wasn't used to having so many people around. And interested. She'd felt so comfortable with Delaney earlier when they'd been sharing about their losses. And watching Delaney and Tucker together was enough to make even the least romantic person yearn for a little of what they had. But then they'd talked about TJ's mom's reaction to Hope being a vegetarian—meaning she might actually meet TJ's mom and eat more of her food—and Delaney had invited Hope for tea and...yeah, it was all intense. Especially for a girl who was used to having only her mom, and a fairly hands-off mom at that, in her life.

She'd been here for a matter of hours and she'd already met and had deep conversations with three of his family members.

Being involved with TJ clearly meant being involved with everyone he knew.

On the other hand, if TJ Bennett needed a woman to truly appreciate him for a little while, it really might be her. Showing someone they were amazing and worth some attention and effort could be done in a moment, but the impact could last a lifetime. Look at how her mother's memory had lingered with Dan. And vice versa.

This didn't have to be intense with TJ. In fact, it would be a good thing if it *wasn't* intense.

She got the impression that TJ took things seriously. Everything. Too seriously. She could feel him putting expectations and pressure on her already—pressure to not upset Dan's family, pressure to not let Tucker and Delaney too close or to know the truth, pressure to not mess with his heart, and now his insistence that things needed to go *his* way.

She didn't mind. She was teaching herself to go with the flow. This was the perfect opportunity to practice. And if he wanted to boss her around in that low, gravelly voice in the bedroom, she wouldn't put up a fight there either. It had been a long time since she'd felt as connected to someone as she did to TJ. Already.

"You think I'm his type?"

Tucker shook his head. His gaze settled on something behind her and she knew TJ had moved into the light from the porch.

"Not at all. And that's what gives me hope." He grinned up at her with the unintentional use of her name.

She met his smile. "What's his usual type?"

"Hope." TJ's low voice interrupted before Tucker could reply. "Go inside."

Tucker said, "In the past? Difficult and impossible to get rid of. Lately, super easy and very short-term."

"Tucker," TJ said warningly.

From his voice, Hope could tell he'd moved closer. She glanced over her shoulder. TJ did not look pleased. "It's not like I'm not going to learn every one of your secrets anyway," she told him.

"Inside. Now."

Bossy. And hot.

She rolled her eyes—and made sure he saw it—then left the boys out front and headed for the kitchen. She found Delaney just finishing loading the dishes in the dishwasher.

Hope crossed to the sink and rinsed the last two bowls before handing them to Delaney.

"What did Tucker mean when he said that TJ used to like difficult women who were impossible to get rid of and now he goes for super easy and short-term?" she asked. She wasn't really a beat-around-the-bush kind of girl.

Delaney looked at her, both eyebrows up. "Tucker said that?"

"Just now."

Delaney sighed as if she wished Tucker hadn't done that.

"Okay. Well, there is a woman in TJ's past who was...difficult. And who has been in and out of his life for years."

Hope leaned back against the sink, bracing her hands behind her. "His ex?"

Delaney turned to fully face her. "You know about Michelle?"

Michelle. So that was her name. "Yes. Is that a good thing?"

Delaney grabbed a towel to dry her hands. "It's a surprising thing. He doesn't like to talk about her."

"Here's what I know," Hope said. "They were married, she caused him a lot of trouble, cheated on him, they broke up, but she still calls him sometimes."

Delaney's eyes widened. "That took me almost a month to get out of him, and Tucker still had to tell me most of the details."

They moved to the table. Hope took a seat and folded a leg up underneath her. "And now he goes for women who are...what?"

Delaney took the chair next to her. "Women he doesn't know well. He never dates women from Sapphire Falls. He only sees them for a short time. Never introduces them to family or friends."

Hope thought about that. Either he was protecting himself from finding another Michelle...or he was leaving himself open in case Michelle changed her mind.

Neither was good.

"So tell me some of these details about Michelle that you've learned," Hope said.

"I don't know if I should. Shouldn't TJ tell you?"

"He will," Hope said with confidence. TJ already trusted her, and she loved that he did even as his head was telling him he shouldn't. "But I want your interpretation of it. As someone who knows him and loves him." She wouldn't ask just anyone she ran into in town about TJ. This was personal stuff. But this was someone he was close to, and Hope was working on a short timeline here. She wanted to know TJ and knew Delaney could tell her something that would take months to get out of TJ.

Delaney took a breath and seemed to be considering that. Then she nodded. "Okay, well, I know that she doesn't deserve the attention he gives her."

"Why does he give it to her then?"

"I think he feels obligated. I think *he* thinks that he loves her, but I don't think he really does."

Hope hated that TJ thought he was in love with this woman. And it didn't surprise her that she cared. She had a compassion for people in pain of all kinds, and adding that to her physical and emotional attraction to TJ seemed like the perfect recipe for caring—a lot.

"Tell me about her."

"They've known each other all their lives. They had a relationship in high school."

"After he protected her from her stepfather," Hope filled in.

Delaney shook her head. "Wow, he told you that too? Tucker had to tell me that part."

Hope shrugged. "People always tell me stuff." Sometimes even things she didn't want to know. "I'm easy to talk to."

"I guess so," Delaney agreed. "But I think it's great. TJ doesn't lean on people—ever. He doesn't open up. He doesn't let people close easily at all."

And all of that made him even more attractive to her. Hope loved a challenge. As the temporary help on her nursing assignments, she'd often been given the tough cases—the kid scared to death of needles, the woman who heard four different voices in her head, the old man who thought any woman under the age of fifty couldn't be trusted. And she'd won them all over.

TJ Bennett didn't scare her.

He fascinated her.

"I'll help him with that," Hope said. "Tell me more about Michelle."

Delaney looked surprised and impressed by Hope's confident declaration. "She lives about an hour away with her husband—the guy she cheated on TJ with. But she's from here, so she comes home a lot to visit. She's here at least once a month. She'll go out partying, get drunk or in a fight or a sticky situation, or all of the above, and she calls TJ."

"And he shows up every time," Hope said.

"Every time," Delaney said with a nod. "He'll go pick her up, bail her out, smooth things over and let her sleep on his couch—or I'm sure he gives her the bed and he takes the couch."

"They don't...do they..." Hope wasn't sure how to ask the question that was nagging her. Or if she *should* ask. It wasn't her business. But it felt like it was.

"They don't sleep together," Delaney said. "Not since she left him."

"That's what he told Tucker?" Hope asked.

"That's what Michelle told her girlfriends," Delaney said. She grimaced slightly. "This is a very small town. It's hard to keep a secret long."

For which Hope was grateful in that moment.

"Do her parents still live here?" Hope asked.

"Yes. And her sister."

"So if she and TJ aren't sleeping together, why doesn't she sleep on her parents' couch?"

Delaney sighed. "Because it's TJ. It's not his style to dump her off on someone else when she's called *him*. It's their very complicated, dysfunctional...thing. She loves knowing that he'll always be there for her, and she has to test it on a regular basis."

Fascinating.

"Her husband doesn't come visit with her?"

"He stays home with their son."

A son. Okay.

"So he stays home with their kid while she goes out partying and calling up her ex," Hope said. "I'm guessing that gets her husband's attention too."

"You nailed it."

"So TJ thinks he's still in love with her?" It didn't exactly bother her to think that. Mostly because she was fairly certain it wasn't actually true. But Hope really wanted to help him get *over* that.

Delaney shrugged. "Maybe. TJ will do anything for the people he loves. I can't figure out why else he puts up with her crap. But I think he's also afraid of what she'll do to get his attention if he tries to ignore her or tell her no. If she calls when she's just a little drunk and needs a ride and he goes to get her, it keeps her from doing something stupid or reckless or dangerous."

"This also gives TJ something he needs," Hope said thoughtfully.

Delaney leaned her elbows in on the table and looked at Hope closely. "I think you're right."

"Where do you think this need to help her over and over comes from?" Hope asked. Delaney seemed to really care about TJ, and if he'd opened up to her at all that meant he trusted her, at least as much as he trusted anyone.

"TJ believes that being in someone's life means you're always in their life, no matter what happens, for better or worse."

That sounded nice, on the surface. Until it led to an unhealthy dedication to a woman who used him repeatedly. Hope frowned.

"It's almost as if..." Delaney paused as if thinking through what she wanted to say. "It's almost as if the harder it is to love someone, the more it means to him."

Hope thought about that. Something else that sounded nice but could mean a lot of heartache. "Where's that come from?"

"Partly his mom and dad, I think," Delaney said. "Evidently some stuff went down in the past—I know TJ ended up in jail for beating some guy up. Because of Michelle, of course. I know he got kind of dependent on the whiskey bottle after she left. But through it all, his family was there, especially his parents."

"I happened to meet his dad earlier," Hope said. "He seems great."

"He's the best," Delaney said with true affection in her expression and tone. "He's the textbook father figure."

Hope inwardly grimaced at that. It would have bothered most people to find out their father might have cheated on their mother and had a child with another woman, but by all accounts, Thomas Bennett was revered. No wonder TJ had reacted so strongly to Hope's initial claim that Thomas was her father too.

"So TJ wants to be like his mom and dad."

"And Dan."

Hope froze. Dan. Was there another Dan in these peoples' lives? "Dan?"

"Dan Wells is Thomas's best friend. He's like an uncle to the boys."

Nope. Same Dan. Okay. Hope worked on not revealing anything with her expression. "You think TJ wants to be like Dan?" She was happy that she didn't stumble over the use of her father's name.

"Kind of," Delaney said with a nod. "Dan only has a daughter—who also gets into a lot of trouble."

Two daughters, actually, but Hope kept her expression carefully stoic.

"The Bennett boys are like sons to him. Especially TJ."

TJ was like a son to Hope's father. That was also...interesting.

She was once again grateful to the heavens that none of this was actually biologically true.

"So Dan also stuck by him through those tough times?" Hope asked. She didn't want to push too hard to get this information, but she suddenly felt hungry to know everything Delaney did about everything related to TJ.

"Definitely," Delaney said. "And he's seen both his dad and Dan really prove that love means toughing things out even when the other person doesn't seem to deserve it."

Hope coughed lightly and cleared her throat. For some reason, that choked her up. Probably because it reminded her of her mom. Hope had rebelled against almost everything Melody believed in. They'd had a number of heated arguments about medicine and healing, and Hope had accused her mother of being out of touch and worried that *real* medicine would cut into her livelihood. But Melody had never said a harsh word back. "How so?" she finally asked.

"Dan's wife suffers from some pretty serious issues. A lot of depression. I know she's attempted suicide twice."

Hope felt her mouth fall open. Suicide? *That* might have been worth TJ and Thomas mentioning more specifically. No wonder they were freaked out about how Dan's wife might react to her.

"Wow," she finally managed.

"Yeah. And their daughter, Peyton, is a challenge. She's a lot like Michelle—loves to party and get into trouble. She has terrible taste in men. She picks losers who move in with her so they don't have to pay rent and run up her credit cards and push her around."

Hope felt her heart clench at that. Her sister had some issues. She had a depressed, suicidal mother and boyfriends who treated her like garbage.

The feeling of protectiveness shocked her. Hope had never felt protective of anyone in her life. Not her mother—Melody had been completely self-reliant and had never needed protection. Not her patients—she was there to care for their illnesses and injuries, but she didn't take that on herself. Not her friends—she didn't have many who were all that close and she tended to migrate toward people who were strong and confident.

So the idea that she wanted to take care of a little sister she hadn't even known she had before today and that she'd never met was entirely foreign.

"And Dan's always been there," Delaney said. "For them both. He's never left Jo, even though I'm sure that would have been easier. He's toughed it out. He's shown everyone what real love is."

Hope was torn at that.

Part of her loved the idea that her father knew how to love deeply and had been there for Hope's sister. Sticking by someone's side through it all was admirable, for sure. Not that she would know firsthand exactly. She'd been pulling herself through things on her own forever.

But it didn't feel quite right either, that love had to be hard to be real. She loved that Thomas and TJ's mom had been there no matter how much he screwed up. She loved the idea that a man could love a woman so much that there was nothing she could do to make him walk away. But part of her resisted it at the same time. First, that loving someone had to be a chore to be strong and real. And second, that people would put their loved ones through that. Everyone was ultimately responsible for themselves—their actions, their reactions, how they handled things. Everyone had bad things happen to them. Dragging the people they loved down with them didn't seem very...loving.

Again, Hope worked to keep her expression mild. "So TJ thinks that it's really love with Michelle because it's hard."

Delaney looked at her with a little frown. "What?"

"That's been TJ's model of love—the hard times, toughing it out, being there no matter what."

"Isn't that really love?" Delaney asked. "When the person is there for you no matter how bad things get?"

"Maybe," Hope said. Honestly, she didn't really know. If she had decided to drink herself into a stupor over something gone wrong, her mom would have left her alone to figure out that hangovers were no fun and weren't productive. Of course, Hope had always met things head-on. She would never have thought that whiskey was the answer. "That's part of it, I guess. But what about the good times? What about the things to celebrate?"

"Well...they're there for that too," Delaney said. "This family gathers for happy occasions too. All the time. They have dinners, barbecues, birthday parties, you name it."

"But do they say the words or do they leave quiet, grumpy TJ alone because they think that's what he wants?" Hope asked, her thoughts spinning.

"Say what words?"

"I'm here for you, I love you, you're amazing, I'm happy you're happy," Hope said. She flashed back to that morning with TJ's dad when the men had embraced and he'd told his dad he was the best man TJ knew. That had obviously been an unusual thing for both of them.

"I, um..." Delaney pondered that. "I don't know if anyone specifically says that to TJ. But he knows it."

"And does anyone go out of their way to want him around when things are good?" she went on. "Or does everyone play into his belief that the only time he can show *his* love is when someone is in trouble?"

Delaney's eyes widened. Hope didn't worry about it. They were all supposed to think that she was strange. If ranting about how they should be treating TJ was strange, then it would go right along with the plan.

"I should warn you," Delaney said. "TJ doesn't do drama."

Hope studied Delaney's eyes. "What do you mean?"

"Well, that's not exactly true," Delaney hedged. "He does. With his family. Like with me and the boys—there's been some drama. A trip to the ER, for instance. And he's there for anything we need. There's drama with Dan and Jo and Peyton," she went on. "And with his brothers and friends and…"

"Michelle," Hope filled in when Delaney hesitated.

Delaney nodded.

Hope couldn't get off the thought of Dan and Jo and Peyton, though. Clearly, TJ was closer to them and more involved with them than she'd initially assumed.

"So now with women, he avoids it at all costs," Delaney said. "The minute one of them has a fight with her best friend or her dog gets sick, he's out of there."

Yeah, that didn't surprise her. He'd warned her about the monkeys. "Seems like he overreacts."

Delaney laughed. "I agree. And I'm sure the women agree."

Hope was still thinking about all of that when they heard the front screen door open and Tucker and TJ's voices.

Delaney reached out and grabbed Hope's hand, lowering her voice. "With your mom just passing away and everything, don't be too hurt if TJ pulls back. He's trying to protect himself. I know it isn't really fair, but if you need someone to talk to, you can come to me. I don't want you to get hurt trying to lean on him."

Hope squeezed Delaney's hand. That was really sweet of her, and Hope would love to talk with Delaney more about both of their losses. But not because she *couldn't* lean on TJ.

Because she *wouldn't*.

She wasn't much of a leaner in the first place, and she understood that was the last thing TJ needed.

She had a better plan for him than dumping family drama on him. She didn't know anything about family drama anyway. Melody had been her only family, and she had been the complete opposite of needy and melodramatic. Eccentric and different, definitely, but not dramatic.

Hope had set out in her mother's car with her mother's camper, determined to get in touch with things that had made Melody who she was. Having a magical summer fling in Sapphire Falls seemed the perfect way to connect to her mother, and now she knew it would give TJ something he needed too—some no-strings-attached fun with a woman who would appreciate him, who would care for him, make him laugh, and give him some memories that would last a lifetime.

Tucker and TJ stepped into the kitchen and Delaney rose.

"So the bakery tomorrow morning for tea," she said to Hope as if they'd simply been making plans for the next day.

"Can't wait." Hope remembered the oil and pulled the jar from her pocket. "This is for you." She handed it to Delaney. "Rub just a dab into each of your temples and at the base of your head tonight before you go to sleep. It should help you fall asleep easier and stay asleep and will bring sweet dreams."

Tucker and Delaney left and TJ stood looking at her from the doorway.

"Sweet dreams? Oil can do that?"

Hope shrugged and gave him a smile. "If she anticipates good dreams, the chances of having them are better."

"So the oil really has nothing to do with it."

Hope stood. "It won't hurt. And it *will* help her fall asleep faster." She moved and pointed to the chair. "I have some for you too."

"Some sweet dreams?"

She tipped her head. "I can work on that too."

He looked at the chair. "What did you have in mind?"

They were alone in the house. They had the whole place to themselves. And she had decided to have a fling with him. The things she had in mind would probably shock him. Instead of giving him that list, however, she said, "Sit. I'm going to work on your shoulder."

She pulled another jar from her other pocket. He eyed it suspiciously but took a seat.

"Need your shirt off." She opened the jar and set it on the table.

She'd given Delaney a mixture of peppermint, lavender and sweet almond oil for her stress and tension, but for TJ she'd used some of her favorite whipped coconut oil and added marjoram for his muscle pain. The whipped oil was more like a lotion and her fingers tingled with the thought of rubbing over those firm muscles again. Yes, she'd massaged his shoulder earlier to help give him some pain relief, but touching him was definitely something she didn't mind repeating.

TJ kept his eyes on hers as he lifted his shirt, breaking eye contact only when he tugged it over his head.

"Here." She stepped forward and unhooked the strap on his shoulder sling. "You don't need this anymore."

He didn't say anything, but she felt the need to explain anyway. "You're well past the time needed for tissue healing. The longer you keep it immobile due to pain, the stiffer it's going to get." She slid the brace off his arm and tossed it onto the table.

TJ finished taking his shirt off, and Hope felt her heart rate pick up. He was gorgeous. His skin was golden from the sun, smooth but for the scars and the soft fan of hair over his pecs and stomach. He also seemed to put off an incredible amount of heat. Or maybe that was her. Either way, standing close to his bare skin made the temperature of the air around them climb.

She dipped two fingers in the cream and rubbed it between her hands, warming it and lubricating her palms and fingers. She moved behind him into the best position for acupressure on some key points and put her hands on him. Not able to see his face, she couldn't read his reaction other than to note that his body tensed when she touched him. She hoped it was good tension.

Hope stroked her hands over both of his shoulders and up and down his neck several times, gradually increasing her pressure. Slowly, she moved until both hands were on his sore shoulder. She stroked over the firm muscles, closing her eyes and feeling the tissues underneath.

Yeah, he generated a lot of heat.

She worked over the entire surface of his shoulder blade and down into his deltoid before returning to the top of his shoulder, where most of the tightness was, and settling on a couple of acupressure sites she knew would release some tension.

His head dropped forward and she heard a low groan. Hope fought to keep her hands on his skin. Sure, in her mind she'd decided that a fun summer fling could be what they both needed—a lot. But touching him, feeling his body heat soak into her hands, feeling his torso move as air flowed in and out of his lungs, feeling his muscles softening under her touch and then feeling and hearing that sound of pleasure from him, was overwhelming her.

She wanted to absorb him, wrap herself around him, press against every inch of him. She felt a hunger building unlike anything she'd ever felt before. And that made her want to pull her hands back and turn and run.

There had been something about TJ Bennett from the very first moment that had affected her. A pull, a draw, a sense that he had something she needed—and vice versa. Even growing up with Melody Daniels, where weird and wacky were everyday occurrences, hadn't prepared Hope for meeting TJ and wanting *something* from him—something that went beyond sex and physical desire or simple like and attraction. It was something much more, something that she knew she'd never had, never even knew she wanted to have.

Rubbing his shoulder at the pond had been different than this. Maybe because while it had made his shoulder feel better, he'd really just been tolerating that. This was...giving him pleasure. And that pulled at something deep inside her. She wanted to do a lot more of it.

Then it occurred to her—the reason this was different for both of them... "It was the kiss!"

TJ's head came up and he looked over his shoulder at her. "What?"

She'd said it out loud unintentionally, but that didn't make it any less true. "At the pond we hadn't kissed yet."

Heat flared in his eyes. "I'm aware."

She couldn't smile in the face of that heat. She could barely breathe. "That's why touching you then was different. Now, I touch you and all of that heat and awareness and desire shoot through me and—"

"Hope." He held her gaze.

"Yes?" The breathlessness was very unlike her.

"Come here."

She somehow understood what he meant. She stepped around in front of him. He put his hands on her hips, moving her between his knees as he spread them. "You said you'd let me take charge."

She nodded.

"Seducing me isn't letting me take charge."

She gave him a half smile. "Am I seducing you?"

He lifted an eyebrow. "Aren't you?"

Hope licked her lip and was thrilled to see his gaze follow the motion closely. "I think it could be fun."

"I told you I don't want any drama."

"It wouldn't be dramatic," she said. "I promise. Just good, hot sex. Lots of it. But no costumes or toys or...whatever you're worried about."

He sighed, his expression pained. "That's not exactly what I'm worried about."

She tipped her head. "I'm guessing that you've had a lot of angry sex."

He straightened on the chair and his fingers curled into her where he still held her hips. "Excuse me?"

"With Michelle. The sex was often after she'd gotten into trouble and she was either making it up to you or you were fighting and she used it to keep you from leaving."

His jaw tightened. "You and Delaney got a lot of talking in."

Hope hated the tension that was now emanating from him. Acting purely on instinct, she climbed onto his lap, straddling his thighs. She took his face in her hands.

"That's not how sex has to be, TJ. It can be passionate, but it can be fun. It can be goofy and silly. It can be adventurous. But no matter what, it should make you feel good. It should make you happy. It should be about liking the other person and wanting to pleasure them, not about manipulating their emotions or paying some emotional debt or patching something that's dysfunctional and painful."

He sat staring at her. He still dug his fingers into her hips and was frowning, but she saw something else in his eyes—bewilderment. That was the best word for it. He was looking at her as if he didn't know what to do with her. But also as if he *wanted* to do something.

"It's not the *sex* that I'm worried will be dramatic, Sunshine."

Sunshine. Hmm, she kind of liked that.

"*Nothing* will be dramatic," she insisted.

He lifted one eyebrow. "Honey, you're dripping in drama."

Well, she clearly wasn't dripping in pheromones. She was on the guy's lap talking about sex and he was still holding back.

"I'm not," she told him. "I'm one of the most straightforward people you'll meet."

"The whole reason you're here is all about drama and emotions."

"I changed my mind." She ran her hand back and forth over his jaw. His evening scruff abraded her palm, sending tingles to other parts of her that wanted to rub against other parts of him.

"You changed your mind about what?"

"Why I'm here."

"Nope." He pulled away from her hands as he pushed her back on his thighs. "No way."

To avoid getting dumped on her butt on the floor, Hope scrambled to get her feet down and stand. She propped her hands on her hips. "What?"

"I'm not doing this." TJ got to his feet, towering over her. "You're beautiful and sweet and you smell amazing and the way you helped Delaney and Tucker made me want you even more and I can't stop looking at your earrings, but *I'm not doing this*. You need to focus on why you're here."

She blinked a few times. He thought she was beautiful and sweet and smelled good. That was all positive. She wasn't sure what to make of the earring comment, but she couldn't help her smile. "I'm focused. In fact, I'm *more* focused now."

"On me." He didn't look pleased.

"Yes. On you."

He sighed. "Stop it. You want to meet your dad."

"Yes. I'll meet Dan. I'll talk to him, get to know him a little bit. But I don't need him to know who I am or what I want. No drama, TJ. Nobody gets stirred up. Nothing has to change. Dan and I will have a cup of coffee and everything will be fine."

"All so you can have sex with me?"

She thought about that. Then gave him a big smile. "Yes."

He shoved a hand through his hair. "I was starting to think the crazy thing was mostly an act," he said, almost as if he was talking to himself.

"You need to have fun, hot sex with a girl who likes you. Who really just *likes* you and wants you to feel good."

He frowned. "I like it hard and dirty."

Her entire body went soft and hot at that. "It can be hard and dirty. You can put me up against the wall. You can say wonderful, naughty things to me. But the whole time, you'll be having fun, and you'll know I'm there just because I *want* to be. No agenda. And you'll know that *you're* there because you like me and want me to feel good. Nothing more complicated than that."

He stepped close, looking down at her intently. He put a fingertip against her cheek and stroked back and forth. "I'm not sleeping with you the very first day we meet, Sunshine," he said softly

God, she really liked that Sunshine thing. And the gentle touch. And that intense look in his eyes.

"Okay then, tomorrow is good for me."

He stood just looking at her for another moment. Then he stepped back. "You can take the room at the top of the stairs."

He turned and was gone a second later.

O-kay.

Hope thought about that as she went to the camper and gathered what she'd need for the night.

He hadn't said *no* about the sleeping together entirely.

And he thought she was beautiful and sweet and smelled good.

And he called her Sunshine.

So far her trip to Sapphire Falls had been full of surprises. Good surprises.

Exactly like her mother's trip had been twenty-six years ago.

7

TJ was pissed the next morning.

For the first time in months, his shoulder hadn't bothered him during the night.

He should have been able to sleep the sleep of the dead and should have awakened refreshed and happy.

Should have.

He'd still slept like shit. Because of a throbbing body part.

Just because it wasn't his shoulder didn't mean it was any less bothersome. It might have been *more* bothersome. There was no one to really blame for his shoulder pain. The surgeon had done what he could.

But there was a colorful, pixie-ish hippie girl to blame for the other throbbing.

TJ threw the empty plastic bucket against the side of the barn with exaggerated force.

The ankle bracelets and the earrings and the tattoo weren't enough—she had to be sweet to Delaney and she had to kiss him like it was her sole purpose in life and she had to want to take care of *him*.

Fuck.

That should *not* be appealing. When his mother and sister-in-law and friends hovered and fussed, it made him cranky. When Hope said she was going to focus on him... Well, it wasn't just his cock that responded.

Of course, her straddling his lap and looking at him with those big green eyes and smelling like something he'd like to stick his nose into for a good long time had made his cock very responsive as well.

She was a *vegetarian*. That alone should make him steer clear. And she had pink hair, and claimed that she could *read* him, and mixed up strange concoctions from a big wooden apothecary box in the back of her teeny tiny trailer with the Arizona license plate.

She should be the last woman he wanted anything to do with.

Instead, he'd lain awake most of the night thinking about her proposal to basically have a fun, hot fling this summer.

TJ stomped up toward the house. He needed to get things moving with her meeting up with Dan. Whether or not she told Dan who she really was, he didn't care. He just needed her to meet Dan and have that over with. Surely once she actually met her father she would be thinking more about him and their relationship than she would be paying attention to *him*.

TJ approached the front of the house with some trepidation.

That he was wary of a woman who was almost a foot shorter than him and weighed less than half of his body weight should have been funny. TJ, however, preferred to think of it as a gut feeling he should give a lot of respect.

He climbed the porch steps at half speed and took a deep breath before he pulled the door open. He'd left the house at daybreak, as usual, and hadn't seen or heard Hope in the house. Maybe she was the sleep-'til-noon type. That would also make her *not* his type. He was a farmer. There was no sleeping in. Or time off. Or snow days. No matter what was going on, his farm, especially his animals, needed him.

The house was quiet and he tread carefully across the floors that tended to creak in the middle of the hallway and just to the left of the couch.

He was practically tiptoeing. In his own house. Because of a girl who he was going to eventually have to face. And what was he so afraid of anyway? That he'd grab her and lift her up against the wall like she'd given him permission to do last night? While he talked dirty. He couldn't forget that part. Literally. He could *not* forget that part, no matter how hard he tried.

Disgusted with himself—his lack of self-control and the fact that he was feeling anxious about being in his own damn house—TJ frowned and started stomping again.

He stomped through the living room and into the kitchen.

But the noise didn't bring Hope running.

And as he stomped across the kitchen to the refrigerator, he saw why.

The back window in the kitchen looked out over his backyard.

Where Hope was sitting cross-legged on a purple yoga mat next to his flower garden.

And she was naked.

She was facing away from the window, but she was definitely naked.

There was a silky pool of multicolored material around her, as if she'd shed her clothes sitting right there. But her back was bare from the tops of her shoulders to the dimples at the flare of her hips.

TJ gripped the glass in his hand and was grateful it was plastic. He could have cut himself on the shards from crushing anything made of glass in his fist. As it was, the plastic bent with the pressure he applied and he almost cracked it anyway.

What the fuck was she doing sitting in his backyard naked?

It looked as if she was sitting in a yoga position. He'd dated another girl who was into yoga and he'd seen enough to recognize the mat and the pose. But Hope wasn't just doing yoga. He was pretty sure she was also trying to make him nuts.

And, yes, he did think it was at least partially intentional.

He could easily conjure the exact shape of her breasts and the color of her nipples from the day before, and his tongue tingled with the urge to lick every inch.

He supposed he could turn around and find something else to do until she was done out there. Then again, there was a beautiful naked woman in his backyard. Turning away from the window seemed silly. If not impossible.

TJ forced his hand to relax and unbend the plastic cup before filling it with water. He drank. Refilled it and drank again. Without ever taking his eyes from the woman by his flowers.

She really did something for him.

It wasn't as if he hadn't been with beautiful women. He had as much female attention as he wanted. Her beauty and even her sweetness weren't what called to him. Sapphire Falls and the surrounding area—hell, the entire state of Nebraska, in his opinion—was full of beautiful, sweet women. They grew them right here.

Hope shifted to cross one leg over the other and twisted her trunk the opposite direction. The position brought the side of her breast into view, and he couldn't help but take a moment to appreciate how very, very nice that view was.

He cleared his throat and filled the glass again.

It also wasn't Hope's independence that called to him, though that was certainly appealing. He liked a girl who could take care of herself. He really did. No, his history did not support that theory. Michelle's dependence on him for everything from car care to assuring her she was attractive and loved had gotten to him from minute one. But he was older and wiser now. That was not the way to sustain a long-term relationship. He knew that a healthy, solid relationship was about *both* people. Theirs had always been all about Michelle. He'd made her feel safe, desired, worthy and loved. But it had never been a two-way street with Michelle. It had never been a partnership. And Hope had been completely accurate last night when she'd said that Michelle had made it all up to him with sex.

The sex had been good. Really good. From a physical perspective anyway. Michelle had been willing to do anything and was as wild and adventurous in bed as she was in every other aspect of her life. For a young guy, she'd been a dream come true. There wasn't much they hadn't done.

Of course, looking back now, he definitely saw that sex was the only thing she'd given him. It was the only thing she *could* give him. She hadn't loved him. Maybe hadn't even cared about him all that much—at least not as much as she'd cared about herself.

So Hope's independence was attractive. As was her confidence. She seemed to know exactly who she was, what she needed and what she wanted. He liked that. A lot. Michelle had never been sure about anything—except for *him*. With him as a sure thing, she didn't *have* to know anything else for certain.

Hope shifted again, twisting her body in the other direction, and he got to check out that breast as well. Yes, very nice.

Okay, so naked yoga in his backyard wasn't a *terrible* idea. If he treated it like a spectator sport, he'd be fine. He watched football but didn't actually get on the field and get sweaty. This could be the same.

He immediately felt sleazy. He was watching a woman without her knowledge. Yes, she was in *his* backyard and she had to know that he was here somewhere. Plus, she'd been happily topless in front of him yesterday with no encouragement.

Still, he should probably say something.

She moved so that her legs were straight out in front of her and then bent forward until her head touched her knees.

And TJ simply couldn't help but take another moment to note how flexible she was.

He shook his head. He needed to get away from the window. He also needed to set up the first meeting between her and Dan.

But then she moved again. She stood, lifting her hands to the sky, elongating her spine. He could imagine how that looked from the front as well. Her breasts high and proud, thrusting forward, the tight nipples begging for his hands...and mouth.

TJ shifted and set the glass down. He *really* needed to move. Or go out there. To tell her that he was here, of course. Not to join her. Not to run his hands and tongue all over that smooth, golden skin and those tight muscles. Her body would be warm from the sun and her skin would have that sweet, flowery smell he already associated with her, accented by the fresh air and actual flowers around her. *His* fresh air and flowers.

And he could not deny that the idea of something of *his* scenting her body was damn erotic and too fucking tempting.

He tossed the cup into his sink and started for the back door. Why had he thought he could resist her? The minute he'd seen her on the hood of her little yellow car, he'd been a goner.

He stepped off the back step as she shifted her pose again, this time drawing one foot up to rest against the opposite knee. Her arms were still over her head and the position of her leg opened her thighs.

TJ's whole body reacted. He knew yoga was an incredibly healthy practice. It was a way of stretching and toning the whole body. But the poses were also very sexual. Hands down. He was not the only person who thought so. He knew he could poll a million people and a million people would agree that yoga poses were sexual.

And what had Hope said last night? Sex should be fun and should make you feel good and happy?

He was in.

She shifted again as he crossed the grass. She moved to pull her leg up behind her, balancing on the other leg and reaching back with one hand to grasp her ankle and extending her other arm out in front.

TJ almost swallowed his tongue.

He couldn't see *everything*, but he could see enough. More than enough.

He stopped several feet from her. If he got any closer, she was going to have grass stains on all that gorgeous skin.

"Hope."

She held the pose but looked back at him. "Morning."

So him watching her didn't seem to bother her. That didn't surprise him.

A lot of things about Hope *had* surprised him since she'd blown into his life, but he was starting to figure her out, it seemed. She was the most comfortable-in-her-skin person he'd ever met. It wasn't that the people in Sapphire Falls were uptight—okay, some of them were uptight, definitely—but mostly they were simply...conservative. And in Sapphire Falls, the people you met and the things you experienced were wonderful, but they were...not particularly diverse.

There had been some new people coming to town over the past few years. Mason Riley, a hometown guy, had moved back and brought his world-renowned agricultural engineering company and most of its employees with him. His partner, Lauren, had come to town from the big city and married TJ's younger brother Travis. Joe Spencer, a millionaire playboy who'd grown up in and around the nightlife in Vegas, had come to Sapphire Falls and fallen for a local girl, Phoebe. And then Joe's brother had come from Vegas and met and fallen for another out-of-towner, Kate.

All of them had brought new things to town. Money, for one. The Spencer brothers had invested in several projects and initiatives in town. But there were other changes as well. There was tofu at the grocery store now. The bakery sold green tea. The local bar, the Come Again, now had several imported beers and a much wider wine selection. There was a group of senior citizens who got together weekly to learn French. The book club at the library had branched out beyond Nicholas Sparks. And the summer Movies-In-the-Square series included films by Alfred Hitchcock and Orson Welles along with the usual animated movies and, well, Nicholas Sparks.

The town was changing. All of it for good.

And it hit him that Hope could bring some good changes, some new things to think about as well.

Fuck.

She wasn't staying. She was here for a single purpose—a single purpose that would take only a few days, truly—and then she would be gone again. She was a free spirit. Clearly. In every way. She wasn't the type to settle, especially in a little farming town in Nebraska.

They used herbs for *cooking* here. For cooking *meat*, as a matter of fact.

Sapphire Falls was not for Hope.

He shoved his hands into his front pockets and took a few more slow steps. "I'm going to make some calls and set up a barbecue for everyone. Dan will be there. Do you want to go ahead with the girlfriend story or do you want me to tell him who you are?"

Hope dropped her pose and then knelt to gather the silky material pooled around her feet. She drew it up over her body and TJ was equally grateful and disappointed.

As she reached behind her neck to tie the two strings together at the top, he realized it was a loose sundress. It left her shoulders and arms bare and a good portion of her back, but it covered everything else, falling to mid-calf.

Of course, he'd seen everything else now. And knew she had nothing on under the dress. The silky multicolored garment was so loose that it seemed to not even touch her body as it draped over her. Except her breasts. Those glorious curves filled the bodice and he itched with the urge to run his hand over the warm silk and feel the firm mounds under the smooth material.

"I thought we'd already talked about this," she said.

Now that she was covered, TJ expected his brain to start working again. But he realized it wasn't when he said, "Naked yoga?"

She grinned. "There is nothing that opens your body, mind and soul like yoga first thing in the morning outside completely naked. The fresh air and sunshine can touch every part of you—"

"Yep, got it." Sunshine and fresh air on every part. Every part that he would very much like to touch himself. He wasn't going to be getting *that* image out of his mind anytime soon.

TJ shoved a hand through his hair. She was going to kill him. She'd been here less than twenty-four hours and he really thought she might kill him.

"Hey, you're using your left arm," she said, clearly pleased.

He rotated the shoulder and nodded. "It feels really good. Best morning I've had in a while."

And his shoulder was a small part of that. He was sleep deprived, but he'd gotten a spectacular view from his kitchen window, so he couldn't be too upset.

Horny and achingly hard behind his zipper, but not upset.

"I'm so glad."

Hope reached out as if to touch him and TJ jerked away instinctively. Certainly not because having her touch him was unpleasant or painful—exactly—but because those grass stains were still a definite threat.

Her eyebrows went up at his strange reaction and he quickly covered with conversation. "So you're sure you don't want Dan to know who you are when you first meet?"

Not that conversation was something he was especially good at.

"I'm sure. It takes all the pressure off everyone. Let's just see how it goes." She paused. "Will your dad be okay with that? Like we said about Delaney and Tucker last night, now he has to lie to people he cares about."

TJ had thought of that. He sighed. "I think he'll consider it the lesser of two evils."

"Dan's wife is really that unstable?"

TJ hated to admit it. But... "Yeah."

"How hasn't she gotten any help? How has Dan not insisted she get help?" Hope asked. "I understand love and devotion, and I guess I admire that he hasn't left her, but if he loves her, don't you think he should be getting her the help she needs?"

TJ frowned down at her. Did she understand love and devotion? "You *guess* you admire that he hasn't left her?"

Hope took a tiny step closer. Not the reaction most people had when he frowned.

"Everyone deserves to be happy, TJ. Does JoEllen make Dan happy?"

This woman. She turned him inside out. They'd gone from naked yoga to questioning what it meant to be devoted to someone in a matter of minutes.

"What if he didn't stay with her and she got worse, or drank herself to death, or ran off and he never heard from her again and didn't know if she was alive or dead?" TJ asked.

"Would that be worse than her dying?" Hope asked, studying his eyes in that *way* she had.

"Not knowing what happened or if she was okay?" TJ asked. "Yes."

"Because you would assume the worst."

He didn't hear a question mark at the end of that sentence but he answered anyway. "What's that mean?"

"I mean, it would be possible that she would run off and end up in exactly the right place and find exactly what she needed and would live happily ever after."

TJ's frown deepened.

He also wanted to kiss her.

She was pissing him off. The way she studied him, the things she said, the way she got so fucking close to truths he hadn't even admitted to himself...and he still wanted to kiss her. And untie those little ties behind her neck and let that dress fall back to the ground.

"It's also possible she would get hurt or in trouble."

"And that's the first assumption you would make," Hope said. "Why is that?"

"Because that's more likely than her going off and finding some happily ever after like some damned fairytale," he said, letting his exasperation show.

"You think that being unhappy and hurt is more likely than being happy?"

She was psychoanalyzing him or something. Did the fucking perfume she wore have truth serum in it or some other hypnotic property? Because he didn't *talk* to people like this. TJ didn't like it. "Not in Sapphire Falls," he said with conviction.

"No one is unhappy or hurt here?" she asked.

TJ folded his arms. "In Sapphire Falls, people take care of each other. People are safe and happy here."

"And that's why Dan should do everything he can to keep Jo here?" Hope asked.

"She's better off here than anywhere else."

Hope's eyebrows went up, but after a moment, she simply

nodded. "Okay, I'm no expert on Sapphire Falls, so I'll take your word for it."

He also got the impression she was simply placating him when she said stuff like that.

"You can definitely take my word for it."

She paused for just a breath and then said, "But what about Dan's happiness? Is he getting the same chance to be happy?"

No. Dan's life revolved around JoEllen. And, no, she wasn't getting the help she needed other than some mild sedatives she took when she got really over-anxious and the insomnia hit. The doctor hesitated to give her anything more because she wouldn't stop drinking.

Most of the time everyone just kind of covered for JoEllen. For Dan and Peyton. People made excuses or ignored her crazy behavior or provided help without her realizing it. People in town had gotten really good at finding reasons to bring dinner over for Dan and Peyton when Peyton had been a kid, or taking turns looking after Jo when she was in one of her moods so that Dan didn't have to miss work, or showing up to take Peyton to school or practice when Jo couldn't get out of bed.

TJ didn't know how they always knew Peyton and Dan needed help, but he knew that his own mother and father had done a lot of caretaking in the Wells household.

"*I* have always admired Dan's devotion to his family," TJ said.

"Are we really still taking about Dan and *his* family?" Hope asked.

There was that psychoanalyzing thing again. Fuck, he hated it. And she was good at it. It had to be the herbs.

Ignoring her hadn't been working. Not even slightly. Getting deeper into the conversations with her had only resulted in him sharing far more than he'd wanted to. He needed a new tactic for dealing with Hope.

TJ stepped close, grasped her upper arms and pulled her up

onto her tiptoes. He sealed his mouth over hers in an instantly hot, aggressive kiss.

But *he* wasn't the aggressor.

Hope opened her mouth, licked along his bottom lip and then nipped it lightly.

Heat and want and the need to give as good as he got slammed into him, and TJ yanked her against his body, put both hands on her ass and ground into her. Hope wrapped her arms around his neck, pressing against him and making a soft needy sound that further fired his blood.

Damn the lack of a firm vertical surface. He wanted her up against a wall. Right. Now.

But he wasn't inclined—or able—to take even one step away from this spot.

He reached behind her and pulled on one end of the ties holding her dress up. The bow came loose and the bodice fell —at least as far as it could go with their chests plastered against one another. TJ shifted back so the silk would shimmer down her body.

It worked like a charm. The slick material slid over her breasts and dropped to the ground.

Hope was bare-assed naked in his arms.

TJ leaned back and looked down the length of her body, then raised his eyes to meet hers. "Say yes."

He didn't recognize the gruff voice that came from his throat.

"Yes."

He knew that she knew what he was referring to, and she said it clearly, without even the slightest waver in her voice, with full eye contact.

Naked woman. Gorgeous breasts. Lots and lots of lust between them. And she'd said yes.

He wasn't much of an analyzer. That was everything he needed to know.

He ran his hands from her butt to her shoulders and back down, then skimmed his palms over her waist, running his right hand up and down over the tattoo along her side an extra time. Her skin was every bit as smooth and warm as he'd imagined. Now he had to know if it was as sweet.

He cupped both breasts, running his thumbs over the hard tips, relishing her quick intake of air and the way she arched closer to his touch.

"Harder."

TJ's eyes went to her face. Her lids were heavy and she was breathing fast.

She put her hand on the back of one of his and pressed his thumb harder against her nipple.

He followed her lead and rubbed more firmly, then took the tip between his thumb and finger and squeezed.

"God, yes." Her head fell back, her long hair slipping over her shoulders to spill down almost to her butt.

"Your hair is blue today." The realization was late in coming and stupid to comment on in the middle of playing with the most gorgeous nipples he'd ever seen, but the words slipped out.

Words did that a lot around Hope.

She lifted her head to look at him with a smile. "I felt like blue today."

"The streaks were pink yesterday," he said stupidly.

"It's all temporary color, all natural, but it's a fun form of self-expression when I'm in the mood," she said. "I don't usually use any color at all, but it's felt right lately."

She didn't usually have pink hair. Or blue hair. Usually it was just blond.

That felt significant, though he wasn't sure why.

Though it was fair to assume his inability to scrutinize his thought and emotions at the moment might have something to do with the nipples he still had in front of him.

He tugged on her nipple and was rewarded with a hissed, "*Yes.*"

He didn't give a shit what color her hair was.

TJ leaned in and licked the hardened tip. She tasted even better than he'd imagined.

Hope ran her hand into his hair and gripped his head as he licked and kissed the entire surface of each breast, returning to the first to suck hard on the nipple, making her arch her pelvis closer to him, as if offering him more of her body.

And he knew she was.

Hope was pretty easy to read too, really. She was open and free, all for living in the moment, appreciating every detail of what was going on around her. Sex with her would be...new. He'd never had lazy, slow, take-his-time sex. And he wanted that with Hope.

Oh, he wanted to put her up against the wall and thrust deep right now.

But more, he wanted to appreciate her. Like a fine wine. Or at least, how he understood people treated wine—he was a beer guy.

He was used to hard, sweaty, push-the-envelope-to-keep-it-exciting sex. It seemed like sex needed to have extras to really work. Out-of-the-ordinary places, toys, lingerie, dirty talk and, yes, liquor. Those were the ingredients to his sex life.

But with Hope...

TJ knew as he worshipped her breasts that he would be unable fuck her until he'd tasted and touched every inch of her in full sunlight. He'd already spent more time on her nipples than he sometimes did on the entire act. He wanted to know every freckle, every *pore* on this woman's body. And he somehow knew that she would treat him to the same. Hope *enjoyed* things. She relished things. She absorbed things. She would make sex so much more than what he was used to.

And he couldn't wait.

"TJ!"

He froze at the intrusion.

No. No, no, *no*. It couldn't be.

A female voice that was not Hope's was the last thing he wanted to hear.

Especially the female voice belonging to his mother.

He pulled back and looked up at Hope. Her cheeks were flushed, she was breathing hard and she had a slightly dazed look in her eyes that he fucking loved.

And his mother was in the front yard.

"More family coming to check on you?" she asked. Definitely breathless.

Dammit.

His mom would go into the house to find him. It would take her about a minute to get to the kitchen—and the kitchen window.

He reached for Hope's dress and pulled it up her body. The body that seemed made for being *uncovered*.

He retied the strings behind her neck and gave her a wobbly smile. "My mom."

Hope's eyes widened. "No kidding?"

"I'm absolutely positive Delaney was the first person Mom talked to this morning," he said.

Hope took a deep breath. "She has good timing."

"*Good* timing?"

"Five more minutes and you would have been naked too."

His cock swelled at that and he almost reached for her again.

She must have read it in his eyes, because she put a hand on his chest and stepped back. "Mom."

He huffed out a breath. "Right."

Hope turned toward his flowers in the bed at their feet. "I love your herb garden." She knelt on the grass at the corner where he'd planted sage and mint and oregano.

TJ pulled in a deep breath. Okay, they were going to talk about herbs.

"Uh, thanks."

"You use these for cooking?" she asked, looking up at him.

And all he could think was that she was on her knees in front of him.

The screen door off the kitchen slapped shut behind him and he heard his mother's voice again. "TJ!"

Herbs. Garden. His little hippie girl kneeling in the dirt and grass that was as much a part of his home as the house behind him.

Even that thought stirred him, and TJ had to force his attention away from Hope and the way the sunlight caught in her hair and made the stars and the tiny pink gem in her ear sparkle.

He turned toward his mother, hoping that his emotions weren't plastered all over his face.

"Hey, Mom." He didn't pretend to be surprised to see her. He wasn't, and she knew he wouldn't be.

"Good morning!" Kathy Bennett's smile was wide and sincere as she approached.

TJ smiled in spite of himself. He and his brothers had inherited their height and brown hair from their father, but their blue eyes came from their mom. Their love of the land, their work ethic, their appreciation for home and roots, and their dedication to family and friends came from both parents.

"I brought banana bread," Kathy said. She smiled up at TJ but brushed right past him to get a good look at Hope. "Hope, I'm Kathy, TJ's mother."

Hope rose and gave Kathy a smile that TJ would have labeled ethereal. And he had never in his life used that word, even in his head.

But the girl looked like a pixie or an angel or a fairy or something standing in the morning sun with the breeze ruffling her flowing dress, her blond hair falling around her in waves with the light blue streaks and her big eyes and her sweet smile.

His entire body clenched at the idea that she was here with *him*. She was his. For now. Temporarily. But who would pass up a chance of even an hour with an angel?

"It is so nice to meet you," Hope said, extending her hand.

"Oh, you too, honey."

Kathy reached out to shake it, but Hope sandwiched Kathy's hands between hers and held on, stepping closer.

"I've now met two of your sons and your husband. I have to tell you that you are surrounded by wonderful men."

She couldn't have said any more perfect words to his mother, and looking at Hope's face, TJ was again torn—was she saying it to win Kathy over or did she mean it? She seemed sincere. But she was also really good at reading people and finding the right things to say and do to get on their good side.

Complicated. That's what this was. How could he forget?

Oh, yeah. Naked breasts.

"Well, they all seem very taken with you as well," Kathy said. "Tucker said he's never slept better than last night after you...pulled on his ears?" She finished the sentence with a question mark.

So Tucker had been the one singing Hope's praises, not Delaney. Interesting.

Or something.

Tucker was a pushover for a pretty girl. That was no secret. But once Hope had helped Delaney feel better, Tucker was president of her fan club. Well, maybe vice president. Delaney might head it up.

Hope laughed. "It's a wonderful technique for tension in the head and headaches."

"Maybe you could give me some ideas for the arthritis in my hands," Kathy said.

Sneaky. That's what his mother was. TJ shook his head. She wasn't over here because Tucker's earlobe story had made her think of her arthritis. She was here because one of her sons had a woman staying with him. Period.

But...

TJ glanced at Hope. If she could help his mother with her painful joints, he'd...want her even more. Which seemed impossible.

"I have something wonderful I could put into a cream for you," Hope said, rubbing his mother's hand between her, sliding over the knuckles that had grown larger and crooked with the arthritis. "And I can show you some acupressure points for pain relief."

"I would love that."

Something in his mother's voice made TJ look closely at her eyes. She was watching Hope's hand work over her own with a look of surprise. She wasn't grilling Hope about where she was from or her family or her interests. She wasn't insisting Hope come to dinner—for more grilling. She was quiet and still. Those two words were as rarely applied to Kathy as they were to Delaney and Tucker's four boys.

"Mom, you okay?" TJ asked.

She nodded. "That feels so good."

"Come with me to the bakery this morning," Hope said. "I'm going to talk to some of the other girls about essential oils and meditation and some other things you might find helpful."

Kathy looked up at Hope and a small smile curled her lips. Not her usual friendly, outgoing smile. Not her devious smile. Not her I'm-on-to-you smile. A small, sweet smile that TJ wasn't sure he'd ever seen.

"I'd love to."

TJ watched them walk back toward the house together, still hand in hand, and all he could do was shake his head.

Hope was pulling his mother in.

It was usually the other way around. Kathy Bennett was impossible to resist, and she gathered friends like she gathered flowers for the dinner table—in colorful bunches because they made her happy.

But now Hope was gathering Kathy up. Hope was drawing Kathy into *her* world. She was doing something for Kathy, where Kathy was usually the one doing for others.

TJ ran a hand through his hair.

He was completely screwed.

He was never going to get this woman out of his system. And it didn't even have to do with her breasts. Much.

8

Scott's Sweets was the most adorable shop Hope had ever been in.

She didn't eat sugar and sweets, and yet she knew she could sit at one of the little round, white wooden tables for hours and simply inhale the scent of coffee—which in truth she thought was one of the best substances ever created—and baked goods. She'd lived on coffee for years. But when she'd decided to go caffeine-free for the summer, she'd had to break up with her favorite morning lover. Same with sugar. She'd discovered the addictive white stuff after leaving her mother's house for college and had indulged for a long time—and several pounds. Kicking that habit had been as hard as the caffeine. Resisting the Oreos on TJ's table last night had required considerable effort. Of course, distracting herself by touching and leaning on TJ had helped.

And it had been good for their story.

The story she'd repeated for the girls Delaney had gathered in the shop off the town square.

"A lot of people think that because essential oils come from plants, they're harmless," Hope said. She had four bottles of different oils in front of her on the table and all of the women gathered had taken a chance to smell and look at them. "But that's not true. They're very concentrated and can cause skin irritation, respiratory distress and other problems. That's why we mix them with carriers—other oils, lotions and butters." She picked up a bottle. "It's important to know how to mix them properly because the carriers offer different things as well. Butters absorb slowly, so you'll get a longer-acting effect. Lotions absorb more quickly, so they're great for sore muscles and such. Oils are somewhere in between as far as absorption."

Hope was in her element. She got excited about this stuff. It was new to many people but could be so helpful. She loved the idea of giving people possibilities for pain relief, improved sleep and mood, and all the other things essential oils could do. The oils had worked for her for everything from stomach upset to improving her memory.

But she was hardly an expert. She often talked from her own personal experiences, so in preparation for today, she'd studied her mom's journals and a couple of Melody's favorite reference books last night to brush up. She was also sticking with the basic oils and not getting into combinations that she knew even less about.

"Different oils have different effects, of course, and the way you can use them also varies. You can use them topically, aromatically, you can even ingest some of them."

"Are these okay for Lauren while she's pregnant?" Phoebe asked.

Lauren was a gorgeous, very pregnant brunette who was sitting next to Kathy across the table from Hope. She was married to another of TJ's brothers, Travis.

Hope was good with names and details about people. The group around her included Delaney and Kathy and the shop owner, Adrianne, all of whom Hope had met. In addition, there was Lauren, the bubbly redhead Phoebe, and another beautiful blond, Kate.

Initially, there had been two other tables of customers in the shop having coffee and visiting, but they had also joined the mini-class when Hope had started talking.

The only other person in the shop was a girl working behind the counter and moving in and out of the kitchen. She wore a Scott's Sweets apron and a nametag, but Hope hadn't been able to read it and no one had introduced her.

"We always err on the side of caution and assume the oils do cross the placenta," Hope said, concentrating on the topic at hand rather than the fact that she was surrounded, literally, by women who cared about and were a part of TJ's life. There really were a lot of them. And she could have sworn they were slowly inching their chairs closer to her. "It's best if they're used only for nausea or insomnia, and not every day. Same for when you're breastfeeding."

"I've heard that there are oils for sinus infections," Kate said. "Adrianne has a hard time with those."

"Oh, absolutely," Hope said. "You can breathe them in, or my favorite is a Neti pot. It looks like a magic lamp you rub to get a genie at your beck and call." She grinned. "You can add a number of oils to a saline water solution for the irrigation."

She was impressed, and a bit amazed, by the fact that these women cared for one another as much as they did for themselves.

What would it be like to have so many people involved in your life and aware of your issues? Hope wondered. Stifling? Or comforting?

"Delaney said you did some acupressure on her last night too," Kate said. She was sitting on the edge of her seat and looked excited.

Hope nodded. "For stress relief. There are pressure points in the hands and feet."

"And she said you mentioned improved orgasms," Kate said.

All of the women focused on Hope at that.

She nodded. "There is a lot that can be done to improve your sex life. Oils, acupressure, massage, meditation, yoga."

"Levi doesn't believe they can get any better," Kate said.

Hope lifted an eyebrow. "Levi is your husband?"

"Fiancé," Kate said and grinned. "Do you have anything that can shrink an ego?"

Hope laughed. "I'm thinking if the orgasms get even better, he'll just take credit and it will make his ego even bigger."

Kate laughed too. "You're absolutely right. Have you met Levi?"

"How about bitchiness?" Lauren asked. "Do you have anything that can cure that? Because I have a lot of it."

"You do not," Adrianne protested. "You're two weeks away from your due date. You're uncomfortable and hormonal. That's all it is."

Lauren looked at Delaney. Delaney got very interested in buttering her muffin. Then Lauren looked at Phoebe. Phoebe picked up the bottle of lavender oil in front of her and studied the label intently.

"Red?" Lauren said.

"Hmm?" Phoebe asked, turning the bottle to read the back label.

"You didn't tell Adrianne about how I blew up at Delaney the other day?"

Phoebe blinked at her innocently. "Did you blow up at Delaney?" She looked at Delaney. "I don't remember that, do you, D?"

Delaney shook her head. "Nope. Doesn't ring a bell." Then she stuffed a third of a blueberry crumb muffin into her mouth.

Lauren sighed and looked at Adrianne. "I was a raging bitch the other day. Phoebe and I went home at lunchtime to see what Delaney was doing with the kitchen remodel at our place. She had knocked out some cupboards I wanted to keep and I came unglued."

Delaney started choking and Kate patted her on the back and slid her ice water closer.

Adrianne looked at Delaney. "Really?"

"Yes, really," Lauren said. "I was yelling and cussing and then I threw two plates and broke into tears."

Adrianne didn't look shocked by the news.

Hope sat back and watched the women around her.

Fascinating stuff.

"So I went to the fridge and pulled out her most expensive bottle of white wine," Phoebe replied. "And I drank right out of the bottle, right in front of her. I figured if she was going to yell at someone, at least I'd give her something *real* to yell about."

Adrianne's smile grew. "That was brave."

"And it worked," Lauren said. "I realized that we had talked about removing those cupboards. I brought Delaney dinner that night to make up for it."

"You cooked?" Kate asked. She looked confused. "How is that an apology?"

"I didn't say I *made* dinner that night," Lauren said. "I *brought* dinner. Pizza."

"Oh, good." Kate looked relieved. "Did you forgive her?" she asked Delaney.

Delaney nodded. "Of course."

"Well, it's not really her fault," Adrianne said. "It's hormones and swollen feet and a sore low back."

Delaney grinned. "It's actually because I know that every time Lauren has a dinner party and two guests have to eat on plates that don't match, she'll be sorry all over again."

They all laughed and Hope found herself completely hooked. She'd never experienced a group of women like this. Friends, clearly, who could be totally honest and loving at the same time. She'd never had someone else worrying about her sinuses or defending her emotional outbursts or teasing her about her cooking.

Of course, she took care of her own sinuses, didn't have emotional outbursts and rarely cooked for anyone else.

Watching these women together touched and overwhelmed her at the same time.

The bell over the door tinkled and another beautiful woman stepped into the store. The other women around the table were all very pretty, but in a more understated way. This one wore a black pencil skirt, an electric-blue silk blouse and black heels that hoisted her an additional three inches into the air. Her long, straight blond hair was perfect, as was her makeup and nails.

Wow, maybe there was something in the water or air here. All the women were beautiful and the men good-looking.

"Well, anyway," Lauren said to Hope. "If you have something for Raging Bitchitis, I could use some."

"Embrace it," the newcomer said. "It's rare around here. You'll be a novelty. Like me."

Lauren snorted. "Novelty is not the word I've heard people use, Hailey."

Hope watched Lauren and the other woman curiously. She might be a nature-loving, yoga-practicing, meditating free spirit, but even she knew about alpha females. And she was looking at two of them. She could read it plain as day. She was interested in who would concede the top spot to the other.

"Am I late?" Hailey pulled up a chair, sat and crossed her long legs.

"Of course you are. Exactly as you planned it," Adrianne said with an affectionate smile. "Do you want tea?"

"Water with lemon is fine," Hailey said.

"Good thing you didn't miss the part about how to relax and

kick back," Phoebe said to Hailey. "If anyone needs to learn to chill out, it's you."

Hailey focused on Hope when she replied. "I don't really like to relax."

Yep, she could read that easily as well. Hailey was wound tight. She appeared cool as a cucumber, but Hope sensed she was always alert and ready. She was clearly sharp and confident —or at least wanted people to think so.

Hailey had come in and taken over the conversation and focus on the instruction, but Hope got the impression from the other women's expressions that it was typical.

"Do you sleep well at night?" Hope asked.

"I go to bed at the same time every night and get up at the same time every morning," Hailey said.

That wasn't really an answer to her question. "And during those hours in bed, do you sleep well?" Hope asked.

Hailey met her gaze steadily. "Yes."

She was lying. Hope could tell. This woman was restless. Hailey might call it energy or chalk it up to being highly driven and a Type-A personality, but she was restless and filling her mind and her life with activities and plans and schedules to keep from having to think about other things.

Hope would bet Miss Hailey hated yoga and meditation.

"How do you feel about yoga?" she asked.

Hailey wrinkled her nose. "I prefer more *active* exercise."

She preferred more motion and noise, Hope guessed. "I'll bet you're a runner."

Hailey's right eyebrow rose just slightly. "Yes."

And Hope would bet she was a competitive one. "Do you train for races?"

Hailey lifted her chin a bit at that. "Yes. I do half-marathons."

Hope didn't smile, but she had Hailey pegged. And she'd

win her over. "I have some amazing cream that you can apply to your arches for pain and inflammation," she said.

This time, Hailey didn't hide her surprise quite as easily. "How do you know I have foot pain?"

"You're a runner." Who likely pushed herself through any hint of tightness or pain. Hailey seemed exactly the type to subscribe to the no-pain-no-gain theory. "And those killer heels," she said. Hailey had walked across the smooth tile floor of the shop in three-inch heels like she'd been born in them. Women that confident on heels that high wore them a lot. "But I'd really like to show you some acupressure techniques and some stretching," Hope didn't add that they were actually yoga positions, "that could help with your back pain."

Hailey flat out stared at her this time. "How did you know I have back pain?"

Hope couldn't fully explain it. Her nursing instructors and classmates had marveled at her ability to read the body as well.

"I'm very intuitive," she said, using the same line she'd used on TJ. "I'm good at sensing things about people."

Hailey narrowed her eyes, clearly skeptical, but she nodded. "Okay."

Hope smiled at her, then at the other women around the table. "You should all come out to TJ's farm in the morning for yoga."

They looked interested and Kate, Delaney and Phoebe all agreed. Hailey said she'd need to check her schedule. Adrianne needed to check to make sure the morning in the bakery would be covered and Lauren decided she'd come watch even if she couldn't participate fully with her belly in the way.

"We can modify everything for you," Hope assured her.

"I'll bring my lawn chair and orange juice," Lauren said. "We'll go from there."

Hope let it go. She *would* get Lauren doing yoga in the morning. But Lauren didn't need to know that right now.

"Kathy said you were talking about some cream for her hands too," Delaney said. "Is it the same stuff you rubbed on TJ?"

She said it innocently, but Hope noticed the twinkle of mischief in her eyes. Again, she had the full attention of everyone in the bakery, including the helper she still didn't know the name of, who was wiping down the next table. Slowly and more thoroughly than it needed. Hope had noticed her eavesdropping the entire time. She would have invited her to join them, but the girl was Adrianne's employee and Hope didn't want to step on toes.

"It's similar," she said, not intending to deny there had been rubbing between her and TJ. "For his sore muscles, I used marjoram in whipped coconut oil. For arthritis, my favorite to start with is wintergreen." She smiled at Kathy. "I love the aroma. But then there are lots of other options. I also love juniper berries for arthritis."

"Sounds wonderful." Kathy gave her a big smile.

"I'll make some for you tonight," Hope promised. "TJ can bring it over to you."

"Oh, please promise you'll come too," Kathy said.

Hope simply nodded. She really shouldn't make promises of any kind. This was TJ's world, his family and friends. She shouldn't get any more involved with them than she already was. Looking around the table, she realized that she really liked these women. Even uptight Hailey obviously fit in.

Hope didn't know how to do that.

It wasn't that she always felt out of place or anything, but she was used to feeling like...a visitor wherever she went. A welcome visitor most of the time, but someone who was just passing through nonetheless.

She and her mom had lived in Sedona all through Hope's high school years, but Hope had been homeschooled until ninth grade, and even after she'd known the other kids in Sedona for a couple of years, she'd still felt different.

College was the first time she'd had a group that she'd spent time with over a significant period. And it had been a learning experience. Living with a roommate had actually been the first time Hope had fully experienced someone who wasn't used to taking care of herself.

Taylor had driven Hope crazy. She'd asked for advice and input on *everything*. She'd known nothing about how to care for her car or how to handle her finances or how to tell their neighbors that they needed to turn their music down.

Hope had tried to be patient. She'd helped Taylor as much as she could, but it hadn't taken long before she'd decided to push Taylor to be more independent. Taylor hadn't liked it. They'd parted ways after that first year when Hope had decided she'd rather live in a tiny, crappy apartment on her own than coddle someone in a bigger, less-drafty dorm room.

So she wasn't so sure about this close, in-each-other's-business circle of girlfriends. It was obvious they cared for one another and each seemed confident on her own, but they'd clearly shared a lot of details about their lives with one another and were comfortable with the others having input on everything.

Hope wasn't sure how she'd do with that long-term.

She was completely open about who she was, the things she knew, her background and views. She loved talking to other people and getting their stories. It was when it came to having people want to help her that she got frustrated. Anything she needed done, she could do herself.

Not that it wasn't sweet when TJ tried to help her. In fact, it made heat swirl through her when he begrudgingly did something for her.

The heat thing, and the liking it thing, were very disconcerting really.

"Okay, Hope?"

She focused on Adrianne. She hadn't heard a word of the discussion around her as the women talked about yoga and the things they'd learned about the oils so far and possible uses.

"I'm sorry, what?"

"We were thinking that we could just make a bunch of the oils and creams right now. I have coconut oil in the back and plenty of bowls and mixers and things. We can all pile into the kitchen and mix up a bunch of stuff together. I'll make lunch for everyone too. We can make it a day. Unless you need to get back to the farm?" Adrianne said.

Everyone's attention swung to Hope. They were clearly waiting to see if she *needed* to get back to TJ.

She kind of did.

They'd definitely been interrupted in the midst of something wonderful that morning. Hope could still feel his big hands, his hot mouth... Her nipples tightened and she felt her panties heat.

The panties she'd slipped on underneath another sundress to come to town with Kathy. She liked going with as few clothes as possible. She had, of course, always dressed in scrubs at work, but she'd inherited her mother's free-clothing style, preferring loose, flowing garments that were not restrictive or fitted whenever possible. Bras drove her crazy.

She shifted on the chair, aware of her panties not because they were restrictive exactly, but because they rubbed over flesh that was sensitized just thinking about TJ.

That boy was going to have to scratch this itch soon. Especially after watching her do yoga, stripping her naked in the garden and showing her just how delicious work-roughened hands felt on her skin.

"I didn't have any specific plans for the day," Hope said honestly. This summer was about going with the flow, so she'd avoided making plans and schedules. She had intended to explore more of TJ's land...and more of TJ. But she supposed that could wait.

She really did want to make this cream for Kathy's hands. She also wanted to win Hailey over with her massage technique for her arches and she wanted to help Lauren feel less fatigued and even bitchy, if Lauren was truly concerned about that. Some relaxation techniques and aromatherapy could help her a lot.

"I'd love to stay," she finally said. "Are you sure it's not a problem to use the restaurant's kitchen?"

"Not at all." Adrianne waved away her concern. "We've got today's baking done and Peyton can watch the counter and wait on anyone who comes in."

"Peyton?" Hope perked up.

Adrianne pointed at the girl in the apron Hope hadn't been introduced to. "My new employee."

Hope turned to find Peyton unloading a tray of cupcakes into the display case.

Peyton.

Of course, Peyton was a common name. There had to be more than one, even in a little town like this. But Adrianne's employee was about the right age to be Hope's half-sister.

Hope felt her heart kick at that thought and frowned. Strange. She really wasn't here looking for a long-lost family. Especially a sister she hadn't even known about.

Still, she couldn't deny the urge to go to Peyton and talk with her, look into her eyes, to confirm that they shared a father.

Hope put a hand over her heart. Wow, that was a lot all of a sudden.

"So we can use the kitchen all afternoon," Adrianne said, sliding her chair back and standing. "I'll make some chicken salad for lunch."

"Oh, Hope's a vegetarian," Delaney said as everyone stood

and started moving the tables and chairs back where they belonged.

Everyone paused at that. Lauren was the first to speak. "You're a vegetarian?"

Hope nodded. "Most of my life. And actually, I'm vegan." She'd had a brief love affair with bacon in college and she did eat fish on occasion, but she'd never developed a taste for other pork products and couldn't do beef.

The vegetarian thing was no problem for her. The vegan and gluten-free thing definitely was. She hadn't always been vegan, but her mother had been for the past ten years and had said over and over how wonderful it was.

The hardest thing was the Oreos.

She'd been shocked to find that TJ kept Oreos on hand at all times. The man was practically perfect.

Except that she was trying not to eat Oreos.

"Oh my gosh, Hope, I'm so sorry," Adrianne said. "Here I was pushing sweets at you all morning and now the chicken salad. I guess I don't know any vegans anymore and it didn't even occur to me."

Hope smiled at her. "No worries. I'm a big girl. I just say no to the things I don't eat." She'd passed on all of the baked goods that morning, sticking with the green tea that had turned out to be delicious. Maybe not as delicious as the bold-roast coffee Adrianne had poured for several others, but good all the same.

"I had some friends in Chicago who were vegan," Adrianne said as they all started for the kitchen. "But you don't run into many in the middle of Nebraska."

Hope laughed. "I don't suppose. But I'm fine, really. I always have staples with me."

"Staples like what?"

"Dried beans, quinoa, dried fruit, things like that."

Adrianne stopped her by the door to the kitchen. "Show me how to make some amazing vegetarian thing for lunch."

Hope glanced at everyone else. "Really? You want to eat quinoa?"

"Why not?" Adrianne asked, looking at the other women. "We're adventurous."

"I really like quinoa," Kate said. "I've had it a lot."

"I've had it too," Lauren said. "I'm game."

"Never had it," Phoebe told her. "But if I hate it, there are plenty of cupcakes here to cleanse my palate."

Hope laughed and shrugged. "Okay. I know an easy recipe for quinoa and veggies with peanut sauce."

"Perfect," Adrianne said. She gestured toward the kitchen. "Let's get going."

Everyone filed in, Hope jotted down a quick list of ingredients she needed and Phoebe and Delaney headed out to get what Adrianne didn't have from the grocery store. Adrianne had never had the need for soy sauce in her bakery. She did, however, make quiches, so she had broccoli and red bell peppers, along with every spice and plenty of peanut butter to work with.

Kate helped Hope retrieve her full apothecary box from the car along with her stash of quinoa. She was glad she hadn't asked TJ to unhook the camper after all. She'd felt silly pulling it into town and parking it on one of the main streets around the square, but now she was happy she had it. She was impressed with the women wanting to learn new things and was feeling better about the togetherness they inspired.

They spent the afternoon whipping coconut oil into light, fluffy creams for everything from Kathy's arthritic knuckles to Hailey's tight arches. Hope made a lavender oil for Lauren to use on her pillowcase at night, showed Kate a couple of acupressure sites that would drive Levi crazy, gave them all a lesson in deep breathing and a five-minute meditation exercise she loved personally, and introduced them to homemade peanut sauce and quinoa.

She was at the sink helping with the dishes when she felt someone bump her arm.

"Oh, sorry."

The soft apology made Hope turn. It was Peyton.

"Peyton, right?" Hope asked.

She nodded. "Right."

Hope lowered her voice after glancing around. None of the other women were close enough to overhear. "What's your last name?" she asked. No time to beat around the bush. If this was Dan's daughter, Hope needed to know.

Peyton looked up from the bowl she was scrubbing. She met Hope's gaze and Hope felt a jolt of recognition go through her. Which made no sense. She'd never met Peyton before that day.

But there was something so familiar about her eyes.

"Wells," Peyton answered. "Why?"

Peyton Wells. Her half-sister. Hope worked to keep from reacting outwardly. "I, um, thought maybe you were also related to the Bennetts," Hope said. "Seems everyone is somehow."

Peyton smiled at that. "It does seem that way. Actually, most people are just friends. Like Kate and Levi," she said, glancing over to where Kate was helping Lauren off the stool she'd been sitting on. "But friends are like family to the Bennetts. My dad and TJ's dad are good friends."

Dan's daughter. For sure.

Hope blinked against the sudden stinging in her eyes. Holy crap, what was that?

But this was her sister. Some emotion was understandable. Of course, if she started crying, Peyton would want to know why. Or would think she was crazy.

Crazy. Right. She was supposed to be convincing these people that she was a little kooky and so obsessed with TJ that she'd driven all this way to take care of him while he was hurt.

Crazy could work in her favor. Not only did it give her a reason for being in Sapphire Falls, but it could give her a reason to do something that she suddenly really wanted to do.

She threw her arms around Peyton and hugged her tight.

"Any friend of TJ's is a friend of mine," she told Peyton, loud enough that the other women would hear and not be suspicious of the hug.

Peyton's hands slowly came up, as if she wasn't sure what was going on, and she patted Hope's back. "Uh, thanks."

Hope pulled back, schooling her features into an expression of pure excited happiness instead of the I'm-fighting-tears-because-I-have-a-little-sister that she was feeling. She had not been ready for those emotions. Until TJ had told her about Peyton, she'd had no idea she had a sibling. It wasn't as if she'd felt a sense of emptiness in her life. She couldn't remember even wishing for a baby brother or sister as a kid. But ever since TJ had told her the truth, there had been an ache in her chest. It made no sense.

Hope looked into Peyton's eyes, this time more prepared for the impact. "Do you have allergies?" she asked, the red rimming Peyton's eyes and the dark circles underneath an indication.

Peyton looked surprised. "I do."

"Here." Hope took Peyton's hand and pulled her over to the apothecary box. "I have something great for that." She uncapped a bottle of peppermint oil. "Hold out your hands." She put a dab of oil on each of Peyton's palms. "Rub them together." Peyton did. "Now cup your hands over your mouth and nose and breath deep." Hope demonstrated and Peyton copied her. Peyton's eyes grew wide as she inhaled the aroma.

"Wow," she said a moment later, dropping her hands. "I can feel it clearing my sinuses."

"Here." Hope mixed the oil in with some carrier oil and poured it into a bottle. "Take this. You can dab it at the base of your neck or you can rub it on your chest at night. It should help."

She pressed the vial into Peyton's hand, stupidly desperate for Peyton to take it and use it and feel better.

It was the weirdest feeling she'd ever had. She was feeling protective toward this girl she'd known for five minutes.

Peyton's hand curled around the glass bottle and she nodded. "I definitely will. Thank you."

"And did you try the quinoa?" Hope asked, sounding even to her own ears as if she was talking too fast and like the pitch of her voice had risen.

Peyton shook her head. "I was working."

"You have to eat lunch," Hope said. She took Peyton's hand again and moved toward the bowl of leftovers.

"I had a sandwich during my break," Peyton said, following behind. As if she had a choice.

"But this is so good for you," Hope said. "Lots of vegetables. And the quinoa is really high in protein."

"I'm—" Peyton was clearly puzzled by Hope's sudden attention to her eating habits. "I'm full, right now," she finally said.

"Then you can take some home and eat it later." Hope pulled in a huge breath, realizing that she was sounding and acting nuts. Fortunately, she wanted these women to think exactly that. She wasn't quite as happy thinking it of herself though. What was going on? "You can share some with your dad," she added. Then frowned. Where had that come from?

Peyton's eyes were wide and she nodded slowly. Like someone would when faced with a real crazy person. Hope sighed.

"Okay. That sounds great," Peyton said.

Her sudden and ridiculous urge to feed this girl overrode her urge to not scare Peyton off. She grabbed a plastic container with a lid from one of Adrianne's shelves. She dished up a portion of the leftover quinoa and handed it to Peyton. "I hope you like it."

And she really, really did hope that. Which was completely crazy.

Peyton took it and looked ready to turn away when she hesitated. "You're really interesting," she said to Hope, a wrinkle between her brows. "I've never met someone like you."

"Someone with blue hair?" Hope asked with a smile, bothered by how much she liked Peyton thinking she was interesting.

Peyton smiled. "That too. Not too many people around here do stuff like that."

"It's temporary. Totally natural. Will wash out tonight," Hope said. "It's just something fun to do once in a while."

"Well, I like it."

"I could show you how to do it. It's not much different from changing your belt or shoes. It's just another accessory," Hope said. Her mother had been against chemically treating hair, including permanent hair colors, but instead of telling Hope she couldn't do it, she'd helped Hope find a natural way. Hope had been honest when she'd told TJ she didn't typically color her hair. She'd done a lot of it as a teen, but as she'd gotten older, she'd grown out of some of that. But now, for some reason, this summer seemed like the right time to do it if the mood struck her.

"Really?" Peyton asked.

"Sure. If your mom wouldn't care." Hope almost bit her tongue off after the words came out. She hadn't meant to get any deeper or more personal about Peyton's family. Hope knew who Peyton was now, and that was enough. Or it was supposed to be enough. And now she was offering to see Peyton again to show her how to color her hair and asking, indirectly, about her mom?

Peyton's expression changed instantly. "My mom probably won't even notice."

Okay. Yeah, she did *not* want to get into all of this.

"I'm sorry to hear that," Hope heard herself say.

Peyton shook her head. "It's okay. Nothing new. I would love to try purple, is that an option?"

"I make my own hair chalks, so anything is an option," Hope told her. "And I do have some purple. I can show you how to use it or even how to make your own, if you'd like."

"You'd just give it to me?" Peyton asked.

"Sure. I can make more."

And she could, of course. But she had to make it sound like no big deal so Peyton didn't realize how much Hope wanted to give her stuff.

It made no sense to Hope, and it might go a bit beyond the delightfully kooky thing she'd been going for.

Peyton nodded. "Okay. I mean, I'd love to learn to make it. Actually. If you don't mind." She suddenly seemed shy.

"I don't mind at all."

"I'd love to learn to make some of this other stuff too," Peyton said, looking around the room. "The lotions and stuff are amazing."

Hope felt a surge of pride at that. "I can show you how to make shampoo and perfume and stuff that's great for your nails." She couldn't help herself—she took Peyton's hand again and lifted it. "Working here, you'll be washing your hands a lot. I have a hand mask that would be great for your dry skin and cuticles."

"A hand mask?"

"Like face masks—and I have some awesome ones of those too—but you put it on your hands and leave it for a while. Softens everything right up."

Peyton looked up at her. "See, you're so interesting."

It was so similar to what Hope had said to TJ yesterday as

she was getting to know him that she was unable to reply for a moment. Finally, she took a breath and forced a smile. "When's your day off? If you're not busy we can play around in TJ's kitchen."

She was going to assume he wouldn't mind. He, after all, was the only other person on the planet who knew who Peyton was to Hope.

"Not until next Thursday," Peyton said regretfully.

That was several days away. It looked like Hope had another reason to stay in town. She *had* to teach Peyton these things. Something lasting. Something Peyton could do and think of Hope—even if she didn't know who Hope really was.

That idea caused a twinge in her chest, but Hope ignored it. She didn't actually want Peyton to know her real identity. That would be messy.

This was fine. She could stay here as TJ's girlfriend, give him what he needed while still giving something to Peyton too. Peyton didn't need to know that Hope was her sister to enjoy and benefit from learning about the soaps and chalks and lotions.

"You've got to go with us to the Come Again tonight," Phoebe said, crossing the room to retrieve more of the plastic containers for the women to take creams home in.

"Me?" Hope asked.

"Yeah. We're going down there for burgers and margaritas," Phoebe told her. "Not that you'll eat the burgers, but Lauren needs some cheese and grease."

Hope glanced at the pregnant woman. Lauren grimaced. "This baby is a Bennett for sure. I mean, I like a good burger once in a while, but I ate a lot healthier before this kid started bossing me around. He loves fried food, especially onion rings." If it was possible for a woman to look disgusted and tempted at the same time, Lauren pulled it off.

"It's a boy?" Hope asked, finally letting go of Peyton's hand

and wondering if the girl thought the hand holding had gone on past the appropriate stage.

"It's gotta be," Lauren said. "No lady would act like this."

Phoebe snorted. "What makes you think she'd be a lady?"

Lauren arched a brow. "Excuse me?"

"Oh, sure, hoity-toity city-girl genius scientist," Phoebe said. "You can try to act all superior, but I've seen you chug a beer faster than *I* can and belch afterward. And you dance in the back of Travis's truck in boots and short shorts with the best of us when you're not knocked up."

Lauren sighed. "I so hope I can wear short shorts again after this."

Phoebe laughed and turned back to Hope. "There's not much to eat there for you, but margaritas are vegan, aren't they?"

"Think they would use agave syrup?" Hope asked.

Phoebe hesitated. "I'm not sure they would *have* agave syrup."

"I can supply it," Hope said, fighting a smile.

Phoebe nodded. "Then, yeah, they probably would. Especially if Derek's tending bar. You flash those big green eyes at him and he'll probably let you behind the bar to make whatever you want, however you want."

That she could do. She didn't drink alcohol often, but she did happen to have an amazing recipe for margaritas. "Great, then I'm in." She turned to Peyton. "You want to come?"

Her sister had to be twenty-one. Probably.

Peyton's attention went to where Adrianne was cleaning one of the huge mixers they'd used to whip the coconut oil. Peyton lowered her voice and moved in closer. "I just got this job and I don't want to mess it up."

"You'd be off the clock, right?" Hope asked. "Surely Adrianne doesn't care what you do in your off time?"

"Well, I..." Peyton trailed off. She studied Hope for a

moment and then took a deep breath. "I tend to get into trouble when I drink tequila."

Hope could tell Peyton was surprised she had confessed that to a near stranger.

"We'll have to keep you away from the tequila then," Hope said.

"And rum. And whiskey. And vodka."

Hope bit the inside of her cheek. Okay. TJ had told her that Peyton tended to get into trouble. She'd assumed it was more the bad-taste-in-men thing.

"So maybe you can just stay away from all of that."

"At the Come Again?" Peyton asked, clearly skeptical. "That's why people go."

"What about just having a good time talking with friends and maybe dancing?" Hope suggested.

Peyton shrugged. "Everything is more fun with alcohol."

Hope decided to change her mind. "I'll prove that's not true," Hope said. "You come out with us tonight, I won't drink either, and I promise you'll have a wonderful time."

Peyton studied her again. "Why do you care if I go out with you?"

She had to be careful here. "I like you."

Peyton's eyes widened with surprise. "You do?"

Hope's heart clenched again. Was that really so surprising? "I do."

"You barely know me."

"I'm very intuitive," Hope said. That word was getting a lot of play in Sapphire Falls. Was everything black and white here? Was everyone here the I-have-to-see-it-and-touch-it-to-believe-its-real type?

"I heard you tell the other girls that."

"It's true. I get senses about people. And I'm almost always right."

"And you get the sense that I'm likable?" Peyton asked.

Hope wanted to hug her again. "I really do."

"We'll have to go to Julie's," Lauren said, waddling to the sink with her plate and cup. "You'll need some new clothes."

Hope looked down at her dress and sandals. "I will?"

"You're going to need some denim." Lauren put a hand on her back and took a deep breath. "Red, tell her about the denim. I'm too tired."

Phoebe chuckled and took Lauren's plate and cup. "Do you have any blue jeans, Hope?"

She did. Back in Arizona. And she didn't particularly care for them. They were too confining and denim was too rough for her. "No, sorry."

"Then we'll go to Julie's and hook you up," Phoebe said.

"With blue jeans?" Hope asked.

"And then Phoebe will cut them off," Lauren said.

"Why?" Hope wanted to know.

"To make shorts," Phoebe said with a shrug.

"I have to wear denim shorts to the bar?" That was a strange dress code.

"TJ wants you to wear denim shorts to the bar," Lauren said.

Hope's eyebrows went up. "He does? How do you know?"

Lauren smiled. "Denim is like Viagra to the men around here."

Phoebe laughed. "Especially short denim."

"And I personally can't wait to see my brother-in-law's face when he sees you in short denim," Lauren said.

Hope was starting to feel her tolerance for denim growing. "Really?"

"TJ's the gruff introvert of the group," Lauren said. "But he's a great guy underneath all the grumpiness. I want—I *need*—to see him happy and having fun and...ruffled."

Hope agreed with the happy and having fun stuff. She liked Lauren. "What do you mean by ruffled?"

"Not so sure of himself, crazy about someone, distracted

and...ruffled," Lauren said. "He usually acts bored and under-whelmed or even uncomfortable in social situations. But I'm thinking if he's got you in a pair of short shorts, that might be different."

Hope would love to see TJ ruffled too. Or maybe it was rumpled—as in, his clothes had been thrown all over the floor on the way to the bedroom...

Okay, she could put up with denim for a few hours.

"I thought he was pretty outgoing and into partying at one time?" she asked. That was what he'd told her, wasn't it?

"Nope," Lauren said. "TJ's always been the dependable one. But he used to know how to have fun. He used to be happy."

Hope didn't need to know anything more about Lauren to like her immensely. She cared about TJ and wanted him to be happy.

"That was why Michelle was attracted to him," Delaney added. "That's what Tucker says anyway. Michelle needed someone who was stable, to be her rock. That was TJ. But because he *wasn't* a big partier, she would get bored and they'd end up fighting and breaking up. Then, eventually, she'd be right back, needing his help."

Lauren sighed. "When she showed up on his doorstep, pregnant and pathetic, he went way beyond responsible. He worried all the time. He was uptight, perpetually pissed off. Being with that bitch twenty-four-seven ruined him."

Hope didn't move. She didn't even breathe deeply. She didn't want these women to realize they were spilling all of TJ's secrets and stop. She wanted to know *everything*. Michelle had been pregnant? With TJ's baby? Was that the boy Delaney had mentioned Michelle left behind when she came to party in Sapphire Falls?

"Then she told him the baby wasn't his and left to be with his real father and he hasn't been the same since," Phoebe said. "I didn't know him before all of that, but Tucker and the other guys say that he's really withdrawn into his own bubble now. I think he's great, but he definitely seems unhappy a lot of the time."

Michelle had *lied* to TJ about the baby being his? And had then left him? Hope hadn't known TJ long, but she knew deep, deep inside that losing the child he'd thought was his son had been worse than losing Michelle.

She really wanted to slap Michelle. Hard. More than once. And Hope had never wanted to do harm to another person.

"So you can see why we would love for him to really fall for someone," Delaney said, focusing on Hope again.

"Delaney and Tucker said it was so nice seeing him happy last night," Lauren said. "I'm so glad you're here."

The breath caught in Hope's chest. She looked around the room and saw the same thing on everyone's faces—hope. Ironically.

Including TJ's mother's.

Oh...crap.

She wanted TJ to be happy too. She'd already surmised that he needed to have some fun, to spend time with a woman who truly liked him and had no other agenda. But it was *some* time. Short-term. The summer, at most. Now these women, who she was growing to actually like, in spite of the fact they knew a scary number of details about everyone's lives, were looking at her as if she was some kind of savior.

She really liked TJ. And she thought that some fun with her could go a long way toward healing his heart. But she was going to leave eventually. And these women would all hate her then.

"TJ and I are just getting to know each other," she started.

Adrianne laughed. "You guys are scaring her," she said to Lauren and Delaney. She turned to Hope. "Don't worry. We know you just got here."

"But this is Sapphire Falls," Phoebe said with a grin.

Hope looked at her, worried for some reason. "What does that mean?"

"People fall in love fast here," Kate said.

Love? Yeah, she was going to have to be careful here. She wanted to have a fun fling. She wanted *TJ* to have a fun fling. Love was something else altogether.

"Fast?" Hope repeated. "Like how fast?"

"Two or three days," Phoebe said happily.

Two or three *days*? Hope shook her head. "But not TJ. He's way too..."

"Grumpy?" Delaney asked.

"Cynical?" Lauren offered.

"Serious," Adrianne supplied.

"Ooh, suspicious!" Phoebe said, as if they were playing a game.

"Yes, all of that," Hope said. "TJ does *not* seem like the type of guy to fall in love easily or fast."

"But he's a Bennett man."

This comment came from the woman sitting at the counter, sipping a cup of coffee and smelling like wintergreen cream.

Kathy Bennett.

Delaney and Lauren nodded in response. The other girls just grinned at Hope.

"What do you mean?" Hope asked Kathy, almost not wanting to know but not able to *not* know.

"My sons are hardly perfect," Kathy said with a smile full of affection. "But they know what love is, and when they find it, they figure it out quickly and hold on tight."

Hope felt an almost painful twinge in her...all over...at that.

"But at this point," Kathy said. "I'm just thrilled you're here to help with his shoulder and make him smile."

"He hasn't done *a lot* of smiling yet," Hope said honestly.

"Oh, I saw how he was looking at you this morning. He was smiling on the inside," Kathy said.

Smiling on the *inside*? And how had he been looking at her?

"How can you tell if he's smiling on the inside?" Kate asked.

"Mothers just know," Kathy said. "And that's all I really need for TJ right now. Fun and friendship come first anyway."

"And sex," Lauren said. She looked at her mother-in-law and pointed at her pregnant belly. "Pretty obvious we do it."

Kathy almost choked on her coffee but she gave Lauren a grin. "And I hope you keep it up. I want lots of grandchildren." She glanced at Delaney.

Delaney held up her hands. "I gave you *four. At once.*"

"And I love them to pieces," Kathy agreed. "Makes me want four more just like them."

Delaney laughed. "Just like them? I thought you liked me, Kathy."

"So, honey," Kathy said to Hope. "We're not talking grand-kids from you. Lauren and Delaney are on that. If you can just make TJ smile and realize that sometimes people want to take care of *him* too, I would be eternally grateful."

Oh, God. His mother wanted to be *grateful* to her.

Hope took a deep, cleansing breath that didn't do one thing to calm her down.

But she couldn't ignore the truth—she wasn't the only one who thought TJ needed and deserved happiness. She also wasn't the only one who thought she could be the one to help him find it. And she couldn't leave that alone, even if she should. If they all hated her when she left, well, there wasn't anything she could do about that. Because if she could give TJ one fun, sweet, hot summer, she was going to do it.

"So you think TJ will be at the bar tonight?" she asked.

"He will if you are," Phoebe said.

"Even before he knows about the short shorts," Lauren added. "But I really need to be sitting facing the door when he comes in and sees you."

"Okay, I'm going tonight," Peyton said.

Hope turned to her. "Really?" That was great. Hope could get to know her better and show her that alcohol didn't have to be part of a good time. Then when she left Sapphire Falls, she would feel as though she'd been a good big sister.

"Yeah," Peyton said. "Michelle is in town this weekend."

Hope's stomach knotted instantly. "*Michelle* Michelle?"

"TJ's ex," Peyton confirmed.

"And you think she'll be there tonight?" Oh, wow, how Hope wanted to meet this woman.

"Oh, definitely. And she'll probably be looking for you."

"For me?"

Peyton smiled. "You don't think you could be in this town for twenty-four hours and not have people know all about you, do you? And I guarantee Michelle knows you're here. With TJ."

"And that's going to be a problem?" Hope guessed. Based on Peyton's tone and on the history Hope knew about, she was sure it was going to be a problem.

"Oh yeah. But I'll be there." Peyton patted her shoulder. "I can take her."

"Take her?" Hope felt like a parrot.

"If she tries to start something with you. I'll have your back."

Peyton moved off to help finish cleaning up the kitchen while Hope pondered her new situation.

TJ's mother wanted her to make him happy. All of his sisters-in-law and friends wanted her to make him happy. No pressure there.

And her sister who didn't even know she was her sister would have her back when TJ's ex came looking for her at the local bar.

And she was going to be wearing short cut-off denim shorts. Great.

None of that sounded dramatic at all.

TJ would be thrilled.

9

Hope hadn't come back to the house all day. TJ hadn't seen her at lunch when he'd gone in to eat at three p.m. when he'd come up with an excuse—that he hadn't needed—to stop at the house, or at six when he'd finished work for the day and come home.

Where the hell was she?

And why was it driving him so insane?

She'd been here for one day. One freaking day. And she wasn't *actually* his girlfriend. She was his houseguest, at best. It didn't matter where she was, and she had no reason to keep him apprised of her agenda for the day.

It was still driving him insane.

Too restless to make dinner and settle in for the evening, and not in the mood to face his mother's dinner table and all of the inevitable questions, he headed to town. He could grab some food and catch his nephew Henry's baseball game with Tucker and Delaney.

Henry was twelve and loved all sports. Getting involved with the summer baseball program in Sapphire Falls had been the perfect way for him to meet kids his age and make some friends before the school year started.

TJ grabbed some concessions and headed for the field. Tucker was standing at the fence, coaching Henry during their warm-ups, and his brother Travis was seated on the metal bleachers. He chuckled and climbed up to settle next to Travis.

"Staying out of the house?" he asked.

Travis's wife, Lauren, was hugely pregnant, two weeks from her due date, and had been...difficult...over the past two months.

Travis grinned and dug into TJ's bag of popcorn. "Actually, Lauren's out of the house too."

"What's she doing?" And did she know where Hope was? But TJ managed to keep the last question to himself.

"She's going out with the girls."

"The girls" usually included Adrianne Riley, Phoebe Spencer, Delaney almost-Bennett and Kate Leggot-soon-to-be-Spencer. He wondered if it included Hope tonight.

"Including Hope," Travis added with a grin that said he knew TJ had been wondering.

Travis was actually a really good brother.

"I'm glad the girls have hit it off," TJ said casually, lifting his root beer for a drink.

It didn't escape him how strange that was. He never wanted the women he was messing around with to get involved with his family. They'd been through enough because of Michelle. But something about Hope being a part of the circle of women that TJ thought of as some of the best on the planet felt good.

Maybe because he wasn't messing around with her. Or hadn't. Really. Yet.

"How's it going with her?" Travis asked.

"I'm having a hard time keeping her clothes on her," he admitted.

Travis looked at him with wide eyes. "Oh?"

"Topless sunbathing yesterday. Naked yoga this morning," TJ confirmed.

"Not topless yoga, but *naked* yoga?"

TJ nodded grimly.

Travis looked surprised, then impressed, then amused. "I can't think of a single reason why any of that is a bad thing."

"It makes it ha—difficult to remember that I've known her just over twenty-four hours," TJ said.

Travis laughed. "If Lauren had taken her top off within twenty-four hours of meeting me, it would have saved me two years of blue balls."

TJ couldn't help but laugh at that.

"And look at Tucker and Delaney. He had her out in the barn the first night she was in town."

TJ shook his head. "I know." And he'd really thought that was rushing it, going too fast, but seeing his brother with his fiancé now, there was no question they were meant to be together.

TJ sighed. Maybe he didn't know anything at all. That actually wouldn't surprise him that much.

"And Lauren said Hope's hot," Travis said. "Enjoy the view, I say."

TJ felt the root beer slid down the wrong pipe and he had to hack for a moment before he could reply. "Oh yeah?"

Travis grinned and held up his phone. The message from Lauren read, *It's HOT in this kitchen and we're not even using the ovens. Hope is something.*

TJ coughed lightly. Hope definitely was something. And hot. "Pregnancy hormones?"

It was a well-known fact that Lauren was bisexual. Travis loved to brag about the fact that he'd won her over even with her having twice the options to choose from. Most of the time, Lauren thought that was funny and would make a smart-ass quip back, or simply roll her eyes. Once in a while, she'd go off on a rant about how being bisexual didn't mean that she'd simply fuck anyone who came along or that she was attracted to *all* women any more than Travis was attracted to *all* women.

The *last* time Travis had said it was about five weeks ago when bitchy-pregnant Lauren had replaced happy-and-glowing-pregnant Lauren. The Lauren who had been fortunate enough to have an incredibly easy first two trimesters had been kidnapped and killed by the third-trimester Lauren. Nobody messed with third-trimester Lauren.

When Travis had made his dumb-ass comment, she'd whirled on him and ranted for ten straight minutes about how a person's sexuality couldn't be so easily defined and how society's small-minded assumptions about things they didn't understand was only contributing to more fear and hatred when people should be embracing each other's differences and diversity or, at the very least, minding their own fucking business.

"Not hormones. Hope's Lauren's type," Travis said to TJ's question.

TJ marveled, not for the first time, at his brother's open-mindedness and confidence. It didn't bother Travis a bit that Lauren occasionally found women attractive—and commented on it. Having known Travis for thirty-three years, that was a level of maturity TJ was happy to see and hadn't really expected.

Travis turned his phone again so TJ could see the photo he had pulled up.

It was of Hope. Her hair was down, the blue streaks bright on Travis's screen. She was smiling, the look on her face the same one he'd seen in his kitchen when she'd been talking about oils and stuff with Delaney and Tucker—passion and happiness.

Two things he'd love to see in another room in his house.

Or any room actually, but in regards to another topic entirely.

And with fewer clothes.

TJ looked up at his brother and knew instantly that he had not hidden his feelings well. Travis was looking at him with a knowing grin.

"Wait for it." Travis touched his phone's screen, reducing the size of the photo.

As it shrank, more of the scene was revealed.

Like the fact that Hope was standing in front of Kate. Kate was seated on a wooden stool in Adrianne's shop's kitchen. She was wearing shorts and had one foot propped up on the countertop next to her.

And Hope's hand was on Kate's inner thigh. High on her inner thigh.

"Acupressure for increasing sexual excitement," Travis said. "Or so I've been told."

TJ couldn't look away from the screen. "Holy..."

"That's exactly what I thought." Tucker dropped onto the bleacher in front of them. "Levi's gonna flip when he sees that picture."

"Already forwarded it to him," Travis said with a grin.

"Reply?" Tucker asked.

"Nope. But Lauren said Kate went home to change her clothes and hasn't shown back up yet."

They all laughed. And TJ felt a little jealous.

Not that the envy was something new. He was surrounded by happy couples—more all the time. Seeing his brothers and friends fall in love and make homes and build families was amazing. If not hard to take once in a while.

He had wanted the same thing. So much so that he'd let the desire blind him to the fact that he and Michelle had been missing some very key components—like mutual respect, friendship and trust. Just to name a few.

Did he wonder sometimes what it would be like to be in a relationship where you not only wanted to be naked with your girl all the time, but where you laughed and shared and *liked* each other? Sure. And he did believe it could happen. There were examples all around him.

But he also knew it didn't happen that way for everyone.

There were examples of that all around too.

They sat through the first three innings of Henry's game, talking and joking, cheering and coaching.

Delaney showed up just in time to see Henry snag a line drive up the middle and turn a double play. She climbed into the bleachers with a huge grin. "Hey, guys."

She leaned in to kiss Tucker. When they parted, Tucker smacked his lips. "Margarita."

She laughed and nodded. "Had to have one with the girls before I headed over here."

"You didn't drive, did you?" Tucker asked with a frown.

"I walked. It's like six blocks," she said with a shake of her head. "But Lauren asked me to send you over to the Come Again," she said to Travis. "She's really tired."

"Well, I know she's not drunk," Travis said, stretching to his feet. "How's her mood?"

"Great."

Travis looked skeptical.

Delaney laughed. "Seriously. Hope did this massage to her lower back and gave her lavender oil. It's supposed to help her sleep at night but it's also really mellowed her. Said her back feels a lot better. She's pretty content."

Travis looked at TJ. "I'm telling you right now, if you don't want to keep her and she's managed to soften up third-trimester Lauren, we might just have to make it a threesome at my house."

Travis was kidding. Well, he was ninety-percent kidding.

And TJ knew it. But it still bugged him to think about someone else wanting Hope.

"You're hilarious," TJ told him.

"You might want to go with him," Delaney said to TJ.

"Why's that?"

"Hope's at the Come Again too."

Yeah, he'd figured. But clearly she was having a good time. She'd come to Sapphire Falls on an adventure, and Lord knew, meeting some of the other people in town could be adventurous.

"Hope's pretty used to doing her own thing," he said. "Doubt she's missing me."

"Oh, come on," Delaney said. "She's hanging out with Peyton and Lauren and Phoebe and Kate right now, but I'm sure she'd love it if you showed up."

"Peyton's with them?" TJ asked, trying to act nonchalant. Hope's little sister. The first family she'd really been with since her mom died. One of two people who were the only family she had left in the world. He swallowed hard. How was she? Happy, upset, regretful?

"Yeah, she's working at the Sweet Shop now," Delaney said. "She was there when we were talking about it and Hope asked her along."

Uh huh. And how *was* she? Was she sad? Was she considering telling Peyton who she was? Had she already?

But he couldn't exactly swoop in there and ask her all of those questions.

"And Michelle's in town," Delaney said. "According to Peyton, anyway. We didn't see her down there, but it's early."

But for *that*—he could definitely swoop in there.

Hope had been in town all day. If Michelle was back this weekend, she would have heard about Hope. She'd be looking for her, in fact.

Yeah, he needed to go to the Come Again.

"Okay, talk to you later," TJ said as he stood.

Delaney grinned. "Call if you need backup."

He wasn't going to need backup. Michelle was going to mind her manners and everything would be fine.

Probably.

Ten minutes later, TJ strode through the doors of the Come Again.

He glanced around quickly but didn't see Hope or Michelle.

Peyton was sitting at one of the tall tables in the corner across the dance floor with a friend. He couldn't see who it was, with her back to him, but it looked like Peyton was drinking soda. Interesting, but not his biggest priority at the moment.

"TJ!"

He turned toward the voice and found that Travis and Lauren were still there. They were sitting at a table with Phoebe and Joe.

He pulled out a chair at their table. "So false alarm."

"What do you mean?" Phoebe asked.

"Heard that Hope was here with you guys and that Michelle was in town."

Phoebe's eyebrows went up. "Is she? Oh, this will be good."

"She's not here," TJ pointed out.

"Not yet."

"Even so," TJ said, admitting that the chances of Michelle showing up at the Come Again were about as good as the sun coming up tomorrow. "Hope left." And he was wondering how long he had to sit here and bullshit with his friends before he could leave to go back to the farm without it looking pathetic.

"Hope didn't leave," Phoebe said with a grin. Her eyes focused on something behind TJ and she pointed. "In fact, it doesn't look like Jason's going to be letting her go for a while."

TJ turned slowly, already sure he wasn't going to like what he was about to see.

Hope was involved. Which meant it was going to drive him crazy.

Sure enough, it took him only three seconds to locate her this time. She was on the dance floor in the arms of another man. And not just any other man. Jason Gilmore—*Doctor* Jason Gilmore, if they were being specific. Jason was twenty-eight, good-looking, charming, a hometown boy who had returned home with his medical degree in hand to heal the sick and improve the lives of those in Sapphire Falls.

To hear people talk, the man could cure any illness with the simple laying on of hands.

And until that moment, it hadn't annoyed TJ one bit.

Now, however, Jason was laying his hands on Hope. And TJ cared a lot.

Then there was the matter of her clothes.

She was wearing cut-off denim jeans, and he suspected Phoebe had something do with how they'd been chopped. She had a tendency to cut them short.

Hope was also wearing a fitted baby-blue T-shirt and had her hair pulled up into a high ponytail.

And the I'm-so-fucked clincher—she wore cowboy boots on her feet.

They had to be borrowed. TJ could tell they were scuffed enough that they'd been worn by a girl who actually *wore* boots for reasons other than dancing on a Saturday night. But scuffs or not, they looked hot.

Hope looked hot.

She looked like...a Sapphire Falls girl. And that did something to TJ's gut—and lower—that he could no more stop than he could prevent snow falling at Christmas time. He was a country boy who had been raised to love, appreciate, respect and want country girls. Reacting to denim and ponytails and boots was in his blood.

His brain might know that Hope wasn't a true country girl,

but his body only saw denim and skin. A lot of skin. A lot of skin that he knew smelled like wild flowers and felt like silk.

Dammit.

That woman.

TJ sighed and turned back to the table. Everyone was watching him for a reaction, and hell if he knew what that reaction should be. Part of him wanted to stomp over there and pull them apart. That would be an understandable response if she was really his girlfriend, he supposed. Though Jason wasn't doing anything inappropriate.

On the other hand, the fact that he *wanted* to stomp over there and pull them apart made him nervous. He didn't want any more drama. He didn't want jealousy and distrust and fights and stress. Even if it was fake. His entire relationship with Michelle had been about those things. Michelle had flirted— and more—with men to get TJ's attention and to goad him into reacting to show he cared.

He'd cared all right.

She'd made a damn fool of him repeatedly.

She'd always known exactly the right buttons to push to get him going, and his possessiveness had given her some kind of strange thrill.

He was not going to do that with Hope. Or anyone. But definitely not with Hope. She was a sham girlfriend who was leaving. Sometime. Eventually.

In any case, he was not going to be a fool over her. He was not going to make a scene. He was *not* going to get possessive and stupid and crazy.

"You okay?" Phoebe asked him.

Phoebe had grown up in Sapphire Falls. She'd left for a few years to get her teaching degree, but she'd come home to teach as soon as she'd graduated. She was a hometown girl through and through. Which meant she knew every bit of his history with Michelle and had been there to witness a lot of it.

"I'm fine."

"You're not going out there?"

He shook his head and grabbed the glass of root beer the waitress automatically brought for him. Everyone knew that he'd given up alcohol...and why. He and Michelle and alcohol had never been a good combination.

"Really?" Phoebe asked. "*You're* not going over there to cut in where another guy is dancing with your girl?"

Yeah, yeah. It was unusual for him to be relaxed and laid-back about a woman.

He was laid-back about the women he dated in other towns, but no one here got to see that or got to know those women. And he was laid-back about them because he didn't really *care*. He liked them. He treated them well. He loved the time he spent in the two towns about thirty minutes in either direction from Sapphire Falls. But he wasn't invested. He wasn't committed. Those relationships were not even exclusive.

One woman was a veterinarian who was devoting all of her time and energy to her practice and didn't have time for a relationship. She and TJ got together when they needed to let off some steam. She liked it hard and fast and dirty and kicked his ass out of bed at five in the morning when she headed to work.

Another was a single mom of two who had a girls' night out once a month and needed a guy she knew and trusted to remind her that she was a woman in addition to being a mom. She needed someone who knew his way around a G-spot but who was happy to head home to his own bed after rocking her world for a couple of hours. The kids stayed at Grandma's house and she got an orgasm *and* to sleep in the next morning without having to make breakfast for anyone. TJ loved the phone calls from both of those women.

"She's dancing with him," he finally said of Hope. "No big deal."

He wasn't committed or invested with her, either.

Except...he was.

TJ's grip tightened on his glass but he didn't show a bit of the tension to Phoebe.

"Hope is completely different from Michelle," he said. That was absolutely true. And he'd do well to remember it too. Hope didn't seem like the type to play games. She wasn't dancing with Jason to make TJ jealous. He was sure she was dancing with him because she'd wanted to dance and Jason was a willing partner. Or something.

Of course, she was playing *his* online-girlfriend-gone-crazy game. And she seemed to be enjoying it.

And what did he really know about her anyway? Everything she'd said to him from minute one could have been a lie. She seemed to be rolling with all of the other lies—like being madly in love with him, for instance—easily and happily.

He hadn't known her since she was finger-painting in kindergarten like the other women he'd dated in Sapphire Falls. He had no idea if she was even really into essential oils and such. She could be dumping vanilla extract into hand lotion and *telling* him it was a cure-all.

Hell, maybe his shoulder wasn't even better. Maybe she'd just talked him into it. Maybe her sweet smile and sexy ears and gorgeous breasts had brainwashed him into *believing* he felt better.

Maybe—

The scent of honeysuckle hit him a millisecond before he heard her say hi.

He looked up at Hope standing by his side, smiling at him as if she had never been happier to see anyone. And that was all it took for him to be right back under her spell.

"Hi."

"Dance with me." She held out her hand.

He stood and took it. Without a glance around the table—

that would show only knowing smiles—he pulled her to the bar. They needed to talk.

There were people clustered at the bar as well, but he wasn't going to be seeing any of them around his mother's table in the near future. If any of them overheard anything stupid or pitiful come out of his mouth, at least they wouldn't bring it up over pot roast.

"Come on. Let's dance," Hope said, tugging on his hand when she realized they were moving away from the dance floor.

He pulled her around in front of him, tucking her between him and the bar and lowering his voice. "I don't do jealous, Hope. If you're trying to get me worked up dancing with Jason, it won't work. If you're trying to get *him* worked up by dancing with me, you can forget it."

She looked up at him. She had to tip her head back with him so close. "You don't do jealous?"

Of course he did. He didn't *want* to. He'd thought he was over it. He was thirty-four and knew better. But did he fucking *hate* seeing her with another man? Definitely.

"I don't do games," he said.

"Good."

She pressed into him and TJ was sure she could feel that being close to her was affecting him.

"I was just dancing, TJ. He asked and I like to dance, so I said yes. No games. Nothing underneath it. Nothing more to it."

He couldn't help himself. He lifted his hand and ran his fingers over the ends of her hair. He liked it up away from her face. He could see the length of her neck and every one of her earrings and the way her freckles started darker over the bridge of her nose and got lighter as they dotted her cheekbones toward her ears. But he couldn't help the thought of gripping that ponytail and using it to angle her head perfectly for his kiss or to tip her head back and expose her throat for his lips and tongue. And he could easily imagine pulling the elastic band loose so that her hair would spill over his pillow while he...

He took a deep breath. "Sorry. Maybe I do still do jealous."

She tipped her head to one side and got that look in her eye that said she was realizing something, and TJ cursed internally. Why did he do that? Why did he say stuff like that? *Dance with me, TJ. No thanks, Hope.* Why couldn't he have *that* conversation with her?

"So she used other guys to manipulate your feelings, huh?" she finally said. "She liked it when you were jealous? Geez, TJ, the sex must have been *really* good. You put up with a lot of bullshit."

Her reaction surprised him. Which shouldn't have surprised him.

"Yes, I did," he said. "And...it was."

It had been. The sex had been really good. And he was mature enough now to admit that he'd chosen getting laid over his pride more than once.

"Dance with me," she said. But she didn't try to move him from the spot he was on. She just looked up at him with challenge in her eyes.

"I don't really—"

She put her hand on his chest, directly over his heart. "No manipulations. No one else. Just you and me. And dancing. And seduction."

She slipped around him and started for the dance floor. He still held her hand, so he turned with her, the word *seduction* distracting him enough that she got him out in the midst of the other couples before he stopped.

"Seduction?"

Hope smiled up at him and he was, as of that very moment, completely seduced.

"I want you," she said simply. "I want to get you naked and know every inch of you. I want to feel you against every inch of me. I want to stay up all night learning what you like and giving it to you over and over again."

He stared at her. *Holy shit.*

What word went beyond seduced? Consumed? Obsessed?

"Hope—"

"I also want to dance with you. And I want to rub your shoulder. And I want to know your favorite movie. And I want to tell you my favorite poem. And I want to ask you to take me for ice cream. And I know you're not the poetry type and I don't eat ice cream anymore. So all of this is a little overwhelming for me too. So I was hoping that maybe we could just dance. For now."

Consumed and obsessed it was.

"I don't dance," he told her.

Her smile fell, and TJ wasn't sure the last time he'd felt an actual loss when someone stopped smiling.

"But to show you just how far gone I am here," he said, moving in closer. "I'm going to tonight."

She lit up just like that, and TJ had a premonition of absolute heartbreak when she left town.

Then he was pulled out of anything even close to melancholy by Hope beginning to dance.

She swiveled her hips, she moved her shoulders, she moved her head, her hair swinging, and TJ just stared. With a stupid grin on his face. Watching her move in one of her flowy skirts or dresses would have been enticing, but the fitted denim and cotton showed every curve and every shimmy and was almost as good as naked yoga.

But the truth was she was not doing those boots justice.

"What are you doing?" he asked after a moment.

"Dancing."

"Sunshine, *that* is not how you dance to Dierks Bentley."

She stopped. "Who?"

He shook his head and stepped toward her. He took one of

her hands and put his other on her lower back, bringing her up against his body.

"*This* is how you dance in Sapphire Falls." And he began to two-step her around the dance floor.

Hope caught on easily, letting him lead her, allowing her body to move with his. Like every man who had ever two-stepped, twisted or tangoed with a woman he wanted, TJ was caught up in the sensuality of the dance, regardless of the tempo or lyrics to the music.

"I thought you said you couldn't dance," Hope said, looking up at him with a smile of pure pleasure.

"I said I don't dance, not that I couldn't." He took the chance to twirl her, making her laugh. He felt his own mouth curl. "Boys in Sapphire Falls learn to country swing and two-step early on because it's the best way to get a girl up against you when you're too young to have a truck."

"Trucks get girls up against you?" she asked.

TJ gave her a full grin at that. "There's somethin' about a truck." It was also one of his favorite songs.

Hope seemed to be thinking about that. "I guess I hadn't really analyzed why I want to be up against you," she finally said. "I thought it had something to do with your wide shoulders and gruff exterior and sweet underneath, but maybe you're right—it might be the truck."

"Gruff exterior and *sweet underneath*?" he repeated. "What's that mean?"

. Except he knew. The gruff exterior was something he'd been working on perfecting. The sweet underneath—well, that was something Hope was seeing that no one else did. Anymore.

The sweet stuff had been what convinced Michelle that he was the perfect sucker to give her everything she wanted.

But it seemed he couldn't help it with Hope. Because he trusted her? Maybe. Because she didn't seem to really want *anything* from him? Possibly. Because he wasn't even sure he could help give her what she did want from her trip here? Probably. Or maybe it was because *she* was sweet.

He didn't typically go for sweet girls. Hope certainly had a spicy streak in her too, it seemed. But her caring and kindness, her sincerity, her outlook on things and the way she seemed to truly see him—and like him anyway—all gave her a sweetness he was having a hell of a time resisting.

Maybe that was bringing out the sweetness in him.

He cringed even thinking that. Sweetness was for saps.

But he couldn't remember the last time he'd hidden in the dark with a girl, whispering and giggling so they wouldn't be found. Or the last time he'd turned down sex because it was too fast, too soon, too—whatever. He had never called a woman Sunshine before. He hadn't called a woman by an endearment in what felt like forever, as a matter of fact. He steered away from female tears, yet he'd instinctively pulled Hope close when she'd cried. He stayed far away from crazy, but he had this one already moved into his house, along with her potions and creams and insights and auras.

Yep, he was showing his sweet underbelly.

Fuck.

"You *are* sweet," Hope told him as they made their way around the dance floor. "And I know you don't like that. So I thought maybe you'd want a chance to show me how...unsweet you can be."

TJ tripped over his own feet.

She smiled up at him as he made himself focus to re-find the rhythm.

"Dammit, girl," he muttered.

"It's not my first night in town anymore," she said.

He frowned down at her even as heat coursed through him. It wasn't her first night in town and, as *crazy* as it was, it felt as if she'd been here a lot longer than she had. He'd never gotten to know a woman as quickly and as easily as he had Hope. She was an open book. Or, more accurately, an open diary. She felt her feelings and thought her thoughts out loud. And she'd inspired that in him as well. She'd figured things out about him that he doubted even some of the people in this very room knew. When he'd been wild and happy and in love, he'd let his feelings show. Then Michelle had made a fool of him, and he'd determined not to do that again.

But Hope had gotten under his skin. Fast.

"And there you go propositioning and offering everything to a guy you barely know."

Maybe she did that all the time. Maybe that was her thing —finding guys in all of the towns between Sedona and Sapphire Falls and having flings. Maybe he was nothing special.

But the way she looked up at him didn't feel practiced or calculated or routine. She actually looked as amazed by all of this as he did.

She was just the type to embrace being amazed.

"I do know you, TJ."

"So you say."

"But you're trying to protect me from something," she said. "What is it? Heartbreak because there won't be a diamond ring in the morning? Or maybe disappointment because there won't even be breakfast in the morning? Or are you telling me that the sex isn't going to be any good? Because…I have a cream for that."

The smile she gave him was full of mischief and sass, and TJ felt everything in him respond to it. He wanted all of that mischief and sass in his bedroom. Because with her, he felt like he could dive into it. He wouldn't be wondering what she was really thinking about, he wouldn't worry about doing or saying something wrong, he wouldn't have to just follow her lead. He felt like he could take the lead. With Hope, he knew he could give into *his* desires.

"I have a cream...and a few other things...for that too," he replied easily.

She lifted an eyebrow.

"But I don't know how to cook breakfast for a vegan."

"You wouldn't anyway. You wouldn't want me to think you wanted me to stick around."

"You're living in my house, Sunshine. That's kind of sticking around."

"But I'm not living there because of you," she said. "That's different, right?"

It was. He nodded.

"So I need you to know that tonight when I go home with you, it *is* about you," she said. "When you take me into your bedroom, it's not about anything or anyone but the two of us. No matter what brought me here, tonight is because I want *you*."

He felt as if she'd sucked all the air from his lungs.

Hope was completely up front about everything. He loved that about her. He loved a lot of things about her. Like the fact that he truly felt as if he could be himself.

He liked the wild, crazy, hot sex that Michelle had been into. But that was all it had ever been—a physical release, a dirty fantasy.

With Hope, he wanted the—*shit*—he wanted the sweet stuff. He wanted to talk to her while he undressed her and kissed every inch of her body, but he didn't want to talk dirty. He wanted to tell her how beautiful she was, how amazing she made him feel, how he wanted to make *her* feel. He wanted to kiss her, long and deep, and *only* kiss her, for hours.

What was wrong with him? The girl who was leaving? The girl who had blown into his life *yesterday*?

The vegan girl who talked about energies and practiced acupressure and God knew what else? The hippie girl with pink—or blue—hair who carried an apothecary box in her car with her?

Of all of the women in Sapphire Falls at that moment, she was the *last* one he should be getting sweet with. He should put her up against the wall in the back room of the Come Again and fuck her.

And be done with it.

"I'm into some kinky stuff," he said. Maybe he could scare her off.

"Like what?" She seemed legitimately interested.

Of course. That was just like her. And was the opposite of what he wanted. So...of course.

They were still dancing, but at some point the music had slowed considerably and Hope had moved close and wrapped her arms around his neck. It had all happened so naturally. As if they'd been doing it forever. She fit with him. As if she'd been made to be there in his arms.

And these whimsical thoughts were making him nuts.

His hands rested on her hips and he was suddenly acutely aware of the feel of the denim rubbing against his palms as her hips moved.

Maybe it wasn't his thoughts making him nuts. Maybe it was just this woman—and the way she looked and moved and laughed and thought and felt.

"I might want to dress you up as a sexy secretary and pretend I'm your asshole millionaire boss and insist that you give me a blowjob on my desk." There. He needed to add some hard reality into all of this fanciful stuff that seemed to be swirling around him since Hope hit town.

Okay, so dressing up in costumes and role-playing wasn't maybe *reality*, but it sure wasn't in the same category as auras and energies and a new obsession with sparkly earrings.

But his comment didn't make Hope look *less* interested. "Uh huh," she said mildly.

He narrowed his eyes. "Maybe I'll put you over my knee and spank your ass when you say 'uh huh' to me like that."

She laughed at that. Laughed.

He clearly needed to work on his scowling or his dominant tone of voice. Or something.

"What about Ben Wa balls?" she asked.

TJ almost reacted to that. Almost.

It had turned into a sexy game of chicken. That he was going to win.

"What do you know about Ben Wa balls?"

And wow, did he suddenly want to take her out dancing in public knowing that she was wearing some.

"They're great for pelvic floor strengthening," she said conversationally. "A strong pelvic floor is important to having a good core. And I have amazing strength in my pelvic floor. Yoga, you know."

He'd love an in-person demonstration of that strength.

So much for scaring her off. So much for worrying about being sweet with her.

The way it was going, they weren't going to make it out of the parking lot.

They danced for a moment without talking. But this was Hope, so it really was only a moment.

"Just so you know, I'd do anything for you."

He tripped again.

He tried to recover his cool but was very afraid he'd never have a lot of cool where she was concerned. He would swear that she knew exactly the moment to say exactly the words that would make him fall all over himself.

Except that she wasn't Michelle.

Hope was saying what she was thinking when she was thinking it because she couldn't *not* say it. Not because she was plotting or scheming or trying to get a reaction from him. She was seducing him just by being her.

Hope was into him. Everything about her body language, her eye contact, her words, her...*vibe*—and TJ knew he was losing it then—told him that she was all in here. With him. Because of him. Not because of something he'd done or because she was trying to keep him on the hook as her plan B, but because she wanted him.

Scars, wounds, frowns and snarls and all.

"Do you want me to make you use Ben Wa balls?" he asked.

"I would use them."

"Really." He knew she would.

And he might die from oxygen deprivation to his brain.

"Whatever you need, TJ."

And in that moment, he wanted it all. It *all*. He wanted her against the wall in back. He wanted her naked, wriggling on his truck seat, condensation running down the insides of his windows from their heat. He wanted her on the dock in the moonlight. He wanted her bent over his kitchen table. He wanted her spread out on his bed. And he wanted her next to him at Sunday dinner and holding his hand in the town square and beside him on the bleachers at Henry's next game and dancing with him, just like this, every time he danced for the rest of his life.

He let go of her and stepped back as if she'd suddenly turned into a pissed-off mountain lion.

Fuck.

The woman was messing with him. Bad.

Michelle leaving had devastated him, had changed him, and that was after *years*.

Hope had been here for two days.

He was going to be so thoroughly fucked when she left. He should stay away from her.

And that was never going to happen.

"Jesus, Hope." He grabbed her hand and pulled her off the dance floor and to a less-populated corner of the bar. "You don't

ERIN NICHOLAS

even know what you're doing," he said, turning her back to the wall so he could talk to her without anyone hearing.

They could leave, of course, but she'd be naked in his truck before they hit the Welcome to Sapphire Falls sign.

"I know what I'm doing," she said calmly.

"Because you do this a lot?"

"I never do this." She didn't even look offended at his question. "I never *want* to do this. Which makes me think I *need* to do this with you."

"This is part of your magical Sapphire Falls summer?"

She grinned at that. "Hey, I'll take magical sex anywhere I can get it, any time of the year."

He sighed and pushed his hand through his hair. His left hand. Because his shoulder still felt great.

Like magic.

"What if I want to tie you up and share you with three of my friends?" he asked, giving one last attempt at pointing out that going home for sex with a stranger was a bad idea. Even if that stranger felt more connected to you than he maybe ever had to anyone.

"You don't," she said.

"You're so sure?"

"I am." She gave him a nod. "Though maybe you should tie me up. You need to take charge, you need to be totally able to do whatever you want, and you need to feel the power of someone being at your mercy because they totally trust you and want you that much. But you won't share me."

The feeling of power was already coursing through him.

He'd thought she was crazy for claiming she knew him from the very beginning, but right now, he got it. He looked into her eyes and he *knew* that everything she said was right—she liked him, wanted him, she trusted him, and he needed to let her give all of that to him.

"Time to go," he said.

He turned and started for the door with her wrist in his hand.

"Hang on." She was laughing. "I'm ready. Just let me grab my bag." She pointed in the direction of Peyton's table.

He met her eyes. "Hurry."

Her smile died under the intensity of his look. She wet her lips. "Maybe I don't need my bag—"

TJ made himself take a deep breath and relax his expression. "Go get it." He didn't have to haul her out of here like a caveman. No matter how much he wanted to.

He headed for Phoebe and Joe's table. "We're heading out."

"Yeah, got that," Phoebe said. "You two were putting off so much heat they had to bump the AC up."

"Tell everyone..." He thought about it. "Nothing. It's no one's business."

"You're right," Phoebe said with a nod. "But not everyone feels that way." She nodded in the direction of Peyton's table as well.

And TJ felt icy unease trickle down his spine even before he turned.

10

"I'm heading home with TJ," Hope said to Peyton.

She knew her cheeks were flushed and she was breathing and talking too fast. But she didn't care. TJ Bennett was letting her close. He was letting some of his walls down. She wasn't just turned-on—she was feeling pretty damned proud of herself.

The big, grumpy, anti-social farmer was going to rock her world. And vice versa.

"Have fun," Peyton said with a wink. "Call me tomorrow?"

"Definitely," Hope said. She eyed Peyton's glass. "Be good, okay?"

Peyton saluted her with the soda. "I will." She set her glass down and gave Hope a small smile. "Thanks for...everything today. Thanks for listening about my mom and stuff. I know we don't know each other—"

"Hey, we're...friends." Hope prayed Peyton didn't notice the tiny pause. She really had almost said "sisters". For the third time since meeting the younger girl. Damn. It just seemed the longer she was with Peyton, the stronger the feeling became.

Peyton gave her an almost shy smile. "It's weird since we just met, but I feel like we're already close."

"Sometimes it just happens," Hope said. And Peyton wasn't the only one she was feeling it with. She smiled at Peyton. "TJ said something about having a barbecue tomorrow night. Could you come?"

"I'd love to."

Peyton's eyes lit up and Hope felt her throat tighten. She hoped Peyton had friends, but she was afraid maybe they were more drinking buddies.

Well, Hope was going to change that. Hope was going to show Peyton that she didn't need to rely on anyone else for approval or to feel good about herself.

They'd talked for almost an hour after leaving the clothing store with Hope's new ensemble. They'd settled at the table in the bar and ordered non-alcoholic drinks and talked like girl-friends who'd known each other for years. Peyton had confided in Hope about her mother's bipolar disorder and her drinking and that Peyton acted out to get her father's attention. It seemed the only time Dan pulled his focus off JoEllen was when Peyton was at the police station or the ER. Peyton tried not to let it get to her, but every once in a while, she'd break down and do something that she knew would land her in one of those places.

Hope took Peyton's hand and leaned in to give her a hug. "We'll talk more." They had already exchanged phone numbers. "I'm here for a while. We'll have lots of time."

She didn't have to tell Peyton who she was to have a positive influence. Everyone needed friends. And if she could teach her little sister about being more self-sufficient and about seeking her own happiness and approval, then Hope would feel that her trip to Sapphire Falls had been completely worth it. She would not only connect with her half-sister, but she would be able to pass Melody's lessons on to another young woman who needed that strength. She'd come seeking a greater understanding and appreciation for her mom. With Peyton and with the healing she'd done with the women today, she already felt she was honoring Melody and the things she'd tried to pass on to Hope.

And then there was TJ.

Her trip to Sapphire Falls had already been completely worth it.

Maybe it was in the water or air here, or maybe it was in her DNA to go for hot Nebraska farmers, but Hope was very much appreciating this town where her mom had spent a formative summer.

Hope was more than ready to head to the farm. But when she turned to find TJ, a woman was blocking her way. "Oh, excuse me."

She felt Peyton stand up behind her.

"Michelle, don't. Just leave her alone," Peyton said.

Michelle.

The one and only.

Oh boy.

Hope was struck by three things at once about TJ's ex. One, she was gorgeous. Two, she had cold eyes. Three, she smelled like she'd washed her hair in rum.

That was really all she had a chance to catalog, but that was all she needed.

"Hi, Michelle. I'm Hope," she said.

"So he's been talking about me, huh?" Michelle flipped beautiful long black hair over her shoulder. "Don't feel too bad. He's been in love with me for years. It's really more about me than it is about you."

Hope felt her blood pressure rise slightly, and she hated it. She really didn't care what Michelle said or thought of her. Michelle was nothing to her.

Except that she was something to TJ. And TJ had become something to Hope.

Which made the urge to slap Michelle not all that shocking. Foreign, yes. Shocking, no.

However, on the heels of the urge to slap the other woman was something Hope was more familiar with. Empathy.

Something had happened to Michelle to make her like this. Besides, Hope could easily see why it would be hard for her to get over TJ. Hope didn't think *she* was ever going to, and that was after only two days.

She shook her head as that thought wanted to take root for further analysis. Now was not the time.

"I'm very sorry," she said sincerely.

Michelle frowned. "For what?"

"For whoever made you feel like you weren't worth more than this."

Michelle's eyes widened. "*Excuse* me?"

"It's clear that you feel the need to constantly test TJ's friendship. I'm sorry someone made you feel like you can't trust anyone to really care about you even when you're not in trouble or needing help."

Michelle drew herself up tall. She was a couple of inches taller than Hope even without her heels. She was also at least a cup size bigger than Hope and her waist was a good three inches smaller. Dang. Hope could totally see what attracted TJ. Physically anyway. Other than her stunning looks, Michelle absolutely had bitch-on-heels written all over her.

"I can assure you," Michelle said coolly, "that it isn't TJ's *friendship* that I get when I come to town."

Hope nodded. "Right. You get the reassurance that someone will be there for you no matter what." She felt sorry for this woman, she realized. And that was when Hope knew that her mom was with her in spirit.

Seeing beyond Michelle's exterior bitchiness and trying to understand her was completely a Melody thing. Melody would have wanted to reach out to Michelle. She would have taken Michelle's hand and led her to a table where she would have talked to her in a calm, soothing voice about getting centered. She would have taught her breathing and meditation. She would have recommended some time away by herself along with yoga and exercise, healthy eating, affirmations and prayer, or whatever other form of spiritual support Michelle was open to.

Of course, Melody was a nicer person than Hope would ever be.

And all of that would take a lot of time.

"But you really need to find a way to feel strong and worthy *without* TJ. At least for tonight."

Hope understood there was more to Michelle. And she understood that she and TJ had a complicated history. TJ needed to get over being the one to rescue Michelle, and Michelle needed to find her own inner peace. But Hope could only focus on one of them at a time. So right now she was going to choose the hot farmer she wanted to get naked with.

"Oh, and you should google how to get centered and find a peaceful core," Hope said. "That would be a good start."

Peyton was looking back and forth between them as if she didn't know what to think.

"Michelle."

Hope heard TJ's deep voice and looked to find him coming forward, scowling.

"You know what would make me feel better right here and now?" Michelle asked.

Well, crap. If the woman needed to open up to someone, Hope couldn't very well shut her down. Could she? "What?"

"This." Michelle drew her hand back and swung, slapping Hope hard across the cheek.

Intense stinging and burning erupted in Hope's cheek and

her hand flew to cover the spot as she stared at the other woman, speechless. She wasn't sure if she was more hurt or more shocked. She had never been struck by another person in her life.

But she didn't have time to respond. Peyton knocked the table out of the way and lunged at Michelle. Michelle shoved Peyton back, but Peyton grabbed a handful of Michelle's hair.

"You hit like a girl!" Peyton told her.

Peyton definitely had an advantage, being in flat shoes up against Michelle's heels. Not to mention Michelle's blood-alcohol content. Michelle wobbled as Peyton pulled her hair and fell against the chair when her ankle turned. She grabbed Peyton's wrist and swung with a fist at Peyton's stomach.

And then they were being pulled apart.

TJ grabbed Michelle's arms and a good-looking guy wrapped an arm around Peyton's waist, pulling her back.

"You've got to be fucking kidding me," TJ said darkly as he backed Michelle up a couple of steps with his body.

"Dammit, Scott!" Peyton struggled against the other man's hold, but Scott wasn't letting go.

"And keep your fingernails to yourself, P," he said. "It's assault even if I'm not in uniform."

Hope stared at all of them, rubbing her cheek. Wow, TJ hadn't been kidding when he said there was a lot of drama around here. There was also a lot of emotion. And history.

Hope shook her head. She might be in over her head. She wasn't used to people...*expressing* themselves quite like this.

And who knew a slap could hurt that much?

Michelle smirked at Hope from around him. "Nothing to say now, Chatty Cathy?"

"My mother was a pacifist," Hope told her. "She raised me to solve problems by *talking*."

"Well, your voice makes me want to hit someone. And you're the closest someone," Michelle told her.

"Knock it off, Shell," TJ said, stepping in front of Michelle and blocking Hope's view of her.

His back was to Hope, but she definitely heard the nickname, and the way he crowded close to Michelle spoke of how comfortable he was up against the other woman.

That made Hope want to slap her back.

"But my mom and I didn't see eye to eye on everything," Hope told her, advancing a step.

TJ looked at her over his shoulder. "Don't," he said simply.

Hope stopped and looked at him. "I was trying to be nice."

"Well, TJ doesn't really go for *nice*," Michelle said. She'd stopped fighting him but sure hadn't put any space between them.

"Enough," TJ said to Michelle firmly.

He looked at Hope again. "Are you okay?"

She rubbed her cheek once more and then dropped her hand. "Yes."

"I'll take care of this," he said.

Hope wasn't sure she liked how that sounded. "Let her go. I'm fine. We'll just leave."

"Or I can kick her ass for you."

Hope turned to look at her sister. Scott had let go of her, but he grabbed her wrist when she took a step forward. "I don't think so."

"Who—" Hope started.

"I've got it," TJ said firmly to Peyton.

Hope swung back to look at him. She was surprised to find Joe, Travis and Jason suddenly standing behind TJ looking grim.

"I'll take her home," Joe said. He didn't look happy about it.

"I'll help," Travis added, frowning at Michelle.

Jason didn't say anything, but his stance and expression said he was in too.

Hope felt a hand on her shoulder and glanced over to find Lauren and Phoebe standing beside her.

"TJ, think about it," Lauren said. "Don't screw this up."

TJ focused on Hope. Hope met his eyes. In them, she saw a plea to trust him.

Like all of the other things she'd sensed about him, she knew that he needed to know that she was on his side, whatever he did.

She looked around. Things had definitely gotten dramatic. And she was right in the middle of it. She gave him a single nod. "Go."

TJ took Michelle's upper arm in a firm grip and started for the door.

"You're taking her home with you?" Peyton demanded. She elbowed Scott, but he had his thumbs through her belt loops and she didn't get any space.

"I'm taking her to her mom's," TJ said, stopping by a table and grabbing what was evidently Michelle's purse. He gave Hope a pointed look. "I'll see you at the farm."

He herded Michelle out the door. As it shut behind them, Hope became aware that the only sound in the bar was the song playing overhead about trucks being better than cars. Or something.

"What an *ass*," Lauren breathed.

But Hope didn't think he was an ass. He was trying to contain the situation and reduce the drama by removing the instigator. Of course, Michelle had completely instigated the whole thing specifically for the purpose of getting his attention and, probably, getting him alone.

He helped *everyone*. Even the woman who had hurt him more than anyone. And the fact that it made him even more attractive to Hope was confusing as hell. Didn't anyone stand on their own two feet around here? And why was she sort of crazy about the guy who was most often picking them back up?

"It's okay," Hope said, mostly meaning it. "This is their... thing. He needs to have a talk with her, but it can't be tonight when she's drunk and jealous."

"She has no right to be jealous," Lauren said. "*She* left *him*. He's not hers anymore."

But he wasn't really Hope's either. She lifted a shoulder. "He's not the type to leave someone. Even if that person's drunk and bitchy in bar."

And that was something she loved about him. Even as it pissed her off because it hurt him over and over again.

"He's not," Lauren agreed. "I guess it's hard to consider him an ass when he's actually doing something good."

"You have nothing to worry about, you know," Travis said to Hope. "Nothing ever happens between them."

Hope knew that. TJ wouldn't mess with a married woman. The man had integrity coming out of his ears. Hell, Hope wasn't married and had climbed on his lap last night after he'd seen her half-naked and he'd still sent her to bed alone.

"I know," she said. "I'm fine. Really." She looked over at Peyton. "Are *you* okay?"

Peyton glared at Scott, who grinned at her in return. She pushed the table back where it belonged and righted the chair Michelle had knocked over. She sighed as she dropped into it. "I'm fine. She's not as tough as she thinks she is."

Hope sat down across from her. "Well, thanks for defending me. But you didn't have to do that."

"Probably not," Peyton agreed. "TJ was right there. But it felt good." She grinned. "That girl needs more people to stand up to her and tell her to fuck off."

Hope didn't comment on that. Though she kind of agreed.

"Well, you're not going to the farm to wait for him," Phoebe declared, taking another of the chairs at the table.

Hope wished she hadn't vowed to show Peyton that alcohol wasn't always the answer.

It wasn't always the answer. It was rarely the answer. It had probably been over a year since Hope had put anything other than a bit of wine into her body. But she hadn't forgotten the nice warm, fuzzy feeling a shot of something stronger could give.

She wanted to go to the farm and wait for TJ.

He deserved to have someone waiting on him for a change. But she also wished that he'd chosen tonight, had chosen *her*, to be the one to break the Michelle habit.

It was an old, deeply ingrained habit—she got that. Michelle had big problems—she got that too. But the not-quite-as-at-peace-and-enlightened part of her wanted to be reason enough for him to finally say no to his ex.

"See," Hope told Peyton. "You can't let other people steal your happiness. Michelle demands and manipulates TJ into putting her needs first, and when he does, it sucks away *his* peace and sense of self while building Michelle's up. That's not how it should work."

Peyton nodded. "That's what my mom does."

Hope focused on her. "What is?"

"She takes my happiness. She always has to be the most important thing to my dad, and taking care of her sucks so much of his energy that there's nothing left for me."

Hope sat forward and took Peyton's hand. "You can't depend on your dad giving you your energy and happiness anyway," she said. "You have to make your own. Be strong. Do what makes *you* happy. Don't make it about other people. That includes the drinking and partying and the things you do to get his attention," she added. "That's still all about *him*. You need to do things for *you*."

"How do I do that?" Peyton asked. "Just ignore my mom and dad?"

"No." Hope knew about being independent, but she'd never had to *become* independent. That had, essentially, been forced on her. "But when something happens that makes you *unhappy* or makes you feel like you're not important, you need to tell them. And then you need to get away so that you don't keep feeling that way."

"Show them that they can't treat me like that," Peyton said with a nod.

Hope squeezed her hand. "No. Not about them. It's not about how they feel or showing them anything. You need to make yourself feel better. It's about realizing that you have the power to choose and you don't *have* to stay in a situation that makes you unhappy."

"Like what you just did with TJ?" Peyton asked.

Hope glanced toward the door. "Yes. Like I just did with TJ."

Then she immediately looked at the clock over the bar's cash register. How long was he going to be gone? What was he going to do when he realized she wasn't waiting at the farm?

"Hey, who's the guy?" Hope nodded toward the man who'd grabbed Peyton off Michelle. He was leaning against the bar under the clock.

Peyton looked at him with a frown. "Scott Hansen. Our cop."

Hope's eyes widened. "He's a cop?"

Peyton nodded. "I've known him forever. He grew up here too. He was a few years older but I knew him...you know, even before he started hauling me down to the police station."

Scott Hansen was very good-looking. And he was keeping his eye on Peyton.

"He seems interested in using his handcuffs on you," Hope teased.

Peyton snorted. "He's only ever done that *once*. I bitched so loudly that he finally took them off to shut me up."

Hope laughed. "Let's dance." Hope pulled Peyton, Phoebe and Lauren out onto the dance floor. She also caught Jason Gilmore's eye and motioned for him to join them.

Hope didn't know the names of the bands she was dancing to, but she did know that if she was going to be upset about TJ choosing Michelle over her, the music definitely helped. It seemed that a lot of the songs were about kissing in pickup trucks and drinking—also in pickup trucks.

Six songs in, Hope felt a strong hand around her upper arm.

TJ pulled her around. "I went out to the farm."

Hope looked up at him. She didn't say a word, just cocked an eyebrow.

TJ had the good sense to look contrite. "She listens to me. It was faster this way."

She still didn't say anything. She was glad he was back. She knew nothing had happened. She knew that it would take time for him to truly be done with Michelle—if he was *ever* going to be completely done. She knew that she had just gotten to town and had no right to judge him or lecture him or be upset about anything.

He took her hand and pulled her close. "I'm really sorry. I maybe should have let Joe and Travis take her. But—"

"You were protecting them."

He looked at her with mild surprise. "Yes. And her."

Hope lifted both eyebrows.

"They would have chewed her out. Told her she was messing with me. Told her to stop. They would have made her cry."

"Because they would have been trying to protect *you*," Hope said.

He blew out a breath and then gave her a quick nod. "I guess so."

"It's okay to let people help you once in a while. To defend you. To take on some of your problems," she said.

"I'm not good at that."

"I know." She did. And she was again struck by how that

fact about him was something she loved and hated at that same time.

"But she's taken care of now. We have the rest of the night," he said, putting his hands on her hips and pulling her close. "I'm all about you now."

She looked into his eyes. She'd meant what she said to Peyton. Her happiness couldn't be about the things TJ did or didn't do, or should or shouldn't do, or the commotion and emotion in his life. Her happiness was in her control. And being with him tonight would make her happy.

"Then let's go," she said.

His eyes heated and he took her hand. "Hope—"

"I can't believe you went with Michelle." Peyton pushed in next to Hope, frowning at TJ. "Why do you keep giving her your happiness? You need to be stronger than that."

TJ's jaw tightened. His gaze went from Peyton to Hope and lingered. Then he met Peyton's angry glare. "Being there for someone no matter what takes strength."

"She knows you'll always help her. She uses you," Peyton said.

TJ focused on Hope. "I know."

"Why do you let her do that?" Peyton asked.

"Because that's what good guys do. We help people. Even when they don't deserve it or don't help back. Especially when they don't deserve it. Because that's sometimes when they need it the most." He turned to Peyton. "Nobody's alone here."

Hope felt her breath lodge in her chest.

He was so...magnificent when he was all stubborn like this.

He'd tried to be stubborn with her. She knew that from minute one, he had tried to keep his distance, keep his walls up high. But it hadn't worked. And she loved that about him—the softness and sweetness that he couldn't help underneath it all. He might be acting all annoyed and determined right now, but it was fueled by a caring spirit that he couldn't suppress.

They couldn't be more different. She did it all alone and, regardless of his stance on monkeys, he was a fricking circus ringmaster. But his unwavering confidence, his assurance in what he knew, his faith in the things he believed was—strangely—attractive.

For just a moment, she kind of understood Michelle.

If someone was floating, unanchored and unsure, knowing that TJ was there and would always show up, it had to give that person an incredible sense of security.

In fact...

But no. She liked her free-flowing life. She might be floating a bit, but that was because she *chose* to float. She wasn't insecure. She was an adventurer. Like her mother.

"Michelle doesn't appreciate you," Peyton told TJ.

"I know." He didn't seem bothered by it.

"And you just left Hope here. That wasn't very nice."

TJ looked straight at Hope. "That's because Hope doesn't need me to be okay."

And again, she couldn't breathe for a moment. Because those words—they were supposed to be true. Forty-eight hours ago, they had been true. But now...

"I haven't felt okay since you walked out that door," she told him.

All hint of teasing was gone when he said, "You jealous, Sunshine?"

Was she? No, not really. Because Michelle didn't really have TJ. They might have both thought she did for a long time, but TJ didn't respect Michelle. And Hope suspected that he didn't even like her a lot of the time. She didn't have his heart.

Hope shook her head. "You feel sorry for Michelle. That's not what *I* want from you."

He stepped in close, his eyes on hers. "What do you want from me?"

She put her hand on his chest, over his heart. "I want you to let me be the first person to give you what *you* want."

"I want you in my truck in the next sixty seconds."

Hope gave Peyton a quick hug. "I'll call you tomorrow." Then she swung her bag onto her shoulder and headed for the door.

She could feel TJ right on her heels and noticed that he didn't speak to anyone on their way out. As she reached the door, he leaned around her to open it, one big hand on her lower back.

His touch soaked through the soft cotton of her T-shirt and she felt the heat spread quickly through her body.

"TJ—"

He nudged her out the door and onto the porch of the bar. "Just get in the truck, Hope."

"My car—"

"We'll get it tomorrow. Need you with me," he said.

He didn't glance down at her but stayed focused on keeping her moving toward the truck.

She liked the sound of that, so she went along. Why not? They both wanted this. They both knew exactly where this was going to lead.

They got to his truck and TJ more or less lifted her onto the seat and quickly crowded in behind her. He started the engine while she was still getting settled and they were on the highway a moment later.

The drive wouldn't take long, but it was a chance to breathe before things got really good.

"Can I ask you about two things before we get home?" she asked.

He stared straight ahead at the road. "Fine," he said tersely.

"Michelle has a son."

There was a beat of silence before TJ said, "That's not a question."

Hope noticed how his hand tightened on the steering wheel though. "You thought he was yours at first. Do you ever see him?"

"Nathan was only six months old when Colby came back and Michelle told us the truth. We all agreed that it would be confusing for Nathan if I was in his life. He was too young to remember me, so, no, I don't see him."

Hope could feel the sadness coming from him though. "You were there when he was born?"

"Michelle showed up on my porch when she was about three weeks pregnant. She figured it out right away, about a week after Colby dumped her and left town. She got me drunk one night and we slept together and she told me two weeks later that she was pregnant with my baby. We got married the following weekend and I was there for everything from then on."

Hope absorbed all of that. Did TJ miss Nathan? Of course he did. She was sure he'd loved the baby. She was sure that whole period had been horrible. She was sure that he was angry with Michelle. And yet, he was still there for her when she needed him.

Hope had only one other question. "You've mentioned all this kinky sex and we talked about Michelle using sex to manipulate you."

He sighed. "That's also not a question."

"Do you really like the kinky stuff or was that a Michelle thing?"

He didn't answer at first. Then he finally glanced over. "Michelle called all the shots."

Hope wasn't surprised to hear that. Not so much that Michelle had run the show, but that TJ had let her. "So she was into the kinky stuff?"

"Not always kinky. But...it was like she needed more than just the usual. She was into sex in public places, lingerie...

extras. And I still—" He broke off. Then he muttered, "How do you do that?"

"Do what?"

"Get me to say stuff I don't want to say." He sounded more puzzled than angry though.

"You trust me," she said simply. But the realization warmed her almost as much as his touch did. TJ Bennett did not trust easily. At least, he didn't trust the women he slept with easily.

A thought occurred to her. "You still do that stuff? With other women?" she asked.

He sighed and she knew she was right.

"So are we talking Ben Wa balls here?" she asked.

TJ shifted in his seat and muttered something that sounded like, "This should be easier than this."

"TJ? What kind of stuff?" she pressed, sensing it was important.

He turned the truck onto a gravel road off of the highway. "Okay, fine," he finally said. "I think Michelle was into all of that stuff because that kept *her* interested. I don't know—or care—if she's still into all of that or if she needs that with Colby, but for her and I... She needed the extra stuff."

Hope stared at him. She had no idea what to say. TJ thought Michelle hadn't wanted him enough to want him without bells and whistles.

He glanced over. "Speechless, Sunshine? That's gotta be a first."

"You have to be kidding," she finally answered. "You think you need that stuff with the other women too?"

"I just..." He shoved a hand through his hair and turned onto the long lane to his house. "It makes it... It's easier that way." He looked over at her. "How do you get me to say this stuff?"

"People always tell me stuff," she said. But she wasn't done with their conversation. "TJ, there is no way those women need to have toys and role-playing to want you."

He pulled up in front of his house and killed the engine. "I need it. It keeps some distance," he finally said in the quiet. "If we're role-playing, or doing something that's unconventional, it doesn't feel as personal. The women I...date—"

Hope snorted at his choice of words.

"*Anyway*," he said, giving her a look. "The women are looking for an escape from real life for a little bit. I'm looking for an outlet, an escape too, I guess. It's sex. That's all it is. But that stuff keeps it fun and not so heavy."

It kept him from getting too close to them.

Hope got it. Completely. She was also impressed with his insight into all of it.

"We're not going to need anything extra," she told him. She scooted across the seat and climbed into his lap, straddling his thighs. "You and me. No clothes. And a large horizontal surface. That's all."

TJ looked into her eyes for three heartbeats. Then he opened his truck door, scooped his hands under her ass and slid out with her. As his feet hit the ground, Hope wrapped her legs around his waist, her arms around his neck and put her lips against his neck.

She breathed in deeply, pulling in his scent and the heat from his skin as he walked with her up the porch steps. He shifted her to one side so he could open the front door.

"Hey, your shoulder is a lot better. You're holding me up with your left arm," she commented.

"Yeah, well, my shoulder is getting no attention from my brain right now." He stepped across the threshold and kicked the door shut behind them.

"Oh?" she asked, wiggling against the part of him that was getting the majority of *her* attention.

"Yeah." He turned and put her back to the door, pressing his erection against her. "I'm surprised I can even form words."

The porch light shone in through the front window, but mostly it was the bright moonlight that gave a glow to the foyer where they stood.

"You don't need a lot of words," she said, putting a hand on either side of his face. "Yes. More. Hope. Sunshine. Those are the only ones you need."

He squeezed her butt. "You like Sunshine?"

"I do."

His lips covered hers almost before she got the two words out. His kiss was demanding. He immediately opened his mouth and thrust his tongue against hers, stroking hard and deep. He pressed his hips into hers, his cock right against the zipper of her new shorts. The pressure against her clit made her groan and curse the material. If she were wearing one of her skirts, sans panties, they'd be a lot further along already.

As quickly as he'd taken her mouth, he lifted his head. "I'm going to spread you out on my bed, but I have to do something that I can't wait for."

"Anything," she said breathlessly, meaning it with every fiber in her being.

He stepped back and set her on the floor. He quickly stripped her shirt off, tossed it to one side and reached to unhook her bra. She was topless before she was even fully balanced on her feet.

"God, yes," he said fervently as he cupped her breasts. "I love your breasts."

She couldn't respond. Her entire focus was on her nipples as he strummed his thumbs over them, making need course through her and settle deep in her belly. "More," she managed to murmur.

He responded, rolling a tip between his thumb and finger and tugging gently.

Had it really been just that morning that he'd nearly given her an orgasm in his garden just by playing with her breasts? Of course, his mouth had been involved too—

TJ dipped his knees and took one nipple in his mouth, sucking hard immediately.

Hope cried out, her hand coming up to hold his head, her fingers gripping his hair.

"Fuck, I love that sound," he muttered.

One hand continued to tug and roll while his other hand went to the fastener of her shorts.

"I can—" she started, moving her hands to help.

But he knocked her hand away. "I've been unhooking blue jeans one handed in the dark since I was fifteen," he told her.

The wicked grin he gave her made everything in her tingly, and she could only press her palms against the door and let him at it.

Sure enough, a second later, Hope felt the button and zipper on her shorts give. He swept the denim over her hips, somehow taking her panties with it. They stopped at the top of her boots.

But TJ didn't stop. He rose to his full height, his blue-jean-breaching hand cupping her sex as he dragged his mouth up the side of her neck to her ear.

"I've wanted to touch you since I first saw you stretched out on the hood of your car," he said huskily. "Spread your feet, Sunshine."

Hope was powerless to do anything but follow his commands. She widened her stance as far as her shorts would let her.

"You're bare," he said, as he ran his flat fingers over her mound, his middle finger skimming her clit.

"I like how it feels," she said softly.

"I like how it feels too," he said with a small chuckle. "But it wouldn't matter. It's you."

Her heart flipped at that. If it turned out that TJ was romantic too, she was going to have a really hard time packing up her camper.

That should have maybe felt like a warning sign, but all Hope could think at that moment was that she needed as much of this man before she packed that camper as she could get.

"You're wet for me."

"I think since you first saw me stretched out on the hood of my car," she told him honestly.

That got a soft growl from him, and he moved his finger deeper, up and down over the slick heat below her clit.

Hope's head fell back against the door and she gripped his forearm. "Thank God this arm is feeling better."

He moved his middle finger, sliding into her to his first knuckle. "Trust me. There's nothing that would keep me from this sweetness." He moved the finger in and out, only going as deep as that knuckle each time, then sliding up and over her clit again.

Hope gasped as he circled her clit with a pressure and rhythm that would take her over the edge in only a few seconds if he kept it up.

He didn't.

"Damn, you look good with your shorts and panties around those boots," he said huskily. "But I need more of you. Can't get my tongue on you with those in the way. And I *need* my tongue on you."

Hope felt her muscles clench around his finger with those words.

TJ felt it too, because he chuckled softly. "Yeah, let's do that."

God, she loved that chuckle.

He took his hands away, but he went to his knees in front of her and Hope felt *her* knees get a little weak. He lifted one foot, slid the boot off and flung it toward the couch. The other followed, but his eyes were on her pussy rather than his actions. The boot hit the end table and the lamp wobbled slightly. Hope wasn't sure TJ even noticed.

She had never felt more wanted. His desire was clear on his face, even with the lack of light, and Hope wanted nothing more than to spread her arms and legs and let him take over.

She knew he'd never taken what he wanted, never had what he wanted offered to him, with Michelle. Hope wanted him to take from her. It sounded strange even in her mind, but she wanted TJ to take—to know that he could, to indulge, to whet every appetite, satisfy every craving with *her*.

She kicked free of the shorts and her panties, leaned back against the door, pressed her arms against the wood, and spread her legs.

"I'm all yours."

And it wasn't as if she wasn't going to get anything out of this. Her orgasm was already building and he'd just gotten started.

TJ met her eyes for one long, hot moment. Something hung in the air between them—desire, anticipation and even more, a feeling of familiarity. It didn't make any sense, even to the girl who was used to things seeming strange but true. But Hope embraced it. She felt as if she'd made love to TJ a thousand times already, as if she was already completely fulfilled and yet hungry, as if she'd never have enough.

"TJ," she whispered.

With that, he put his big hands on her ass and drew her to his mouth.

His tongue licked over her clit, sending spirals of heat and need careening through her body. Then he took a longer, deeper swipe.

"TJ!"

And his gasped name from her lips seemed to be the key to getting his *full* attention.

His lips and tongue traveled over every hot, wet centimeter of her, returning again and again to her clit, winding the pending orgasm tighter and tighter each time. He held her against his mouth firmly, not letting her escape even long enough to draw a deep breath. He ate at her for long minutes, alternating between full, long strokes and small, fast flicks of his tongue. Hope was gasping, crying out his name, begging by the time he again went to her clit. He slid first one thick finger, then a second into her heat. Her muscles gripped him immediately and when he finally, *finally*, sucked on her clit while pumping into her with his fingers, her world exploded.

She shouted his name as she dug her fingers into his scalp and her legs began to shake. The ripples of her climax seemed to go on and on and traveled in a wave through her body.

When all that was left were tiny shocks of pleasure sparking along her nerve endings, she opened her eyes.

TJ still had two fingers deep inside her and he was watching her from his kneeling position, his gaze the intense, hot one that she loved so much.

"I could watch that over and over again," he said.

He moved his fingers and she felt the sparks intensify again. She gasped. "Oh my God."

"Making you come is now my favorite thing in the entire world," he told her, moving his fingers again.

"I'm a fan," she said. Barely. She didn't have enough breath to even remain upright much longer.

"Again," he told her.

"No, I—"

He put his mouth back on her clit, licking and sucking, fucking her with his fingers at the same time, and Hope felt another orgasm building immediately. *Holy crap.*

Hope gave herself over to the sensations. She'd never been one to hold back on feeling good, and she followed the instinct to move her hips and rub against his mouth and hand.

"That's right," he murmured. "Let me feel that sweet pussy come again, Hope. I want to feel you lose it."

She was so, so close, and when she lifted her hand and cupped her breast, squeezing her nipple, she felt everything pull tight and then let go.

"Yes," TJ said against her. "Fuck, yes." He worked her with his fingers and tongue through another orgasm that rolled up and over her, less sharply than the first but lasting longer.

TJ stretched to his feet, rubbing against her as he did, the fabric of his shirt abrading her nipples. He caught her chin with his hand and covered her mouth with his, stroking his tongue along her lower lip and then in along her tongue, tasting her thoroughly as he had between her legs. She could taste herself on his lips and tongue and she wanted him right back where he'd been *again.*

"Need to spread you out, Sunshine," he said when he lifted his head.

"Yes." Oh, yes, that's what she needed. He was good with his fingers and tongue, but she needed more.

She started to move toward the steps, but TJ caught her around the waist and swung her up into his arms. He strode to the steps and climbed them quickly.

11

"You have to tell me if I go too fast or hard," he told her as he strode through his bedroom door. He crossed the room and set her down next to the king-size bed. He reached over and switched on the lamp on the table. "But damn, I want to..." He pulled in a deep breath and looked at her. "You're so fucking beautiful," he finally finished. "I want you more than I've ever wanted anyone. I might...I might need...to take the edge off."

"I'm not scared of you or what you want to do," Hope told him, reaching for his arm. She pulled him closer. There was plenty she *hadn't* done sexually, but she would do anything with TJ.

"I'm seriously going to hurt you," he said, cupping her cheek. "I want to fuck you *hard*, Hope. I don't think you understand."

She shook her head. "It's okay."

He stepped back again, but this time he stripped his shirt off. Her gaze traveled over his shoulders, chest and stomach greedily. She was going to have her hands and tongue all over *him* now.

He unfastened his jeans and she had to work not to lick her lips. That might be a little much. Then again...

He kicked his shoes off and then shoved his jeans and underwear to the floor, stepping out of them and then standing, feet braced apart, letting her look him over.

And there was a lot to look over. He was huge. All over. Everywhere. From his wide shoulders, to his hands, to his feet, to his cock. He was easily the biggest man she'd ever been naked with.

Her gaze went from his cock to his face.

"Oh," she said simply.

The corner of his mouth curled. "I could pound railroad spikes right now," he said. "I'm so hard, I'm hurting. And you simply looking at me is almost enough to make me go off."

"Oh," she said again. She loved that he wanted her that much. She hated that he was hurting. "You can have me, TJ. Right now. Whatever you need."

He closed his eyes and tipped his head back, pulling in a long breath through his nose and then letting it out slowly, his hands gripped at his sides.

Finally, he looked at her again. "I can't take your pussy like this," he said bluntly. "I'll hurt you."

"So...what?" She moved forward. "I can—"

"You can't take me in your mouth either," he said, reading her intent.

"Then what?"

"Lay back on the bed."

She did as he asked. Hope got onto the bed and lay back, propping up on her elbows.

He moved to the bottom of the bed. He had his cock in one hand, holding it in a firm grasp.

The sight made Hope wet all over again. This time she couldn't help but lick her lips.

He gave a strained laugh. "Yeah, this won't take long."

"You want me just to lay here?"

"Not quite." He grabbed one of her ankles and pulled her to the bottom of the bed so her feet were dangling over the end.

He stroked up and down the length of his cock as he looked her over. "Damn, you're gorgeous."

"You're amazing," she said sincerely, her gaze traveling over him again.

"Open your legs."

She bent one knee and let it fall to the side. Just his gaze on her pussy was enough to have her starting that delicious climb. "I can tell you one thing," she said, watching him watch her. "There's no way any of those other women needed anything but you."

Something flickered in his eyes, and he said simply and directly, "I need to come, Hope. Because I want to be buried deep inside the sweetest pussy I've ever had, and I can't do that until I let off some steam."

God, he was hot. This was exactly what she should have expected—intense, even a little brusque, but somehow sweetly reverent at the same time. It was overwhelming. He was overwhelming. In the best possible way.

"Tell me what to do," she said.

"Touch yourself."

Oh, well, that was easy enough. With him as visual inspiration, she was going to have no trouble with this.

"But don't come," he said.

His voice had tightened, and she watched his hand moving up and down his shaft with a firm pressure. She wanted to touch him. She wanted to wrap her hand around him, grip him, stroke him.

"I could do that for you," she said, her eyes on his cock. Her hand slid between her legs and she rubbed over her clit.

"This is what I need," he rasped. He increased his speed.

When she glanced up, his eyes were riveted on *her* hand.

And she decided to make it a good show. "If you're sure," she said. She lay back and opened her legs farther. She slid one finger into her heat, moaning his name as she did it.

His strokes were long but faster now.

This was the hottest thing she'd ever done. She slid a second finger inside, then pulled them up over her still-sensitive clit, circling slowly, then faster as he increased the speed of his strokes.

"Do not get yourself off," TJ commanded. "I'm going to come and then *I* will make you come."

She circled faster. "I'm so close though." She tugged on one nipple and felt the ripples of her climax starting.

"Hope," he said roughly. "*I* make you come."

"But you're going to come and then it will be a while before you can take me."

It might have been the "take me", it might have been the sight of her masturbating for him, or it might have been that he was really that close, but TJ gave a low moan and came, the warm fluid of his release hitting her stomach.

She couldn't pull her attention away from his hand milking his cock. She would have never expected having him do that to be so hot, but that was enough to get her climbing faster.

Her fingers started moving more rapidly and she felt it winding up. But before she could go over the summit, TJ grabbed her wrist and pulled her hand away.

He quickly replaced it, though, with his mouth. He went down on her at the end of the bed, licking and sucking for the minute it took to shoot her into another hard orgasm, crying his name as she came.

He licked her thoroughly through the mini aftershocks before climbing up onto the bed beside her. He had his T-shirt in hand and used it to clean her up before he rolled her onto her side and tucked her against his body, moving her as if she weighed nothing at all. She wasn't typically one for being handled, but having TJ do it felt comforting and hot at the same time.

She was lying on her right side, so her tattoo was on the side he could see. He began tracing the letters with his fingertip.

"It seems like a year ago when I first saw this playing peek-a-boo and driving me crazy."

Hope tucked her hand under her cheek. "It does seem like I've been here longer than a day."

He was quiet for a minute. Finally, he said, "We should talk about your experience."

"My experience?" she repeated. "You mean sexually?"

"Yes."

Okay, Mr. Protective had shown up again.

"What do you want to know?" She was facing away from him, so she couldn't read his expressions. Interestingly, she already knew the various tones in his voice. There was concern there, an earnestness about the topic, but also a deeper tone that said he was still turned-on and a note of cockiness that she loved. TJ was stubborn and tough, but cocky was not a word she would have used. Until now. She loved that he was sure of himself, and of her, at this moment.

"Everything." He paused. "No, never mind. I don't want to know anything really."

She smiled to herself. Was he jealous? Jealousy was really a sad, wasteful emotion, but a small part of her liked that he might not like thinking of her with other men.

"But you think you need to know something?" she asked.

He sighed. "Yes. How many men? What have you done? What are your limits?"

"Are you going to push my limits, TJ?" she asked. "I'm into adventure, remember? Especially with you."

"Why especially with me?"

"I trust you. You would never hurt me. And I want you more than I've ever wanted anyone."

He didn't say anything again for a moment and Hope wondered what he was thinking.

"How many men?" he asked again.

"Four."

He paused and she thought she heard teeth grinding.

"Were you in love with any of them?"

She started to roll back to look at him, but he tightened his arm around her, not letting her move. Okay, fine. "One of them, yes."

There was definite teeth grinding then. She smiled.

"Have you ever used Ben Wa balls?"

"No."

"A vibrator?"

"Well, yeah," she said. Didn't all women have a vibrator?

"Have you ever been blindfolded during sex?"

"No."

"Ever had sex in public?"

"Once."

He paused and she was ready for him to ask where. She could almost hear the battle in his head—curiosity versus jealousy. She knew because she felt the same battle in her about *his* experiences.

"Ever used food during sex?"

"Like whipped cream? Once."

"Like German chocolate cake frosting."

She laughed. "That's very specific. And, no."

"Do you like German chocolate cake frosting?"

"In my mouth? Yes. In my..." She trailed off.

He put his lips against her shoulder and began stroking her stomach. "Well, if it's in your...it will end up in *my* mouth and I *do* like German chocolate cake frosting."

Her body heated and she suddenly had a craving for

coconut. "In that case, I freaking *love* German chocolate cake frosting."

"Have you ever had anal sex?"

On the heels of cake frosting, that threw her. "No," she finally said. She waited for him to ask if she would consider it. She waited to see if she *would* consider it.

Instead, he said, "How do you feel about cowgirl?"

His hand was stroking lower now and he glided his finger over her clit. She felt his erection pressing into her butt. He was ready to go again. Yee haw.

"Love cowgirl."

"I think that might be best this first time," he said, flicking his tongue behind her ear.

She shivered as goose bumps danced down her arms.

"That way you can take me slowly and easy. You can set the pace."

Hope felt her inner muscles clench in delicious anticipation. "This is supposed to be about what *you* want from me," she said. Even though she really wanted to ride him.

"Oh, Sunshine, watching you work my cock into that hot pussy is exactly what I want."

She wanted to roll over, flip him onto his back and climb on. But his hand was between her legs again and she couldn't quite pull herself away from his teasing fingers.

"I have to say though," he told her as he pressed on her clit and then slid down into her heat, quickly adding a second finger, and then a third. "I could play right here for days."

"I want to come with you inside me this time," she said, trying to tamp down the building need. "Please."

She didn't think she'd ever been this horny in her life. Or this easy. She had never come like this with anyone else.

She heard TJ pull in a sharp breath and he eased his fingers out of her.

"Ride me."

Yes.

He rolled back as she turned over. She went up onto her knees and focused on his cock.

It had definitely recovered. It was big and thick and she was aching with the need to take him in and feel him stretching and filling her.

She wrapped a hand around him, squeezing gently.

"Easy." He put his hand around hers. He didn't pull her away but he kept her from stroking him. "I'm still wound pretty tight."

"Good." She grinned up at him.

"I want this to last more than thirty seconds," he said, giving her butt a pinch with his free hand.

"Hey!"

"Get on already." He grabbed her hips and pulled her up.

She swung a leg over, straddling him.

"That's better." He kept his hands on her hips. "Take it easy with me."

"No way." She took him in hand again. "Where are your condoms?"

He reached out for the bedside table and pulled a box from the drawer. He quickly ripped one open and positioned it above the head of his cock. They rolled it down his length together, his breath catching as she brushed her fingers over his balls.

Then she lifted herself over him. Still holding him, she moved into place, his head at her entrance.

He dug his fingers into her hips. "So hot. So good."

She licked her bottom lip and eased herself down.

"Take it slow. Let me in easy."

"I can take you, TJ," she panted.

"You're *going* to take me," he promised. "All of me. I'm going to fill you up and fuck you thoroughly. Just take it slow."

His words definitely made it easier. It seemed she got hotter and wetter every time he spoke. She moved, her body opening and accepting him inch by glorious inch. She felt the stretch through her inner thighs as well as her pussy, but it was such a good stretch, causing pulses of pleasure to ripple through her.

The way she wanted him, the multiple orgasms, the fact that her body *needed* him, all combined to make it easy to take him, and soon she was fully seated.

"Holy shit, Hope," TJ breathed. "Holy shit."

Yeah. It was that good.

"I have to move," she said. "I...have too..." She began her motion, sliding up and down his length.

"God. Yes." He gripped her hips and helped her move, slowly at first, but with increasing speed. "You feel so fucking good. God, Hope, I knew it would be amazing."

Yeah, she'd known it too. Even before she'd realized that she could fall in love with him. Which had occurred somewhere around the time he'd refused to turn his back on his needy, sad ex. Or maybe it had been when he pulled her back from almost diving off the end of his dock. Or maybe it was when he wrapped himself up in her situation to protect Dan and Peyton.

Whenever it had happened, it had happened fast. The big, tough guy had awakened protective instincts in *her* that she hadn't even known were there. She wanted to make him laugh and relax and open up and know that he could, and should, be loved.

Yeah, she could definitely fall for TJ Bennett.

Especially when he insisted on taking care of her. That was the strangest thing of all. She'd never been taken care of. So why did that turn her on so much from TJ?

Like when he started to lift his hips to thrust up into her but then stopped, as if he'd remembered he couldn't do that.

"TJ, don't be careful with me," she said breathlessly. "Take me. Hard. If I can't walk tomorrow, I'll just have to stay here in bed and teach you all the massage techniques and acupressure points to make me feel better."

His gaze burned up at hers for three seconds before he flipped her over onto her back.

"I'll show you an acupressure point." He was teasing her, but his voice was rough. He moved his hips forward, pressing deeper. "Right about..." then he thrust, "...there."

She gasped. "Yes!" Her instinct was to widen her legs so she could take him completely. She wrapped her legs around his waist, locking her ankles at his lower back.

"You with me?" he asked. He was propped on one elbow, his other hand under her ass, holding her against him.

"So with you. Yes. Definitely with you." She wanted to feel the bed rocking, feel him pounding into her, feel her muscles screaming as she took all of him.

TJ seemed to sense her desperation, because he began moving, pulling out and thrusting back in with long, delicious strokes. He stretched and filled her over and over again, touching her deeper than anyone ever had. But it was the way he was watching her that made her feel so completely overwhelmed, lost and found at the same time. He was so intense in everything he did and, of course, he could never make something all about *him*. Of course he'd be tuned in and determined to make *her* go out of her mind.

"Harder," she begged.

His jaw tightened and she felt him grip her butt. "Hope—"

"Please, TJ." She pulled his mouth down to hers and kissed him, opening and taking his tongue, pressing back, showing him that she was all in. "Harder," she whispered again against his lips. "Please. I want all of you. I want everything you've got."

He rested his forehead against hers, breathing hard, seeming to struggle for a moment. Then he lifted his head, met her eyes, and thrust hard and deep.

"Yes," she moaned. "Yes. More."

Watching her closely, he shifted so he was on his knees, both hands under her ass. He lifted her hips and thrust hard. *Hard*. And deep. So deep.

Hope felt her orgasm bearing down almost immediately. His hands held her in place to take his hard thrusts and the angle had him hitting a spot that made her entire body feel electrified. She couldn't breathe, she couldn't think, she just *needed*.

And he gave it to her.

"*Hope*."

He was giving her everything. She could tell he was finally holding nothing back as he pounded into her, and the realization that he was letting go took her hard and fast into an intense climax she felt everywhere.

She lay limp, barely able to even focus her gaze on him. But she couldn't look away. His pace slowed slightly. He watched her, then looked down to where he was still thrusting in and out of her body. He ran a palm up along her tattoo, over her breasts and up to her mouth. He traced his thumb over her lips.

"Sunshine," he said softly.

Then she felt him tense and he closed his eyes, tipping his head back as his orgasm claimed him. She felt the hot throbbing of his release and she instinctively tightened around him.

He groaned and tensed again. He held the position, buried deep, one hand on her ass, the other with his thumb against her lips for several long moments.

Hope just enjoyed studying him. This was beauty. This was what sculptors should be sculpting—the combined look of power and satisfaction on the face of this magnificent man.

A feeling of power washed over her as well. She'd made him look like that. She'd made him *feel* that.

Damn right she had.

Her muscles clenched around him again and he groaned, pulled from the quiet moment.

He opened his eyes and locked his gaze on hers as he pulled out of her. He reached for the tissues on the bedside table, took the condom off and tossed it to the floor before propping on his side and pulling her against him again.

This time, she wasn't on her side. She was on her back and could see everything in his face.

TJ traced his thumb over her lips again, looking down at her with a look of bewilderment she found endearing.

"You okay?" she asked, lifting her hand to his cheek and rubbing over the stubble.

"So okay."

"Why do you look like you can't believe we just did that?"

"Because I can't believe we just did that. You've been here for two days."

"Sometimes magic just happens."

He didn't respond to that. He leaned in and kissed her though. A sweet, hot kiss that was very different from the hot, needy, possessive kisses of earlier. This was a kiss of contentment, and Hope drank every bit of it in.

Content was something she didn't think TJ had felt much. She was so happy to give it to him that it was almost startling.

He put his head on the pillow next to hers and wrapped a big arm around her. He was hot and hard, but she settled into him, more comfortable than she'd been in a long time.

Now they could talk. She could get to know him even better. While they rested up for round two. Or was it round three? Hope grinned to herself as she thought about what she most wanted to know from him.

But strangely, she couldn't come up with anything. Either her brain had ceased working with that last orgasm, or she was completely satisfied with what she did know. She knew there was more to learn about him, but she didn't feel a driving pressure to know everything right now like she had since meeting him.

She took a deep breath and let it out, thinking that maybe *she* hadn't been totally content in a while either. Because that was sure what *this* felt like.

A ringing cell phone startled him awake, and TJ realized they'd both fallen asleep.

Squinting at the clock next to the bed, he saw it was one a.m.

He had to roll away from Hope to reach for the phone in his jeans on the floor, but he knew she was now awake too.

That was perfect. He needed her again.

He also feared that need would never go away. But taking her again right now would certainly help for the moment.

"What?" he asked into the phone a moment later. He was going to kill whichever brother was purposefully calling to interrupt.

"Do you know where Peyton is?"

TJ pushed himself up in the bed. "Dan?"

That got Hope's full attention, and she shifted to sit next to him, pulling the sheet up over her breasts.

"Yes. We had an argument and she left. It's been almost an hour and she's not answering her phone. Scott hasn't seen her, but he said she was with your girlfriend tonight. Do you know where she is?"

TJ glanced at Hope. "No, I haven't seen her since we left the bar."

Hope frowned. "Who?" she mouthed.

"Peyton."

Her expression went from annoyed to concerned in an instant.

Hope scooted to the edge of the bed, taking the sheet with her. "Let me check my phone."

Which was downstairs, either in her shorts that were somewhere on his living room floor, or in her bag in his truck outside.

"Hope, wait—"

"I'm good. I'll be right back."

"I don't know where else to look," Dan said.

"I'm sure Scott's checking on her," TJ said. He was *sure* Scott was checking on her. In addition to being the town cop, TJ knew the other man was intrigued by the troublemaker. "And Hope will try to get a hold of her."

"This Hope girl," Dan said. "Are you sure she's okay? Okay to be hanging out with Peyton?"

TJ bit his tongue. For one, Dan was hardly in a position to judge other people's positive or negative influence on his daughter. For another, Hope had a special reason for being connected to and concerned about Peyton. One that TJ couldn't share with Dan. Yet.

He'd seen Hope with Peyton though. He knew she was feeling a bond, and he loved it. She had been insisting that she could keep her distance, meet them without telling them who she was, but now that she had gotten to know Peyton, she was feeling attached. Already. Yeah, he loved that a lot.

"Dan, Hope is really good for Peyton, actually," TJ said. "You'll see...they're going to be good friends."

"I thought you just met her yourself," Dan said.

"Yes, but—"

"I'm coming over."

"No, you don't have—" But the line was already dead.

Dammit.

If Peyton and Dan had argued tonight, then Dan was riled up. He always put his wife first, and TJ knew that he felt guilty about that. So he overcompensated when Peyton was in trouble by acting the concerned, protective father.

TJ got out of bed and pulled on his clothes as well. He

should at least warn Hope they were about to have company so she could get dressed.

"Hope?" he called as he descended the steps.

She wasn't in the living room and her shorts still were, so he assumed she'd had to go out to the truck. He headed for the door and pulled it open.

To find his porch filled with people.

Including Hope. Still wrapped in a sheet.

"No, she didn't say anything to me," Hope was telling Delaney.

"What the fuck are you all doing here?" TJ demanded.

Travis and Lauren were there, along with Phoebe and Joe and Tucker and Delaney.

"Dan called us worried about Peyton," Travis said.

"Who's with your kids?" TJ asked Tucker.

"Kate," Tucker said.

"So you got Kate and Levi out of bed to come babysit so you could come over *here*?" TJ asked.

"Everyone was at our house," Delaney said. "We were just hanging out. Tucker was showing Levi how to wire a ceiling fan and we were talking," she glanced between him and Hope, "about you guys."

TJ sighed. Just his luck they'd all be here together when Dan called.

"We were making a German chocolate cake for you," Lauren said with a grin.

TJ frowned at her. "No, you weren't." Lauren, Delaney and Kate didn't bake. But Phoebe did. German chocolate cake was a tradition of TJ's mother's. She made them for engagements and anniversaries in Sapphire Falls. It had been the first cake she'd made for Thomas and had won his heart—or so the story went.

The story also went that she frosted the cakes extra thick and that recipients found fun, sticky uses for the extra frosting.

In their family, a German chocolate cake meant a love match had been made.

"German chocolate?" Hope asked. She looked up at TJ. "You just asked me about that earlier. That's strange, isn't it?"

Travis chuckled. "Not really all that strange."

Hope was obviously confused, but further conversation was interrupted by Dan's arrival.

"*No one* knows where she is?" he asked, approaching the porch steps. "How is that possible?"

"Dan, settle down," Tucker said. "Phoebe and Joe confirmed she was still at the Come Again when all of them left."

"Well, she's not there now." Dan's attention zeroed in on Hope. "You're Hope?"

She nodded. "I am. Nice to meet you."

TJ stepped closer to her, taking in her look of surprise and excitement and trepidation.

He had never seen Hope look unsure, and he was certain it was a rare thing for her to feel.

"What did you say to my daughter?" Dan asked, frowning at her.

TJ moved in front of her. "This isn't Hope's fault, Dan. Peyton does shit like this all the time."

"But we can always *find* her. Where the hell could she be tonight?"

He looked at Hope again, who had, of course, stepped out from behind TJ.

"What did you say to her?"

"We talked about a lot of things," Hope said. "She shared with me about her mother's mental illness and her desire for more of your attention, and I told her she needed to make her own happiness and not to worry about the choices *you've* made."

TJ felt everyone suck in their breath at the same time. JoEllen's bipolar disorder was one of those things that people knew about but never mentioned out loud. And *never* to Dan. If they referred to it at all, people talked about her being sick. Like she had the flu or something.

Dan's eyes widened in surprise. "She told you about her mother?"

Hope nodded. "And you. And how it all makes her feel."

Of course Hope wouldn't tiptoe around Dan. Sure, she'd been willing to hold back and not head directly over to introduce herself after she understood their situation. But now that it was front and center, TJ realized that she was going to meet this head-on.

She wasn't addressing Dan as her long-lost father. She was addressing him as the father of a girl she cared about.

TJ realized that he was falling for her in that moment.

She was being protective of her own monkey.

TJ also became aware that she was still wrapped in only a bedsheet. Her hair was tousled and she had whisker burns along her left collarbone. And he felt a primal streak of possessiveness seeing her like that. Part of him wanted to parade her around town so everyone would know she was *his*.

Another slightly larger part of him wanted her covered up and away from any other male eyes immediately. She needed clothes on. Now.

"Hope, maybe you should—"

"Mind your own fucking business," Dan said.

TJ felt his spine go rigid. His brothers and Joe stepped back slightly, widening the space around TJ. He turned slowly to face the man who had been like a second father to him.

"Dan, you need to be careful," TJ said firmly.

"She needs to stay out of it," Dan said, glaring at Hope. "This is between my daughter and me."

"Stop it!" Suddenly Peyton appeared from around the corner of the house. "She didn't do anything wrong."

Everyone swung to face her.

"Where did you come from?" Travis asked. "Are you all right?"

Peyton nodded and then looked sheepishly at Hope. "I needed to get out. Like you said. I saw your car and camper were still at the bar so I...brought them out here for you. I was just going to sleep in the camper for the night."

"I have my keys," Hope said. "How did you start it?"

Peyton glanced at her dad, then back to Hope. "I can hotwire cars."

"Jesus," TJ muttered.

"It's okay," Hope assured her. "As long as you're safe, that's all that matters."

"That is *not* all that matters," Dan declared. "You told her she needed to get out?" Dan asked Hope.

"If being around you makes her unhappy, yes," Hope said. "She deserves to be happy and she needs to figure out how to make that happen without depending on someone else."

"Who the hell do you think you are?" Dan asked.

"She's my *friend*, Dad," Peyton said. "She cares about me."

"You just met her and you think she cares about you more than your own father? You don't even know her!"

"I *feel* like I do know her! She *listens* to me. She wants me to be stronger."

"That's ridiculous!" Dan yelled. "You just met!"

"Sometimes people connect," Hope interjected. "Sometimes...there are...reasons...that people feel drawn to one another."

Was she working up to telling him who she was? TJ watched the scene before him, torn. He wanted to jump in and protect Hope from Dan's anger and whatever stupid thing he was about to say—TJ knew Dan well. He *was* going to say something stupid. But if this pushed Hope to confess who she was, TJ was all for it. She deserved to have a family, to have a sister who would bring out her protective instincts, who she could be there for, who would look up to her. God knew, Peyton needed Hope. And with her mother gone, Hope needed a place to belong, and a father who... Okay, Dan didn't have a lot to give. But Hope was a healer. Maybe she could heal Dan a little too.

Dan turned to Hope with wide eyes, clearly dumbfounded. "Drawn to one another? Are you kidding me with this crap?"

TJ glanced at Hope and his chest tightened at the wounded look on her face. "Dan, watch yourself," he said, warningly.

"You just pulled into town, and within a day, you're my daughter's new best friend?" Dan went on. "That seems really creepy, you know that?"

TJ flinched at that. So did Hope.

Her father was calling her creepy because she was trying to take care of her sister. Dan didn't know who she was, but Hope knew who *he* was. Rationally, she would understand that he was a concerned father looking out for his daughter who was being suddenly influenced by a complete stranger. But TJ knew better than anyone that being rational was hard when the heart was involved.

And no matter how tough and independent she tried to be, Hope's heart was involved here.

"Hope is *my* friend," TJ said. "You can trust her."

"She's your *friend*, TJ?" Dan said, his gaze going to Hope again. "You wouldn't be biased where she's concerned, would you?"

TJ didn't want to throw Dan off of his property. But he fucking would. "Okay Dan, you need to go."

"I'm not going anywhere without Peyton."

"Peyton's fine," TJ said. "She can stay here tonight. But you need to go. Now. Don't make me *make* you leave."

"No," Hope protested to TJ. "Don't do that." She turned to Peyton. "You decide. You need to choose what you do. You can stay here or you can go with your dad or you can take my camper and go someone else entirely. But it's *your* call."

"Hope—" TJ started.

"Peyton, no—" Dan said at the same time.

But Peyton talked over them both. "I don't want to go home, Dad. I don't want to fight anymore. And I can't keep trying to get your attention. It's just hurting me. And I know you don't want me to be hurt.

"Goddamit!" Dan roared. He turned on Hope. "Why do you care? What business is this of yours? Leave my daughter alone. She's nothing to you."

"Dan!" TJ said sharply. "Stop. Hope cares about Peyton. You don't understand. You should be *glad*."

"That some strange woman showed up and started brain-washing my daughter against me?"

"She's your daughter too!"

Everyone froze.

Including TJ.

Oh...*fuck*.

"TJ!"

He looked down at Hope. She was clearly shocked.

"I'm sorry, Hope." TJ wanted to reach for her, but she stepped back before he could, as if reading his mind.

"I can't...you shouldn't have told him." She cast a glance at Dan. "Not like this."

"It's...fine," he said, praying to God it would be fine.

She frowned at him. "It's not fine. That wasn't your secret to tell."

"I'm so sorry," he told her sincerely. He shouldn't have blurted it out but listening to Dan raging against her had been too much. "But maybe it's better this way." For all of them. The secret was out. Now they could work through their issues and maybe even be a family.

"Better for *who*?" Hope asked, gesturing toward a completely stunned Dan and Peyton.

Dan moved to sit on the steps and put his head in his hands. "She's..." He took a deep breath. "She's Melody's daughter," he said quietly.

TJ looked from Dan's slumped back to Hope. Hope was chewing her bottom lip.

"Hope?" he asked. He inclined his head toward Dan.

"What do you want me to do?" Hope asked. "You told him. I don't have a lot else to add."

He stared at her. "You don't have— Are you kidding me? This is your *father*, Hope. The whole reason you're here."

"So it's true?" Peyton asked. "You're...my *sister*?"

Hope focused on the younger girl. "Yes. Half-sister."

"Oh my God." Peyton crossed her arms over her stomach and hugged herself hard. "Oh my God."

"Peyton, I—" Hope started.

"That's amazing!" The words seemed to sink in and Peyton ran up the steps to enfold Hope in a hug. "Oh my God!" She squeezed Hope hard and then leaned back, tears in her eyes.

Hope gave her a smile but TJ could see it was forced.

She had to force a smile while being reunited with her family? With her sister? A girl she'd already bonded with?

"Hope," he said quietly. He looked from her to Dan and back.

Hope followed his gaze, resting on her father's bowed head. She sighed.

She stepped around Peyton and moved to the top of the steps. "Yes, I'm Melody's daughter," she said to his back. "And yours."

Dan shook his head back and forth on his hands. "She told me she was never going to tell you who I was."

Surprise shot through TJ. "You knew you had a daughter with Melody?" he asked.

He looked at Hope. She was frowning at Dan.

"I knew she was pregnant. I never knew if it was a boy or girl."

"You...knew?" Hope repeated, her voice scratchy. "You knew about me?"

Dan took a deep breath and rose, turning to face her from two steps down. "Melody called me from Arizona three months after she left. She wanted to come back. I told her Jo and I were engaged and...I couldn't do it."

Hope took a step back and TJ moved in behind her. He rubbed his hands up and down her upper arms, offering his support. And resisting the urge to punch Dan.

"She always told me it was just us, just her and me. She said that she hadn't told you because I was *her* gift from the universe."

Dan nodded sadly. "Another great adventure."

Hope nodded.

"Okay, I *really* hate to bring this up right now."

Everyone looked at Lauren.

She was standing near the front door, one hand on her belly, the other gripping the front of Travis's shirt. There was a puddle of water at her feet.

"But I'm gonna need to be going now."

There was a second of absolute silence. Then everyone started talking at once.

Travis immediately swung Lauren up into his arms. Tucker and Delaney offered to drive.

They started for the steps and TJ noticed Hope biting her thumb nail as she watched them. She said nothing.

But as they got to the car, Hope asked him, "How far is the nearest hospital?"

"Twenty miles."

"Damn," she muttered. Then called out, "Hang on!"

Everyone turned to look at her.

"How long have you been having contractions?" Hope asked Lauren.

Lauren hesitated and Hope gave her a look. "Be honest," she told the soon-to-be mother.

"Two days. I thought they were Braxton-Hicks. And then they got worse. But the class and the doctor and all the books said the first labor takes forever. I didn't worry. Until...now."

"Jesus, City—" Travis started.

"Later," Hope said. "You can go over all of that later. How far apart are they?"

"Pretty close."

Hope nodded. "Okay, then. Guys," she said to Travis and Tucker. "We need to get her in on the sofa so I can check her and make sure they can make it thirty more minutes or so."

Travis turned with Lauren and headed back into the house. Everyone else followed close behind. Hope hung back, taking big, cleansing breaths, her hand on her stomach.

"Do you know what you're checking for?" TJ asked.

She looked up at him. "A baby's head. If I don't see that, we're still good for a while."

Right. "And if you do?"

"We might be in trouble."

He shook his head, but he couldn't help but lean in and kiss her. "You don't have to know everything. Just...convince Lauren that you do."

She met his eyes and held his gaze for a moment. Finally, she nodded. "Yeah. Okay."

There was something new in her eyes. Something soft. Not the sparkling sweetness or the bright optimism or even the glint of mischief that he was used to, but something...more. Almost wistful.

"You okay?" He stroked a finger over her cheek.

"I can see why Michelle won't let go of you."

He pulled his hand back. Damn. He hadn't been expecting

that. Because her comment stirred up a bunch of stuff he'd been thinking about for the past day and a half.

Michelle used him, yes. But she also needed him on some level. She turned things dramatic so he'd come to her rescue, but him being there met a deeper need in her. And she admitted it.

Hope didn't think she needed anyone. She didn't want to need someone. She didn't really know how.

And it might make him the biggest ass in Sapphire Falls, but sometimes having Michelle need him met a need in him as well.

A need that Hope might not be able, or willing, to meet.

"Hope—"

"Hey, uh, you guys?" Peyton poked her head out the door. "We could use you in here."

"Yeah, I'm coming," Hope said. She looked at TJ. "Will you go to the camper and get the bottle of lavender and a clean washcloth?"

"Of course." He shook off the previous thoughts. Now wasn't the time. "What will the lavender do?" he asked, already moving.

"For labor? Nothing," Hope said. "But I'm going to tell Lauren it will help with her pain."

"Will it?"

Hope shrugged. "It won't make it worse."

That would have to be good enough. TJ jogged off in the direction Peyton had come from. Sure enough, the girl had brought the car and camper back and parked behind the garage where no one would see it.

He rummaged through Hope's apothecary box and found the bottle labeled lavender. But it was empty. He looked over the other bottles but had no idea if any of them would be an adequate substitute.

He headed back for the house with the empty bottle. He

was pleased to see that Hope had pulled her clothes on at some point and he resolutely kept his mind *off* wondering if she'd bothered with underwear or a bra.

She was kneeling next to the couch where Lauren lay, her lower half draped with a big blanket.

"How far apart did you say your contractions were?" she asked Lauren.

"Really, really not very far apart," Lauren said through gritted teeth. She was squeezing Travis's hand on one side and Tucker's on the other. Both men were grimacing.

"Okay, well, I believe that." She looked at Phoebe. "You need to call the ambulance."

12

"I do not want to have this baby in an ambulance," Lauren said, struggling to prop up on her elbows.

Hope met her gaze. "I don't think that's going to be a problem."

"She'll make it to the hospital?" Travis asked.

Hope shook her head. "Your baby will be here before the ambulance."

"Of course." Lauren slumped back onto the couch. "Just like a Bennett to make this into a big deal."

"Just like a stubborn-assed city girl to think she didn't need to mention that she was in *labor*," Travis said. He leaned in and smoothed Lauren's hair back from her forehead. He looked into her eyes. "You're a handful, you know that?" He kissed her forehead. "And I love you with all my heart."

Lauren's eyes filled with tears. "I'm sorry. I didn't want to go yet. It's not time."

"Well, baby doll, I think our kid gets to decide if it's time."

Lauren just took a deep breath and nodded.

Travis looked up at Hope. "You got this?"

TJ moved in behind her and handed the vial over her shoulder. "She's got this," he said with confidence.

Hope had to know *something* about delivering babies. She'd been to nursing school. But no matter what, she was the most caring, warm, positive person he'd ever met, and she had a way of drawing everyone in. She would calm and encourage Lauren and everyone around them would feel completely confident in everything happening and all would be well.

Hope took the vial and obviously noted it was empty. She covered it with her hand so no one else could see and pretended to tip it into her palm. "Okay, Lauren, your baby is on the way." She took Lauren's hand and began massaging it with sure, firm strokes. "We're going to do some stimulating massage to make your contractions more effective and some deep breathing to calm your system so you can focus on this delivery." She continued to massage and talk. "I'm a believer in natural childbirth and I think that being on your back is a tough position. I'd rather have you up walking as long as you can and then squatting. What do you think?"

Lauren looked at her with wide eyes, and TJ would have sworn Lauren looked scared.

But this was Lauren. Kick-ass businesswoman, genius scientist, humanitarian and political activist.

"Lauren?" Hope asked. "You can do this. It's a beautiful night to have a baby." She tugged on Lauren's hand, helping her to sit and then stand. Hope held her hand all the way to the door and out onto the porch. "Think about it," she said. "This is Sapphire Falls. Look at that sky. And this land. This is your home. This seems like the perfect place to bring your child into the world, don't you think?"

Lauren finally nodded and took a deep breath. "Okay. Yes. Definitely."

"Travis, Tucker, walk with her. Deep breaths. All of you." Hope gave Travis a pointed look. "Do *you* have this?"

He nodded. "On it."

But TJ knew his brother was scared too.

They moved off the porch, walking with Lauren toward the garden.

"How long for the ambulance?" Hope asked Phoebe softly when they were out of earshot.

"Twenty minutes."

"What about Jason Gilmore? Does someone have his number?"

"I do," Joe said. He pulled his phone from his pocket and dialed.

"Okay, the rest of you," Hope said, turning to the group that was now back on the porch. "I need blankets. We're going to need towels. Water—for her to drink and for her face, and also some boiled so we can sterilize a knife to cut the cord. We'll need some orange juice. And a heating pad. And crackers. Plain saltines. Also, if there's anyone who isn't here who should be, call them. We're going to have another Bennett very soon."

Everyone scattered and TJ took Hope's hands. "See? You know exactly what to do."

She looked up at him and laughed softly. "I'm completely faking all of this."

He looked over his shoulder. "But the blankets and stuff..."

"Well, I assume we will need blankets and towels."

"And the boiling water to sterilize the knife?"

"There's no way in hell I'm cutting that cord," Hope said. "The ambulance will be here by then. Or Jason."

TJ shook his head. "You came up with all of that to keep them busy."

She nodded. "They need to feel part of this and like they're helping. If anyone thinks too hard, they're going to get scared."

"And Lauren's walking? Is that to keep her distracted too?" he asked.

"No, that's actually really good to progress the delivery."

TJ laughed and pulled her in close, wrapping his arms around her. "And what do *you* need?"

She hugged him back. Tightly. And TJ felt his heart clench.

"Another orgasm, a shower and Double Stuf Oreos. Not necessarily in that order," she told him.

He felt the urge to press her against the wall, kiss her, laugh, hug her tighter and take her straight to the kitchen for Oreos all at once.

"I can actually deliver on all of those," he said against the top of her head.

"Hope!" Travis yelled from the middle of the yard.

"Rain check," Hope said, pulling away. "I'm up."

"I'm right here," he told her. "Through it all."

Her eyes went to something behind him. "Keep the monkeys occupied, okay?"

He smiled and nodded. "Bananas on the house."

She looked like she wanted to say something more, but instead just took a deep breath. "Here we go."

She headed across the lawn and TJ went to grab the towels and blankets they would need.

The next twenty minutes were a blur of activity.

When TJ got back outside, Lauren was squatting in the grass, Travis and Tucker holding her up. They spread the blankets underneath her and surrounded the make-shift bed with lanterns. Hope coached her through pushing with her contractions while also rubbing her back and pressing on what TJ assumed where acupressure sites in her lower back, wrists and even ankles.

The ambulance arrived, as did Jason, before the baby was actually born, but Lauren was too far progressed for anyone to do anything more for Lauren than what Hope was providing as the labor continued at a steady rate.

When the baby was crowning, Hope started to move out of the way for Jason but as Hope tried to stand, Lauren cried out.

Tucker and Travis lowered her to the ground and Hope just got her hands in position in time to catch the baby.

There was a long, stunned silence. Then Hope called out, "It's a girl!"

Jason moved Travis into place. The EMTs supplied him with the scissors—and how-to instructions—to cut his daughter's umbilical cord. Then Hope swaddled the baby as if she'd done it a thousand times and handed her to her father.

"Oh, wow," Lauren said, slumped back on the blanket. "I was sure she was another Bennett boy."

Travis was staring at the tiny girl as if he'd just come upon a two-headed dog. He looked at his wife. "I have a daughter."

Lauren looked at his face and burst into laughter. "A stubborn little girl who's already raising hell," she said. She nodded. "Yes, this is perfect."

Travis looked pale.

"Travis," Hope said. "Pull yourself together."

He shook his head. "I don't think that's going to happen for the next eighteen years."

TJ was pretty sure it was going to take even longer than that.

Then they bundled both baby and Lauren onto a gurney and into the back of the ambulance.

They sped off, Jason in his car right behind them. Everyone from TJ's porch piled into cars and headed for the hospital as well.

Somehow, Hope ended up in the car with Phoebe and Joe, while TJ found Tucker and Delaney in his truck with him.

"Congratulations, you guys!" Delaney said, kissing him on the cheek. "Our new niece is gorgeous, isn't she?"

He grinned at that. "Thanks and, yes, she takes after her mother."

Delaney laughed. "And she clearly loves excitement already."

TJ thought about that. More excitement. Another person to

worry about. Another female to bring drama to his life. He was torn—he'd love for her to be a shy, quiet bookworm on one hand. On the other, Travis deserved a hellion.

"I'm so glad they had a girl," Delaney said, settling back in the seat and smiling happily. "We have *a lot* of testosterone in this family."

TJ loved that she already referred to the baby as *their* niece and their family as hers too.

With thoughts of family and belonging with the Bennetts, his mind went immediately to Hope.

She had a family here in Sapphire Falls too. And now they all knew it.

Wow, had he fucked up.

He'd outed her to Dan and Peyton. To everyone.

And they hadn't had a chance to fully process it or talk about it.

Damn. She had every right to be upset with him about that.

But was it really so bad that they all knew now? It was the simple truth—Hope was Dan's daughter. It didn't have to be any more complicated than that.

But it was. It would be.

"Hey, Tuck," TJ said. "Think there's a place we can stop and get some pancakes?"

"You don't want to go to the hospital?" Tucker asked.

"I'll take them to go."

"At almost three a.m.?" Tucker laughed. "I don't think so."

Yeah, dammit.

The coffee in the cafeteria at the hospital was terrible. Which really sucked. Hope had the perfect excuse to have coffee without guilt for the first time in weeks and the coffee was bad.

Figured.

Going to fetch the terrible coffee, however, had been an excellent excuse to leave the tiny waiting area where Lauren and Travis's friends and family were gathered.

Or maybe the room just seemed tiny with so many people and emotions filling it up.

So. Many. People.

The baby was fine, Lauren was fine, Travis was as fine as he could be expected to be now that he had a daughter. Everyone had seen Lauren and Travis and baby Whitney. Everyone had thanked and congratulated Hope on her role in Whitney's arrival. Everyone had done *everything*.

So why were they all still hanging around here?

It was four in the morning. And not a single one of them looked or seemed tired. They were all happy, elated even.

Except the family's friends, Dan and Peyton.

Hope sipped her horrible coffee in the hallway *outside* of the waiting area, watching through the window.

Not everyone in the room was bubbling over with joy and excitement, but everyone in that room was filled up with intense emotions, and Hope felt the hallway was the best place for her.

No, actually, back at TJ's farm would be best. Or maybe even another town altogether.

What was she doing here?

She didn't need to be here. She didn't belong here. She wasn't really a friend. She was no longer the only healthcare provider on the scene. She wasn't family.

She shouldn't be here.

She pushed away from the wall just as she heard someone call out to her.

"Hope!"

Hope turned to see Kathy Bennett coming toward her, a huge I'm-a-new-grandma smile on her face.

The pure joy in Kathy's eyes made Hope choke up as the

woman came to stand in front of her.

"Lauren told me how amazing you were. How you kept her calm, and used the lavender to relax her, and coached them all through everything." She took Hope's hands in hers. "Thank you so much for being there and doing what you did."

Yeah. What she'd done. A big fat nothing. The lavender bottle had been empty and Lauren's delivery had been progressing nicely. Sure, she might have had Whitney on the couch or on the front seat of Travis's truck, but that baby girl had been in charge all along.

Hope had pretty much bullshitted her way through the whole thing.

"I just reacted," Hope said. "I'm so glad everything turned out well. Whitney is beautiful."

"She is, isn't she?"

Kathy was positively glowing, and Hope couldn't help her smile.

TJ's mother squeezed her hands again and then let go. But she didn't go back into the waiting room. She leaned back against the wall beside Hope, taking in Hope's view of Kathy's family.

"I'm so very blessed," she said.

Hope looked at her. "Your family is..." She couldn't find the right word.

Overwhelming probably wasn't the appropriate term—or at least not one that Kathy would appreciate. Boisterous would also maybe not be taken well. "They're unlike anything I've experienced before," she finally said.

Kathy laughed at that. "Very political answer."

Hope smiled. "Well, it's true. It was always just my mom and me. It was a lot...quieter."

Kathy laughed again. "I'm sure. But you'll get used to it. Or you'll learn to tell them they need to shut up. Or you'll learn to appreciate long walks in the countryside."

"I do like the countryside."

"And you have a good ten acres between TJ's place and Travis's place," Kathy said. "Ten acres is a good buffer."

Hope felt her heart trip. Kathy was talking as though Hope was staying.

"Kathy..." Hope wet her lips and took a deep breath. "I didn't come to Sapphire Falls because of TJ."

"You came because of Dan," Kathy said. She looked over at Hope. "You look so much like your mother."

Hope wasn't sure what to say. "You knew?"

"Thomas told me before I came over that morning. But I would have known the minute I saw you. I'll bet Dan almost fell over when *he* saw you."

"He was, um, distracted when he first saw me. And it was kind of dark." Her gaze went back to where Dan was sitting on the opposite side of the room from Peyton. He looked miserable.

Kathy nodded. "Well, he knows now. Give him time."

Hope's throat constricted and she felt stinging in her eyes. "He actually always knew. He's had about twenty-six years to adjust."

Kathy pushed away from the wall. "He knew Melody was pregnant?"

Hope pressed her lips together and nodded. "She wanted to come back here and he told her not to. He chose JoEllen."

Kathy's eyes filled with sympathy. "Honey, I'm sorry."

Hope hugged her arms to her body. "I'm not. I had a wonderful mother who loved me enough for both of them. And I only came here to meet him, not to start a relationship. I wasn't even going to tell him who I was. So this is fine."

"But now that you're here—"

"I'm not staying," Hope said, cutting her off. She couldn't. *That* would be crazy. "I did what I came to do." She'd met her father. And she'd had a hot fling with a farmer she would never get out of her system.

She'd definitely followed in her mother's footsteps.

Kathy frowned slightly. "What about TJ?"

Hope's eyes went to the waiting room window again. TJ, big, gorgeous and—no matter what he said—in his element in the midst of all the people and emotion of the moment, was lounging on one end of a sofa, talking to Tucker.

She didn't know what to say. About him or *to* him.

In his yard, with the adrenaline pumping from the baby coming and the chaos with Jason and the EMTs arriving, she'd welcomed his hug. She'd felt right, up against him. In the midst of the swirling craziness around them, he'd felt like the calm spot where she could catch her breath.

But now...

He'd outed her to Dan and Peyton. To everyone. All of the women she'd started friendships with now knew she'd lied to them. She'd caused a rift between Dan and Peyton. She'd confused Peyton about *their* relationship and Peyton was either going to realize that Hope had lied to her too, or she was going to want to get even closer.

Hope didn't do closer.

Basically, he'd complicated everything. He'd been defending her, sort of, but for a guy who claimed to dislike drama, he'd sure jumped into the middle of it.

"TJ's wonderful, of course," Hope said. "But you know our story now." She focused on Kathy instead of the man she was afraid she might be falling in love with. "You know we just met."

Kathy looked into her eyes. "You made him smile again."

Hope's breath caught in her chest.

"And that makes me greedy to have you stay. I'd love to see him smiling for a while. But I understand."

Hope felt her stomach tighten. She loved that TJ was

smiling again. That his shoulder was better. That he knew what it was like to be with a woman who sincerely *liked* him. That he knew he could leave Michelle at her mom's house and everything would still be fine.

But to stay and give him more than that? She didn't know how to do long term. She had no role model for that. She had no context. Except a few days in the midst of the Bennetts. And her head was still spinning from all of that.

"My mom talked about her adventures and the greater journey she was on," Hope said. "I've never entertained the idea of being in one place with the same group of people for life."

Kathy nodded. "I know. But I do wonder if Melody had everything she wanted, or if she told herself she did because she couldn't have what she really wanted."

Hope stared at Kathy. A part of her felt as if she should argue. She could tell Kathy that Melody had been the happiest person Hope had ever known and that she'd experienced things that some people had never even heard of outside of story books.

But she couldn't make the words come.

Because...Kathy was right.

Melody *had* entertained the idea of settling down, in one place, with one man, and making a home and family. She'd called Dan after she left. She'd wanted to come back.

What if he'd said yes? What if he'd wanted to marry her? What if Jo hadn't needed him?

The realization that she could have grown up in Sapphire Falls rocked through Hope.

She could have grown up with Phoebe and Hailey and the Bennett boys. Phoebe might have been her BFF. She might have dated TJ. She would have had a crush on him for sure.

Hope shook her head. That was all too weird. But had Melody *really* thought about settling down here? Marrying Dan and raising corn and chickens?

Hope knew she had. She'd wanted to come back to him.

Suddenly everything seemed jumbled. Everything Hope thought she knew now seemed off-kilter. Melody had been a free spirit, enjoying learning new things, meeting new people, going to new places.

But...was that because she couldn't be where she really wanted to be? Where she truly belonged?

Maybe she'd been searching for another place or other people where she could put her roots down. When she'd been twenty, she'd wanted to see the world. That was normal twenty-year-old stuff. But most people didn't live their entire lives that way, just blowing in the wind, bouncing around in the world.

Unless they never found a place to be happily settled.

Hope knew her mother really had been happy. She really had enjoyed her lifestyle, she'd believed in the things she taught people, she'd always been open to learning or trying something new.

She hadn't been unhappy.

But she had been restless.

Had Melody been so determined to be independent, and to make Hope independent, because that was easier than trusting and depending on other people? People who weren't there for you when you called, scared, pregnant and alone? People who could break your heart?

Hope felt her eyes fill with tears. Her mother had found a home and had fallen in love. But she hadn't realized it until it was too late.

This was so stupid. Coming to Sapphire Falls, trying to find Dan, had all been so, so stupid.

Hope didn't want to know what could have been. She didn't want to leave Sapphire Falls with her heart broken by Dan Wells. She hadn't wanted to follow in *those* footsteps of Melody's.

Hope wiped at her eyes. She wanted to remember her mom

as a sweet, open soul who was *happy*, who was living her life fully and without regret.

"I'm not really comfortable with all of these relationships and this closeness you all have," she said, forcing a steadiness into her voice that she didn't feel. "I'm not used to thinking about other people. I do what I want, when and how I want to. The way you all have your lives all intertwined with one another's is completely foreign to me."

Kathy nodded, sympathy in her eyes. "I understand."

"You do?"

"It can all be overwhelming for *us* sometimes, to have so many people who know everything about you, who care about everything that happens to you, who are always *there*."

Hope got the impression Kathy meant that everyone was always physically there, actually present, along with being supportive. That was certainly what Hope had witnessed in her few days here.

"So I'm sure it would seem that way to someone who isn't used to it."

Hope nodded. "I don't know how to function that way. I don't usually have to think about how my actions and feelings and words affect other people." She looked at Peyton again. "I might have messed things up for Peyton and Dan," she admitted. "I told her she needed to be stronger, to stop making her happiness and unhappiness about her dad and mom."

Kathy shook her head. "That sounds right on to me. Coming from you, she probably listened too."

But that was the problem. Hope was giving relationship advice? To a daughter about her relationship with her father?

What the hell did Hope know about any of that?

She shouldn't be messing with people in areas she didn't really know. Especially in areas that the people she was talking to knew *better* than she did.

Like relationships.

Peyton was surrounded by people who knew about relationships of all kinds. And Hope was teaching her to be strong based on what she'd learned from her mother—the woman who had been using the quest for independence as a way to protect herself from further hurt, not because she really didn't need anyone else.

This was all so confusing.

"I think I need to leave Peyton alone," Hope said. She took a deep breath. "And TJ. He deserves someone who knows how... to do this." She gestured toward the waiting room.

Kathy pressed her lips together. Then she said, "This maybe isn't my place, but I think I would regret not saying it more than I might regret saying it."

Hope hugged herself again. "Okay."

"Dan chose Jo because Jo needed him to be happy. Melody might have missed him, she might have been happier *with* him, but she was able to be happy without him too. He knew that. So he let her go."

But it wasn't fair. Everyone deserved to be as happy as they could be. But Hope said nothing. She simply nodded.

"TJ won't do that."

Hope felt surprise rock through her.

"TJ wants to be happy. He knows that's important. And now that he's found you, he's not going to let you go easily."

Hope stared at Kathy. It had only been two days.

"Michelle treated TJ like crap. I'm glad I was able to show him that he deserves more than that," Hope finally said with conviction. That much she did know. "TJ shouldn't have to wait around for or chase after someone anymore. He needs to let people closer. And I really hope he's realized that now."

Kathy didn't say anything to that. She simply stepped forward and pulled Hope into a hug. Hope hugged her back tightly before letting her go. Being hugged by a mom, even if she wasn't yours, always made things feel better.

"Bye, Kathy," Hope said softly.

Kathy cupped her face in one hand for a moment and smiled at her with sincere affection in her eyes. "'Til we meet again, Hope."

Kathy turned and headed into the waiting area. Her foot hadn't even hit the threshold of the room before TJ was up off the couch and coming for Hope.

"Are you okay?" he asked as he approached. He looked concerned.

Hope took a deep breath. "I'm not sure."

"Did my mom upset you?" he asked with a frown.

"Of course not." She paused. "Dan upset me."

TJ's frown intensified. "Yeah. Me too."

"But I got my chance to meet him," she said with a shrug. "Mission accomplished."

TJ moved closer and peered down at her. "That's it?"

"What else is there? I met him. I got his side of the story. And I didn't even want that much," she said. "I just wanted to be able to say I'd had a conversation with him."

"And you met Peyton. Got close to her."

Hope nodded. "Unfortunately."

TJ frowned. "What's that mean?"

"I should have left her alone. I should have said hi to her at the bakery and left it at that."

TJ reached out, took her upper arm and pulled her closer. "Peyton needs a big sister, Hope. In one night, you have her feeling more confident and cared for than she has in...maybe ever. She needs you."

Hope so wanted to bury her face into his chest and wrap her arms around him. Like at the farm, when everything was swirling around them and he'd anchored her, she felt as if he could make all of the emotions stop tumbling around inside of her.

But that wouldn't fix anything. Ignoring them, trying to

forget about them, wouldn't make them less real.

She shrugged out of his hold. "Exactly. I don't want that."

"You don't want *what*?" he asked.

"To have Peyton need me. To have some big heart-to-heart with Dan. To have your mom thanking me for bringing her first granddaughter into the world. To have everyone looking to me for answers and help."

Hope was aware her voice had risen slightly and people in the waiting room were looking. Including Peyton.

TJ noticed too and again took Hope's arm, this time turning her and steering her down the hall. It was impossible to shrug out of his grasp this time.

He didn't stop until they were outside the hospital doors and around the corner in a more shadowed area.

He let go of her but stood close, towering over her, displeasure and concern on his face. "What is going on?" he asked.

"You told Dan and Peyton who I am!"

He grimaced. "I know. I'm sorry. It just came out. But it's not bad. Dan would have realized it eventually. And Peyton is thrilled."

"Because she thinks I'm going to fix all of her problems," Hope said. "But there's no oil or acupressure site that will fix her stuff."

"Probably not," TJ agreed. "So you'll have to use something else."

Hope threw her hands up. "I don't have anything else, TJ. That's what I've got. And even those are borderline bullshit."

His frown was back. "Borderline bullshit?"

"Yes. The lavender bottle was empty!" she reminded him.

"Hope—"

"I'm a fraud," she said. "I've been trying to live like my mom, follow her principles and beliefs. But...that's not the real me. I do drink coffee. I've been trying to kick the habit but I *love* coffee, TJ. I also love Oreos. Like hardcore addiction—sugar, fat and preservatives—all of it. I wear underwear almost all the time. I do yoga, but almost never naked. And I only know the basics about essential oils. I use them but my mom always mixed them for me. I'm a nurse, but I travel because it's easier than getting pulled into a community where you care for the people through *everything* they need for all their lives. That idea intimidates the hell out of me, frankly. And I have only been on the road in that camper living a simpler life for about five days and I already miss my internet connection, my big screen TV and my pillow-top mattress."

Hope stood, slightly out of breath, staring up at TJ, praying she wouldn't cry.

Wow, that had felt cathartic. But she feared the coldness she was about to see in his eyes when he realized that she'd been fooling him too.

He didn't say anything.

So she said, "And I love bacon."

With that, he slowly nodded. "Me too."

Her eyes widened. "Are you listening to me? I'm not all of these things you think I am. You think I'm this wonderful healer and this sweet spirit that wants to reach out and help everyone, but I'm not. I don't do relationships. I don't know how. I don't know what it's like for people to need things from me that don't have to do with herbs and plants and ibuprofen. All my life, I've had to solve my own problems, and it makes me crazy when people won't help themselves. And that's not what you all do here."

"But you don't eat bacon. Even though you love it."

She frowned. "No. I don't eat bacon."

"Or Oreos."

"No—" She hesitated and sighed. "Actually I do. Not often, but sometimes I just have to."

"And you really have a big-screen TV?"

She nodded. "It's gorgeous."

"Well, that's nothing to be ashamed of."

She shook her head. "You're not listening."

"I am, actually. You're not perfect or totally in touch with yourself and the universe. I heard you."

"TJ—"

"I am wondering, though, how you feel about the no underwear and naked yoga now that you've tried them."

She sighed. He was being difficult.

"I kind of like the no underwear and naked yoga," she confessed. It was true.

"Good," he said with a nod. "Because I'm a big fan. And, for the record, I have a pillow-top mattress."

She shook her head, feeling the tears stinging again. She'd known it would be hard to say goodbye to him, and his mother had warned her that he wouldn't make it easy. That was kind of nice, really. She wasn't sure anyone had ever tried to hang on to her before.

"I don't do the kind of relationships you all do. The kind you all want," she said.

"Yes, you do," he said simply.

"I've messed everything up for Peyton!" she exclaimed. "I've made Dan miserable. JoEllen doesn't even know yet."

"Dan and Peyton have been messed up for a while, Sunshine. That's not on you."

"I made it worse."

"Do you believe the things you told her? About being strong and making her own happiness?"

"Yes. But what do I know? I've never had a father who worried about me."

TJ's expression softened at that. "But you know about being happy and at peace. Maybe more about it than anyone I know."

"I learned it from my mom," Hope said. "But that was all a lie too. She wasn't really happy. She was running from memories, trying to fill gaps in her heart and in her life."

TJ shook his head. "You don't really believe that."

But she was afraid maybe she did.

"I can't stay. I came for something and got way more than I expected. I need to quit before it gets worse."

He scowled. "Why do I feel like you're working up to saying you're leaving?"

She smiled sadly. "Because you're very, very intuitive."

"No," he said firmly. "Not yet. You said you were spending the rest of the summer."

"That was a sister running away from home, a dad who knew about me for twenty-six years but didn't want me and a baby on the front lawn ago."

Not to mention falling in love with his mother, getting a glimpse into what it would be like to have a group of girlfriends and seeing a glimmer of just how fun it would be to watch Travis Bennett raise his little girl. For starters. She wasn't even going to go into all of the things the big, grumpy, sweet, loving farmer in front of her made her feel.

"*I* need you to stay."

Hope stared up at TJ. She couldn't believe that he'd just said that. "Your shoulder should keep doing well if you keep moving it."

"Actually, after our trip to my bedroom, it hurts like a bitch again, but it was worth it. And that's not what I'm talking about."

She felt her cheeks—hell, her whole body—flush with heat with that simple reminder.

"Yeah," he said, noticing her reaction. "Don't tell me *that* isn't worth sticking around for."

"You've just been having the wrong kind of sex before me. If you let someone close, someone you really like, you'll be fine." And the idea of him being with another woman made her want to throw up.

"Now *that* is bullshit, and you know it," he said. He stepped close and lifted his hand to her face.

She knew she should pull away. When he touched her, she felt that sense of contentment and that everything would be okay.

"I get it. I'm freaked out too," he said softly.

"*You're* freaked out?" she said. "I come here for a cup of coffee with my dad, and three days later, I'm immersed in all of...this. Your family and friends and everyone wants me involved in all of...everything. And I'm probably falling in love with you and just had the best sex of my life and I don't know what to do." She took a deep breath. "Why are *you* freaked out?"

"For all of those reasons."

"Because I'm involved in everything?"

"Yes. And that I'm probably falling in love with you too."

The look on his face and the tone in his voice when he said those words made everything in Hope clench with want.

But he went on. "When things went to hell before, it affected everyone in my life."

She understood that. And now, knowing his close relationships with his family, she knew that was as important to him as his own broken heart. "And things with us will go to hell. Eventually. Right?"

"I'm not so sure, actually."

"But eventually we'll fight about...something," she said.

"Yeah. But we'll make up."

"We will?"

"I'll lean in and catch a whiff of that shampoo, which will make me think about how you always remind me of sunshine... and how can I stay mad then?"

Hope felt her determination melting.

"You stayed mad at Michelle."

"She used me. Nothing was ever real. That's not a problem

here."

"I told you I don't drink coffee, but I do. I told you I knew all about oils, but I don't."

"Do you really think that's what I'm talking about?" TJ asked. "I could remind you that you are *trying* not to drink coffee and that you know more about oils than anyone else here. But that's not what I mean. This thing between us—it's real."

She took a deep breath. "You sound crazy, you know that?"

"Yeah."

"*That* freaks me out."

"Me too."

They stood looking at each other, and Hope felt everything in her start to want—she wanted him, she wanted to know it would all be okay, she wanted to know that Peyton would be okay, she wanted to hear stories about her mom as a young woman from Dan and Kathy and Thomas. And she wanted to drink coffee. Lots of it. At Scott's Sweets. Maybe every morning for the next ten years or so.

She pulled away from his touch. That was what was doing it to her. "I know what you're doing."

"Begging you to stay?"

Determined. She had to stay determined. Even when he was clearly getting better at showing her that soft layer he had underneath. "You're *making* this into a circus. I told you I wasn't dramatic, that I didn't want all of that either. So you had to *make* drama with me by telling Dan and Peyton who I am. You say you don't want it, but then you shake the monkey cages and let them all loose so you can go chasing around after them."

"Why would I do that?" he asked with a frown.

"Because you feel like that's the measure of true love. If things aren't hard, they're not real."

"And you think things should never be hard," he said.

Things had always been easy with her mom. They'd

disagreed from time to time, but Hope had never worried about Melody. She'd never given Melody advice and then had to worry about it being wrong. If her mom would have taken off in the middle of the night with her camper like Peyton had, Hope might have wondered where she'd gone, but she wouldn't have worried. Loving Melody had been easy. Melody was a happy, optimistic, curious, adventurous, independent woman. She'd been easy to be around and had never had a problem she couldn't fix on her own. At least, as far as Hope had ever known.

Even her death had been undramatic. There had been no long, drawn-out illness or injury that needed caring for. Melody had simply gone—quickly and without fanfare.

Hope felt her throat tighten. She nodded, fighting the tears. "Why do you think I'm attracted to you, TJ?"

"Because I'm the one you're supposed to be with forever."

She sucked in a sharp breath. Holy crap. "This crazy stuff is contagious, I guess."

He shrugged. "I was probably already borderline anyway."

Hope laughed lightly. In the middle of it all, he still made her laugh. "I'm attracted to you because you can take care of yourself. You're not needy. You don't need me to advise you or build you up or help you through."

"Don't I?" He moved closer, pinning her in place with that intense stare. "When you got here, I was keeping everyone at arm's length. I didn't want people close. I didn't want people taking care of me, because I didn't know how to do that either. Michelle never took care of me. She just took what I gave. I didn't know how to have a two-way relationship. Then you show up. Like a rainbow and a tornado all wrapped up into one, and you turned me all around. Now I want to be close to someone."

"Someone who doesn't know how to do that, TJ."

"So we'll figure it out together."

"I just got here *yesterday*."

"Technically two days ago."

"It doesn't happen that fast."

"You haven't been to Sapphire Falls before."

She took a deep breath. He wasn't saying he was in love with her, but he was saying he thought it could happen.

She knew exactly what he meant.

"I came to Sapphire Falls to have a memorable summer like my mom did and to see the world the way she saw it. I thought she had all the answers. That she was strong and independent and wise. But I think she got some of it wrong."

"So she was human too."

Hope pulled in a long breath and then nodded. "Yeah, I guess so. But I don't know what she was right about and what she was wrong about."

TJ studied her face for a long, long moment. Finally, he said, "And you need time to figure everything out."

She nodded. "And you can't wait around for me to call for help."

Her heart was tearing in two, but she knew it was the right thing. TJ had spent too long waiting for Michelle to love him back, trying to make it work when she wasn't trying at all. He couldn't do that for Hope too.

"You won't call me for help anyway," he said gruffly. He looked resigned and a touch affectionate as he said it.

Everything in her ached. "It's not you. I don't call anyone for help."

He nodded. "I know." He dug in his front pocket, pulled his keys out and handed them to her. "But you can call for other reasons."

Hope somehow managed to keep from sobbing until she was inside his truck and on the road back to Sapphire Falls.

And all the way back, she wondered if she loved him more because he hadn't wanted her to go, or because he'd let her.

13

Three days later, Hope sat in a truck stop just east of the Nebraska state line.

From where she sat, she could see Colorado.

She'd been able to see Colorado for two days from the window in her motel room. She just hadn't been able to make herself cross the state line. She wasn't ready to leave Nebraska just yet. For some reason.

And, yes, she was staying in a motel. She'd wanted to live in her mother's world for a while, but the truth was, the tiny camper was making her claustrophobic and she wasn't really the sleep-under-the-stars kind of girl.

She picked up her cup of coffee and sighed. Caffeine was good.

"See you for dinner?" Paula, the waitress who had been taking Hope's order for breakfast, lunch and dinner over the past two days, asked.

Hope looked out the window again. She should cross that line today. She should just do it and get it over with. She should leave Nebraska behind.

But she looked up at Paula and nodded. "Yep."

"Okay." Paula smiled and laid Hope's lunch bill on the table. "Talk to you then."

Hope knew it was pathetic that she couldn't leave the state. For one thing, it wasn't even a real line. The dirt on the Colorado side was the same dirt as on the Nebraska side.

But it seemed different.

TJ was in Nebraska. So was Peyton. So was Kathy and Lauren and Phoebe and...

Okay, so she'd been waiting to see if TJ would come after her.

He shouldn't. If he did, she would be disappointed. He shouldn't have to chase someone. Anyone who would leave him was a complete idiot and he deserved better.

But she'd still kind of wanted him to.

The tears that had been just beneath the surface since she'd left Sapphire Falls threatened again.

Her phone chimed with a text message and she almost didn't look. The odds were about twenty to one that it was Jason Gilmore. Offering her a job. Again.

He'd not only been impressed with how she'd handled Lauren's delivery, but Lauren and Travis had been pretty insistent that she needed to join the medical team in Sapphire Falls. The medical team that consisted of Jason. Just Jason. He wanted and needed the help.

Hope was flattered, but really? Talk about a job completely opposite from what she'd been doing. The traveling had been perfect because she hadn't formed long-term attachments. That would not be the case in Sapphire Falls.

If she joined the clinic there, she would not have only delivered Whitney Bennett, but she'd give the girl her first stitches, set her first broken bone, do her kindergarten physical, give her a tetanus shot after she stepped on something on the farm, treat her for the flu and strep throat, be the one to confirm *her* pregnancy and deliver *her* baby. Hell, it was possible Hope would give Whitney's daughter her first stitches too.

That was how healthcare worked in small towns.

That was a lot of pressure. That was a lot of being involved with someone.

It was also kind of tempting.

Hope would love to see Whitney dressed up for school on her first day of kindergarten.

The damned stinging in her eyes was becoming stronger.

She finally flipped her phone over and read the text message from Jason. But it wasn't an offer of more money.

The mayor is determined to talk you into the job. You've been warned.

The mayor? Hailey was going to call her? Why?

"What can I get you?" Hope heard Paula ask someone.

"Coffee please," a deep voice said from right next to Hope's table.

She looked up. And froze.

Dan Wells stood there, studying the plate in front of her. "Is that Oreo pie?" he asked.

Hope glanced down and nodded numbly.

"I'll have a piece of that too," he told Paula as he slid into the booth across from Hope.

Hope just stared at him.

"I loved your mother with everything I had," he said. "Not going with her when she left Sapphire Falls was the hardest thing I've ever done."

Dan Wells was here. Her *father* was here. He'd come after her.

No one had ever come after her before.

Her phone started to ring and Hope silenced it without even looking. She couldn't deal with Hailey right now too.

"And when she wanted to come back?" Hope asked.

Paula set his coffee and pie down in front of him. He stirred in one cream and two sugars.

It was exactly how Hope drank her coffee.

She sat back and crossed her arms and waited.

"I told her the truth—I had proposed to JoEllen and we were getting married."

"And that you wanted nothing to do with your baby," Hope said, trying to sound detached from the whole thing. She had never missed having a father.

Until now as she was facing him over Oreo pie.

He nodded and Hope felt her chest ache.

"I was scared. I was scared of what Jo would do. I didn't know how to possibly make it work over such a distance. I couldn't leave Jo and if Melody had moved back closer..." He sighed. "I never stopped loving and wanting your mom, Hope. If she'd been close, it would have ruined my marriage."

Hope bit her tongue against all of the things she wanted to say. How pathetic that all sounded, how wrong he'd been, how he'd hurt her mom. And her.

The thing was, she hadn't been hurt until now. She hadn't known that he'd turned his back. Her mom had protected her from that, had always made her feel like a gift and the best adventure of Melody's life.

Hope didn't know if her mom had done the right thing or if maybe Dan had even done some of it right. Or if they'd both done everything wrong. But none of it really mattered now. It was over and done.

"You missed out," she said simply.

He met her eyes. "I know."

She sighed. "So now we're going to have a big happy family reunion? Jo is going to love me? Peyton's going to straighten up? You're going to get to assuage your guilt over not being there for me for twenty-five years?"

He shook his head. "I'm here to make an offer on your car and camper."

She stared at him. "Excuse me?"

"I want to buy the Fiat and camper."

She frowned. Maybe the crazy thing was genetic. On both sides of her family. "*Why?*"

He leaned in on the tabletop with his forearms. "Peyton and I checked Jo into a rehab facility yesterday. It's a thirty-day program. We can't visit or see her. She's totally immersed in the program. I've decided to take some time to myself and do some camping and reminiscing and soul searching. Thought it might be easier if I'm off by myself."

Hope wasn't sure how to process all of that. Jo being in rehab seemed like a great thing. Dan having some time to think about the past and his choices would also probably be good. But she wasn't sure what it had to do with her exactly.

"And mine is the only camper you want to buy?"

"Yours is the only camper that belonged to Melody."

"This is...strange," Hope finally said. "You tracked me down to buy my camper?"

"I tracked you down because the last time I let a beautiful blond walk out of my life, I spent the next twenty-six years regretting it. I'm hoping to learn from a few mistakes."

Hope swallowed hard. "So you do want to be in my life?"

"As friends. As the sort of clueless father of a new friend of yours. As some guy who lives in town and you see at the grocery store once in a while. Whatever you want it to be."

"But not my father? Because of Jo."

He leaned in closer. "Hope, I will gladly tell the *world* that you're my daughter. If you will let me try to be some kind of father to you, I will be grateful for the second chance. But I'll warn you, I'm not that good at it."

She gave him a small smile. "Well, I've never had one before, so I might not know the difference."

He smiled back and she could see that he was touched.

"How did you find me?" she asked.

He shrugged. "I headed west for Sedona. TJ told me that you made a habit of stopping at truck stops to eat."

TJ. Just hearing his name was enough to make her heart throb painfully.

"I drove past this one and saw the yellow car—hard to miss —pulling the camper."

"You would have gone all the way to Sedona?" she asked.

"This time, absolutely."

So he wanted a second chance to get it right with her. It was twenty-six years late, but...

"I don't know a lot about it, but I'm guessing families give each other second chances," she said.

Dan nodded. "And third and fourth and tenth." He picked up his coffee and sipped. "If you need to know anything about families, there's no one better than TJ."

Hope had to swallow hard again. "He gives second chances?"

"TJ lets people try until they get it right."

The tears were *right there*. "What if they never get it right?"

Dan looked completely sincere when he said, "That's kind of his specialty."

Hope felt her heart thump and one tear finally escaped.

"If you take my Fiat, how will I get back to Sapphire Falls?" she asked.

Dan smiled and pushed his keys across the table. "Just so happens my truck knows the way."

F our hours later, Hope pulled up in front of TJ's house. He was on the porch by the time she'd turned off the ignition, and by the time her feet hit the dirt, he was down the steps and standing on the front walk, feet braced apart, hands on his hips, waiting for her.

He didn't look surprised to see her. In fact, he looked impatient even as she made her way across the grass and came to stand in front of him

"I want it noted that I didn't call you, text you, call the cops or come after you," he said.

"Noted."

"But these were the longest three days of my life."

Her heart tripped. "And you had your phone fully charged, on and with you every minute, didn't you?"

He nodded, and she was astounded by how good it felt to know that he had been there. She could have called at any time, for any reason, and he would have done anything she asked.

She wasn't going to have to call him very often, but there really was something about knowing she could that made her feel...loved.

Yep, she totally got where Michelle was coming from.

"I'm going to need to have a talk with Michelle," she said. "We need some boundaries."

"Agreed."

"But sometimes she's going to call you to pick her up and *sometimes* that will be okay."

He smiled. "We'll see."

She spread her arms out. "So the thing is, I don't know how to do this. How to not just want to slap some oil on a problem and be done with it."

"I know. But I can show you."

Her heart started pounding. She was going to do this. Her mom had been good at a lot of things. But she'd made some mistakes as well. The biggest in Hope's opinion was when she'd driven away from Sapphire Falls.

It looked as if she was still learning things from Melody.

"I've learned about healing from the things my mom did

right. And I've learned about love from the things she did wrong."

TJ stepped close and cupped her cheek. "I love you, Sunshine."

"I love you too," she said past the tightness in her throat. "So, I'm here and I'm willing to try."

"That's all I need," TJ said sincerely. "*Here* is what I do best."

She laughed lightly at that. "That's an understatement."

"And everyone else? They know how to be here too," he told her.

Even her dad. Kind of. She nodded. "I know."

TJ shook his head. He looked pained. "I mean, they'll be here all the time. In everything. All. The. Time."

She grinned and moved in to wrap her arms around him. "Yeah, I know."

His arms came around her, his hands stroking up and down her back. "So I was thinking. Maybe we could take the camper somewhere for a while. Alone. Far away. Maybe for a long while."

She laughed. "You are never going to be able to fit in that camper. And besides, it's Dan's now."

"Not that camper."

She pulled back and looked up at him. "What do you mean?"

"*That* camper."

She turned to look. A huge motorhome was rolling up the drive.

"Oh my God."

"Well, I would never be able to fit in your camper."

"Yeah," she agreed distractedly. "But that thing is *huge*, TJ."

"Oh, we both know that you can handle huge."

She looked away from the RV and up at him. Her huge, hot farmer. Who was giving her a very wicked grin. "I can't believe you just said that."

He laughed and her heart expanded. God, she loved when he laughed.

"That baby has a king-size bed in the back."

She shook her head in wonder. "You knew for sure I was coming back?" She liked that. She liked that he could sense some things about her too.

"I didn't know for sure," he said.

Oh. Okay, maybe she was still the more insightful one.

"I was coming to you."

His answer was simple and he said it as if she should have known.

She teared up. Again. "I told you not to wait."

"And I wasn't. I wasn't waiting. I gave you a few days to think things through and then I was coming to be with you."

"To bring me back?"

"To be wherever you were."

"But—" She was speechless at that. But only for a moment. "This is your home. Your farm. Your family."

"Yeah, well, it's not like I wouldn't have been able to ever come back. And there are plenty of people around here who need more to do," he said dryly. "They've all somehow managed to find time to come over here every day since you left to give me a hard time about letting you go. I'm thinking they could put that free time to good use."

She laughed and hugged him. "But they're your *family*."

"Yep. Which means I can't get rid of them. So if I need a break, I have to be the one to leave."

"Well, if you want to do some traveling, I'm your girl."

He tipped her chin up. "You're my girl no matter what."

The RV's horn started blaring and another car came speeding up the drive and pulled to a stop in front of the house, dust flying.

Hailey Conner was driving the car—a red sports car that matched her heels perfectly. She got out and Hope braced for her to head directly over and launch into a spiel about the clinic job.

Instead, she slammed the car door and stomped to the RV.

"Who's in the RV?" Hope asked.

TJ grimaced. "Everyone."

"What's Hailey doing here?"

"Not sure. But my brother Ty is in the camper. Odds are he did something to piss her off."

"What's that about?" she asked as the door to the RV swung open and everyone stumbled out, talking and laughing, raving about the amenities and how horrible the gas mileage would be. The party included Delaney, Tucker, Joe, Phoebe and another good-looking guy who was absolutely related to TJ, Tucker and Travis.

"No one really knows," TJ said as they watched Hailey head directly to Delaney. "They drive each other nuts. Ty constantly pokes at her, Hailey reacts every time."

"Uh," Hope said, watching Hailey breeze past Ty as if he didn't exist and his resultant grin.

"Uh, what?" TJ asked, looking down. "Your amazing magical insights telling you something?"

She rolled her eyes. Her insights *were* kind of amazing sometimes. But in this case... "It's obvious."

"It is?"

"They're sleeping together. Or want to be."

TJ's gaze snapped back to the scene in front of them. "No shit," he muttered.

Hope thought it was all pretty clear.

"Someone is moving in next door to me," Hailey said to Delaney.

Delaney looked at Tucker, then back to Hailey. "Yes, I know."

"You sold the house and didn't tell me?" Hailey demanded.

"The house?" Hope said to TJ.

"Delaney bought and flipped a house in town. Right next door to Hailey," he explained.

"Okay, got it." She focused back on the mini-drama.

"The buyer asked me not to say anything to anyone," Delaney said. "I'm sorry."

"You agreed to that?" Hailey asked.

Delaney shrugged.

"Well, they moved in in the middle of the night, I guess. I haven't seen anyone yet, but there was a bunch of racket going on this morning at six a.m. I went over and knocked on the door but no one would answer."

Delaney shot a look around at the group. "Sorry?" she offered.

"This is a very small town and I'm the mayor. How can I not know these things?" Hailey asked.

"The next time you go over, you should probably take brownies or something, don't you think?" Ty asked. "Isn't that the neighborly thing to do?"

"How do you know I didn't?" Hailey asked him.

He snorted. "You're not really the sweet, baked-goods kind of neighbor, I'm guessing."

"And what kind do you think I am?"

"The you're-making-a-lot-of-racket-at-six-a.m.-and-disturb-ing-me type," Ty told her with a grin.

"What are you doing here anyway?" Hailey asked. "Don't you live in *Denver*?"

"Sapphire Falls will always be home," he said easily, giving her a charming smile.

Hope was positive that smile had caused lots of swooning.

Hailey Conner didn't strike her as the swooning type.

"Yes, how could I forget with that huge new sign on the edge of town?" Hailey asked.

"You mean the one that reads *Home of Tyler Bennett, Olympic Silver Medalist*?" Ty asked.

"The one that the city council approved in spite of my protests," Hailey said. "The one with the huge photo of you with your medals and that obnoxious silver font and the lights for at night. The one that looks like it's some kind of shrine to you. *That* one."

Ty nodded. "Oh, the one that the town had a fundraiser to put up. The one that all the kids wanted pictures in front of."

Hailey turned away from him with an exasperated sigh to focus on Delaney instead. "I'm going to get it out of you."

Delaney pressed her lips together and shook her head.

"He paid her extra not to tell anyone," Tucker said.

Hailey narrowed her eyes. "He? It's a he? Not a family?"

Tucker groaned and Delaney elbowed him.

Hailey pointed a finger at them all. "This isn't over." Then she turned and paced to where Hope was standing. "I can't believe you're not taking my calls."

"Uh..." Hope felt everyone's eyes on her.

"Why is Hailey calling you?" TJ asked.

"To talk me into taking the job with Jason," Hope told him.

"Jason offered you a job?"

She shrugged. "Guess I impressed him by delivering a baby in a front yard in the dark."

"Uh huh."

She squinted up at him. "What's that mean?"

TJ shook his head. "Nothing."

"He means that hot blonds are kind of Jason's type," Joe called.

"You mean the good-looking, funny, charming, intelligent doctor who's returned home to serve the medical needs of his hometown?" Phoebe asked. "That Jason?" She gave TJ a huge grin.

TJ gave her an irritated look.

"He offered me a job as a *nurse* in the clinic here," Hope said.

"Which you would be amazing at," TJ said, hugging her against his side.

"Thank you."

"I wasn't calling to talk you into taking the job," Hailey said, propping a hand on her hip.

"You weren't?" Hope frowned.

"I assumed you were going to take it," Hailey said. "What with being in love with TJ and all."

"Then why were you calling?" Hope asked.

"To talk you into taking it *part-time* so that you can also do things with your oils and acupressure and yoga."

Hope stared at her. "Really?"

"My feet and back haven't felt this good in years."

"That's...great." Hope was amazed. It all felt really good. Right.

"Hey, yeah." Ty approached. "I heard about this oil stuff," he said. "Tuck said something about incredible orgasms afterward."

"Tucker!" Delaney exclaimed.

"I did not!" Tucker protested.

Ty gave him a look. Tucker glanced at Delaney. Then he sighed. "I didn't say that *exactly*."

"Then again, I'd better be careful with anything that makes me even better," Ty said thoughtfully. "That could be dangerous."

"You're such an ass," Hailey muttered.

"Oh my God. Please make it stop," TJ moaned.

Hope laughed. "How do you feel about a quick trip to Arizona?" she asked him. "I have a few things I need to pack up in Sedona for my move."

"There's going to be a move?" He looked down at her with a look that made her catch her breath.

"I think there is. Another adventure."

"This adventure is going to take a while," he said, as if warning her.

"The one to Arizona?"

He looked at the group gathered in his front drive. "Yes," he said. Then he focused on her again. "But I also mean the one with the two of us. Wherever life takes us."

She nodded. "I happen to be available for the next hundred years or so."

TJ opened his mouth to reply.

"By the way, the bed in there is awesome, TJ," Tucker said, ruining the moment.

"Tucker, Joe and I all fit on that bed, and we could have squeezed a hot blond or brunette in easy," Ty added.

"What about a redhead?" Phoebe asked.

"Well, we would have had to boot Tuck out for that. I know from personal experience that you need *extra* room to move when a redhead's involved," Joe said.

Phoebe laughed and kissed him.

TJ groaned again. "*Seriously*. We're taking the long way to Arizona. And back."

Hope just grinned. The important thing was that they were coming back.

———

Thank you for reading TJ and Hope's story! I hope you loved *Getting Lucky*!

And next up Hailey and Ty's story, **Getting Over It!**

Hailey Conner has been driving Ty Bennett crazy for years.
And vice versa.
It's kind of their thing. But Ty is ready to make their thing into

something more. And he's moved in next door to make it happen.

But is he *really* ready?

Ty loves the confident, sassy, sexy mayor's Ice Queen act...because he loves making her melt. But he soon finds there's more underneath all that frostiness. And things are about to come to a full boil...

Grab **Getting Over It** now!

———

The Sapphire Falls series

Getting Out of Hand
Getting Worked Up
Getting Dirty
Getting Wrapped Up
Getting It All
Getting Lucky
Getting Over It
Getting His Way
Getting Into Trouble
Getting It Right
Getting All Riled Up
Getting to the Church On Time

And more at
ErinNicholas.com

———

Join in on the fan fun too! I love interacting with my readers and would love to have you in the two places where I chat with fans the most--my email list and my Super Fan page on Facebook!

Sign up for my email list! You'll hear from me just a couple times a month and I'll keep you updated on all my news, sales, exclusive fun, and new releases!
http://bit.ly/ErinNicholasEmails

Join my fan page on Facebook at Erin Nicholas Super Fans! I check in there every day and it's the best place for first looks, exclusive giveaways, book talk and fun!

ABOUT ERIN

Erin Nicholas is the New York Times and USA Today bestselling author of over thirty sexy contemporary romances. Her stories have been described as toe-curling, enchanting, steamy and fun. She loves to write about reluctant heroes, imperfect heroines and happily ever afters. She lives in the Midwest with her husband who only wants to read the sex scenes in her books, her kids who will never read the sex scenes in her books, and family and friends who say they're shocked by the sex scenes in her books (yeah, right!).

Find her and all her books at
www.ErinNicholas.com

And find her on Facebook, BookBub, and Instagram!

CPSIA information can be obtained
at www.ICGtesting.com
Printed in the USA
LVHW090232050321
680663LV00007B/114

9 780986 324574